SECOND TIME ROUND

GUY WILSON

First published in Great Britain in 2000

by Benchmark Press

Little Hatherden Near Andover SP11 OHY.

Cover: By A.D.Lucas. 1878.

A CIP catalogue for this book is avaliable from the British Library.

ISBN: 0-9537674-0-X

Printed and bound in Great Britain by Henry Ling Ltd, The Dorset Press, Dorchester. DT1 1HD.

BY THE SAME AUTHOR:

<u>NOVELS</u>

The Industrialists (Dent)

A Touch of the Lemming (Bles)

The Ardour of the Crowd (Chatto & Windus)

A Healthy Contempt (Images)

The Art Thieves (Rampant Horse)

The Carthaginian Hoard (Harold, Martin & Redfern)

<u>SHORT STORIES</u>

The Three Vital Moments of Benjamin Ellashaye (Chatto & Windus)

Brought up in Devon, Guy Wilson was educated at Marlborough College and Gonville and Cauis College, Cambridge. After a stint in the Royal Marine Commandos and a statutory attempt at being a schoolmaster, he determined to be a novelist. He and his wife, Angela, set off to Spain on a motorbike. This was the start of an adventurous and precarious existence. They spent three years in Spain, two in Algeria, three in Italy and one in Paris, supplementing literary income by starting and running English language schools. Then they found themselves in charge of Padworth, the international sixth-form college for girls, which they ran for twelve years. The Wilsons now live in Hampshire.

Also available from Benchmark Press:

By Guy Wilson:

'A Healthy Contempt.' Maynard Temple, a worldly Cambridge don and successful TV historian lives with his talented wife, Rachel, a biographer. They have a young son. Their relationship is open, loving, rooted, until Rachel's sister, Rhoda, comes out of prison where she has served a sentence for an episode of violent idealism. Maynard contains his distaste for Rhoda's strident martyrdom to causes until he suspects her attitude to him goes beyond random dislike. Against all his liberal principles, he is driven to an extreme act which tears his life apart. (Hard back. First published in 1993. UK price: £14.95. UK postage included).

'The Carthaginian Hoard.' Sir Alan Silverman, eminent archaeologist and discoverer of the legendary hoard in the Central Sahara in 1936, is buried in Westminster Abbey with full state pomp. But does he merit the international reputation he has won? Claudia Drake, his biographer, thinks so. But left-wing freelance journalist, Michael Strode, has another opinion. He guesses Silverman knew a lot more about the murder of one of his British assistants than ever came out. In an unlikely alliance the two go out to Sahara, now independent and a vicious dictatorship, to find the truth. Amid unforeseen perils and hardship, they find their courage challenged and their view of each other changed. (Hard back. First published in 1997. UK price £15.95 UK postage included).

By Angela Mack.

'Dancing on the Waves.' The motto of the WRNS was 'Never at Sea', but this soon became outdated. Wrens were required to handle coded signals on board the 'Monsters,' the peace-time liners stripped for war-time action, which brought over the American forces and which were a prime target for U-boats. This was only one of the highlights of the writer's war-time adventures. She worked at Submarine Headquarters, and then was chosen to attend the Yalta Conference. A small cog but an eager witness, she writes entertainingly about the details of this great event. Behind the light-hearted approach is the author's interest in the changing role of women which the war brought about. (Paper back. First published 2000. UK price: £6.99 plus postage.)

The Benchmark Press, Little Hatherden, Near Andover, Hampshire SP11 OHY. Fax: 01264/ 735205 Tel: 01264/ 735262

PART 1.

1.

They all had cut and dried remedies which included rent-a-muscle. 'You've got to frighten him,' one of her woman friends said, 'that's the only thing a man like him understands.'

Jocelyn Cunningham didn't think she had lost her ability to listen to good advice, but how did this woman know what Leo 'understood'? What did she know about her own ability to inflict such treatment on her pathetically vulnerable ex-husband, whatever he had done?

With a mote more reality, her daughter Sally, who now lived in London and whose present partner was a budding lawyer, lectured her on the law of harassment and how she could get a court order. When Sally saw her turning her head aside in tolerant doubt at this, she got quite cross, accusing her of allowing 'the man' (by which she meant her father) to erode her will. Did she want to drown with him, Sally asked, in a tone that suggested she, her mother, was the one aged twenty.

She did think about Sally's neat solution. Could it be that she lacked will? Perhaps it wasn't understanding which detained her but some trivial squeamishness like the inability to wring a chicken's neck. But long before she saw the advertisement, she had known there was only one real remedy. People who haven't had seriously to do with the law in such complex emotional matters don't know what a cumbersome and ineffective animal it's likely to prove with someone involved as artful, determined and damaged as Leo.

Nonetheless, especially after she had applied and apparently been short-listed for the job, she had plenty of second thoughts. Now the divorce was through, was it possible Leo might accept the situation and leave her alone? There were as well all the practical impediments - the house (which though rented she felt was hers de facto by dint of years of occupation), her job at the clinic, the life she had so painstakingly reseeded for herself in spite of everything. In the end she thought it was the excitement which made her make the journey, something new even if it came to nothing, action instead of inaction. She was also drawn by Henry Bordeaux's handwritten letter, which had, she thought, a certain vigour and lack of formality.

'Dear Mrs Hammond, (She had used her mother's maiden name),

'I liked your letter. What about coming down for a chat? I have to say, though, you're the only female applying. Do you really want to haul and draw, which has to be a part of the job description? Nature's a relentless opponent, even down here in balmy South Devon. If you come by car, bring your wellies by the way. Our bog outbogs the Irish moors.'

A touch of male chauvinism there maybe? Why shouldn't 'females' haul and draw? Horticulture was surely carried out by women, some as beefy as men? But the script was strong, somehow careful. And he had taken the trouble to say in a noticeably less carefully written p.s., as if money though important was not a headline priority in life, that 'naturally' expenses would be paid. That someone else could assume any financial responsibility for her would make a change.

She decided she wouldn't go in her car, which was proving unreliable lately. A long train journey would be part of the adventure. The first leg, to London, was stimulating. Was this the beginning of a new life? But from Paddington onwards she had increasingly the feeling she was voyaging away from her life, not into a new one. She found no solace in her fellow passengers, at whom she foolishly looked for some sign of similar unease. Rocking complacently with the motion, talking and reading and sleeping by turns, they all seemed entirely unconcerned at their displacement. Several times she had crises of self-pity.

These largely fastened on the open question of what sort of accommodation she would have if she landed the job. 'Living-in accommodation available if required,' the advertisement had said. Living-in accommodation would be necessary. Even with Sally off her hands there was no money of the sort she would need to take out a mortgage on the smallest property. She thought what this would probably mean - a bed-sitting room in a strange house with strange people? Wouldn't she be like one of those unfortunate governesses in Victorian novels, having the pretence of social equality without the comfort of comradeship below stairs? At least her present job at the clinic had status and was the kind of thing some well-to-do women did. It also stopped at five and at week-ends. She had to calm herself by thinking that either she wouldn't get the job or that she would turn it down if she did.

Pulling out of Exeter, they began the traverse of a long estuary. On the wet mud of a low tide there were large colonies of birds feeding busily - sanderling, dunlin, oyster-catchers, she identified, two or three heron standing stock-still. Sundry gulls loitered in the air. Unusual nostalgia attacked her. It was on rare childhood visits to the seaside she had learnt these names from her father. How far away and lost were those times she had once thought, though dull, secure.

They were precipitated from the estuary on to a bright coastline of red sandstone cliffs, which had figured, she remembered, with a train drawn by a green steam locomotive, in a jig-saw puzzle she'd had. There were several quick tunnels, glimpses of empty beaches and beyond them the immensity of the Channel glistening to the horizon in the yellow March sunshine. She panicked again. In the scene she felt such an alien permanence. It had all been here for so many years. Who was she, even to herself?

Assuming she would come by train, Henry Bordeaux had rather unexpectedly rung her two nights before with all the travel arrangements precisely worked out. He had told her to get off at Totnes and take a taxi.

At the barrier a substantial neatly-dressed figure was standing in fawn-coloured whipcords, a tweedy shirt and tie and a well-cut brown corduroy jacket which had a smart slit up the back permitting a glimpse of coffee-coloured silk lining. She was sure it was him before his mildly anxious eyes scanning the few people who had got off focused on her. She saw he was good-looking in a square-cut sort of way, reminding her of Jack Hawkins in those heroic second world war films.

'Jocelyn Hammond?' Stooping, he took her small case in his left hand in the same movement as shaking hands with her. 'Thought I'd save you waiting for a taxi. Sometimes you have to from the London train.'

She rather liked it that he didn't immediately try to launch into small talk. He didn't even ask her about her journey as he led the way out into the forecourt of the station with a muted stride deferentially turned to her. His vehicle was a huge dark green new-looking Land Rover, which stood a lot higher than the other cars. He saw her up gallantly into the passenger seat, parked her case in the back and climbed in beside her. He shut his door, put the key into the ignition, then sat back in his seat, frowning, not looking at her.

'Look, I've a confession to make. The local hostelry where I was going to book you in is unexpectedly full, there's an antiques fair on. Hotels are never normally full at this time of year - and I'm afraid I left it till this morning to phone them. Hope you don't mind, I didn't try any others. I thought actually it might be better if you put up at Combe. Might give you the feel of the place?' She said she didn't mind at all, it would be nicer. 'Good,' he said, with a faint, she thought shy, smile and apparently a small relief. He reached forward to start the car.

They drove through the outskirts of the town whose picturesque quality, he explained to her, wasn't widely known. He talked of its history - something about a castle, a priory, and a fine medieval Guildhall. But though such knowledge was in her estimation something of importance, she was a little ashamed to find she wasn't fully listening. She had been looking at his hands on the wheel, rather nice muscular well-used hands - *he* certainly hauled and drew. She observed also his voice. The accent inclined towards upper, she supposed, but not ostensibly so, there were no consciously-identified, archetypal vowel-sounds. His abundant brown hair with no trace of grey was conventionally, almost boyishly, parted at the side. She remembered for some reason - was it in this context? - he had been a colonel in the Commandos. She had looked up the house and the garden in a guide book she found in the public library. Some of the entries had short biographies of the owners. Maybe it was that she thought of Commandos, of all ranks, as rather effective, classless individuals, a law unto themselves.

He startled her from her thoughts. 'You know the west country?'

'Er - no.'

'I didn't till I bought High Combe.'

'But you do now of course, very thoroughly?'

'Oh yes.'

She hesitated. Who was interviewing whom? 'And you obviously love it?'

He turned his head away and looked serious. 'South Devon has become my life - the climate, the soil, the flora and fauna, and increasingly the people, who are perhaps a bit difficult to get to know. You wait for them, they won't allow you to force things. As indeed is proper, relationships can't be pushed - don't you think?'

She ignored the question, which she wasn't sure was one. 'And had you done anything like it before - gardening, I mean?'

'I was a soldier.'

'A Commando.'

'Yes.'

'It was a big change then?'

'Shall we say it's a different kind of warfare.' He turned to give her another brief smile. Was it shy, or ironic? She was no longer sure.

The question she had been itching to put was on the edge of her tongue. He had said 'stay the night at Combe', not 'stay with us.' Was there no us, had he done it all alone? But she funked so suggestive a change of subject. 'So you had to learn everything from scratch - about plants and so on?'

'About plants, and also about aesthetics - landscaping.'

She risked a compliment. 'Well it seems you've done marvellously. The book I looked you up in, which said you were a Commando, also said your garden is one of the most renowned in these parts.'

'I'd like to think it is, yes. His expression was realistic, she thought, certainly not smug. If anything, it was the smallest bit sad.

They had crossed a river he informed her was the Dart, mounted a hill, and now drove through the lushly-green hilly countryside whose soil was ubiquitously a rich red. They turned off the main road on to a smaller one with high hedges which only here and there permitted glimpses of the wide valley to their right. They drove through a charming village of pink-washed thatched houses, which smelt not unpleasantly of manure, and several times caught sight of water which he said was 'the estuary.' 'The Dart's a drowned valley,' he explained. 'When the Ice Age finished and the ice melted, the sea-level went up and invaded the river valleys. You might say it's a fjord. Rather beautiful up here, isn't it?'

After a while, having drawn away from the estuary, it seemed they were now approaching it again. Keeping to a contour, they were dipping in and out of re-entrants, some of which were thickly-wooded.

They arrived without warning. The road was running through trees on either side. He slowed suddenly, looked in the mirror, and turned off to the right through an open white-painted gate into a newly-gravelled drive. Set back slightly and inside the gate was a large white board with 'High Combe Garden' painted in neat black letters. On the other side of the drive was an 'In' sign. They wove between thickets of fatly budding rhododendron, and debouched into a large circular parking area which had an exit road marked 'Out' at the other end. In the centre was a raised round bed stuffed with budding daffodils edged with healthy polyanthus plants also getting ready to bloom. Beyond a new-looking limestone wall, against the near end of which a shop had been built, rose the upper floors of the red-tiled, gabled Edwardian house.

'You're well defended from the buses.'

'How clever of you to notice. Yes, surprising what a difference the wall has made. We had up to ten loads at once last summer. And it corrals the visitors. They now enter and, more important, leave the garden through the shop, which so becomes a kind of fly-trap.'

There were no cars. The place seemed deserted. She had forgotten until this moment that she had read they didn't open until next week. He drove to a black-painted iron gate at the far end of the wall. It was marked 'Private' and opened electronically. They passed into a small gravelled area in front of the porched entrance of the house, where he parked. A young labrador appeared round the corner of the house and bounded ecstatically to the car on Henry's side.

Briskly caressing the reaching head he ordered it down. As they went in, he told it to stay outside. Disappointed, the dog obeyed.

He showed her up the pleasing heavily-carpeted white-painted staircase to a large room on the first floor with a bay window - surely one of the master bedrooms? It had an adjoining bathroom. It was handsomely rather than beautifully furnished with faint blue, striped wallpaper and a darker blue wall-to-wall carpet. There was single bed with a white velvet bedhead and a heavily embroidered royal blue bedspread, two comfortable upholstered chairs and a mahogany dressing-table with a solid-looking triptych mirror, beside which a vase of daffodils had been placed. Had he put them there? Her question lurked again.

She made for the large window and was faced with her first breathtaking view of the garden. Immediately below was a broad Italian terrace, its ornate ceramic pots of varying shapes and sizes ranged attractively here and there on the pinkish limestone flagstones and along the balustrade. Several were stuffed with spring bulbs sturdily sprouting. Below this was another wider level, a rose garden laid out round a rectangular pool which had flat water plants and a central fountain. The well-dug well-manured beds were spaced artistically, stocked with roses pruned and labelled and already breaking into reddish leaf. On either side of the vista she suspected there were other planted areas shielded by the huge magnolias, and there before her, descending the valley in which the main garden had been created, was a wild miscellany of (surely) rare trees - she recognised only a cedar and a wellingtonia - exotic-looking shrubs, numerous areas and levels planted with flowers, and everywhere huge plots of daffodil and narcissus. Here and there a stream appeared as it made its devious busy way down, twice crossed by small wooden bridges. Right at the bottom was a glimpse of the estuary through a final glade of trees.

He had moved beside her and was waiting as she took it in, allowing her time and space. She felt he was looking at the scene with as much intensity as she was. 'It's a magnificent achievement,' she said finally. 'No wonder they come in bus-loads. You must be very proud of it.'

'Yes, I suppose I am.'

'And surely unique? I've never seen anything like this anywhere.'

There was a small awkwardness for her as they continued to stand together for a moment. He didn't move until she did. Then he suggested she made herself at home and met him downstairs for a cup of tea - say, in twenty minutes?

When he had closed the door and his footsteps descending the stairs had died away, an eerie silence fell. She found herself listening to it. Was he the only person here? Was that why he had been anxious about not getting her a room in a hotel? A fear sprang. Had she been wise? Stupidly, before she could correct herself, her eye flew to the door. Was there a key in the lock? 'You're the only female applying,' he had written.

There was a key. Cinema stuff, she told herself. It wasn't the first time she had found her instinctive reactions being governed by relations with Leo over the last years. Of course Henry Bordeaux was an honourable man - a Commando Colonel? And if he had amorous intentions, or were to have any at any time in the future, she would know how to deal with them.

She washed, took off the bedspread, and unpacked her few things into a handsome antique tallboy he had indicated was empty. Really to kill time she sat finally at the dressing-table and did minor repairs. Her few actions had not taken her more than five minutes.

He was in front of a sparking newly-lit log fire when she entered the long sitting-room. Having entered by the other door, with practised movements which told her he had done it many times before he was just lowering a silver tray on to the glass coffee table.

'Good timing. Until we open I'm on my own, I'm afraid. I just have Edith Applecote, my gardener's wife, to do the cleaning and some of the cooking. Most of my own food I do myself in the winter. Milk, sugar?'

He handed her the steaming brew in the cup from the pale-yellow porcelain tea-set. Her eye flew to the open door of a glass corner-cupboard whose door was open and which had two half-empty shelves. Was the set in daily use? She couldn't think so. Fortunately he didn't see her looking. He was busy extricating a plate of crumpets from the other crocks.

'Do you like these? They're a childhood obsession of mine and I tend to assume everyone lusts after them as much as I do.'

She took one, and the simultaneously offered plate, and quite decided he was either a bachelor or had lost or been divorced from his wife. It was now surely inconceivable that there was a Mrs Bordeaux at large. She decided if he wasn't going to get into the action straight away, she would. 'I'm afraid I didn't bring my wellies,' she said.

'That doesn't matter. We can avoid the wet bits. We'll do a round before it gets dark if you'd like to. I want you to see the main outlines of the garden before we talk. As I explained, in the summer the job will be in large part administrative - a great deal of it now is the publicity and dealing with party bookings - but in the autumn, winter and spring, with the green-houses greatly extended last year, there's more than enough for three working full-time. That's why I've been envisaging giving the job to a man, even though the admin would be as well done, perhaps better, by a woman.'

'I'm ready for hard labour. Though, as I explained, I've no professional skills, I do understand and like gardening. I used to have quite a sizeable patch. I am quite strong physically,' she added with an element of riposte.

His mind was on something else. 'Skills can be learnt, knowledge can be acquired,' he murmured. He paused, frowning, stirring his cup, level with his chest. 'But I hope you're not going to mind if I ask you a question. Because of the way I worded the advertisements, most of the serious applications have been from men in their early twenties who've had training and/or experience and who as far as one can tell are bent upon some kind of a career in horticulture. You, by your own statement, have had neither. What I suppose I'm really asking you is whether you have any longer term intentions in the business.'

She found herself blushing. Had she thought him over-sensitive? She could see he was more than capable of bluntness. For a moment she was annoyed. How could any employer expect even qualified guarantees of this sort? And she was now even more suspicious that a male assumption of superiority was lurking. Why should he think a woman less capable of professional constancy than a man? She took refuge in a levity she didn't feel.

'You mean, being a woman, I might be filling in between husbands and that in six months I might scarper with all you'd taught me?'

It was for him now to blush. He did so in dismay. 'No, of course I didn't mean that. How dreadful of me to have given you that impression. It's certainly not to do with your being female. Simply that you're not at present in a career structure. I'm sorry to have been so clumsy.'

She'd had no intention of discussing her private life. Either, after talking to her, she was capable of doing the job in his estimation or she wasn't. It was the unhappiness on his face which changed her mind. What he was asking her was perfectly reasonable. Before she could stop herself she was into a headlong rush.

'I'll tell you exactly my position - if you offered me the job and I took it, I'd be telling you anyway. I was married. My marriage began to break up some time ago when I discovered my husband was a conster and in some ways criminal. I'm now divorced and live alone. Unfortunately, though, my husband has been pursuing me in a quite intolerable way. I could take some legal action to try to protect myself, but I don't believe it would work. It's for this reason that I recently decided I must get away from where I live, as this is the only way I'll escape him in any clean way. You might well think this makes me an unsuitable candidate. I don't think it does. It's because of this, not in spite of it, that I think if we were both to survive that trial period, you'd find me a stayer.'

She had surely put it much too forcefully? He put his teacup down carefully. The half-eaten crumpet lay on his plate on the arm of the chair. 'I'm so sorry - about your marriage,' he said.

'Thanks for saying so. But there's no need to be. The pain's long over. What I'm looking for now is, as I say, something new to work for, a new purpose.'

'Yes, yes I can see.'

Surprising her, he cut it off there, like luggage left behind on a platform for a porter to handle. There was one obvious explanation of this, she thought, as he launched into the details of the job, her outspokenness had decided him against her. It was just that being the very decent man she was now sure he was, he was going through the motions of the interview. Tomorrow, on parting, there would be a polite phrase about writing to her.

When he had finished about the job, he leaned forward, holding a knife over a glutinous calory-dispenser of a cake that had garlands of candied peel. 'Now I hope you're going to have a piece of this. Edith makes it. She'll be upset if she finds more than three-quarters of it left tomorrow morning.'

He had already plunged the knife in when she was startled by a bell shrilling in the hall. At first she thought it was a fire-bell it was so loud. But it rang insistently three times. It couldn't surely be the front door?

She saw a weary look cloud his face as he finished cutting two slices and rose. He picked up the teapot and the milk jug. 'My wife is a total invalid,' he said with simple desolation. 'Excuse me for a minute. I'll have to go upstairs. Help yourself to the cake.'

The garden was even more remarkable at close hand. She could see how every bit of it represented, first a vision, then a great deal of hard work. When they had done the tour, he packed her off upstairs again. 'I thought I'd don a suit,' was the last thing he said. 'That is if you've . . .

'Brought something? Yes, I have.'

She had a bath, partially redressed and felt at a loose end again. She had never been one for lengthy toilet preparations. More from idleness than wishing to be nosey, she began to prowl the room. She opened one of the top drawers of the bow-fronted chest. It was full of male socks. Visible under the wool she saw a leather photo frame. She shut the drawer on a guilty impulse. What on earth was she doing, snooping like a common thief? But then, even more guiltily, she reopened it and drew out the frame. It was of him and a slim blonde woman, both in bathing suits, sitting under a huge sunshade - taken about ten years ago, would it be? The place looked somewhere foreign - Central America? Belize perhaps, weren't the Commandos there at some stage? It was a beach, with a jungly background. There were two little girls in sunhats playing in the sand in front of them, twins by the look.

Her guilt took control again. She stuffed the photo back under the socks. Had she unconsciously learnt some of Leo's underhand stealth? Never in her life had she caught herself doing something like this.

She'd also had another thought. She was now sure this was Henry Bordeaux's room, which he must have cleared of some of his things. If it was so, she didn't like it. It was surely just a bit too gallant. If he was going to treat her as different just because she was female, it wasn't going to work. Nonetheless she was touched. Those children - were they his? If so, where were they now, at boarding school? They would presumably be teenagers. She was left with a sharpened sense of sadness. That woman - an aged version of the blonde in the photo? - must be in the room, perhaps identical to this one, at the other end of the house, which also had a projecting bay. She had sensed he had gone up with the teapot to that side of the building and, drawing the curtains while waiting for the bath to fill, she had seen the light on over there. She imagined a terrible incapacitating injury. Why had he not said anything about her before the bell rang? She read herself another lecture. It was no possible business of hers. She must expunge her ill-gotten knowledge from the records until she came by it legitimately. She put on the dress she was glad she had packed - a faithful black well-cut but years old - a string of pearls, dabbed a small quantity of her inexpensive toilet-water, and applied a minimum of lipstick.

He was waiting for her in front of the sitting-room fire when she went down. In the dark surely tailor-made suit, he was even more good-looking - and pleasingly unselfconscious about it. They had gin and tonics, then he suggested they went in to the small dining-room adjoining where the highly polished table had been laid carefully for two with quite a glitter of silver. There were two antique candlesticks, which he lit as they entered. Ready placed were two delicious-looking starters which looked suspiciously like caviare heaped on top of a mound of brownish jelly and cream. As she sat on the comfortable high-back chair which had embroidered upholstery he uncorked a half bottle of white wine and replaced it in the silver ice-bucket.

'I'll let you into a secret,' he said. 'I'm really rather enjoying your visit - quite apart from the business side. I've got quite interested in cooking in the last year or two and I don't often have the chance of doing something out of the ordinary. When we're open it's practically out of the question - Edith does it all - and in the winter, well, people from afar don't come, and I don't seem to have an enormous number of local friends.'

'The first, visible, part of it looks absolutely delicious. I also suspect you're spoiling me.'

He laughed. It was the first time he had done so with any conviction. 'Taste it before you pronounce,' he said as he stood beside her to pour her glass.

She did so. 'You *are* spoiling me,' she said.

He sat down, unfolding the white linen table-napkin. 'What do you think it is?'

'Well, caviare.'

'No, it isn't. Monk fish roes at a fraction of the cost. A tin of good old Campbell's beef consomé, a spot of gelatine to set it, cream, seasoning, and you're there. I found it in a magazine.'

Because of his cooking - the entrée was veal in a delicious Marsala sauce - conversation was easy. She saw he liked to talk of functional matters. She had only to feed him with her interest in what he had to say. Was it really going to be one of those interviews where the interviewer makes all the running and forgets to interview? She took it as a further sign that she had got the thumbs down.

Was she pleased, relieved, she pondered, as the interesting but uninterrupted recitatif continued - now he was talking of the coming summer problems? Would she really want to come into this set-up? How could she live alone with this very marketable man, even with an invalid wife at hand?

Perhaps it was the wine - a surely expensive Hermitage had succeeded the temporarily suspended Alsace. The safe conversation, which had seemed so well-established, came to a sudden end.

'But look, I'm wittering and probably boring you out of your skin. I'm sorry. It's just that, living virtually alone in the evenings, it all comes out in a rush when the sluices are opened. Perhaps you have the same problem? You say you live alone. No, I bet you don't have the same problem. I'm sure you have lots of friends.'

'I don't know that I have at all.'

'I'd guess you're very much in demand.'

She considered. A gambit, to be stone-walled? Possibly, but she had again an impulse to be frank with him. 'I'm not in demand actually,' she said seriously. 'It's not, either, that I've chosen not to be. I think, given the option, I'd rather like to be the life and soul of the party. It seems to be sometimes that, although I'm well and truly severed from Leo, the fact that he has pursued me and made my life such a burden - which you might think would be a source of people's sympathy rather than the reverse - in some ways adheres to my person as if I was almost infected by it. People are outwardly kind and helpful, but it seems sometimes that they almost need to inoculate themselves against me because if they didn't they might be infected by the contagion. Does that sound fantastic?'

He was dabbing his mouth gravely with his napkin. 'No, it isn't fantastic at all. I know exactly what you mean.'

What had she done? She sensed that what she had said did, fortuitously, apply to him as well, but also that he didn't care for such an intimacy. There was a long silence in which she dived into the food in a panic.

When she reemerged, he had switched the subject. 'By the way,' he was saying, 'we were so busy on the garden we haven't discussed what from your point of view is probably the most vital thing if you took the job. You certainly wouldn't want to live in this house. I don't know what you'd want to do if we came to an agreement - buy or rent a property perhaps? I forgot to say that, as an alternative, there is a small independent flat I built over the garage, which I'm offering to the successful candidate. It's rather small, but comfortable with all mod con. I'll show it to you anyway in the morning.'

She decided overnight this had been perfunctory, and no more than a necessary change of subject. He did show her the flat in the morning, but cursorily, and he didn't offer her the job. He apologised for not being able to take her to Totnes, and rang for a taxi. He asked her to say if she definitely didn't want the job. She said she would natually want to think about it if it were offered, but that she felt very positive. He said he would also like to think about it, and that he would be seeing two other people. He handed her an envelope - which contained a cheque, he said. He hoped it covered everything. 'Whatever happens, I thank you for coming down,' he said. 'From my point of view it was a quite delightful time we spent together. I hope it wasn't a complete bore for you.'

These were his final words as they shook hands. Later, she realised a fact which seemed curious to her. Apart from his first greeting at the railway station, they hadn't once addressed each other by name. They had certainly been nowhere near a 'do please call me Henry' and its reciprocation. It portended one thing. At best from her point of view, the owner of High Combe had been giving himself a perhaps infrequent opportunity for female company.

2.

Jocelyn would be the first to say her childhood in the fenland city of Ely had been happy. She was an only child, but had been cherished by both her parents. On the other hand, if pressed, she might have admitted her early existence had been uneventful, even dutiful. This dutifulness she would probably have associated largely with the church.

Her father was a canon in the cathedral clergy, and they lived within the Close under the very shadow of the massive Norman structure whose stern octagonal tower rose like a monitoring finger over the surrounding fens. Every Sunday since she could remember she had attended early Communion with her mother, followed at eleven by Matins, and on at least one weekday evensong. These attendances were never acts of devotion on her part, involving emotion, but ones of habit. The liturgy, repeated so often, was meaningless to her. When she entered her teens she was given some instruction in its significance but the words remained as they always had to her, part of the rather static furniture of the place, a reminder - as were equally the stout pillars and the lofty roof and tower of the great church - of people in history to whom presumably they had once meant something and which you could therefore look upon with some respect. What engaged and always uplifted her was the glorious music of the organ and the choir. Where would the Church of England be today, she had often thought, without the magnificent inheritance of its music?

Apart from the music, Jocelyn's churchgoings were part of her duty to her parents. This duty took other forms as well. Her local schooling, which included 'A' levels, distanced her from any of father's views on politics on which he frequently expounded his ultra-conservative views. There were, here and there, a few coincidences of opinion, but she tended not to distinguish these items from the others, for quite early in her mental development she had sensed that all father's statements were not specific views at all on the topics they were alleged to refer to, but some kind of a receptacle for unnamable private emotions about quite different matters - his frustration at being a clergyman at all maybe, and at not being a famous naturalist like Gilbert White, whose books he revered rather more, Jocelyn thought, than the Bible. His opinions were thus not to be disputed, but sympathetically nodded at.

With her mother, Jocelyn's forbearance was of another order. What Beatrice Lotham's expectations of life had once been Jocelyn found it difficult to fathom, presumably she'd had some. Jocelyn was only sure that whatever they were, they were now sunk on a seabed so deep as to be unsalvageable. Her mother was a person of unremitting habit, getting up, donning neat clothes - but ones she wore until they fell apart - going to church, cleaning the ludicrously roomy three-storey flint and brick house which was stuffed with furniture, holding tea-parties for other ladies of the Close and cathedral helpers, visiting, assisting with those regular jumble-sales and fetes which cluster like bees in a swarm round church life, and knitting for dear life whenever there were spare moments. It seemed to Jocelyn her mother was totally cocooned in the kindly proverbs and sayings she had probably inherited from her own family. 'Never mind, dear, no real harm done,' she had chanted rhythmically over the grazed knees and bruised elbows of childhood, 'it's no good crying over spilt milk, is it?' When on a famous occasion Jocelyn lost her entire bowl of goldfish to a predatory Close cat which had developed a habit of burgling their house, there were - not so inappropriately in this case - 'plenty of other fish in the sea.' Beatrice had her own well-thumbed liturgy to match that of the Church, Jocelyn thought, tags and phrases for any eventuality. But it was all kindly, well-meant, affectionate. When she was about seventeen, Jocelyn discovered in herself a capacity for mild irony, but this she never applied to her mother, even though it probably wouldn't have been noticed if she had. She loved her mother, as she loved her father, and only in some deep crevice of her consciousness grieved for them for what seemed some almost genetic predicament in which they were transfixed.

As far as she herself was concerned Jocelyn had no particular problem in her childhood, nor in her early and middle teens. If she began to sense quite early on that the solicitude both her parents showered on her was in some degree an atonement for whatever failures there were in their own relationship and circumstances, why should she question this? She accepted their separately bestowed affection gratefully. Wasn't she perhaps lucky in this way - a tertius gaudens, to quote a famous phrase of Bismark's? When she compared herself with other girls at the local comprehensive she went to, she realised she had even more reason to be convinced of her status as the third one rejoicing. So many of the others seemed to talk bitterly about the shortcomings of their parents, whom they blamed savagely for the restrictions which were placed on them. They spoke of Ely as if it were beyond the pale of civilised life.

There was a period, about the time she entered the sixth form, in which she did feel a mild disturbance. A great deal of the conversation among her fellow girl students now naturally concerned boys, the degree and quality of interest these males showed in the female charms displayed to them and their consequent eligibility for reciprocal favours. The 'medieval' restrictions which were placed on her friends' relationships with boys by their parents was also a matter of deep concern. Jocelyn had a boy-friend, whom she had known since early childhood, but their relationship didn't seem to produce any of the dramatic excitements those of the other girls did. Was there something missing in her, she had to ask, which made her complacent, or deficient in this aspect of life? She thought there wasn't - she had always awarded herself some merit for being able to understand how others felt, which one would have thought would stand her in as good stead in relationships with boys as with girls. But perhaps sexual relationships were different?

Then she was able to reassure herself. It was at this time she was graduating from Mills and Boon type of fiction to serious literature. She discovered the word 'passion'. Passion, she was assured from these enlightened pages, was not something wild and melodramatic to be tossed about in public like a beachball, but an all-consuming deeply private feeling. This was a relief. It would be all right then, she told herself. Passion - 'the real thing' - would come to her in due course. In the meantime she could do without what she now saw was, in her friends' behaviour, only its substitute. All she had to do was wait patiently. With patience she was well-endowed.

Jocelyn left school after her 'A' levels, went first to France for a year as an au pair, then did a bilingual secretarial course, after which she got a job in Cambridge at the Modern Language Faculty. Her life, she felt, was gently opening out. She'd had a couple of affairs - neither she knew being in the category of passion referred to, but enjoyable and sufficient to allow her to believe she was perhaps even a little above average in her attractiveness to males. And now she was beginning to make interesting friends of both sexes, most of whom were associated with the University in some way. She would much rather have got herself a small flat in Cambridge but, feeling her presence at home was more required these days than it had ever been, she continued to live in Ely.

One autumn Sunday they'd had lunch, one of their typical Sunday lunches which had occurred regularly for as long as she could remember, as other Sunday lunches were no doubt occurring all over England - the trussed joint of beef overdone to the point of saddle-leather, brussels sprouts whose green had been left behind in the saucepan, potatoes roasted so thoroughly that when you broke through their blackened carapaces there was a hollow inside, then plum tart which lived up to the inadvertently sugarless suggestion in its name, apologised for only by a small quiff of whipped cream. Father, released from the tedium of Cathedral matins, in which his part as a canon was secondary and almost entirely decorative, was as usual as eager for the food as he would later be appreciative of it. Mother gave herself no pudding. When she had served her husband and daughter she excused herself. 'I shall have to have a lie-down, James,' she said, 'I didn't sleep too well last night.'

Father was pleased. If Mother was feeling active on Sunday afternoon there was an obligation to entertain her, a drive to her unmarried sister's house perhaps, which was in a village ten miles from Ely. He waited only until she was out of earshot.

'Well in that case a good walk, Joss, don't you think?' He

rubbed his hands. 'I'm told shelduck moved into the water meadows last evening. They should still be there.'

Jocelyn had always been happy about this one genuine enthusiasm her father enjoyed. And she had always found it easy, even restful, to take refuge in other people's enthusiasms. It made them happy - happier still if they felt there was a genuine listener present - and what better cover was there, as with cathedral services, for private thoughts?

The duck were there, hundreds of them, feeding vigorously in the Wagnerian afternoon light. She was moved, even a little disturbed by their clamour and by their huge, almost fascist, collective purpose. She was moved also by father as they skirted the scene to enable him to observe the birds from all angles with his heavy black military binoculars. How much more alive he was when out twitching than in the cathedral. She thought he really hated religion - and didn't even care much about the music as she did. It was, for her as well as for him, an afternoon of contentment.

She would always remember his cry from upstairs when they got back. Though certainly not in any way false, it sounded theatrical - like someone doing Lear rather too strenuously. Already fearing from its tone what might have happened, she raced up. Mother lay, her hands folded on the sheet, her face pale, composed, looking young, almost virginal, as if waiting for a treat. Father, kneeling, was sobbing into the bedclothes. She remembered feeling - detachedly even at this moment - that it would have made the most perfect Pre-Raphaelite painting. What did this make her, callous?

The debt William Lotham owed to his wife was monumentally apparent in the coming months. Rendered silent and totally morose without her, he aged visibly by the day - willing himself to die, Jocelyn thought. The lack of faith he had by implication expressed all his life was now overt. 'You know there's nothing afterwards, Joss,' he said to her dismally. 'I've been on my knees half my life, but it's all our own make-believe. It just finishes, as she has finished.' She did what she could to comfort him, but succeeded only here and there and temporarily. His security he'd had on a lease. The freeholder had now called in the property. He was emotionally and spiritually roofless.

A most unexpected result of the death of her father, which occurred only six months later, was the discovery that she was very well-off. The house in the Cathedral Close was the property of the church and reverted to it, but it emerged from the lawyer that there was a huge sum of money her parents had inherited and saved, all of which had been bequeathed to her as the sole legatee. There was also the furniture. She had always been aware that some of it probably had value - most having been handed down by their respective parents - but not to the extent which was pointed out to her.

To possess what amounted to a minor fortune might eventually have to be some kind of an excitement and an opportunity, but for the moment she felt no elation at all. She pondered in dismay why her parents could have scrimped and given all indications of penury all their lives when they could have spent at least some of this money. Why had they not bought nice clothes, a car (which they had never had), taken holidays abroad? Why had father not left the Church, which she was sure he had wanted to do? She had always imagined he couldn't because of money. The discomforting thought occurred to her. She was sure both her parents were frugal by nature and upbringing, but could it also be that they had exercised this gross self-denial mainly so that she could inherit the wealth intact? Would she ever be comfortable at having done so?

Thinking about this was an essential part of the numbness she felt at her loss. She lived through father's funeral and the days after it in a state of suspension. People went through the motions of what they would call 'paying their respects'. She paid back to them an equally perfunctory gratitude. Then this tiresome ritual culminated in a sparsely attended memorial service which Anthony Thwaites, the Dean, had thoughtfully organised a couple of weeks later to honour both her parents.

The few mourners, and Anthony, had emerged from the cathedral afterwards through a side door and were standing on a little patch of grass. Most of them were itching to go, Jocelyn thought, conversation was hard to come by. Anthony, however, did his duty by talking cheerfully to them all, and finally rendered her a service by rescuing her from the attentions of that aunt, her mother's sister, who lived nearby and who was sour because nothing at all had been left to her in the will.

'I have to say,' her aunt was saying, 'I fear your father was never entirely in his right mind after Beatrice passed on.'

'Oh, surely not,' said Anthony, pouncing humourously. 'William was on the ball to the last over. Certainly he was as meticulous about his duties as he always was.'

Neatly, really rather ruthlessly, Jocelyn thought, he severed Aunt Emily, presenting to her just enough of his shoulder to indicate her conversation was ended. 'Jocelyn, my dear,' he continued in another voice, patently on another tack, 'now what are you going to do? You must stay in the house until you have made up your mind - but it's to be Cambridge, I'm sure, isn't it? A nice modern flat with no vestige of ecclesiastical gothic?' He had often been light-hearted to her, some would have certainly said disrespectful, about the Victorian aspects of the Close. She told him that she hadn't really decided yet, but that she supposed she would. 'Then I'm delighted,' Anthony said. 'Delighted because we aren't going to lose you.'

He began to talk about Cambridge, and how much more pleasant it would be for her to live there than in Ely. Archly lowering his voice, he said he envied 'her escape from this social bog.' He listed several acquaintances in various University colleges and explained how these would give him 'alibis' for visiting her when she was installed - 'that is, if I'll be permitted to,' he added with an element of coquetry she was also used to.

She composed a practised smile to acknowledge this performance, and thought what she had thought before, that Anthony was no more devout than her father had been, though for very different reasons. The Church to Anthony, she thought, wasn't a vocation but a ladder set up before him, which he was climbing with dextrous speed. It could surely have been almost any profession he could have set himself to scale - the media perhaps, advertising, advocacy. His deanhood had been secured at a surprisingly young age, and now it was said a mitre was not too distant a possibility. But, she also thought, he was an intelligent urbane man who knew how to charm, especially women. Jocelyn didn't find herself particularly charmed, but she found his company agreeable enough in a town not rich in excitements.

Her attention strayed nonetheless as the jaunty flow of words continued. She became aware of a young man in a smart grey suit standing alone a little apart from the knot of people. She didn't know him, but she had noticed him at the service looking in her direction. She thought he must be someone from another town who had known father - he was again regarding her closely. Quite definitely then, as she briefly met his eyes, she saw him give a little wiggle of his head and make a grimace - one she could only interpret as subversive, as if he were an intimate member of the family with whom she had some long-established accord. Did he refer to Anthony? She was sure he did, and had to turn away quickly. Anthony, thankfully, noticed nothing.

With one or two exceptions, she felt no sentiment about the contents of the house and had decided as soon as her father died that she would sell them by auction. She had imagined a local firm would do the job, first removing the stuff to their saleroom. But Anthony had been horrified when he asked her what she proposed and she had told him. 'No, no, Jocelyn, you can't do that. I can understand your not being able to keep the furniture - you'd have to store it, which would be expensive - but don't engage a local firm, they'll make an appalling mess of it and you won't realise half the proper value. It should be a London firm, I'm sure - and hold the sale in the house, not a saleroom. Sotheby's, no less. They'll jump at it.'

Sotheby's didn't jump at it. It was, it seemed, too small fry for them. But Anthony immediately had a connection who produced another London firm named Brent and Shapley, 'whom I'm told are first rate and, not having yet achieved their classy aspirations, probably won't be so greedy.' Jocelyn concurred. She found herself ambivalent about the matter. She felt on the one hand that keen guilt at being the recipient of such bounty - a fact which inclined her to listlessness about it - but on the other she had the idea that it would be disrespectful to her parents to give away their possessions for less than their worth.

The day after the memorial service, which was warm and spring-like, employees of Brent and Shapley were putting the finishing touches to their preparations. A pink medium-sized marquee with frilly tasselled loops round the edge of the roof had been set up on the lawn at the back of the house for the viewing of some of the less valuable stuff - and for the auction itself, which would be the next day. Two khahi-overalled men were drifting about the house sticking lot numbers on all the larger items and a smartly dressed rather with-it woman was following them, taking notes on a clipboard.

Having nothing better to do, Jocelyn was sitting in the hall watching them, when through the open front door drifted, hands in pockets, the man who had grimaced at her after the memorial service. He was dressed today in a white polo-neck and relaxed but stylishly-cut black trousers, white socks. He saw her, checked himself only for an instant, then advanced towards her. Stationing himself at her side, he looked round amiably at the numbered objects, and nodded approvingly. 'Good idea to flog the lot. Start again afresh - except for a few choice pieces maybe? I think I'd've done the same myself in your shoes.'

The cheek. Who was he? All her upbringing demanded that she should put him in his place. She found she couldn't. Rather, she was intrigued. His resonant actor's voice was assured, and he was obviously no simpleton - another idea she'd had momentarily. It was so immediately apparent to her how electrically alive he was and - a fact she was already guessing - how totally guiltless.

She delayed her stricture. 'Did you know my father?' she found herself saying instead.

'No?'

'But you know who I am?'

'Of course.'

'Why "of course?"'

He grinned pleasantly. 'You know very well I know who you are. I saw you at the service in the Cathedral yesterday, at which you were obviously the principal mourner. After the service, when we were standing outside, our eyes met when you were corralled by the garrulous Dean. I thought of trying to rescue you, but didn't dare.' She was on the verge of denying she had noticed him, but hesitated too long. He had already gone off the subject. 'Bit of a sham the service, don't you think?' he went on, folding his arms. 'I don't mean from your point of view, of course - you were sad, I could see, in a quiet, dignified way. It was your parents who were being honoured after all, which transcended the banality. I mean most of the others. Crocodile tears, I thought. I thought you thought so. Am I right?'

She flushed with annoyance. 'What do you mean?'

'I mean all the people there were pretending, putting on mournful faces while they sang and prayed, but really they probably weren't thinking about your parents at all. The Dean's address was done more for the glorification of the Dean in my view. He rates his prose rather highly, doesn't he? As for that woman you were talking to outside - did she have her nose put out of joint by something? She seemed to me to be castigating you, not sympathising. I thought you were tolerating her with remarkable restraint until His Nibs rescued you.' Again, he allowed her no time to reply and switched the subject. 'Actually I'd've known who you are, you know, even if I hadn't seen you at that service. I'd've known even from the expression on your face just now as I came through that door.'

'Oh? What was my expression?'

'In a way twice removed, but belonging, definitely belonging - spacially - to this house. The way you were sitting in that chair. Haven't you noticed that? Like animals, we're psychologically quite different on our own territory. On home ground the timid fugitive becomes the fierce defender. Your days here are numbered - church property, is it, hence the sale of furniture alone? - but you're still on your chair, your own territory. It shows.'

Against herself, she smiled faintly, and examined his face which surely expressed, not aggression, but humour and light-heartedness in every line. His approach was outrageous but he was unusual certainly. 'The viewing and the auction is tomorrow, you know,' she said, nonetheless introducing a note of censure.

'Well I ought to know that, oughtn't I? But I just thought I'd take a peek beforehand. I always like to know what I'm flogging. That's why I got here a day early - as well as to see your lovely hunk of a Norman church, not hitherto on my cultural repertoire.'

'Do you mean you're the auctioneer?'

'The very same, Leo Cunningham by name, bright, willing, and at your service - madame.' He gave the latter word a ludicrous foreign stress and drew himself up into a stiff bow, as if to mock old-fashioned gallantry and with it all social correctitude. He was extremely good-looking, and his brown open face was - quite definitely she thought now - infectiously humorous. Also, quite probably he was well aware he possessed these attributes.

'You'll no doubt want to carry on with your inspection then,' she said, rising from the high-backed chair which she was beginning to feel exposed her by making her look magisterial.

'I will, but you wouldn't like to give me a guided tour, would you?'

She suspected then what he was up to. Either he was seeking a mild flirtation to fill an empty afternoon or, more likely, he wanted private family information about the lots, which he could use tomorrow in his sales patter. 'A tour?' she said. 'I'm sure you'd be better off looking round by yourself, wouldn't you?'

'One is seldom better off by oneself. At least, I'm not - and certainly not in this instance. You know where everything is and, let's face it - let *me* face it anyway - I'd very much like you to show me round.'

It was the latter remark which decided her no doubt contrary nature to take him round. She was bored, and really, if this was the limit of his subtlety, it might after all be amusing as well as merited if she found a way of quietly blocking any further intimacies he tried.

She took him first into the library because it was the nearest room. To her great surprise he made no effort at looking but moved at once to the red velvet sofa, sat down and patted the cushion beside him. 'Come and sit, will you? I think I'm getting in a lot more vibes about you. Want to hear them?'

She continued to stand. 'What on earth do you mean?'

'What I say. I'm really getting a lot more ideas about you and am dying to try them out. I'm like that. Can't help it. It sort of happens, as it does to a water-diviner.' He mimicked an Irishman. 'Faith, for sure, it's the gift I must be having.'

She decided not to be stuffy. There was plenty of time for that if it became necessary. She lowered herself on to an arm of one of the chairs and crossed her arms over her chest like a hornpipe-dancer. 'Perhaps you should be a fortune-teller then, and not an auctioneer,' she said with a glint of irony.

'I'll remember that in case I ever need to change my job.' He stared into her face and narrowed his eyes playfully. 'All right, here goes,' he said, 'the crystal ball. I'd say for starters that for very noble and philanthropic reasons, despite good talents you've had to rather mark time in your life so far. Elderly parents, the only child, the aged-P syndrome? Dad a very minor old canon - I do know that for a fact. Mum tied to cathedral chores maybe? And you providing the yeast to keep their lives going all these years. Anything like right so far?'

'You've got a nerve.'

'Fair amount of it, I suppose - an auctioneer has to. Nothing risked and all that, you have to be slightly dangerous, in fact. Well?'

'My father was a canon. I wouldn't describe my mother as a performer of chores, and I don't have any particular talents.'

'Aha, playing forward, are we? Nicely smothering the spin. OK, let me try a googly on you. I'll re-phrase and put it this way. As I say, you were sad yesterday about your Dad's death, and your mother's some months ago, naturally you're sad. But you're not exactly in mourning, are you, not *deeply* grieving. Grieving's a big word after all. If you're grieving, it's probably about something else, I'm not sure quite what.'

He took her breath away. 'You're quite incredible.'

'Fairly. But am I at all right? That service, or rather the people at that service, were as much a pain to you as they were to me. I'd guess religion's probably a pain to you. I'm sure you loved your parents, but they weren't maybe - what's the word? - weren't necessary to you perhaps? It was written all over your face. I'd say in fact when all this is over and digested, you might even come to think that what you've done is to weigh anchor.'

She turned her head away, but found she couldn't still be annoyed. He was after all perfectly, amazingly, right. And she had just noticed something - that in spite of his social confidence there was an incongrously anxious uncertainty in his eyes, which were of a devastating blue, the blue of innocence. Was he so totally self-assured as he made out? She hovered between simulated rage - for simulated it would have been - and the truth. She had a sense that only the truth would defeat him, less he would winnow like chaff.

'What I'm sorry about is that my parents didn't enjoy their lives more,' she found herself saying.

'Ah.'

'They could have done, but for some reason they went on treading a path they'd always trodden. That's sad.'

'Sad indeed.'

'And now . . .

'Now you must tread a very different path for them. Is that it? Is that what you're thinking? Aren't you limbering up to tread it for them? You should be if you aren't. Sort of in their honour, to compensate. Isn't that right?'

He said this so softly, in such a different, uncocky, surely sympathetic tone, it caught her unawares. It was also true, though she hadn't precisely thought it. Was she so transparent? But she suddenly felt besieged. Through the days of official mourning she had felt nothing at all tangible. Suddenly now she was overwhelmed. It was all so totally sad. She put her hands over her face.

To her amazement he got up and she felt his hand on her shoulder. 'It's understandable you're upset,' he said. 'Of course - it's your past. But it won't last, will it - your being upset, I mean? I suspect that like me you're a free spirit. You'll take wings, soar. By the way, I have news for you. After the auction I'm going to invite you to the biggest wake you've ever imagined.'

When she had recovered sufficiently to look up and attend to this incredible remark, he was on his way out of the room. At the door he turned, raised a hand in mock solemnity, then went out, closing the door behind him.

During the sale the following afternoon, hardly noticing the procession of familiar objects the two khaki-coated men lifted into view, she observed him from the back of the marquee. Back in the fashionable grey suit, today set off with a swingeing orange shirt, toning tie and socks, he was tireless, it seemed, ubiquitously awake and running circles round a placid audience which seemed transfixed by his performance. He reminded her of a sheepdog, rounding them up, cutting off strays, impelling them in the direction he wanted, and all with a light-hearted humour which seemed in a strange way - was it fanciful of her? - to proportion the relative value of possessions. Beautiful and desirable as they were, he seemed to be saying between the lines, was it not really a game, this lottery of property? Shouldn't they remember this even when in the thick of bidding?

Before the sale was over, Jocelyn retreated to the small top floor of the house which had for some time been her living quarters, and which during the viewing and sale had been made out of bounds, with a tasselled red rope across the stairs. In the flat she had gathered a few things from downstairs she wanted to keep, in addition to those which already furnished her two rooms and small kitchen.

She felt tired and lay on the bed, looking forward to the moment when the clamour and bumping below would cease and she would be left alone. She must have dozed. She awoke suddenly to hear her name being called.

It was someone half-way up the stairs, she thought. 'Jocelyn, it's me, Leo,' she heard, 'they've all gone.' Not sure what she felt, she leapt up. Glancing in the mirror she pushed briefly at her hair, smoothed her woollen dress, and went out of the room. He was on the landing below. 'Is something wrong?' she asked.

For answer, he unhooked the rope, replaced it, and continued up. 'Far from it. Am I intruding? I just thought you'd like to know how much we made. I lie. That isn't my motive at all. I've just come to see you. Someone said you were up here.'

It was perhaps her fatigue. She began to feel cross. 'Look, I think you are intruding. You must surely realise that rope was put there . . .

'To keep out the general public, right. But I'm not the general public. Am I?'

'I really don't want visitors just now, and the sale figures can wait.'

He was now standing beside her in the half-gloom. Unbelievably, he put his hand on her arm, as he had in the library. 'I'm serious, you know. I really do want to get to know you. I know what you're thinking - smart Alec, west end salesman. But I'm really not the fast type where girls are concerned. The fact is, the moment I saw you across the pews two days ago in the Cathedral, I just knew you were different. I knew I wanted to meet you. When we encountered downstairs yesterday I was sure. What's bitten me above all, I think - given the fact that you're extremely beautiful - is that, behind your kind goodwill, you have a look of such devastating almost frightening openness and emotional honesty.'

She had an unusual feeling which took her quite unawares. Before, she had been mildly entertained, then he had nearly made her weep, now she found she was suddenly unreservedly furious. She had thought his behaviour absurd, amusing enough to fill a boring afternoon. It was nothing of the sort, she decided. It was nothing more than gross cheek. This was the kind of superficial thing Italian men are supposed to go in for with foreign girls on holiday, wasn't it? She had a sudden desire, of a sadistic force which astonished her, to put him down good and proper, the cocky idiot. She gave a hard, ironic laugh, and his hand fell away without her having to remove it.

'I see,' she said. 'So you're a shy recluse who never makes passes at girls, are you? Do you really expect me to believe that, when in the last hours you've made a series of extraordinarily intimate remarks about me and my family, and now have had the neck to barge into my home without invitation? Look, I've had a rather trying few days. I'd like you to leave at once.'

She was quite prepared for him to be angry, even physical. Let him try anything on, she thought, she would slay him with her rage. But he was neither angry nor physical. Instead, he stepped back as if reeling under the impact of what she had said. Then, after a pause, he seemed to recover and gave a gentle laugh.

'You know - I'm sorry if I sound cocky - but I have to say I just don't believe you're really so angry with me as this. It's something else, it must be. If I am being male and cocky, I'll admit it, but I honestly don't think I am, except maybe a little on the surface - one has to be allowed to show off a bit. I've shocked you coming upon you like this - I can see that - and I'm sure you have had a very trying few days. But the look you had on your face when you first saw me down there on the stairs didn't tell me you were outraged. I could swear you looked intrigued. "Who the hell's this joker - a mere auctioneer, if perhaps a rather posh one - who thinks he can break all the canons of normal social behaviour?" Isn't that what you were thinking? Well, I'll let you into a secret. I'm pretty surprised at my behaviour myself. I've really never done anything remotely like this before in my life. If you really don't believe me and want me to go, of course I will. But will you tell me first, honestly, if it's really me you're angry about?'

She allowed him in, she was to think later - OK, because undoubtedly she found her first reflex anger did abate as suddenly as it had come - but also because she was still curious, curious not so much about his searching provocative remark, but about that gentle laughter of his. Could he really have counterfeited that - and, again, that look of anxiety? She was still convinced he was playing and that sooner or later he would say something absurd which would give away the silly superficiality of his act, but until he did she would allow him a stay of execution. Fortunately she didn't possess a sofa, just the two armchairs, which were a distance apart. Finding an unused bottle of angostura bitters at the back of the kitchen cupboard, she gave him the anachronistic pink gin he asked for and sat opposite him.

'Now, where were we?' he began.

She continued to be tart. 'I don't think we were anywhere very much.'

'We were talking about why you were angry just now.'

'*You* were talking, you mean.'

'OK, I was. But it still intrigues me. It has to intrigue me because if I can't prove my point I'd have to conclude it was me who'd upset you somehow. All right, here goes - the deep end again. Could it be that it's the whole set up here that's making you champ? A sort of delayed action? Start with Mr Smoothiboots, the Very Reverend Thwaites? It was plain to me, standing there outside the cathedral, that you're bored rigid by him.'

'I don't think so.'

'No? I'd've guessed that if you weren't so charitable you'd be classifying him a prize hypocrite.'

'Not at all. He's a lively man, not at all the stereotype clergyman.'

'You can say that again. So much not a stereotype he shouldn't be a clergyman. You can see a mile off he knows it's all a fancy dress party and that he's just manipulating it all for his own advancement.'

'He's probably ambitious certainly. Able people often are.'

'But they don't all invent a spurious ideology to camouflage it, do they?'

'Spurious?'

'Of course it is. He's got a brain, for God's sake. He knows it's all a load of codswallop - perhaps I should say Godswallop.'

Against her will she laughed. 'Having a brain disqualifies him from taking the cloth then, does it?'

'You know it does. You've got a brain, and you know it's all a centuries-old con kept alive by male priests who had an axe to grind and a laity trying to believe there's a heaven waiting for us when we die.' He paused. 'But what you perhaps don't know is that Thwaites is terrified of you.'

'Oh come on, what on earth do you mean now?'

'I mean that he knows from your every inflection that you rumble him. You don't attack him verbally of course. That he'd probably know how to deal with. You could imagine the line he'd take. He'd try and confound you with theology, and if that didn't work he'd be able to write you off as "a young materialist", "a soulless young rebel" - there'd be a number of literary options open to a man of his undoubted communication skills. You don't attack him verbally, you do so with politeness and protocol and, being the nice person you are, even kindness. In your parents' interest I bet you've always been impeccable in that department. But there you were the other day - gentle, apparently tolerant, but all the time under the surface implicitly posing him the question - "how can you, a rational and urbane person of above average intellect, pose as a modern sophisticate and at the same time accept all this ecclesiastical mumbo-jumbo?" No wonder he half wants to bolt in your presence as well as flirt with you. He knows you've rumbled him.'

She began to panic a little. She shouldn't have allowed this. 'Look, this is absurd. Anthony and I didn't talk about religion at all, I don't think we ever have. You're building castles in the air. And it was the Dean's idea to have the service. It was kind of him, I was grateful, that's all there was to it.'

He put his hands up as if in surrender. 'OK, Joss - that's what I'm going to call you by the way if I may, not Jocelyn - I probably am going much too far and being much too fanciful. All this is an irrelevant bore anyway. What I came up here to say is in a very different direction.'

'What direction?'

'A southerly one. Come to Venice with me next week.'

'What?'

'Venice. Have you been?'

'No.'

'Then come.'

'Of course I won't.'

She certainly didn't offer him a second drink and rather surprisingly he didn't ask for one. It seemed he had at last taken the hint. When they had talked a bit more sensibly about the sale, he got up.

'I've got to go back to London tonight,' he said. 'But I'll be back here tomorrow to know your answer about Venice.'

It was the most probable probability of her life that she wouldn't see him again. Nonetheless, she thought later that evening, though ashamed of her outburst of anger - which she had realised by then rebounded more on herself than on him - she was glad the curious episode had taken place, meaningless as it was. Obviously he must have talked to someone in the town about her. No one could have seen so much in a short time. But it had been amusing, and it had taken her mind off the contents of the house, all of which, she found when she went down, had been removed, as if termites had eaten them. She continued to think about him in bed. She found she could conjure exactly his active athletic figure and the quick speech which darted like a bird from branch to branch. She was sure she was sincerely indifferent as to whether or not he reappeared, but she found she thought of him in retrospect with amusement after all. It was not so often one met someone so different, so challenging and unpredictable. Definitely a one-off type. It would be something to tell them in Cambridge.

3.

Jocelyn heard nothing immediately from Henry Bordeaux. Each day when there was no letter she examined her feelings. Was she pleased or disappointed?

She found it depended on immediate circumstances. On Saturday when she was in the middle of an interesting French-to-English translation one of the doctors at the clinic had asked her to do, she was delighted there was nothing. Why should she leave this life she had made for herself? Then she had a letter from Leo, the second this month, asking to see her. If she didn't answer it, it would only be a matter of days before he was in Nottingham again with some new assault on her sympathy. He spoke of 'going straight,' and of being 'guyed up' by the thought that 'in spite of everything' she would find it possible to forgive him. If he was guyed up, it was a result of her attempts last time to bolster up his moribund confidence, which had exhausted and deeply depressed her, and the chance of money which she had also given him before. Of course she would have to go - if not to High Combe to something else. She bought *The Lancet* and began to scan the classified advertisement pages. A post at a London clinic perhaps? She would have a good reference for that from her present job.

The letter was waiting for her on the doormat one lunchtime, vicariously announcing its significance by being the only one that day. She tore open the handsome off-white envelope that looked nearer to vellum than paper. The address was printed elegantly on paper of the same hue and quality.

Dear Mrs Hammond,

I am sorry to have kept you waiting for so many days and only hope that the delay has not worked against me in that you may have found something that suits you better. Her pulses jumped. *But as I told you, I did want to see these two other people. They are better qualified than you are, but as soon as I had seen them I realised that - can I be so bold? - compatibility is a greater factor than expertise. Compatibility from my point of view, I hasten to add. You may not feel the same at all of course.*

Anyway, I am hereby offering you the job. If you decide to take it and would like a contract I will certainly have one drawn up, but as far as I am concerned we don't need legalities. It's obviously an open-ended arrangement both ways. The salary we discussed, the flat which you saw (and liked if I am not mistaken) is offered free of rent if you want it.

I hope with eagerness for a positive reply. If you accept, I know that all of us here will do our utmost to make you feel happy and at home.

He signed it, *Yours sincerely, Henry Bordeaux.*

There was no doubt now it had happened she was pleased. She had read the letter there in the hall where she picked it up. She carried it into the sitting-room and sat down still holding it like a trophy.

She realised all her anti feelings had been a defence against being turned down. She would go. She would leave this house in which she had never been happy and in which she would become a psychological prisoner if she stayed. She realised she had all her plans covertly ready-made in her mind. She would go, with as many suitcases as she could get into the car. The rest she would do at arm's length, using Sally's address in London as her safe house and Sally as her forwarding agent. Apart from Sally, her past life would be severed at a stroke.

She phoned Henry Bordeaux to tell him she accepted the job. He sounded pleased, though somewhat less so than she would have expected from the tone of his letter. 'Oh I'm so glad,' he said, almost matter of factly, as if it didn't concern him directly. 'When do you think you can start?'

She had been thinking of very soon, probably the next day. In the event she said, 'I shall have to take a day or two to clear up here.' Wouldn't he otherwise think her too eager?

'I entirely understand,' he said. 'You'll let me know then? Look, please excuse me, but I must go. There's a bit of a crisis on.'

There were certainly people talking in the background, but was he already having second thoughts, perhaps seeing someone else? Would he phone later and withdraw the offer? She dismissed this idea. The explanation of the muted tone was that he probably regretted the unprofessional atmosphere of their interview and now she was to be his employee wanted to redress the balance. It was surely to be welcomed.

She went shopping that afternoon in the small suburban street which served her part of the town, mostly to buy two pairs of jeans she could wear in the garden and a pair of gardening gloves stouter than the ones she had. She also went into the leather shop for a couple of large cheap plastic suitcases to supplement the miscellany of old luggage - mostly her parents' imprinted with their initials - which had been stowed in the roof loft for years. She was coming out of the shop lumbered with the cases when she saw Leo on the other side of the road.

She drew back into the shop door and watched him, like an animal transfixed by a predator. She had the idea he would somehow hear the pounding of her heart across the din of the traffic, would stop and see her cowering here with the cases, which would give away what she was doing. He continued on with that rapid walk of his she had once thought jaunty and confident and even now had the appearance of being so. With relief she saw him disappear into the Crown and Castle Hotel.

Still with the impression that he was regarding her through a window, she hurried to her car parked on a meter and sped home, abandoning other shopping she had intended to do.

She took the receiver off the telephone and busied herself upstairs, making a list of what clothes she would take. She would have liked to put them straight into the cases and go. But she feared he would come in the middle of her flight, see what she was doing, and her whole operation might be ruined. There had to be this last meeting, she thought. Then, when he came again, she would simply not be there. He would have to realise finally it was over, that she had nothing more for him.

She didn't think he would come until after dark. She had told him (untruthfully) on his visit three months ago that she intended alerting her neighbour to come to her assistance if he came again. But she hadn't done so, would Leo have minded if she had? Leo was not a physical coward. She thought he would creep in through the garden gate from the lane beyond and start talking to her through the door. She was sorry summer time had just started. It would probably prolong the agony of waiting.

It did. Sally had said she should simply refuse to open the door. While staying, Sally had had two automatic lights fitted outside and a spy hole in the front and back doors to enable her to identify him. Perhaps she would do as she was told this time, she thought, as darkness began to fall, or not put any lights on and try to make him think she wasn't at home.

She decided against the latter. There was to be no cloak and dagger. If he thought she was out he would simply break in with the idea of waiting for her return. She would do as she had before - listen to his new tale of woe, try to suggest practical ways in which he might get himself together, resist any attempt to arouse her emotions, and finally give him something. There was no more money, but she would give him a rather good antique silver jug to sell, she thought, which had been valued in the days she could afford insurance at a few hundred pounds. It would be her last gift, and when he realised she was finally gone from his life, perhaps the thought of kindness would outlast the actual monetary value of the gift. Leo had never really been mercenary, as Sally and the others thought. Steeled by her decision, she waited.

But ten o'clock came and he hadn't appeared. She didn't think he would come now tonight. Probably he had met someone in the pub and conned a meal with some story. She hadn't felt like food, but making herself a sandwich with the last of some pâté and a cup of tea, she had a surge of resolution. She would go now, in the dead of night.

It took her less than half an hour to clear the kitchen of anything that might go off, and tidy the house. She did a tour of windows to make sure they were all as secure as they could be. She read the electric meter, then wrote to the Electricity Board and to B.T. to terminate her accounts, giving Sally's address for the final bills to be sent to. She also wrote to her landlord announcing her intention of ending her lease - she would have, she supposed, to pay the remaining three months of the current annual contract. Then she went up to pack. Because she had planned what she would take, it took her under an hour. She then loaded the car, using the door from the kitchen into the garage and keeping the garage door shut. She shut off the electricity at the main. Finally she opened the garage door. She sat for a moment in the darkness, listening quietly to herself after the drama of the day. Was she really walking out on this place and quite a number of possessions, for good? Was it real? As real as anything, she decided. She ran the car back into the drive on the slope without starting it, returned to close the garage, started up the engine, and went.

Since receiving Henry's letter she had looked several times at the battered old cloth road map of England which had belonged to her father. The route was clearly in mind. The map had no motorways, but she knew she could initially take the M.1. south. She knew the motorway went through Northampton and saw on the map that she could branch off here to Oxford and the south-west. There was no doubt a faster route, but she didn't care, she had all night to get there. She filled up at a twenty-four hour garage just outside the town, making use of her credit card in her married name for the last time. From now on she would be Hammond, her mother's maiden name, which Leo never knew. She wouldn't put it past him to trace her via the card.

It was a moonless but fine star-lit night. She felt the darkness of the open road close around her like a protection. A single star ahead burned steadily. She thought how it had been there every night since she had been alive, and millions of years before that. She found this comforting, a steady ally. Most things in the universe didn't change, they circled dutifully, obeying laws. She had a panicked thought that the old Escort would not live up to its name and break down, leaving her dangerously stranded but, as if the old thing approved of the venture, it got its head down and bore her smoothly on at forty miles an hour. At first there were quite a number of cars flashing by, going the other way, some on her side of the road overtaking her. Soon there were many fewer. She voyaged the night almost alone. It pleased her. She switched on the ancient radio and twisted the knob. Home emissions had gone to bed, one was inaudible through atmospherics. She fell upon a foreign station that came to her as clear as the stars. Was it Vienna, Budapest, Prague? They were playing a familiar waltz. She sang with it, and in her mind danced with it, too.

She went off the motorway as planned and found the road to Oxford. She circumnavigated Oxford on what seemed a widely embracing by-pass, and identified the road to Newbury. Later, she came across a motorway to Bristol. Should she take that? She thought she didn't want a motorway again and ignored it.

Further on, she looked at her watch. It was still only one o'clock. If she continued at this rate she would be there much too early. She realised she would have to stop somewhere and take a room. It meant the credit card again - she had little cash. But she was in the middle of England for God's sake. What could this give away? She could be on her way to a Channel port. There would be a motel perhaps, open all night.

She did find a rather third-generation-looking motel with a half-baked man on night duty who made her pay in advance. He took an age to work the credit card palaver as if he had never operated it before. The room depressed her - the cheap burnt lampshades, the thin carpet over the concrete floor, the fitted nylon sheets, the uncomfortable foam-rubber pillows, the faint smell of nicotine and some slightly sweet odour mixed with it - was it some kind of canned polish or an accumulation of stale talc? The window was double-glazed, but though she drew the curtains, car lights beamed periodically across the ceiling. She slept fitfully.

At daybreak she was up. She wanted to be free of this dreary place. She washed cursorily, got into the car and drove off into the fresh rosy light. She had already decided she was going straight there even if Henry Bordeaux thought she was mad or desperate. What was the point of hanging about?

After finding the railway station in Totnes, she was able to remember the way out of the town and drove into Combe's gates just before nine. The daffodils in the centre bed of the car park were fully out. There was nobody about. She parked, got out of the car and peered through the shop door. There was no one.

Then she saw the sign that said opening hours were 10.a.m. to 6.p.m. Should she go away - explore Dartmouth perhaps, which couldn't be far?

She turned the idea down. She didn't think her new employer was the sort of man who would lie in bed. If he was up, he could perhaps show her to her quarters and let her get on with it. He'd said he wanted her to start right away.

She locked the car and walked to the iron gate at the end of the wall which was the private entrance to the house. There was a pedestrian door in the wall beside it, which was unlocked. In front of the porch was the young labrador. It barked once as it got to its feet, then as if deciding she was a bona fide visitor, walked up, head bowed, tail wagging. Just at that moment Henry Bordeaux opened the front door, wearing oldish-looking trousers, an open-neck shirt and a red sweater. There was a biro in his hand, the dog must have alerted him. He stood peering for a moment, his hand still on the door handle, amazed.

'Oh, it's you - er - Jocelyn,' he said, recovering. 'I say, I hadn't expected you so soon. I thought I heard a car.' He ordered the dog to heel.

'I felt I just had to run for it.'

'Run?'

'Yesterday afternoon I saw my ex-husband on the other side of the street. I was quite sure he'd come to cause more trouble. Last night I just jumped into the car and came. I hope you don't mind. I know I should have phoned, but it all happened so suddenly. I half didn't know what I was doing.'

She saw his grave eyes absorbing this quickly. His good manners followed close behind. 'Don't give it a thought, I'm delighted. I thought we'd have to do without you for days, perhaps longer. I'm afraid I haven't aired the flat or anything. But come in, come in. You'd probably like some breakfast? You haven't driven all night, have you, for goodness sake?'

She had blurted much too much again, but her spirits lifted in ridiculous relief as she realised that nothing would be more acceptable than food. She had stopped at a roadside transport stall for a cup of tea, no more. 'I'd love some breakfast.'

As they went in she explained she hadn't driven all night. She told him about the motel and how she had woken early. He was making for the kitchen. She followed him. A bounce in his stride heartened her further. He sat her in a pinewood area in the corner. There was a table and a bench seat. 'Now, what can I get you? Coffee, toast, a cereal of some sort? I can do you an egg and bacon if you like.'

It came out in a rush. 'Do you know, I'd like anything that's going? I'm famished.'

It was the right thing. He looked delighted and burst into action. 'Right. And I'm going to join you. I had my breakfast two hours ago, but it feels like yesterday.' He drew a table-cloth, cutlery and crocks from various cupboards and dumped them in front of her. 'You lay up while I get cracking on the eggs and b.'

He refused to let her help with the cooking. While she downed a huge glass of fresh orange juice, a plate of mixed cereal, then the fry-up which included fried bread, a tomato and mushrooms as well as egg and bacon, he kept jumping up and down to see to things. She saw the immense boyish energy that underlay his gravity.

'I say, that was good,' he said, as he put down the knife and fork on his plate. 'Haven't enjoyed breakfast so much for ages. OK for you?' She said it had been quite delicious.

He poured two more cups of the freshly-ground coffee from the dark blue metal jug, pushed back from the table, and crossed one leg over the other. 'Now look, what you're going to do today is settle into your flat - I presume you *will* be moving in there at least until you decide what you want to do? Tomorrow will be quite soon enough to think about anything. I have to go into Plymouth today, I'm afraid. But if you want to shop for anything you need, Betty, my secretary, could go into Dartmouth with you to show you what's what there. Just tell her what you'd like to do. She hasn't much to do this morning, and for once we can put the phone on answering. Edith Appleton will be in to clean in a minute, and to make lunch for everyone. She can add you to the lunch party if you like. It would be a good chance for you to meet them all. I'll be back at tea-time.'

The little modern flat was over the double garage, facing the front porch of the house. Henry said she could use one side of the garage for her car. She drove it through the gates and parked it next to the Range Rover. The flat was reached by an external iron staircase that ran up the wall on one side. He helped her up with the suitcases, then lingered to make renewed apologies. He really would have wanted to give her a better welcome, he said, but his appointments were a Regional Gardens Committee, of which he was chairman, and then a session with one of the planning officers in Plymouth town hall. He was hoping to convert a barn on the edge of the property into a teahouse.

Through the sitting-room window she watched the car back out from the garage below, its exhaust pluming in the still chilly morning air. As the black gates closed automatically behind him and the vehicle disappeared she felt a rush of reassurance. She was sure she was going to be happy here.

She was about to turn away when she saw two women entering the car park on bicycles. She watched them dismounting on the far side of the shop at the other end of the parking area where she had noticed there was another gate through the wall. Probably they would stow their bikes inside somewhere and enter the house via a back door. They were laughing heartily about something. Jocelyn liked the look of them. She cast the older one as Edith Applecote, the cook-housekeeper. She had learnt from Henry that somewhere down the huge garden Geoff Applecote had been at work since eight. She felt she had joined a friendly and effective team. Would she fit in? She no doubt had a lot to learn, but she thought she would. There was the one sadness - Mrs Bordeaux. What exactly was her affliction? She doubted if her curiosity would outlast the morning.

She set about stowing the contents of her cases. She was glad she hadn't been able to bring more - there would have been no room. She laughed at herself for being able to deploy into a new life so quickly. How Sally would scoff when she knew - Sally, whose multiple possessions were always arranged so meticulously. She spent some time rearranging the furniture a bit, then thought she would go into the house and meet her colleagues. A small car had arrived while she was unpacking and she had seen a third, younger woman enter the house through the gate in the wall this end, which she had used, carrying a baby in a Moses basket. Obviously this was Betty, the secretary.

When she went in, Betty was comfortably installed in the well-heated office at her word-processor. She rose as Jocelyn entered. Plumpish, rosy-cheeked, brimming with health and by all appearances placid and good-natured, there would surely be no problem here, Jocelyn thought, as she introduced herself and they shook hands.

After an admiring look at the sleeping baby parked in a carry-cot on the chintzy sofa there was a hiatus. Betty had answered her questions about the child with a minimum of words. Jocelyn was glad to have another question at hand.

Betty explained eagerly that the second of the women Jocelyn had seen was Lorna Standish, a care-worker who looked after Mrs Bordeaux and came in for two long stints twice a day. It appeared there was also another member of staff, Brenda May Pike, who ran the shop and came in at ten. Betty then returned to Edith who, she explained respectfully, did the cleaning as well as the cooking and housekeeping and was 'a tower of strength.' Jocelyn said she wanted to meet Edith. Betty clearly thought this was the most natural wish any newcomer would have and said she would be in the kitchen.

Jocelyn entered the pristinely tidy room as Edith was taking a tray of small cakes from the huge Aga with a jolly-molly. She made quick and efficient movements. On the large wooden table was evidence of a stew in preparation - pieces of steak being cut into cubes on a chopping-board, onions ready-peeled for slicing. Edith put down the cakes and came forward at once wiping her hand on her apron. 'Mrs Hammond? Delighted to meet you. Henry left me a note to let me know you've arrived.'

'People call me Joss,' Jocelyn said as they shook hands.

'All right then, we do use first names here. I'm Edith, as I expect you know. It *is* friendlier, isn't it? Henry's always insisted we should.'

They exchanged a glance of frank appraisal. Jocelyn liked what she saw. It seemed a reasonable bet that action filled Edith's life, but there was worldly wisdom, too, in the open attractive face - and authority. The captain of the ship - under the admiral?

Apparently Jocelyn also passed the first scrutiny. 'Well, you'd like a cuppa, dear, I expect?' Edith said, the relics of a Devon brogue traceable. She glanced at her watch. 'Not so far short of elevenses anyway. Geoff'll be up directly. You've had a long journey, Henry said?'

It was easy to talk to her - or rather, to listen. After a brief question about her nocturnal journey - which Jocelyn attributed to her preference for empty roads - Edith was off. Jocelyn sat down as the vigorous cutting and de-fatting of the meat proceeded. There was a lot about how welcome another hand would be as Henry had been overdoing it. 'Strength of an ox but even he's human. Last summer it was bedlam. This one promises to be worse.'

A list followed of the kind of things that were always happening in the season to make Edith's life 'a chase' - large coach parties, sometimes sixty strong, which were sprung on her at a few hours' notice wanting cream teas which they served on the Italian terrace if it was fine, the need to take someone's place who was on the sick list - she often had to take over the shop, she said - or someone needed first aid. And this on top of her normal duties. It was in the 'never a dull moment' category.

The account came to an abrupt end. Edith had switched on an electric kettle. It reached its crescendo and clicked off. Jocelyn had noticed there was a tray laid for elevenses on the shelf of the huge dresser with two cups and plates with home-made biscuits on each. The small teapot was warming on the Aga. There was a change in the atmosphere. 'I'll just take this up to Lorna to save her coming down, then I'll make ours,' Edith said in a different voice. She didn't explain who Lorna was.

On her return she made their tea but despite the prompt, like Henry, seemed reluctant to give any explanation of the situation upstairs. Was it really such a taboo subject? Jocelyn plunged.

'Mrs Bordeaux's an invalid?'

'Oh yes.' Edith's voice was lowered, but not in a way to kill the subject, she thought.

'Lorna's the care-worker, Betty tells me?'

‘Remarkable woman, yes - also with the strength of an ox, which she needs of course to move her patients about.’

‘Did Mrs Bordeaux have an accident?’

Edith had taken up the knife again. Her voice continued in a more normal key. ‘I see Henry’s told you, or you knew somehow, that she *is* an invalid. You heard her ring the bell, did you, when you came before?’

‘Yes.’

‘And Henry told you the bare minimum ?’

‘I suppose he did, yes.’

‘The poor soul, his life’s ruined of course. Anyone else would have put her into a home when she came out of the spinal hospital - Dr Finnister’s said more than once that’s what he should do. But he won’t hear of it. For some time he looked after her himself, you know. Feeding, hygiene, everything, and that was before all the gadgets she’s got now. But of course it soon became impossible, running the garden and looking after her. Lorna makes it possible, and I do my bit - but he still never goes away overnight, and of course on Lorna’s day off or when she’s sick, he still copes.’

‘What’s wrong with her? Is it an illness?’

Edith interrupted her work and gazed thoughtfully at the ceiling. ‘It happened five years ago, just when he was leaving the Commandos. He was stationed in the Far East, had been back on leave to buy this place, and gone back. Apparently, when the time came for his final return, the twins were still at school out there. They decided that Henry would come back as there was so much to be done with the house. Mrs Bordeaux would stay until the girls’ term finished and follow on a later plane. That was when I met Henry. Geoff was out of a job about then and the house agent who’d been handling the sale had arranged that Geoff and I should caretake the place until the Bordeauxs arrived. On his second return, Henry asked Geoff to be his gardener and me to stay on as housekeeper.

‘I’ll never forget the afternoon it happened. There was a phone call from a friend of Henry’s in the Ministry of Defence - for it was a charter flight his wife was travelling on organised by the military for a number of returning families. He came out at once to tell me in that quiet way of his - I suppose having been in the thick of it in various trouble spots around the world he's had to cope with plenty of tragedy. There'd been a crash somewhere in the middle of India - the plane his wife and children had been on. First reports were that there'd been no survivors. He said he'd go out there immediately.

'The children were killed, but Mrs Bordeaux was one of the very few who survived. We learnt that it was because Henry went out that she didn't die. He somehow organised a helicopter and got her from some village where she was to a hospital in Bombay. I shouldn't say it, I know, but I often think it'd've been better if Henry hadn't gone out and she'd died, too. What life has she now, and what kind of a life has Henry?'

'She's completely paralysed?'

'If only she was. Her head isn't paralysed, the only thing that isn't. She can use her tongue all right, it never stops. It's a funny thing, Joss, but however much one tells oneself that a person like her needs a bit of rope, you can't stop yourself in the moment thinking she means what she says. I think Henry's the same. He comes down looking like death sometimes, and I know it's because she's been on about something. We're creatures of common sense, that's what I say. It's difficult to switch off being that and to make allowances for someone who's gone beyond common sense.'

Jocelyn didn't regret her inquisitiveness. She felt the air had lightened as Edith continued - as if they had emerged from a tunnel into fresh air again. 'Well, now I've told you,' she said. 'Someone had to. You'd've found out for yourself sooner or later. But it's something we don't speak about much. What's the point? I've said to Geoff sometimes, it's like a ship that's gone down that's marked with a buoy. It's there, but you navigate round it. Better all round really.'

4.

Jocelyn had to go back to work at Cambridge the next day. She still had a week off but the sale was over and she knew the Faculty office would be frantic with the beginning of the University summer term. The day was busy, it was after six before she put her coat on and ran out to catch her bus to Ely. She hadn't thought about Leo at all. He was waiting outside.

'Oh no,' were her instinctive words as he crossed the street towards her, grinning.

'You surely didn't think you'd get rid of me as fast as that, did you?'

She was tired and felt irritated. 'Look,' she said, 'I've had the hell of a day, and I have five minutes to catch a bus. I'm grateful for your work at the sale but I've no wish to know you beyond that. I thought I'd made it clear.'

'You made it clear verbally, but it isn't what you feel.' He paused. 'Is it?'

'It's exactly what I feel.'

He was in relaxed clothes again, an open-neck shirt and a pullover. He stood with his toes over the edge of the pavement, balancing, and put his hands into the pockets of grey flannel trousers. 'I understand. I don't think at the moment you know what you think. How can you - a type like me accosting you as I have, thrusting into your life? You can't think I'm serious, why should you?' She began to walk, fast. He easily kept pace with her. 'I've got my car at The University Arms,' he said.

'I want to catch my bus.'

She kept up the furious pace all the way. They rounded the corner where the bus stop came into view. The bus was just pulling away from the kerb beyond a plume of black diesel exhaust. In desperation she broke into an ungainly run, shouting and waving. The driver didn't or wouldn't see her. Heaving for breath, she gave up and collapsed on to a low wall, her back against some railings. He came up, mildly panting, and laughing. He handed her her silk scarf which had been loosely over her bag and fallen without her noticing.

'You see, you can't escape me. It's the Fates, Joss. Sure, it's all the Fates and Furies working for us.'

She looked at him standing there in front of her and, against her wish, felt something stir on his behalf. Was it that she was flattered after all? With his looks and mental agility he could surely pluck almost any girl off the bush, yet he had come all the way up here from London again. Also, whatever else he was, he was comic. Who was she to be throwing away carelessly so rare a thing as comedy?

'Do you mean to tell me you've come all this way just to try to drive me home?'

'I told you I'd come.'

'You're totally crazy.'

'*One* of my attributes, certainly.'

'I'm not having dinner with you, you know.'

'But I can drive you home?'

'No you can't.'

'When's the next bus?'

'An hour.'

'Then it'll have to be a drink, won't it?'

'I'll have a drink with you. Or rather, you'll have a drink with me. I'll pay.'

It was a small pub she had never been in, the nearest at hand. He didn't object when, standing at the bar, she asked him what he wanted. He asked for half a pint. This at least involved her in no obligation, she thought. She ordered herself a gin. She needed an ally.

They made their way to a table carrying their own drinks. Seated, he guiltlessly took up the beer at once, and swallowed half the glass at a go. This was no macho act, she saw. He was thirsty, and so drank frankly, like a child. 'Not used to all this exercise,' he said, putting the glass down and licking his lips. He leaned backwards easily, hooking his arm over the back of the chair - more, she thought, like a third year undergraduate easily contemplating the complexities of life than a young auctioneer. 'Now I'm going to tell you something, Joss. You can believe it or not, but it's true. I've no doubt you're still thinking I'm a professional womaniser who picks up girls as easily as he knocks down a lot. I suppose, now I think about it, I could be a womaniser if I chose. I might claim, without total immodesty, to have some of the equipment necessary. I can talk, which must be the chief weapon one needs. But I'm not a womaniser as a matter of fact. Never had the inclination. Why not, you may ask? A good question. I'm not, not because of any moral restraint particularly but because I can always see ahead of my own lust. I see the banality of what it would be like afterwards if you go to bed with someone you don't love. I'm my own worst enemy in this respect. Sort of arrest myself on suspicion before I get anywhere.

'I'll tell you my love life in a few sentences. I had a first teenage dotage, a girl I was crazy about who jilted me. Then when I spent a brief period at university there was an older woman who wanted me, a don's wife, and I was too stupid to see in advance what she was up to. End of story. Since then I've been celibate. Gone out with a few girls, but no more than that.

'I even worried once or twice, wondering if there was something wrong with me, that maybe I'm gay. But it's not that. I don't stop wanting women even though I don't try taking bites out of them. Then, when I saw you in the Cathedral it was all different, literally in that moment. I've always believed in burning bushes, haven't you? I was hooked almost as soon as I saw you. I had this overwhelming feeling, you see, that you must be on the same frequency, that like me you're free of all the social lies that enmesh most people. I've had it ever since, more since talking to you. I've been transfixed. I did that auction well, but I did it in a dream. It was me, too, on automatic pilot on that platform, as I'm sure you've been over the death of your parents.'

Jocelyn was sipping her gin a lot faster than she intended. She told herself to discount what she was hearing. Wasn't this the philanderer's art to pick up some truth about his subject then turn it into flattery in some way? But she couldn't discount him entirely. She noted a paradox. From one view he was so laid back and sure of himself, from another wasn't there a nervous fervour - that almost naive *anxiety* about him, which she had noted yesterday, and which was strangely touching? How were the two to be reconciled?

Sense told her she should amuse herself with this interlude, terminable very shortly by a bus timetable. But she found herself looking at his face as he spoke, looking at his mouth and eyes, and listening to every inflection of his voice. All her instinct told her that there was a basic sincerity in what he said. She had the idea, which one almost never had about anyone, that what he was saying to her might be, precisely, exactly the truth, that he had not spoken to anyone in Ely about her, that he was that rare occurrence, an innocent.

He ended the short biography of his love life. He grasped the handle of the glass and stared into the remaining beer. In a gingerly boyish way he began to rotate the glass in a puddle he had spilt on the glass-top table.

'Have you ever seen the Leonardo "cartoon" in the Nat Gall?' he said, looking up. You know, it's that drawing for a full picture he did later - of St Anne, the Virgin and the Christ baby.'

'Yes, I think I have.'

'There's the jolly old Jesus, leaning forwards with hands outstretched towards a lamb, as any child might be attracted to an animal. Mum, on whose lap the baby sits, is as involved as any mum would be, permitting it, thinking the lamb business is all it's about. But there behind is the tall foxily-smiling Anne, who's been around, knows all the tricks, and knows it isn't just a lamb involved. She's *aloof*, sitting in judgement. Well, I saw the picture recently and it occurred to me that, leaving aside the religious aspect, it's a sort of allegory for what happens in life all the time. The virgin and the child are us in our daily actions, but above, all the time, as part of our consciousness, is this other ego. Take us now, for example. On the face of it, it's just you and me. But that isn't the extent of the company. There are also two others, aren't there, looking on? Our respective St Annes. Sort of super me and super you, tucked up in the grandstand with a rug over their knees, watching the game that's going on. Id and Ego, is it, in Freudian lingo? Here are we mortals banging on, and these other two are sitting up there, spectating with a tolerant smirk. That's why my love life has been limited to this moment. If I went the wrong way I got a smirk from my St Anne and was extinguished stone cold. I wonder if you've the remotest idea of what I mean?'

It was uncanny. In similar words it was almost exactly like a thought she'd had. She'd even had the same impression of the Leonardo drawing she had seen on a school outing to London, and of which she still had a postcard she had bought in the gallery shop. As in Ely, her immediate suspicion was that he must have talked to someone she knew, but she was sure she had never confided her thoughts about the drawing to anyone. Could the man bug minds? 'I think I do know approximately what you mean as a matter of fact, yes,' she managed to say, with a total banality she could hear in her own voice.

"You do? You really do? Well, *if* you do, you'll probably guess what I'm going to say next. In my feelings about you I'm getting full cooperation from Her Nibs. She approves. We're on, I tell you. We've got to be on if you know what I'm driving at. It's another omen.'

'We're on for what?'

He gave a quick laugh and sat back in his chair. 'Dinner at the very least, don't you think, now we've got this far? If for nothing else, to celebrate?'

She had to own the fun was back. Nothing heavy, nothing so serious after all, his look and tone conveyed, just part of the reality of things. He was already regarding her having the same thought as his about the Leonardo picture with a merry unconcern - *as if the unusual were to be expected.* He really was wild. She agreed to have dinner.

She decided that evening, with conditions, to reef in her distrust of him. The reason for this was that she began to enjoy his company. He suggested what he called a 'frog place,' he had found, but on her insistance they settled for the more homely embrace of the University Arms, which must be cheaper.

Though she was aware of how it might be committing her beyond her wishes, during the meal she did most of the talking - about herself. During this, she was aware of another positive factor. That he allowed this autobiography was not, she thought, for an ulterior motive. There was no element of the innings about it - 'you bat first so I can have a bat later,' a conversational habit she had always found dispiriting with its implication of no common ground. As she spoke, there was almost a greedy look on his face, as if every morsel of information was of vital interest to him. She told him in more detail about her parents and how sad she was for their spare lives, knowing now how much more they could have enjoyed themselves. She told him about her schooling at the local comprehensive, her rather unexceptional performance, and about her relationships with other girls, which though merry had never been intimate. She told him about her time in France as an au pair, how she had particularly enjoyed that French ability to combine a lack of sentimentality, which was almost rudeness in English terms, with a capacity for strong emotion when the occasion warranted. Finally, she talked with relish about her work in the Faculty, where she had begun to find people she could relate to. She was going to start looking for a flat in Cambridge as soon as she could, and move out of - yes, she agreed - gloomy old, Cathedral-dominated Ely.

It was so rare for her to talk frankly about herself, she forgot for a moment the extravagant declaration of his feelings he had made. 'So, you want to make a life in this town?' he said when she had finished talking.

'Yes.'

'It's a nice place to be, plenty going on.'

'I think so.'

'London's more exciting, though.'

'What do you mean?'

'You know exactly what I mean.'

'I assure you I don't.'

'You could get a super job in London. I could probably get you one in my outfit. You could do the sort of thing Lavinia does standing on your head.'

'Who's Lavinia?'

'The girl who was doing the inventory of your furniture. You could really get to know about antiques, then the world would be your oyster etcetera. The firm's going places.'

She realised what he was up to again. She looked down dully. 'I've no intention of leaving my job here.'

'How are we going to see each other then? Week-ends aren't going to be enough for me.'

She took fright, and knew she was blushing. 'Leo' - she used his name for the first time - 'you've really got to stop this. A joke's a joke. I've sort of joined in for this evening, and talked far too much about myself. But you and I can have nothing in common beyond this very pleasant dinner we're having together.'

'You mean you dislike me?'

'I didn't say anything about liking or disliking.'

'You think I'm brash, pushy - shallow perhaps?'

'I don't think any of those things.'

'Then what do you think?'

She had averted her eyes, but now looked at him. She expected the usual cocky male assurance, hearty daring which was backed by no real knowledge or understanding of the situation, rushing in and leaving it to the woman to be wise. But this was not what she saw. What she saw was that impish anxiety again in the unusually gentle and vulnerable blue eyes. It occurred to her that it really did matter to him what she said. Against any conscious wish, an excitement and a pleasure leapt in her, and with it a quite zany notion which left her breathless and was out before she could consider it. 'What do I think? I'll tell you. Venice, you said? If you meant it, I'll go to Venice with you for a week, going shares. Totally platonic of course. I need a holiday after the last days, and when the term is under way I think the Faculty will let me go, given my father's death and given that I went back before I had to. If there were to be anything between us, which I'm quite sure there isn't, we'll find out. Anyway, we might just enjoy ourselves, like one of Cilla Black's blind dates.'

'Done.'

'There's a condition. If at the end of the week there's nothing, we say goodbye and that's it for good.'

After this the anxiety went. He broke into a berserk kind of joy. 'I knew it, Joss. I knew if I could keep the ball bouncing a bit longer you'd do something utterly daft like this. You're as daft as I am. The fact is, the two of us are bored, bored by the acceptable and the predictable - isn't that the case? We've discovered already that in each other's company we can make it otherwise. I'm certain we can.'

They met on both the two week-ends which must elapse before the magic date. She went up to London and stayed with a lady who owned a basement flat just off Baker Street and did bed and breakfast. She had once stayed there with her father when he was at some clerics' conference. On the Saturday, on Leo's suggestion, they went to Madame Tussaud's and the Zoo, which neither of them had ever done. Then she chose a French film, one of those memorable ones as it turned out - a simple provincial love story which began with a loving, traversing view of a town from a hill overlooking it, as if that in itself was enough to announce that the tale which followed would be sincere, direct, moving, sad and funny by turns, and entirely credible - as it was. After the film they had a subdued meal in a small place in Soho in which they said very little to each other. Both had been affected by the film, she thought, and needed this period of convalescence from its sad beauty, memory of which was a bond between them.

The second week-end he came up to her. She was still in her parents' house in Ely, and on her suggestion he stayed in Cambridge for the Saturday night. She took the bus in each day. She didn't want people in Ely to see him, not because she was in any way ashamed, but because she didn't want to have to face the speculation and innuendo, not to mention the castigation - 'unseemly gallivanting' would probably be the phrase, so soon after her father's death - which would follow in this life-starved, scandal-hungry town.

Jocelyn was relieved that Leo didn't press her any more on the amorous side, as if he knew this would now be out of place. The University summer term had started. Walking through the beautiful colleges thronged with youth, punting on the river, walking to Granchester to commune with Rupert Brooke, they just lived together through whatever happened, in the moment, as if they were brother and sister. She asked about his family and learnt almost nothing beyond the fact that his mother died when he was quite young and that his father, with whom he didn't get on, married again. She gathered he was an only child. Rather pleased to hear this, which seemed not so different a family situation from her own, she probed no further. She learnt that he had been to a minor public school - he didn't even give the name, 'a sort of ghastly pastiche of the real thing,' was how he described it - and won a scholarship to East Anglia University to read a combined arts course. This he had abandoned in the middle of the second year. 'I liked the art history side but I'd had enough of being in an academic cage,' was how he explained his walk-out. He had wanted to act, having done a bit at Cambridge, but then saw the advertisement for a job with Brent and Shapley. He had thought vaguely that auctioneering might be seen as a form of acting, but really only applied as a lark. To his amazement they took him on - on probation as he was so young. In three months he got a contract - and here he was.

On the Saturday night, after another film, he took her back to Ely under cover of darkness in his not so new Vauxhall. They had decided he would leave her outside the Cathedral Close gate, by this time closed to vehicles, and not come in with her.

The dark street, high-walled on one side, was silent and deserted, as it always was from quite early in the evening. In the parked vehicle she thanked him for the day they had spent so enjoyably, and paused before she got out. She felt warm and relaxed in his company. If he wanted to kiss her she would let him, she thought tangentially, a brief kiss on the cheek perhaps which would be in keeping with the mood which had bred naturally between them over the hours they had been together. But he didn't kiss her. He took her hand and held it. He held it for some moments.

'We're on course, aren't we?' he said.

'On course?'

'For next Friday?'

'*Of* course.'

'I'll meet you at Liverpool Street.'

'All right. You'll let me know about the time?' He had undertaken the travel arrangements and he had her telephone number.

He reached in front of her for the door handle, and she felt the warmth of his flesh. He pulled back and waited for her to get out.

'Goodnight Leo.'

'Night, Joss.'

'I think it's going to be fun in Venice.'

'Fates'll decide.'

'Our Ids?'

'Our Ids. And yours had better get it right. Mine will.' His tone was light.

Too light, she wondered, as she made her way alone in the cool spring air to the house? Had she perversely wanted it otherwise? She decided she hadn't. It was all perfectly right. She thought humorously it was like waiting for the result of an exam or a competition. An extra-self authority would pronounce. As she entered the cold echoing house, she realised that in his company she hadn't once thought about the death of her parents.

He paid for the package, which included the hotel, without meals. He wouldn't allow her to return her half. 'You can pay for all the other expenses if you want to,' he said. She said they would see how this worked out and settle any difference at the end. He nodded briskly, dismissing this irrelevance.

It was a small hotel, but plumb on the Grand Canal with the Rialto in view. In the humid afternoon air, the *motoscarfo* delivered them and their luggage from the railway station to an ancient tufa landing-stage which had a striped blue and white post, and a bright canopy to match over the modern glass doors. Around them was the busy jostle of traffic on the ancient curving thoroughfare - several other motor-boats, a large canal bus churning, a long motor-barge loaded with planks making slow progress midstream, and a scattering of black gondolas with raised prows, bobbing and sucking on the bright water. They entered the strongly-lit, spotlessly-tiled hall which had a heavy Venetian green chandelier with matching wall-lights, and immediately were set upon from three directions by the porter, the hall-porter, and the male reception clerk who emerged from behind the counter. Their joint long-withheld ambition, it seemed, was to welcome them.

It was enchantment from these first moments. Their adjoining rooms overlooked the canal. In Jocelyn's room, when she had tipped the porter and he had gone, they threw back the heavy wooden shutters and gazed down. An older couple lolling in a gondola, Americans, waved to them. They waved back.

They couldn't wait. Parting only briefly to wash, they went straight out and walked through devious streets to St Mark's Square. Before them, around them, was the famous scene, but no film or photograph could convey the excitement of being here. From a vendor they bought *gondolieri* straw hats with red ribbons, strayed into the mysterious gloom of the Cathedral for their first view of the ancient oriental interior. On the air was the faint whiff of incense, the flagstones under their feet were worn and uneven, icons loomed. An apparently mascara-ed, morose Christ gazed down on them, other golden mosaics gleamed duskily. Later, outside again in the translucent light, they walked past the soaring brick and marble of the campanile and the great white palace of the Doges - more like the dwelling of a Caliph than a European ruler - then stood on the quay with the wide view before them which so captivated the imagination of Canaletto.

Jocelyn often tried to remember afterwards some moment when she realised she was falling in love with Leo, but always failed. All she could say was that perhaps this moment, when they stood on the edge of the broad lagoon looking across at the dome of Santa Maria Salute, panoramic and wonderful as it was, was the last she could recall as being clearly attached to her old life. From then on it seemed they entered a swirl of activity which didn't stop for three days.

While they stood there on the quay, a dapper Italian approached in a dark suit and tie, a raincoat hanging from his shoulders. He also wore an English-looking brown felt hat, which he raised an inch as he spoke. Gravely, almost quaintly, in slow elaborate English he offered them his services as a guide.

They were amused by his manner, which was so ostentatiously opposite to the Italian stereotype. With a glance at her, Leo engaged him at once.

His English was flamboyantly advanced, full of stretched poetic metaphor, and he seemed to be strongly anglophile. 'We Italians,' he informed them in one of the many solemn asides which punctuated his lectures on art and history - this one when they were in the dank dungeons of the Doges' Palace - 'we Italians are shallow, superficial, corrupt. You English teach us to be otherwise. But I fear my countrymen are too far' - he searched for the word and for once failed - 'too far *sommerso* to be rescued from our villainy.'

It appeared he had been four times to a language school in Oxford, that he had a degree in the language and its literature, and that he taught English in a 'liceo classico.' He also owned to being the author of a guide book to Venice sold by all the stalls and mobile vendors. That evening they hired him for the next two days as well, and in his company saw 'a few of the most priceless jewels which the spilt cornucopia of Venice has so casually, so recklessly to offer.' This included not only the Titians and the Tintorettos, but a glass factory - from which he told them not to buy, as it was - 'what you call it? a "gip-joint"', which rewarded the guides with a thirty per cent commission.

So apparently uncorrupt, he was also totally humourless. They could have done with the information without the florid embellishments, but he was sincere, fervid, and knew his way about the watery labyrinths. Above all, Jocelyn thought, he acted as a kind of chaperon to that tender matter which both of them perhaps - Leo too - tacitly accepted needed protection.

They ate enormously, when not with Umberto laughed a great deal at everything and nothing, and after dinner were too tired to think of much except sleep. But on the fourth day, when they had said goodbye to Umberto after giving him lunch and Jocelyn had paid him rather more than the very reasonable sum he had asked, it seemed for the first time they were really alone.

They sat at a table outside a small restaurant in a back alley, which Umberto had recommended. Together, perhaps jointly aware of the extra service which Umberto had unconsciously provided, they watched him cross a small bridge and disappear.

'What an unusually nice man,' Jocelyn said.

Leo didn't answer, and she knew precisely at this moment what had happened. She looked at him shyly out of the corner of her eye. His eyes were lowered and he was playing with a coffee spoon. The same sensation leapt in her as had leapt in Cambridge, only this time a hundred times more powerfully, energised as it was by the astonishing ease and rightness which had come upon her.

He still wouldn't look at her. His face was, if tense, for once removed, neutral. She knew he was waiting for her. It was right that he waited, she thought. He had made his declaration, he was keeping his side of the contract. She felt a further rush of emotion, and spilt the words at his feet.

'You're still feeling the same - about us?' she said.

'Of course.' His voice was small, clipped, almost for the moment as if hostile.

'I think something's happening to me, too,' she said. 'It could be just Venice, but I don't think it is.'

Perhaps rather more on her initiative than his, they made love in the hotel room that afternoon. If she'd had doubts, which she didn't, they would have been swept away. Not because their love-making was an immediate ecstasy. Far from being the practised Casanova she might have imagined him in England, Leo was not on this first occasion a great success from her point of view. She could tell at once that he was physically passionate, but he was shy almost to the point of prudery, embarrassed at her seeing him naked, which she wanted to do, then rushed and precipitate in the act.

He was apologetic, but not, she was glad to see, abject. She'd had little experience of sex, but enough to know that it wouldn't matter, that they had all the time in the world to get it right, and that she could wait. Perhaps it was the same for him. It was not after all an absence of sensitivity that had caused the failure. She was glad he was not proficient, for it confirmed to her, if she needed confirmation, that he wasn't a professional lovemaker, as he had made plain. Above all she saw his commitment to her. She could now believe the extraordinary directness of his suit. That evening they ate in the hotel. They were merry and very happy. In the middle of the meal he said he was going to tell the hotel they wanted a double room as they had decided to get married. She did want to marry him, didn't she, he asked as an afterthought. They laughed inordinately at this surely unusual and banal way of proposing. She agreed about the room and said, about marriage, that they would see, probably yes. She amazed herself with her delicious pact with fate.

The rest of the holiday seemed to be love-making, recovering from (rather more successful) love-making, and lounging in cafes and restaurants. They took a trip to the Lido, another round the islands, but did no more sightseeing in churches and galleries. In a small jeweller's just by the Rialto he bought her a ring, an emerald. On their last evening, after dining and dancing at the Royal Danieli Hotel, a gross luxury she insisted on and paying for, she discovered the meaning of sexual love. She thought he might have done so, too. The next day, all the way home, they lived in a daze of wonder.

They were largely silent in the plane, holding hands like teenagers. 'We're out of the blue, aren't we?' she said once.

'Yes. Like Napoleon we'll be putting the crown on our own heads, standing up the Pope.'

'Unlumbered, free. That's why we shall be so happy. No in-laws to complicate things, no hidden enchainments to the past.'

'Ex-*act*-ly.'

He said this with a fierceness which surprised her. It fired her with love. She squeezed his hand. Wasn't this what she had been waiting for since she had been a schoolgirl and only at times feared never to find, someone as unlumbered as herself, someone who didn't want to force life into patterns, who waited for it to deliver its joys when it would, and had the intuition to know when it had? Wasn't it this which made sense of all her life so far? They would start untramelled.

5.

For the first days Jocelyn was hectically busy in the office. As it was the beginning of the season, local hotels and tourist agencies were firing in their requests for group bookings, some of them for as far away as August. There were bookings, too, from garden clubs, several American and Japanese, and a great number from private individuals. Most of it came through the post, but the phone also went constantly. Henry had made it plain he wanted her to deal with all the enquiries, especially those over the phone. One of the main reasons he had made the appointment, he told her, was because Betty got confused and had made several double-booking mistakes last season. The interruptions had also had an adverse effect on her typing, which wasn't *créme de la créme* at the best of times.

Jocelyn privately thought it not surprising Betty made mistakes. Henry's booking system was a rather scruffy half-page-a-day diary already littered with pencil entries he had made himself in haste. As she worked, she was already planning improvements, certainly a large professional booking-chart on the wall which would show the season at a glance. Also, though Henry was keen to project the notion of a personal service, there was no reason why the word processor should not be used to produce stereotype letters with spaces left for the mutable bits, which she could dictate and Betty could type in.

When there was a lull, she got herself into the files. She started listing organisations which had sent groups and not returned. They should have a letter and the new brochure. Then she found the advertising file. She was to be responsible for projecting the image of the garden 'nationwide' - and abroad, she added to herself. So far visitors had come only through word of mouth recommendation and through tourist agencies or clubs. Henry had spent quite a lot of money in the first years on advertisements in Country Life and other glossy publications. She knew almost nothing about advertising first-hand, but now there was someone appointed to think about it and take action, surely more could be done on the P.R. side - articles and features perhaps which would cost nothing and have far more effect than expensive advert space?

In a few days she felt she was freeing herself from the weight which had seemed to be poised over her. She began to see one or two things clearly. The first of these was that, Commando Colonel though he may have been, and therefore surely you would think with experience of organising, Henry was not much of an administrator. His instructions to her, for example, though clear in their objective, had been almost casual. 'Now you'll have to pore through some of this bumph, I suppose,' he had said on her first working day, and waving an arm vaguely in the direction of the box files. 'Save a lot of explanation if you see for yourself what we've been up to.'

Plainly his love was the garden, the choice and care of the plants, and above all the physical work. Though always impeccably polite, it was plain he didn't like visitors much. It pleased him to be mistaken for a gardener, and never let on who he was when this happened. Each morning they had a brief exchange in the office, but when he went off whistling to his first task outside she knew he was at his happiest.

A second observation she made was that now she had arrived they had too many staff. Henry had rather naively and charmingly thrown last summer's accounts at her on the third morning - how many bosses would have been so open to a relative stranger? The accounts, he pointed out proudly, showed a small surplus for the first time last year. 'Just as well they did,' he commented, 'there wasn't too much left in the kitty, and Jones, the bank manager, was getting edgy about the money I've borrowed.' Businesses varied enormously no doubt, but with the knowledge of the place she already had and with comments she remembered from board meetings of the clinic which she had attended as an unofficial secretary, one reading was enough to make it obvious that the salary bill was too high a percentage of the outgoings. She was quite capable of doing her own secretarial work, and they didn't need the three people who came in to do guiding. She could do that as well, or most of it.

She closed her mind to further thoughts about this, however. Certainly it was none of her business to suggest rationalisations at this stage. What was plain was that to justify her own salary of nineteen thousand plus free lodging on top of those of the others, she had immediately, this summer, to raise the gate, perhaps by twenty per cent. She silently set herself this goal.

Jocelyn had rather feared that Henry might issue another invitation to dinner. Should she accept if he did? The matter didn't arise. She saw plenty of him, as he was in and out of the office, and all the staff had a communal lunch prepared by Edith Applecote, which they ate in the kitchen, Henry with them. But beyond this, he kept away from her. Their exchanges were professional, even those which concerned her own welfare.

'Do ask Edith for anything you want in the way of food or ingredients,' he said once, 'or anything else you need.'

There was just one exchange they had which was not in an everyday category. This was when he saw that her national insurance card showed Cunningham as her name. Cunningham had been her married name, she explained - which she was in the process of changing now she was divorced. Hammond was her mother's maiden name. She couldn't use her own as her ex-husband knew it.

'I see,' he said quickly.

Seizing the opportunity, she reminded him how important it was to her to maintain her alias. She told him she was certain Leo would try to find her. He said he understood entirely and that she could count on him to guard her secret.

Just for a moment she picked up the kind of vibrations she had imagined were around when she came to be interviewed, for was there not a certain *effort* involved in his holding off? She quickly dismissed the idea as, once again, the workings of her too active imagination. Henry Bordeaux was a naturally shy man, she prompted herself, more so no doubt because of the tragedy. He wasn't holding off at all from probing her private feelings in the way she had so immodestly imagined. She remembered one of Sally's strictures - that her romanticism was of teenage proportions.

Her curiosity about his wife on the other hand couldn't be doused by this self-censure. She was conscious every day of that sinister presence lurking upstairs, not the least when the terrible bell shrieked in the hall, which it often did when Lorna, the care-worker, had gone and Edith or Henry had to take over. On the first of these occasions she asked Betty if she had ever seen Mrs Bordeaux. Betty's fingers froze on the keyboard.

'Oh no,' she said. 'No one has as far as I know - except Lorna and Edith.'

'But why not?' she probed. 'I mean, she's disabled and so on, but she must be terribly lonely up there all day, every day. Lorna is only here for six of her waking hours. You'd think Henry would want people to go and talk to her. Read to her perhaps. Can she read herself?'

Betty looked embarrassed. 'None of us except Edith has seen her,' she repeated, still staring as if she had seen a ghost.

For the first time, Jocelyn felt a little cross with Henry. What was this? Some fine scruple of his to save people or himself embarrassment? If so, what good did this do his unfortunate wife? She determined to tackle Edith on the subject.

She knew Lorna wasn't coming in that evening and Edith was on bell duty until Henry came in from the garden. She decided to approach her at once. Betty was about to return their tea-tray to the kitchen before she left. Jocelyn said she would look after it. Edith was taking a pie out of the Aga - the Bordeaux's supper by the look of it. Jocelyn put the tray down.

'Is it Henry's instruction that none of us meets Mrs Bordeaux?' she asked point blank.

Edith took her time answering, placing the pie on top off the stove whose burnished brass was gleaming like that of a cherished steam locomotive. 'No?' she said carefully.

'It just seems rather odd to me that I've been here in her house several days and haven't met her.' Edith was silent. 'So if one went ahead and did, he wouldn't be annoyed, you think?'

'I don't know.'

'It seems a bit grisly. Betty seems transfixed by the idea that someone might go up and talk to her sometimes. You told me before she can talk.'

'She can talk all right.'

'So why not a visit?'

'You wouldn't get anywhere.'

'How do you mean?'

'She'd simply insult you. Use foul language, too.'

'Does she insult you and Lorna?'

'Not now. She knows neither of us would take any notice if she did. Lorna's a professional and Mrs Bordeaux can't do without her. As for me, when Lorna's not here, I'm at her beck and call, too, aren't I? She's no fool.'

'Well exactly.' She paused. 'What you're saying, I think, is that if she's rude there's a way past it if you're useful to her. Don't you think the thing is she gets very lonely? Isn't it perhaps being alone so much that makes her peculiar? Solitude can do things to people. For goodness sake, I know myself it can.'

'You're saying you want to go up and see her?'

'Yes, if you think Henry wouldn't mind. Even, possibly, if he did. Don't you think it's possible he's got himself into this situation, perhaps out of consideration for other people, and now can't get out of it?'

Edith's face went blank. 'It's not for me to say, Joss. If you think . . .

She took a decision. 'Take me up now. Introduce me.'

By the time Jocelyn had washed up the tea-things, Edith was backing out of taking her up. 'Perhaps it'd be better if you went up alone,' she said. 'Take her by storm. If she senses it's set up she'll take us apart.' Jocelyn understood - Edith didn't want to make trouble for herself. It seemed she had enough already. She went up alone.

Half-way up the stairs she thought she heard a small sound above and panicked. She knew Henry was at the bottom of the garden clearing up the winter's detritus in the giant gunnera bed and wouldn't discover her. But of course she should be making the suggestion first to him, not acting unilaterally like this. What right had she to take the law into her own hands?

Around her the house was still, as if something was holding its breath. She had a vision of Henry's face, the sad endurance etched in lines round his eyes, which his age should not account for. She was sure that if she asked him he would say no, or head her off in some way which would make it impossible. Surely she had a duty to try? He hadn't actually forbidden her to. She heard another sound - she was sure now from the room - and continued upwards.

She stood by the door in the semi-gloom of the landing. She heard a small cough. She knocked. There was no answer. She opened the door ajar and knocked again.

'Mrs Bordeaux. It's me, Jocelyn Hammond.'

'What do you want?' The voice was oddly slurred.

She opened the door fully and saw why. A bulky figure in a wheelchair was parked with her back to her in the window bay. Her head was inclined forwards. In front of her was a table with a half-assembled jigsaw puzzle on it, and in her mouth was a long stick which seemed to have a kind of claw on the end. She was picking up a piece of the jigsaw with it.

The puzzle was a seascape, in the centre of which was a partially assembled sailing-ship. Jocelyn stood beside her and watched her try the piece on one of the half-materialised masts. It seemed she could operate the claw by some movement of her teeth or tongue. It was the right piece. Advancing to her side, Jocelyn watched as it was slowly manoeuvred into position, resisting the desire to push it home for her. The piece was positioned by vicious downward movements of the claw, which had a heavier rounded heel that could act like a hammer. She began to search immediately among the mass of unfitted pieces.

'I expect Henry's told you I've been appointed to do the promotion and so on,' she said. 'I thought I'd come up and say hello.' There was a contemptuous-sounding noise. She ignored it and drew up a chair. 'The puzzle seems to be going well. The sea and the sky must be difficult.'

There was no answer, and the searching went on. Then the claw dropped. On a long string round her neck, it fell to the table from where presumably she would be able to recover it.

'Henry didn't tell you to come up here.' The voice was now bell-clear, upper crust, imperious.

'No.'

'Then why have you come?'

'As I said, I've been in your house for several days. I thought it was time I came up and met you.'

'Why should you think that, nobody else does. Nobody else in the years I've been up here has barged in like this. You're an employee.'

'If I'm intruding I'll go of course. I was thinking actually you might like some company.'

'Why should you think that? Do you imagine I wouldn't have company if I wanted it? Henry's company is the only sort I can stand. I'd make arrangements to go downstairs if I wanted to meet people. Move my chair so I can see you properly.'

Jocelyn realised the poor woman couldn't turn her body. Her two paralysed arms were strapped to the arms of the chair, her feet, similarly redundant, were hidden in a huge fur-lined double slipper. Apparently she had no movement from much below her neck.

Jocelyn moved the chair so that it faced where she was sitting and sat down again. She found herself being scrutinised by the remarkably young, still good-looking face. It was the woman in the photograph she had seen all right, the same soft blonde hair stylishly curled and cut short, and the pretty though hard thin mouth. She had the contemptuous beauty of a twenties flapper.

'I knew he'd choose a woman,' she began. 'He went through the motions of looking for a young man, but as soon as I read your letter I knew he was going to pick you. I know everything Henry's going to do before he knows himself. Widow, are you?'

'I'm divorced.'

'Same thing. But you won't get anywhere with him, you know. Not an inch. Henry's a man of gallantry and principle. Sometimes I have the feeling we're more married now than we ever were. For that matter he was never so marvellous in bed, he's probably relieved he doesn't have to make a fool of himself any more. So if that's what you're after I advise you to piss off before you get your fingers burnt.'

'I've come here to do a job.'

'Oh yes, I bet you have, all dewy, fresh and willing.' She scrutinised further. 'Mm, I can see what appeals to him about you. English through and through. Never let your left hand know what your right hand is up to - that sort of type. All the characteristics of a full-dress hypocrite in fact. Silly old boy.'

Could this be a glimmer of distorted humour, she thought, which indicated that if she kept her nerve she might be getting somewhere? She smiled, let the smile fade, and looked about the room. On one side was a television screen fixed half-way up the wall. On a bedside table there was a machine - apparently some kind of a cassette-player. Beside it was a stack of cassettes.

'I was wondering whether you're able to read and, if not, whether I could read to you sometimes when Lorna isn't here.'

'I've got all I want, thank you.'

She paused. 'You listen to tapes?'

'What I said was I don't need your help, to read to me or in any other way. If what you mean is - which I'm quite sure you do - that you want to know what the opposition is by muscling in up here and sniffing around, I can save you a lot of time. The opposition is total and actually, as I say, unnecessary. Henry Bordeaux loves me. He'll always love me. He'll have his dreams from time to time as any man in his situation would - any *man* for that matter. But they're dreams and will remain so. And just to make it absolutely clear to you, even if by some remote chance you or any woman succeeded in persuading him to a momentary dalliance, he'd always draw back afterwards and ditch her for another reason. Would you like to know that, too?' Jocelyn tried to keep her look even, as if this were some kind of a game which in a moment would break down into normal intercourse. 'Of course you would, even though you're playing the high-minded nurse. I'll tell you. Even if Henry ever were tempted towards another woman, he would soon withdraw from such a foolish enterprise for another reason. The garden, you may have noticed, is his life. He has poured all his strength and skill into it over the last years. But he doesn't own it. I do. Ah yes, I see this *does* surprise you. It's all my money, you see, every penny of it. I gave it to him to use, as I've always given him everything I possess. But the estate's in my name, and I could sell it tomorrow if I chose to. Not that that, as I say, will ever be necessary.'

The truth of what Edith had said was beginning to get to Jocelyn. The woman, the room with its out of date chintzy furnishings which expressed somehow her insistence that everything should stop, Miss Haversham-like, just where she had been stopped, began to appal her. She tried to make herself remember that the poor creature had lost her children - there was no photograph of them she could see - that she was confined for the rest of her life to this wretched existence, and that her aggression was entirely understandable.

Should she say more? She didn't see how she profitably could. She rose. 'I'm sorry I can't be of some use to you. I've no doubt when I've got on top of my job I'll have spare time. If you change your mind please let me know. I think you'd like me to go?'

'You're damned right I do.'

Jocelyn was ready to re-position the wheelchair. It was, she saw, unnecessary. Hanging in front of her and fixed on either side to the back of the chair was a metal block. By placing her chin on it and exerting downward pressure she was able to operate the chair herself. There was an electric buzz, and the vehicle's rubber wheels jerked nimbly through ninety degrees so that she refaced the puzzle.

'If I were you,' she said, 'I'd take your money and go at the end of the month. We don't need you, and you'll save yourself a lot of trouble.' With this, with a sideways jerk of her neck she flicked the claw from her lap back on to the table and recovered it nimbly with her teeth.

Jocelyn fled back to her flat, by-passing the kitchen and Edith by going down the front staircase. She was horrified, both at the encounter and, more, at what she had done. Edith would think she had been foolish, and no doubt Henry would be furious. She had little doubt the woman would have some twisted version of her visit to recount to him. She might even be dismissed.

From her bedroom window she could see down the garden. Henry was out of sight, but she could imagine him working down there, happily absorbed with his rake, and with throwing the rubbish into the attendant barrow. Geoffrey had knocked off, but he would go on for as long as it was light. At any moment she expected the bell to shrill. Edith would by now have gone home with Geoffrey and would have switched it through outside so that Henry could hear it anywhere on the estate.

Perhaps Mrs Bordeaux was right. Perhaps it wasn't the set-up for a woman, as she had thought herself on her first visit, before she knew of this appalling situation upstairs. But as soon as she thought it, she knew she didn't believe it. In a way the ridiculous accusation made it even more imperative that she stayed in order to prove its falsehood. It was so plain to her now why it had been made. Delia Bordeaux - she had seen her first name on a letter in the hall - lived perhaps in the grip of an obsessed terror that she would be deserted. Her own right path was to stay, make - with Henry's blessing and assistance - further attempts to help the poor woman, and over time perhaps, put to rest the anguished fear harboured. This was the right path. But how would Henry behave? Should she do and say nothing until he brought it up?

She started to do some washing in the minute bathroom, still listening for that bell. Before she had taken the first garment from the soapy water she made an abrupt decision. She couldn't play the silent game, it wasn't her nature. She wouldn't let Delia Bordeaux implant whatever venom she plotted before she'd had her say.

There was still half an hour of daylight. She put on a light suede jacket and set off down the garden. She couldn't avoid passing in view of the house. As she did so she had the sensation those almond eyes were on her from the bay window. She hurried to reach cover.

The April evening was chilling fast as she descended the winding path through the budding bushes. The beauty of the garden made her realise how attached to the place she had already become. Some of the drifts of daffodils were beginning to go past their best, but everywhere the spring bloom was rampant - hyacinth, wood anemone, polyanthus and, like massive regiments held in reserve, all the armour of summer was on the march. The candle buds of three giant magnolias were splitting into flames of pinky white. In the trees bluebell spikes were pushing up urgently.

He seemed to have finished the work and had knocked off. He had laid the long-clawed rake across the last barrow-load of detritus and was sitting on a wooden seat placed under a giant cedar. He was staring through the other trees to the view of the estuary which was visible.

When he heard her, he looked round, startled, then got up when he saw it was her. 'Joss, a surprise. What a lovely evening. So full of bustling plants and promise.' She sat on the bench and he resumed his seat beside her.

'Henry, I think I've done something I shouldn't,' she said at once, 'something I shouldn't have done without telling you, that is. I've been up to see your wife. I thought I could make friends, read to her perhaps . . .

He looked away with an abrupt movement but not concealing his face, which clouded thunderously. 'Oh no.'

'I should have consulted you, I know. But I had nothing much to do. I thought it was right I should go up and introduce myself.'

'You shouldn't have,' he said after a moment. His voice was clipped, for once military, and unlike him. 'If it'd been right for you to meet her I'd've introduced you.'

'I realise that now. It was perhaps wrong of me. I've come to apologise - though I think my motive was right.'

There was a long uncomfortable silence in which they could hear the incoming tide gently lapping the shore beyond the trees. She could feel his mind racing in several directions. Was it panicked? 'Talk about it,' she prayed. 'For God's sake, talk, get it off your chest. It was more than any human being should be asked not to share such a burden, and what better recipient was there than a virtual stranger who'd had problems of her own and who possessed, she thought, some discretion?

He stood up. 'You must never do that again,' he said. 'She doesn't want to see anybody. If she did, I'd've arranged it for her long ago. She has a gadget which turns the pages of books for her, as well as a cassette recorder. She can also activate a television screen with a blow pipe, which enables her to activate other functions as well as TV programmes. You must never go near Delia again. And you must immediately expunge from your mind anything she said to you, which won't be the truth. Delia has unfortunately long since lost contact with reality. She lives with fantasies, very distressed ones.'

'But yes, Henry, I think I understand that. I was already . . .

'That's enough if you don't mind. I didn't wish it, but you've done it and it can't be undone. What we do now is forget it happened.'

She reared in opposition to this. Surely there was some way through, particularly if, as he said, Delia's venom was the result of distress. But he had already begun to walk towards the barrow. She watched him wheel it towards the bonfire area out of sight behind the gunnera beds. She heard him shut and lock the door of the shed where the barrow was stowed with other garden implements used at this end of the garden. When he reappeared, he invited her to view what he had done as if nothing had happened.

They walked up in the rapidly ebbing light. He talked of the progress of the new tea-room. A friend in the Plymouth planning department had written that day to tip him off that it was almost certain to go through She saw it would be impossible to re-open the topic.

As the house came into view she saw the light was on in Delia's bay window, the curtains un-drawn. Presumably she could control the lights somehow. She felt an actual physical constriction in her chest. It couldn't be right, this lonely truncation of Henry's.

Although - it occurred to her later - was it essentially any different from that severance of her own about which well-wishers had so many practical views? What right had she to pass judgement? Wasn't she being a busybody?

6.

A month after their Venice holiday - a honeymoon-in-advance Leo called it - Jocelyn and Leo Cunningham were married at a registry office in Cambridge in the presence of a few of Jocelyn's friends. They all returned afterwards to the house belonging to the family of one of these, in which Jocelyn was staying temporarily having had to move out of Ely. The party went on for several hours, and there was no doubt who was the centre of attention during this time. Leo charmed everyone, including the Professor of Modern Languages who had given Jocelyn away and who came to the party. There were no speeches, but the professor took her arm for a moment as he left. 'You've picked a winner, Jocelyn dear,' he said *sotto voce*. 'Lively, witty, kind, and a match for your great talents. Be very happy together.'

She needed no one to tell her they were going to be. Not once since that crucial moment in Venice when Umberto had left them alone had she questioned her rapid decision. She was only ashamed that she had so doubted Leo in those first hours in Ely - though she forgave herself easily for this, for was it any wonder, she asked herself, that she had failed to recognise at once the sincerity of someone who knew so quickly and accurately his own feelings and those of others. It was too unique a quality to be appreciated at first sight. She rejoiced a hundred times a day in the lucky chance of their having met so fortuitously, and not the least part of her joy was even that vulnerability of his which seemed like an insurance policy that his nimble emotions would not lead him off in another direction. 'Don't ever drop the basket, Joss,' he said to her once in an especially tender moment, 'I've got all my eggs in it and they'd be totally scrambled if you did.' How little in danger he would ever be of that.

It was a temporary disappointment that they would live in London. Whatever Leo said about London excitements, Jocelyn regretted giving up her job in the Faculty and being separated from daily contact with her new friends. But she was more than happy to contribute a good deal of the money she had inherited from her parents to buy a long lease on a roomy two-bedroom terrace flat in Bayswater - which seemed to go some way to assuage her guilt over the money - and she soon found herself adapting to London life. A job at Brent and Shapley proved not to be in the immediate offing, so she took a part-time post with a firm of house-agents to keep her occupied. She had leisure in the afternoons to read, also to explore galleries and museums, to go to exhibitions and lectures. She had already realised in Cambridge how truncated her education had been and how much she wished to extend it, here was her opportunity.

Jocelyn took up easily that happiness and content she had always imagined for herself and which she had only ever despaired of in bad moments. Leo's optimism and energy and gaiety were inexhaustible. During the day she was occupied enough, but when it came near to the time of his homecoming she found herself restless with anticipation, waiting for the rapid three rings he always gave on the bell which communicated with the front door downstairs, then the clash of the lift gates, and his first shouted communication as he entered the flat.

'Jossy, we're going out,' he would call. Or, 'Jossy, I'm armed to the teeth with a 1976 Montrachet,' which he had bought on the way home. His news from work was always good. He had doubled the estimated proceeds of a sale, his firm was attracting bigger and more lucrative clients with more valuable possessions, which gave him more responsibility, they raised his salary. He talked of the possibility of one day soon 'leaving the hustings', the phrase he used to describe his auctioneering work, and moving on to the administrative side. He even thought there was a good chance they might make him a director in the not too distant future. And always he was passionately pleased to see her on his return from work, sweeping her into long embraces when she was in the middle of getting their meal, reengaging them at once with the light-hearted existence they led just where it had been left off in the morning. They looked about them from time to time and saw people, as it seemed to them, enmeshed - enmeshed in Laocoon-like family ties and obligations, enmeshed in nervous stressful expectations and ambitions, above all anchored by the need to acquire possessions, often when they had plenty already. How wonderfully free they were, Jocelyn thought for the umpteenth time. Just themselves, what they chose to do in the moment, fun, tenderness - and whenever called for, kindness to others and concern for them. What else was needed?

There was one sadness in the midst of all this. In the first two years of their marriage she had three miscarriages, all in the early part of the pregnancy. The sadness, she thought, was not so much for herself - for though the physical discomfort was unpleasant, as was the sense of anti-climax and wasted effort, she had discovered she wasn't one of those women to whom childbearing is a consuming necessity. She saw so many woman abandon what seemed a vivid existence for one which, however gratifying it must be in other ways, she couldn't help adjudging circumscribed, not because of the fact in itself of having children, which could obviously be a joyful and fulfilling thing, but because of the attitudes it seemed to weave about itself. Was not childbearing in this sense an obedience to external, tribal, ancestral dictates, not to the calling of an individual nature? Jocelyn's sadness was more for Leo, who was uncharacteristically downcast after the miscarriages, much more severely than she would have imagined. Indeed, if Leo hadn't been so devoted to the idea of a child she might have given up after the third attempt. The amusing possibility occurred to her that Leo, no dynast where his own family was concerned, could become one when he had progeny of his own. 'There's got to be someone to brag about our success in life for posterity,' he said once.

After a lot of rest, which bored her silly, the fourth conception seemed to be sticking. Then it stuck. Suddenly there was Sally on the scene. Leo was ecstatic and his homecomings became even more eager and rumbustious than before.

'Where is she, where's my star?' he repeated ritually as he crashed through the front door, often leaving it open in his impatience. He wanted to know from her every detail of his daughter's day, which included her diet. He bought a tome on child care which he pored over. Jocelyn laughed at him.

'You ought to be the nursemaid and me the auctioneer,' she said. With a (fortunately placid) Sally in his arms, doing whirls which would have tired a dervish, he didn't seem to hear.

It was perhaps well-timed that Sally appeared just at the time when Leo suffered a small setback. It became plain to him rather starkly one day that, highly regard him as the directors of the firm did, it didn't appear after all that there was any chance of his ever becoming a member of the board. He had made an indirect sounding via the chairman's secretary, with whom he was on very good terms. 'Oh no, you can forget that, Leo,' she had said, 'they'll never let in an outsider. It's a family business and they'll keep it that way. You'd have to marry one of the daughters if you wanted to crash that barrier.' Typically, Leo was not downcast by this disappointment, but immediately put in for a highly paid job that was going at Sotheby's. A fine arts degree was mentioned in the advertisement as a 'probable' requirement. Leo thought his qualities, and now his experience, would be sufficient to by-pass this difficulty. It wasn't. He didn't even get an interview.

Jocelyn knew it hit him. Had he ever suffered a setback of these dimensions before? She was there when he opened the letter at breakfast one morning and saw what happened to his face as he read. But he seemed quickly over his chagrin. 'Well what the hell,' he said almost at once with a shrug. He tossed the letter into the waste-paper basket. 'We'll jog along as ever. I have a good job, I have you, and Sally - what more do I want?' Jocelyn was lifting Sally into her high chair at this moment. He took over, expertly fitting Sally's plastic bib and sitting down beside her to begin the patient process of spoon-feeding. Jocelyn fell in love with him once again. Wasn't this living proof of the strength of their philosophy on life - that one should take each moment as it comes, that it was absurd to assume that one must necessarily 'get on' and climb ladders like Anthony Thwaites? Here he was practising precisely what he preached.

On the other hand Jocelyn did begin to realise at this time that, joking apart, there was a serious difference between them in the intensity of their feelings towards Sally. Jocelyn loved her sweet wide-staring baby who seemed to take everything in her stride, enjoyed looking after her, and didn't resent the plunder of her freedom this entailed - for to Leo's delight, she gave up her job. But every evening nowadays she had to undergo a barrage of questioning, almost a cross-examination, from Leo. This was conducted in his usual half-joking, give-away style, but she felt there was a seriousness behind the levity which was faintly irritating. She had taken Sally for an outing in her pram in the Park - right, he said, how many blankets had she been wrapped in, what had she noticed, had she been on her back or her side when she was asleep? There were endless questions about diet. A bad fluey cold sent him into uncharacteristic and undisguised paroxysms of concern - what precisely had the doctor prescribed, was he right to prescribe it? He was even concerned about her future. What would she be, a famous QC, somebody brilliant in the City, Prime Minister? Sometimes at odd moments she caught herself experiencing a curious feeling of encirclement. Wasn't Leo overdoing things? *Was* this quite what they had foreseen as their style?

There was then an incident which she was to come to view as archetypal. Brent and Shapley were breaking into the European market and were sending Leo to do a probate valuation job in Vienna for an Englishman who had been living there and who had a houseful of English furniture. 'I'll come with you,' she said spontaneously when he told her about it.

His face clouded with a new kind of mild censure she wouldn't have thought possible. 'Oh no, Joss, you couldn't do that.'

'Why not?'

'You can't lug Sally to Vienna.'

'Why on earth not? I'll pay my fare - and hers if they charge for her, which I don't think they do.'

For almost the first time she saw that he was quite cross and turned pink. 'It's not a question of the money,' he said.

'What then?'

'Well, you can't just whisk babies round the world like parcels. I should've thought you'd've known that as a mother.'

It was the first remark she had heard him make which implied there are things you can and can't do, as if there were canons laid down for babycare, as there were in that baby book of his. And 'as a mother' - what was that phrase supposed to mean? That all mothers thought alike about their children and what was good for them? Could it be, she allowed herself to think, that fatherhood was turning Leo into some kind of a conformist after all? The momentary disappointment this caused her made her joke in an exaggerated way.

'I believe the reason is you've got a girl you want to take to Vienna.'

To her further astonishment he took this seriously, too, turning an even deeper shade of pink. 'Jocelyn, how could you think such a thing? Of course that isn't the reason.'

She didn't go to Vienna. It seemed he was going to be very busy and they would have no time together anyway. She even began to think Leo might be right. Perhaps she wasn't taking her maternal duties with sufficient responsibility. She dismissed the incident from the surface of her mind.

One evening he came home unusually pensive. There was no ring on the bell from downstairs, he didn't call out to her as he let himself in to the flat. Wondering if there was something wrong, she went into the sitting-room. He was sitting blankly in the chair, his head back, staring at the ceiling.

'Leo, are you all right?' she asked anxiously.

'Oh yes, perfectly, thanks.' He sat up sharply. 'Look, Joss, I've been thinking. The plain fact is, as you know, my prospects at the firm aren't as rosy as I thought. The chances have to be that if I take no action, in thirty years' time I'll be in exactly the same position I'm in now, a common or garden auctioneer shouting the odds, and performing like a circus animal.'

She was pulled up short, and it was she now who was serious. 'But I thought you loved the work,' she said.

'The money isn't good enough.'

'But you surely earn enough? We have everything we want.'

'We don't, you know - not now. That is to say we *won't* have in the future.'

'I thought we had. You've had increments, and rises, you'll probably get others. There's my bit to help.'

'It won't be enough when Sally's older. Besides' - he had the grace to look sheepish, and lowered his eyes as if he knew what he was going to say was off course - 'besides, there's another point to be considered.'

'What's that?'

'I've never thought this before and I don't really think it now - for myself - but, well, being an employed auctioneer is pretty low down the pecking list, isn't it? You know that rich banker whose loot I sold, who took us out to dinner? I didn't tell you, but I thought we were getting on rather well together socially - quite apart from the business - and I asked him here for a return match. He turned it down at once with a polite reason, and you could see that *wasn't* the reason. "Dine with an employed auctioneer, below the salt? What cheek of him to suggest it" - that's what he was thinking. We do live in society as it is, Joss. We can't ignore that.'

She was astounded. She had never thought to hear this sort of thing from Leo and could not keep a caustic note from her voice. 'I thought the whole idea of you and me was that it doesn't matter where we are in relation to the salt? We enjoy life as it comes. It's you as much as me who's always said that.'

'I know. It has *been* like that, I'm glad it was, and it should be like that. But now - it's different.'

'What's "now" got to do with it? What matters, surely, is whether you like what you're doing - what you get out of life, what you put into it.'

'You amaze me, Jocelyn. Can't you see how things have to change now? Can't you see *Sally* makes it necessary they change?' He made an impatient movement. 'Anyway, whatever you say, I have to take decisions about the lolly and I've rather decided. What I'm saying is we're going to need a great deal more money than we have at present. It'd be *selfish* not to think so. Sally's going to have the best education going, and London's no place for a child to grow up. We need a place in the country.'

She began to grow desperate. 'But Sally will get an excellent education here in London. Hundreds of thousands of healthy children are growing up in London at this very moment - about a fifth of the nation's children probably. As for schools, in London surely there's less of a problem than elsewhere? She can have the best there is on the state.'

'Sally will go to a public school.'

'Why does she have to do that?'

'Because she's having the best, that's why. Surely you want that, too, if we can afford it?'

They didn't get much further with this conversation. It was as if he had already gavelled the matter down like a lot. What contribution could she therefore make? She couldn't keep tartness from her voice. 'Well, if you feel all this, what are you proposing? How are you going to earn enough to pay school fees and buy this country residence you talk of?'

'I'm not sure yet, not of the details. But watch this space.'

No more was said on the subject until a week later when he came back from two days in Nottingham. They were having a disturbed night, Sally was teething. Leo was up as much as she was. He had just returned from Sally's room, having successfully got her to sleep again. Instead of getting back into bed he sat on the edge.

'I didn't tell you something very exciting happened today,' he said. It wasn't frankly, as she saw it, the moment for excitement. Why hadn't he talked about it before they went to bed? But she made a movement to indicate she was listening. 'Before I went up to Nottingham I heard about an auction-room business for sale there. When I finished work this afternoon I went to see it. It's a snip. We'd have to borrow of course, but there's no reason, right away, why I couldn't make enough from the business to service a loan. In the medium term I'd be repaying the loan as well. We could then buy a decent house and . . .

'And what?'

Out it came. 'We'll be able to live the kind of life Sally won't have to apologise for when she goes to school.'

She was totally amazed at this, and sat up fully. 'But why should Sally have to apologise for anything as things are?' she said. 'We've never apologised for anything in that way.'

'Having a kid makes things different.'

'Does it?'

'Of course it does. Surely you see that?'

Honestly, she didn't, not certainly in this rather grim way. And why *had* he chosen this moment in the middle of the night to make such a statement? She had got the impression it had been in the nature of a surprise bridgehead which would be expanded later. It seemed so. In a moment he put the light out.

He went on about it every evening in the next days - about the bright vision he had for their future. This broadened in its scope each time he talked about it, as if he were persuading himself as well as her. She pointed out to him that if it was status he was after, a provincial saleroom was hardly an improvement on Brent and Shapley, which surely had a growing reputation. He pounced on this.

'Ah, but that's the point,' he said excitedly. 'You're right, it won't be much when we start, but I'm going to make this small business grow into something quite different. Brents started just in this way in the East End. I'll start in a lowly way, then move into the quality market. Joss, I just know I can do it. We could eventually be a Midlands and North Country Sotheby's.'

She didn't like the kind of arguments he used, which more and more looked as if, on behalf of their daughter, he wanted to become respectable - a word they had always applied to other people with humorous mockery. Then she began to think it was rather churlish of her to resist him in a venture that most people would consider a laudable capitalist enterprise. Wasn't it something to do with her provincial background which prevented her from responding to Leo's vision? Surely advancement was to be applauded when its objective was a better life for a child? That remark of his about Sally not having to apologise for her parents was wrong, but perhaps it would be in her interests to go to a fee-paying school. Maybe, Jocelyn thought, in her own happiness, she had developed a selfish attitude under the guise of a convenient philosophy, maybe she hadn't sufficiently considered Sally's future. Then she had an idea.

One evening when he was talking about an encouraging visit he had made to a bank, she made up her mind. 'If you've really decided you want to do this,' she said, 'it's silly to borrow money when we've got it. We'll use the proceeds of selling the lease on this flat, and what's left of my legacy, to buy this business. We can start without debt.'

She was convinced after this that she had done the right thing. At first he said he couldn't possibly use her money. 'I'm supposed to be the breadwinner, aren't I?' he said laughing. But over a period, the scruple weakened. He agreed, and with the decision seemed to get back his old personality in full. There was no more idealistic talk about duty and social status, more of his old vivid excitement in life and sense of fun, applied now frenetically to the new venture.

'We'll probably finish up becoming local benefactors,' he said, 'get on the Council, and have civic statues erected to us in front of the town hall when we kick it.'

'Not *that*, please,' she laughed.

'No, not that, but we'll get stinking rich and throw it about. That's what being an auctioneeer's for. Being a totally materialistic job, it can't have any other *raison d'être.* Any further objections now?'

Put in these jocular carefree terms, what he proposed seemed much more acceptable. Her decision about the money made her happy again. As with the Bayswater flat, she had been pleased to find such a creative cause for the money she had inherited, and it was a small price to pay for her rehabilitation with Leo.

The new move was, notwithstanding, less to her liking than the one from Cambridge to London. Nottingham, though a lively town, she was told, couldn't be London as far as cultural amenities were concerned, and the small two-roomed flat they had to rent was poky compared with their place in Bayswater. Though they sold the lease of the latter reasonably, the business took all the proceeds as well as most of her other money. But Leo's humour made up for it. He was soon speaking of 'scoops' and 'snips' and 'pieces of cake', by which he meant the buying of something valuable for next to nothing then selling it at the auctions for a great deal more. One day he bought for 'peanuts' all the plants and shrubs in a bankrupt garden centre. He advertised a special sale in the Nottingham Post and by his account 'made a killing.' The result was certainly a sapphire ring for herself and a dolls' house for Sally. A side of her suggested they could have done without this extravagance when he was building a new business, but as ever she was won by Leo's sheer exuberance and generosity of spirit. He must know what he was doing. It wasn't for her to be an obstacle to his enthusiasm, rekindled as it was.

They had only one serious difference of opinion in the first months in Nottingham. She would have liked to help him with the business right from the beginning. Why pay a secretary when she could do the work for nothing, she argued? But he had always been adamant about this, 'while Sally was young.' She would have to bring Sally with her if she did this work, and The Yard was no place for a baby. The Yard was what he called the auctioneering premises.

Now Sally was a little older, Jocelyn wanted to put her into an infants' play-group in the mornings. It would be good for her to start learning to be with other children, and she could get a part-time job again. Leo was quick to point out, after a rapid calculation on the back of an envelope, that there wouldn't be much in it financially by the time she had paid for the crêche. It wasn't especially for the money she wanted it, she explained, but for something to occupy her. The spectre which had appeared in London rose again.

'But you don't *have* to work, Joss,' he insisted. 'Very soon I'll have enough to buy a house on the never-never. Then you'll have more than enough to occupy you. Anyway, I thought you wanted to improve your mind. Why don't you do an extra-mural course at the University?'

She did think about this, but found her feelings had changed. She wanted, not hours of private study at home, but something more active, something which would bring her into touch with other people.

She insisted, and got her way, though she had to agree that this would only be until the house materialised. She got a job in a small clothes shop in a precinct in the town centre.

Leo was as ebullient as ever about how the new business was going. His plan was to continue the junk market and at the same time to secure the much more lucrative big house sales which would take place in the properties. These would include valuable objects and would attract the big dealers. He secured two of these, and was triumphant. But Jocelyn had no idea he had done as well as he appeared to have done. Only nine months after their move he pranced in one day in the middle of the afternoon.

'We're there,' he announced. 'Number 15, Woodside Avenue, in one of the most desirable parts of the town. You're going to love it if I get it, Joss. I've put in a bid.'

For a moment she couldn't think what he meant. He couldn't surely have been house-hunting without telling her? When she realised that was just exactly what he had been doing, she only just managed to suppress her anxiety, even her potential annoyance. 'But how can we possibly afford to buy a house yet?'

'How? Because I'm a genius. Another house sale bagged for next month, which includes several old masters and a museum-full of classy furniture. Two building societies and a bank are competing to lend me money.'

'A mortgage?'

'Of course, how else?'

They went to look at the place the next morning. It was certainly a nice-looking house in a peaceful area, but did they really need four bedrooms? They both knew there wouldn't be another child.

'What the hell,' he replied. 'I shall have a study in one of them. Maybe you could take up painting or something and have a studio.'

'But I've no interest in painting,' she pointed out.

'Well, something, Joss - a hobby that'll keep you busy. Perhaps you need a hobby. Picture-framing - or découpage, how about that? I could slip your products into the sales and flog them for you. You have to admit it's a lovely house.'

She questioned him further about finance, wishing she had established a stronger interest in this aspect of things at the outset of their marriage.

Leo was off-hand. 'Don't worry about money, Joss. You know very well I'm no longer a junk-merchant. We can afford it. There's another point you probably aren't going to like.

But if I'm going into the big league, which I am, I *need* to live somewhere like this. Seeing's believing in my trade. If you live in a junky flat as we do, I'm a junk-merchant, and vice-versa. The tail wags the dog. You're going to have to buy some clothes by the way, and why not join the women's luncheon club, get our plate up among Nottingham's senior bourgeoisie? By the way, as soon as she's old enough Sally must go to St Gabriel's, the little infant school I've identified at the end of our road.'

Jocelyn found it hard to believe the rapid change in their fortunes the purchase of such a property must represent, work hard as Leo did. She went to The Yard sometimes. Though Leo said he was working to raise the quality of goods being sold there, she couldn't see a lot of difference. It seemed to her there was the usual miscellany of plywoody sort of furniture with the occasional better mahogany piece, skyscrapers of indifferent crocks, superannuated books and pictures, a big glass case with a cracked pane reserved for plate silver and trinkets. Was he really earning so much from these big house sales?

But, knowing how important a factor confidence was in anything which involved making sales, she put her misgivings to the back of her mind. Leo was happy, and determined. Their loving, playful, easygoing relations continued unabated. Surely anything else was subordinate to this - including the move into the new house, which was effected a couple of months later? She felt uneasy about the property, particularly its size which they could not hope to furnish for some time. But Leo laughed away her concerns. 'We'll occupy it by stealth, room by room,' he joked. She came to accept it.

Some months after this, two men called at about six one evening. She didn't at all like the look of them. One, who never spoke during the whole incident, was stout and muscular. He looked as if he would burst the seams of his shabby suit if he breathed too sharply. The other, a thin-faced individual in a brown felt hat with a curled brim, whose appearance suggested a connection with horse-racing, spoke with a lurking irony, she thought. He said they had an appointment with Leo. She was immediately worried by this fact alone. Leo had always made a point of not bringing business home. 'Home's for you and Sally, not for my racketing,' he had sometimes remarked when she had suggested business entertaining.

She was sure the men didn't have an appointment. She couldn't have said why she knew. However, she could hardly refuse them entry. She put them, not in the sitting-room, which would have been usual, but in 'the library' as Leo insisted on calling one of the downstairs rooms, which had indeed got shelves but which as yet were sparsely inhabited by books. The room was well-furnished with a lot of good furniture Leo had bought recently without consulting her, some of it antique. But she had never liked the room, which had always the aspect of being superfluous and anachronistic. Who had a library these days - as if books were to be quarantined and not allowed all over the house? She left the men in the two expensive-looking clubland chairs of reddish leather.

Leo would normally have been in by this time. When he didn't appear in the next half-hour, she went in to them, perhaps to offer a drink. To her surprise both men were no longer seated but were prowling about the room apparently examining its contents. They didn't seem to be at all guilty to be caught doing this. The one who did the talking merely smirked at her as she entered.

'I'm sorry but my husband seems very late tonight,' she began. 'I hope he hasn't forgotten.'

The man replaced a piece of Meissen to the sideboard. 'I think it very likely he's "forgotten", as you say, Mrs Cunningham,' was the disturbing reply. 'And as he isn't here, you're right, there isn't much point in our staying, is there?'

She burbled conventional regrets and asked if perhaps Leo could phone them when he got in - if they would give their names and a telephone number.

'Don't put him to the trouble of phoning, Mrs Cunningham,' the man said. 'Just tell him me and my partner here'll be in touch.' She asked for his name. 'No need for names. He'll know at once who's involved.'

When she had shut the door on them a shiver passed down her body. She had to keep her hand on the yale lock for several seconds to steady herself.

After a suspiciously short time Leo came in. She thought it was even possible he had been lurking outside waiting for the men to go. 'Oh, those two,' he said with easy levity when she explained.

'You know who they were?'

'I can make a very good guess, yes.'

'They said they had an appointment.'

'Oh did they?'

'You mean they didn't?'

'Of course they didn't.'

'What did they want?'

Leo put both his arms round her waist. 'Very persistent salesmen, I'm afraid, Jossy, hard-sell advertising. I've had two visits from them at The Yard already. Some people just won't accept no. Sorry you were bothered. I'll make sure it's not repeated. I'll have something to say to those two if they reappear. What are we eating, it smells delicious.'

She wanted to pursue the matter. It was hard to accept something sinister wasn't involved. But his manner made it difficult. He seemed in a particularly light-hearted mood.

An evening only a week after this he came home rather late with a black eye. She was horrified, and not at all reassured when he laughed at her concern.

'It's nothing. I did it as I was leaving The Yard. I put the lights out - you know they are some way from the door of the storeroom - and walked into a hatstand. Like bumping into a rutting stag with antlers raised.'

'But it's not just your eye. You've got several cuts and bruises on the rest of your face. It looks as if you've been in a fight.'

He went into the sitting-room and slumped into a chair. 'All right, Joss, you've got me cornered. It wasn't that hatstand. I *was* in a fight. Didn't want to worry you. Saved a woman being raped, I reckon. I couldn't find a parking space outside

The Yard and left the car in the next street. I was cutting through the alley by the brewery to get to it. In the dark there was this fellow in a raincoat wrestling with a woman. I thought they were larking about. Then when I got closer I saw what he was up to. By this time he had her on the ground and was really getting to work. Sorted him out while the woman ran for it. Then he ran off.' He dabbed at his cheek with his handkerchief and looked at a small quantity of blood which showed. 'Yes, damn it, the bastard did land one or two on me, I hadn't noticed.'

She was fully alarmed and suggested that he should let her drive him to the hospital. He could be concussed. He wouldn't hear of it. 'No harm done, a mere scratch or two,' he said.

Later, when he had allowed her to dab his face with antiseptic and affix two plasters, she cross-examined him. He hadn't informed the police and didn't want her to.

'Why not?' she asked. 'The man could do it again. The police should be looking out for him.'

'No point now. I didn't see his face.'

'There must be something you remember about him?'

'Large - white, I think - no more, I'm afraid. Anyway, the woman could have been a friend. She might not want the publicity. It's up to her.'

In the end she didn't persist. Was this because she was not at all sure he was telling the truth? She felt a sudden horrid black cloud had risen in their sky. She had another thought. What if he were lying and he was covering up something he had done and was ashamed of? How would their past avoid being devalued as well as the present? She would have to ask herself when he had ever been telling the truth. Was it possible that an abyss of this magnitude could open before a marriage as happy as theirs?

7.

In early June Sally phoned Jocelyn to say Ken had a couple of days off from 'his frantically busy schedule.' Could they come down? Sally was so anxious to see her in her 'new environment' and to make sure with her own eyes that she was 'as content as she professed.' Also there were 'one or two little matters' which shouldn't perhaps be mentioned on the phone. Jocelyn presumed the latter were to do with her affairs in Nottingham which Sally was kindly helping her with, perhaps the disposal of the belongings she had left behind.

Jocelyn's immediate feeling about the call was one of mild annoyance - particularly at Sally's words. She'd always had an unreasonable resistance to immigrant American phraseology. Why couldn't one just be busy and not have a 'busy schedule?' Besides which Sally did not consider, it seemed, that her mother might also have a busy schedule as well as the young lawyer of bright plumage whom, it now seemed to be clear, she was plumping up to be her life's companion. Neither did she like the renewed tone of patronage concerning her own affairs, as if she were already senile and needed such urbane monitoring.

She upbraided herself for this uncharitable and nitpicking frame of mind. Quite apart from her kindness in helping her with her own affairs, Sally was her daughter, wasn't she, Ken her man? It was quite possible that behind this facade of care for her, Sally was bringing him down for her tacit maternal blessing before tying the last knot. Letters had suggested between the lines a change in Ken's status. Hitherto their association had been described as a 'relationship,' now such a word was not needed, it seemed

She had to tell Henry, for it would involve half Friday as well as the busy week-end. When she did so, before she could stop it, she had a wish that he might show some flicker of annoyance which would enable her to phone Sally and say the dates did turn out to be a bit awkward. But she was saved from the guilt she would have felt had she done this. Henry was charming. His rare smile illustrated by contrast how tautened with care his open face had become.

'But of course, Jocelyn. You've been working like a Trojan. Take as many days as you want. We'll cope. And I shall be *most* interested to meet Sally and her young man.' He paused, thinking. 'Look, where do you propose to put them up?' She told him she was going to find them accommodation in one of the Dartmouth hotels. 'But that's unnecessary. They can have my room, as you did when you first came to see me. It's so easy for me to empty a drawer or two. And that bed would sleep three. I'm presuming of course that . . .

'They do cohabit, yes.'

'Splendid. I had sort of gathered that from you somewhere along the line. That's fixed then. I'll ask Edith to heave my stuff over to the back room.'

She would have liked to remonstrate, not the least for her own reasons. A Dartmouth hotel, with its amenity of reprieve overnight would have suited her better. But she could hardly confess to that, and she had learnt that when Henry had decided something was of use to someone else it was pointless arguing with him. His goodwill was as invincible as were other aspects of his nature. After a token resistance to the room-moving - why couldn't they have the quite decent-sized back room, she suggested? - she accepted gratefully.

She went to meet them at Totnes. Now the moment had come she was excited. Darling valiant little Sally who was really so deserving of her love. How deserving she was, too, of a happy marriage. This was another reason for seeing beyond Sally's occasional prim censures.

Even Inter-city trains these days arrive with no drama or fuss. Immersed in her book, she didn't hear it arrive. There was just a heavy muffled presence behind the station building, then all of a sudden an arpeggio of slammed doors. With a surge of emotion, she leapt out of the car and ran to the exit from which, by the time she gained it, the first of a surprising number of travellers were already emerging. She needn't have hurried. Sally and Ken were the last to appear, a porter preceding them with two substantial suitcases. She might have known Sally would a porter.

'What a beastly crowd,' were her first words. 'You'd've thought a Friday would have been all right. Saturday's their change day, isn't it?' Jocelyn didn't allow Sally to elaborate this superior reference to weekly holiday-makers, but engulfed her in an embrace.

Sally gave her little giggle as she extricated herself. 'Mum-*my*,' she said, 'anyone would think we hadn't seen each other for years.'

Immediately ashamed of her emotion, Jocelyn turned quickly to Ken. A handshake or a kiss? It had always been formal so far. After a slight pause he leaned to her from the waist and pecked each of her cheeks. He was impossibly handsome, she thought again, still in his dark city suit and rather rakish brown trilby - presumably he had gone to the station straight from work. He smelt of an exotic male toilet-essence. 'Jocelyn, how lovely to see you,' he said impeccably and remarked on her appearance as he placed a token arm about her waist without touching it. 'Radiant,' he described her.

For a moment she was ashamed of her old car as well as for her outburst of feeling. Ken, she remembered, possessed a Jaguar. At one time, a lack of material excellence could imply cultural superiority, nowadays it just seemed dowdy. But they were too full of conversation to notice the shabbiness of the car or her awareness of it. And for once the machine started without any pranks, as if it were aware on her behalf that it must be on its best behaviour.

She would have liked to point out one or two things on the way as Henry had done to her, but Sally didn't give her a chance. From the back seat she kept up an astonishing sequence of information about London, their life, and about Ken's career - which it transpired was to be as a barrister. Ken had decided only this week, Sally said. It would mean 'postponing things' a little (what did that mean, marriage, children, improved household arrangements?) but wasn't it wonderful? Meanwhile, sitting attentively in the front seat awarded him by Sally beside her, Ken composed suitable faces to accompany Sally's outpouring, and occasionally, when called upon to do so, to give authoritative confirmation or brief extensions to what she was saying.

Jocelyn was pleased and touched by Sally's new fervour. Fervour was not a commodity she had much displayed as a child. Also she was flattered that Sally should at last pour all this out to her. She had been so reticent about Ken in their previous meetings and had rebuffed her probings. It could only mean, she thought, that things *were* into gear now. She was pleased. She didn't know Ken yet, but he certainly looked a scoop.

Arrival at High Combe involved cognisance of her existence and her changed habitat. 'Gosh, it's quite a place,' Sally remarked tentatively as they entered the drive, as if she had expected a lot less.

'And exceedingly well-kept by the looks,' offered Ken.

Unqualified hyperboles accompanied their arrival in the car park, which was now ringed on three sides by the massive towering bloom of most of the rhododendron varieties they possessed. In the round centre bed spring flowers had long since been replaced with an imperial display of huge purple pansies tastefully mingled with the grey foliage of artemesia. When they had penetrated the wall and saw the main garden falling away beneath them to the estuary, they were transfixed, as most visitors were. The full glory of Henry's superb colour sense was now in evidence - in chosen spots smaller thickets of rhododendron and azalea, the strategically-placed trees, fully-leaved but still in the tenderest shades of spring green, dreamy glimpses of bluebell drifts still out, roses just starting to break into bloom on the lower terrace, deep purple lilacs blazing, the water garden bright with splashes of marsh marigold on its perimeter, budding lilies spreading their fat glossy leaves on the surface.

Henry was not about and Jocelyn didn't like to take them up to the room without him. After a brief introduction to Betty, they went up to the flat leaving the bags in the hall.

Despite her determination to ignore any comments Sally might make, she held her breath while the critical eyes ranged the minute sitting-room which, apart from her few bits and pieces, she had left exactly as she had found it.

'But how very cosy, Mum,' she said at last, patently making the best of a bad job. To hide her thoughts Sally moved quickly to the window. 'And you have quite a slice of the view.' Jocelyn was grateful for the sight of Henry bustling out of the front door of the house at this moment. He must have been upstairs with Delia.

She was doubly grateful to him for the performance he then gave - though performance wasn't the right word. He seemed genuinely pleased at the visitors. He shook Ken's hand with a humorous, almost parental, horizontal movement, Sally's he held for several moments as he scrutinised her intently. Then he quite took over, apologising for not being at hand when they arrived, upbraiding Jocelyn for not taking them straight up to their room. He seemed so much in the part of host, Jocelyn did not go upstairs with them when they went over to the house but sat waiting in the hall. She wanted to thank him again.

She didn't get the opportunity. 'Sally's sweet. What a good-looking pair they make,' he said, voice lowered, as he reached the bottom of the stairs. 'You must be immensely proud. And how nice it is to have visitors again. I hope you don't mind, I told them about six-thirty for drinks. They seem to want an hour or so to settle in. And I thought we'd dress up a bit - don't you think? Sally seemed to think that was a good idea. Have I done the right thing?'

For a moment she did feel a little odd, her family being whipped so immediately from her in this way and all arrangements made. It exposed her to the fact of her homelessness. What had she to do now but go back to her quarters, bath and dress herself, as if she, too, were a guest? She quickly expunged such silly thoughts. Henry was giving them all dinner tonight. Sally and Ken *were* guests in his house. And wasn't she really profoundly relieved at the role he had assumed? It could easily have been so diffe

rent.

When later she saw the full deployment of Henry's hospitality, she was even further reassured. Absorbing a second edition of Sally's exposition of her life, then Ken's, which Henry prompted them to give, there was a surprising development.

Edith had not only cooked the dinner but stayed on to serve it. After a cold lettuce soup, Edith now brought in a triumphant Beef Wellington and its attendant vegetables. Cuffs undone and turned back over the sleeve of his jacket, Henry carved at the sideboard while Edith handed round the dishes. Henry, in the best of spirits, interrupted his carving. He turned amiably to them, holding the knife and fork upwards as he contemplated the scene.

'What a happy occasion this is. You two, Sally and Ken, launching into such a promising life. Edith supplying us with this delicious meal. And most of all, your being with us, Jocelyn.' He looked at Sally before turning back to the carving. 'You do know, Sally, how your mother is transforming us, don't you?'

Sally, radiant from her talk and its reception, was also well-disposed. She gave a sweet smile and transferred its radiance to Jocelyn. Ken, too, with his public school manners and having had his innings, was more than willing for the other side to bat now.

'She's so marvellously efficient,' Henry went on. 'She's reforming my muddled arrangements on the office side, and is already noticeably increasing our bookings. Before we've looked round she'll be running the place. Did you know what a genius of a mother you have, Sally?'

Edith smiled conspiratorially at Jocelyn as she placed a healthy portion of the beef-en-croûte in front of her. An alliance of surprising solidarity had formed between them in the last weeks. Jocelyn was embarrassed, but noted with especial pleasure the look of surprise, even anxiety, which underlay the renewed smile of goodwill Sally directed across the table.

'Oh yes, I think I do,' Sally said, with another run of her little girl laugh.

'She not only does her own job, she takes charge of the shop a couple of afternoons a week and has already learnt enough about plants to take parties round the garden.'

Jocelyn had to qualify this. 'I certainly don't know more than a smattering of the Latin names,' she said.

'As if that mattered. English names are what most people

want, and if you use the Latin tags they think you're showing off, which actually most people are who use them - often quite unnecessarily. And you've already been marvellous helping us in the greenhouses. Where does she get her energy from, Sally?'

Sally had to look at her mother with greater attention. 'I think you've always been a good organiser, haven't you, Mum?' The voice was small, but she had said it, Sally had actually been coralled into paying Jocelyn a compliment. Ken was celebrating the phenomenon with vigorous supporting nods.

Henry's intervention surprised her, for it was a little more, surely, than natural courtesy, and a great deal more vigorous a social output than she had come to expect of him. Indeed, she was glad she had from the first made it plain to Sally that he had an invalid wife who didn't emerge from her room, to whose care he was devoted. Sally was quite capable of reading goodness knows what into such an elaborate compliment.

There was a further incident back in the sitting-room after dinner. Encouraged by Sally to air his expertise, Ken was being given more of the floor than he had occupied hitherto. He was talking about several recent cases reported in the papers where landlords, unable to collect rents from tenants allegedly exploiting weaknesses in the legal system, had taken the law into their own hands and hired muscle to do the job for them. Ken thought such vigilante action was to be strongly discouraged as it was surely on the road to anarchy.

To Jocelyn's surprise, Henry took up the point quite strongly. 'Ye-es,' he said dubiously, 'though there is an alternative thesis one could put forward, for it's not just rental matters which are concerned, is it? The non-payment of rent is after all a relatively straightforward matter, even if there may be a delay before the landlord can evict a tenant. Other cases are less cut and dried - those that concern human relationships. Here the law may never deliver justice. The victim can be left doubly victimised, by the act of the accused and by the verdict. I think one can at least see why sometimes people do reach for other more robust solutions.'

Jocelyn drew her breath in and dared not look at Sally. What did Henry mean? What could he mean other than that he was supporting her over Leo's forced intrusions into her life? She had told him, she thought, far too much on that first visit here. How would Sally and Ken not make the connection?

The moment passed. Ken he cruised them out of any difficulty with an easy application of tact. 'Well, you put the other side very forcefully,' he said with a conciliatory laugh. 'And yes, I can see there's a good counter case to be made. Perhaps the profession will have to speed up its processes.' He changed the subject to a harmless legal anecdote which supported Henry's argument. When Jocelyn dared later to look at Sally, there was no evidence she had noticed anything. Perhaps after all, Henry had meant nothing beyond a generalisation, and her imagination was working overtime again.

Lying in bed later, however, Jocelyn couldn't believe Henry had meant nothing. She was quite certain he had not been talking in general. Surely, what he had been doing was make it plain he supported her in not going to the law about Leo. If so, did she welcome it? It had to be flattering of course but, half-asleep, her mind became confused. She imagined Leo finding her here, appalling scenes, violence, and Leo triumphantly the worse for physical combat. She fell asleep in a limbo nightmare, imagining a bloody battered Leo laughing his head off.

'The heroic spirit of the Commandos,' he was roaring. 'Up the fatal chop to the neck.'

The last she remembered was that she was weeping for him. Poor lovable Leo, he had never really been criminal by nature, only circumstances had made him so.

Jocelyn was woken by a ship's hooter reverberating in the steep valley. Something in the lingering quality of the sound told her it would be a beautiful day. A look through the window confirmed this. Last wisps of morning mist were escaping through the trees like fleeing ghosts. Strengthening sunlight glistened on the dewy lawns. She had a surge of joy.

Sally and Ken were joining her for a late breakfast but the postman came early. She thought she would have time to deal with the mail before they came over and before Betty arrived. She dressed, went down, and collected the large bundle of letters held with a thick elastic band thrown in the porch. Sally and Ken weren't down, and Henry was out in the garden. She had already put into action her idea of standard replies. She quickly identified all the letters concerning booking, marked them with agreed category numbers, and scribbled out for Betty the booking information she was to give to each. One or two paragraphs which needed variant wording she wrote out in full.

Just as she was finishing, Edith came in from the kitchen with a huge basket. Knowing they had not yet decided what to do, Henry had suggested last thing that as the forecast was good they might like to go up on the Moor for the day. He had shown them a route on the map. They had all agreed this would be a splendid idea. Unknown to them, Henry had also left a note for Edith, suggesting this picnic.

She gave in. Why should she resist Henry's kindness if it gave him pleasure? She thanked Edith, who insisted on taking out and showing her each carefully wrapped item and telling her what was inside it. Not only were there two flasks, one of tea, one of coffee, but half a dozen cans of beer. 'You'll have to tell me how much I owe you,' Jocelyn slipped in at a later stage in the conversation. Edith controlled all the housekeeping expenses.

'Oh no, it's on the house, Henry's orders,' she said.

She was going to resist, but realising that with Edith this would be futile, she had a better idea. She went back into the office and called the Royal Castle Hotel in Dartmouth. 'A table for four then for dinner this evening?' she said finally, the man confirmed. She went to tell Edith. She would like to have asked Edith and Geoffrey to join them but couldn't be sure how Henry would regard it. She wrote a note to Henry and left it on the hall table. If he couldn't come they would go anyway.

Breakfast was a success. Ken and Sally were sleepy and amiable. It could be, she thought, that after all the whole day would pass in pure enjoyment with no personal conversation - except about the happy couple of course and their plans for the future. Would a wedding be discussed? She imagined herself putting them on the train at Totnes tomorrow with simple embraces untrammelled by the aftermath of disagreeable remarks. Perhaps a happily married Sally would be different and she wouldn't have to undergo her criticism in the future.

Henry had offered his land Rover, but they went in her car. Ken sat in the front seat with Henry's ordinance survey map and navigated the route Henry had suggested. They passed through Ashburton, began to climb, stopped to admire the wooded and picturesque stretch of the Dart at Holne Chase, then continued steeply upwards on to Dartmoor proper. They parked on the flank of a deserted tor and began a long trek over the springy heather-grown turf towards the outcrop of granite slabs which marked the summit. Now and then they stopped to listen to the silence, broken only by larksong, and to admire the immense view over a large segment of South Devon reaching away to the Channel.

Having reached their objective, they returned to the car pleasantly exercised, lugged the basket, Jocelyn's rug, and two garden chairs some way from the road and found a patch of grass beside a stream. They ate Edith's delicious meal and were finishing coffee. Sally sat pensively, clasping the plastic cup with both hands and staring into it. 'Well, you do seem to have fallen on your feet, Mum,' she said.

'I'm very happy, yes,' Jocelyn said.

'Henry Bordeaux seems a nice man.'

'He's certainly a very generous employer.'

The two exchanged glances, and there was a sudden lurch into tension. 'Mum, what exactly did you tell him about Leo?'

'Tell him? The minimum of course - to explain my name. He saw Cunningham still on my national insurance card.'

'He seemed to imply he knew a lot more last night.'

'Did he?'

'Under cover of the general topic, he was making it very clear that if Leo showed up down here he'd take the law into his own hands to get rid of him.'

'I don't think you can read that into what he said.'

Sally was donning her busy schoolmistress air - dealing with a backward pupil. 'Ken, say your bit. It's up to Mum of course, but I think she ought to hear at least what you think about it.

Mum, Leo appeared at my flat last week. Thank goodness Ken was there.'

Jocelyn's pulses began to race. 'Oh no. You didn't tell him . . .'

'Of course we didn't. But that's hardly the point, is it? The point is that sooner or later he *is* going to find out where you are. When he does, you're going to have to think what you'll do. Surely it's better to think now? Go on, Ken, say your piece.'

Ken gave himself space. Bewigged counsel for the prosecution rises with Ciceronian grip on the lapels of his gown. 'I think the point is, Jocelyn,' he began gently, 'that if Leo is as determined as he appears to be, sooner of later, as Sally says, he *will* find you here. We've been as careful as we can in dealing with your affairs - selling your effects, paying bills, and so on. Everything has come through us, as you know, even stuff from your lawyer. But with a man like him there has to be a risk he'll ferret out something we've missed.'

'Like what?'

'I don't know. Everything we've thought of we've tried to cover. It'll be something we haven't thought of that'll be the problem.'

Sally reentered the lists. 'The trouble is you've been so generous to him in the past, he knows he only has to appear and you'll stump up.'

'I've nothing now to stump up with.'

'There'll always be something he can scrounge - or he'll think there is. Look, what we're saying, Mum, is that what you've done is wonderfully courageous. We both admire you immensely for it. And you do seem to have temporarily at least landed on your feet down here. But what *does* happen when he finds you? You're back to square one. I think you'll then have to do what we suggested in the first place. You'll have to take him to court for harassment. That's what Ken thinks, and he *is* a lawyer. He thinks that what Henry Bordeaux seemed to be suggesting last night would be totally ill-advised, don't you, Ken? The use of any kind of force could land him, and you, in serious trouble, knowing what Leo is capable of.' Ken nodded. 'There's another point, which is linked in a way. Do you really like not having a home of your own? You wouldn't have taken this job if it hadn't been for Leo. It has to be wrong.'

'Wrong?'

'Henry Bordeaux's very generosity feels wrong in a way. Don't you feel that? Don't you miss not having a home of your own? We gather the Nottingham house isn't re-let. Armed with an injunction, you could easily go back. We could help with money if necessary. I'm getting a good salary now. With Leo dealt with, you could go on with your old life.'

She tried to keep calm, to deal with the substantive point and forget the emotion she felt. 'There are odd moments, certainly, when I miss being in my own place,' she said, her head aside. 'But they are only odd moments. I love my little flat, and mostly I'm just grateful to be free and to be doing a job I enjoy and feel I can do well.'

'You don't think it's - well - running away?'

'Of course I don't.'

'It *is* a loss of freedom.' Sally paused. Here it came, with the vicious strike of lightning. 'Besides, one must surely consider - you must have considered - what *Henry's* motives are?'

'Sally, what do you mean?'

'His wife a total invalid? Virtually he's a bachelor. And he obviously thinks the world of you.'

This was too much. 'Look, my relationship with Henry is totally professional, and will remain so.'

'You may feel that way, but will he? His innuendo about Leo last night? It's obvious he sees himself as your knight errant. To me it seems inevitable. Sooner or later he's going to make a pass at you. You must have thought of this possibility?'

The vulgarity of the expression stripped away her last defences. Jocelyn was surprised at the emotion that welled up and engulfed her. For Sally to have an interest in her father, from whose weakness and criminality she could be said to have suffered as much as she had, was one thing, but to intrude into her private affairs to this degree, when she had now left home and had a life of her own, was quite unacceptable. What damned business was it of Sally's? What was this, now in plain nakedness, but a sanctimonious act of being wise for others posing as care for her? She was stony with fury.

'I'm grateful for your concern, Sally - to both of you,' she managed to say. 'But I'm staying here. If we're careful, Leo won't find me. I'm grateful for what you're doing to help me and regret the inconvenience I'm causing, but I've made my decision and I'm sticking to it.'

Her frigid statement at least produced a silence. 'It's nothing to do with any inconvenience to us,' Sally tried to re-begin.

She would hear no more. She got up, brushing crumbs from her clothes. 'That's really all I want to say about it,' she said. 'I'd be grateful if you don't refer to it again.'

For the remainder of the day Jocelyn struggled not to allow Sally's remarks to affect her. In this she was thankful for Ken, whose Haileybury schooling had equipped him with an apparently endless capacity for conversational recitatif. He held forth on several political and economic issues, his views a pianolo version of those familiar tunes to be expected from a bright right-wing City professional with prospects. Meanwhile Sally again sat in the back seat - her silence, if a continuing stricture, not at least an overt one.

Jocelyn was glad she had made the arrangement for the evening in the Dartmouth hotel. She was worried as they drove home that Henry would have some other engagement, or worse an excuse, but he was there to open the car door when she had driven into the garage under her flat. She was quite sure it couldn't be so, but it was almost as if he had been looking out for them. He asked briefly about their day, which they all thanked him warmly for providing, then when she explained about dinner said at once how nice it was of her to include him in their evening. He would love to come.

Jocelyn was doubly grateful to Henry during the evening. Unaware, surely, of the service he was supplying to her, he took over the conversation. The one or two attempts she had made since she had been at Combe to draw him on his service career had yielded little result but, prodded by Ken - even by Sally who began to display an uncharacteristically kittenish response to such a macho male image - he talked at length about his stint in Malaysia. The hair-raising narrative, so modestly told, as if he were talking about someone else's experience not his own, held them all in thrall. Silently, Jocelyn was deeply sorry for him. The display of grit and decency which was being revealed this evening threw into even sharper relief the tragedy to which he was chained.

Because of this evening, the departure the next day was better than she could have expected. Though Sally's silence on the subject of Leo continued to reiterate her immutable views, the topic remained out of order until the very last moment.

'And we'll do our best to keep the enemy at bay,' was the only - humorous - aside made, and this by Ken through the carriage window. Sally nodded beside him. She thanked them in another rush of emotion. Why, after all, busy enough with their own lives, should they have to be bothering about her embroilments?

'Be happy, darlings,' she called as the train jolted and began to move.

She had an irrational desire to weep. They, too, perhaps had more to give than they had communicated. They both craned their necks for the last glimpse, waving. Why is it, Jocelyn thought as she turned away, that so often we get the beginnings and the ends of our encounters right but fail in the middle?

8.

Jocelyn never believed Leo's story about the attempted rape.

For that evening she said nothing, she was in a state of shock. It wasn't so much his injuries and their likely cause which affected her. She had suspected for some time there was something amiss in his business dealings - ever since he said he was going to buy a house - and her misgivings had been confirmed by the evening visit of the two men. What affected her worst was the glib lying. Their marriage had been constructed on honesty, an honesty she had believed to be profound and exceptional.

They lived through the rest of the evening in estrangement. Leo made an effort at brightness when they sat down to eat the meal, but soon gave up when he saw she was silent. At least he made no further effort to get her to believe the story. In bed she felt his alienated presence beside her, also awake and suffering.

It wouldn't last. Neither of them would be able to live with it. Their former frankness to each other, which she still believed in, threw this aberration into too huge a relief. What she was unsure of was what her own reaction would be when the lance that had pierced their love was withdrawn. Would the haemorrhage be lethal? She couldn't believe it would be. They would talk it through courageously and reach some new level of candour.

She went to the shop in the morning. In the afternoon she went back into the town, pushing Sally in the pram, not because she need to buy anything but to get out of the house which had become oppressive, even hateful, to her.

When she got back at tea-time he was in, sitting doing nothing in the kitchen. He got up at once when she entered and began to try to take Sally's coat off. Throwing a mood, Sally wouldn't let him. She wanted her mother to take her coat off, she said. They were used to such caprices, which could be directed at either of them. But taking it as a further rebuff, Leo went out of the room quickly. Did he imagine she had discussed his aberration with the child and that she knew?

She gave Sally her tea, and got her playing on the kitchen floor. She went up and found him in the bedroom. He was sitting on one of the hard chairs, leaning forwards with his elbows on his knees. His usual lively demeanour was absent. She glimpsed a grey, worn look she had never seen before.

'It's debt, but I can cover it,' he said at once, not moving.

'Those men who came - it's them?' His silence gave the answer. 'Is it gambling?'

'It was unnecessary - the way they did it.'

'What sort of gambling?'

'I was going to pay them.' He lowered his head in shame. 'Horses.'

'And you've paid them now?'

'Yes. With a bank overdraft. I'll have to sell some of the stuff downstairs.'

'Is that the only debt you have?'

He raised his head, even brightening a little. 'Yes, Joss, really. It was for us, but I was a fool. I admit I didn't have quite enough for the house. I thought just the one flutter and I'd be through. I'm not really a gambler, you know that. It was a one off.'

She hated herself in the role of inquisitor and judge. She did not believe people should stand in judgement over others. It had always been a part of her ideal that people should be independent. She didn't stand in judgement over him now, it was just that she had to know all of it.

'How do I know you're telling the truth?'

'Because it is the truth.'

'Why didn't you tell me at once about the debt?'

'Because I was ashamed. Can't you see that? I wanted you and Sally to have this house. I wanted it so much I let it cloud my judgement.'

'We shouldn't have this house, we can't afford it.'

He brightened further. 'Yes, we can. I'd worked it out, and even now we'll manage somehow. Now this gambling business is over I'll get down to basics again. I'm going to break my back to make it up to you.'

'I don't want you to break your back, and there's no question of your having to make it up to me. What I want is for us to live as we always have, enjoying life without these - mad ideas of respectability. I'm sure they're not necessary for the business.'

'We can live as we always have. Of course we can. I want to, too. A good house is all I've ever wanted, and now we've got it it'll be enough. I've just got to pay for it.'

She knew she had to say all of it. She turned aside as she spoke. 'No, Leo, a house isn't all you ever wanted. Maybe because of your childhood - or whatever - you've got this obsession with status. It's not just the house you want, for itself, but what it represents. You want to see yourself living in it through other people's eyes, not your own. There's the question of Sally's education, too.'

He frowned lightly, sharpening. 'That's different. *You* want Sally to go to a good school, don't you?'

'Yes, possibly, if it *is* a good school - a school that's good for Sally and not one that other people think is good.'

He seemed to throw off the great weight. 'Joss, am I right in thinking you're beginning to forgive me?'

'I don't know.'

'You know all I want is that. You say I want "status" or something. I'm not sure I know what you mean. What I do know is that what I want is you, and Sally, and that everything else is dust. I've been a stupid idiot, but I've learnt my lesson. I want you to forgive me for what I've done, so we can go on as before.'

She wanted to forgive him, but there was one thing more that must be established before the process could begin. She must make herself say it.

'I want to give up the shop job and come to The Yard to help you,' she said. 'If we can't afford the crêche, we'll have Sally down there, too, until she's old enough for primary school.'

She hadn't thought he would agree to her condition, but he did so with surprising ease There was another pleasant discovery waiting for her at The Yard when she saw the account books, bank statements, and other papers. She had feared debts, maybe a mortgage on The Yard, which was in his name though she had bought it with her money. It seemed there was nothing outstanding. With the new mortgage on the house there was nothing to spare, and certainly no surplus for any set-back, but the turnover was healthy.

He showed her the books proudly. 'So you see, Jossy, I'm not a crook. If we cut costs, we're solvent on the day to day account. I'll have to keep Vince to help with the heaving, and I'll need extra help at the auctions, but poor old Mavis'll have to go if you're doing the bookwork now.'

Slowly she relaxed. It was a nearer thing than he said. They had to cut Vince to half time. But Leo did work hard. On her suggestion they didn't buy everything that came in but improved the quality of what they were selling and made more from a lower turnover of goods. They began to attract one or two of the better dealers. At one of the fortnightly sales a London dealer appeared whom Leo used to know. He was the first of several. It was becoming known that from time to time really good pieces could be picked up at lower prices than they would fetch in London. All the time, every other month, Leo was getting them on-site sales, which sometimes proved very lucrative. Jocelyn made sure the money was banked and invested.

They had less time for themselves, which Jocelyn sometimes privately regretted. It was the house, she thought, which was at the back of it all. If they didn't have the crushing burden of the mortgage and all the other costs which a large freehold property attracts, they wouldn't have to work so hard - quite apart from the fact that it had to be kept clean when they only needed a quarter of the space. But she never spoke of this. It pleased him that they lived at such a 'good' address and had such well-to-do neighbours, and she enjoyed working in the business, contributing to its steadily increasing success. If only he had allowed her to do this from the start.

Their life regained most of its former flavour. They had several seaside holidays, usually in August when business was slackest. This was ostensibly for Sally. Donkey rides, sandcastle-building and sea-bathing were part of a child's birthright, Leo proclaimed. They went to Cromer in Norfolk, which he said had a reputation for being a 'family' resort.

Jocelyn sometimes wondered if Sally thought these pursuits

quite as much much a part of her birthright as Leo did. From her earliest days she had been a grave, practical child.

'Why make a sandcastle, Dad?' she observed once when she was seven, 'when the tide is going to come in and knock it down?' She refused to go on the donkeys. 'They have fleas,' she revealed. It appeared she had overheard this from a genteel parent refusing her child money for a ride.

Sally was happiest, Jocelyn thought, on the day of their return to Nottingham, where her chosen pursuits awaited her. These were largely collections. She collected wild flowers, bottle-tops, stamps, sea-shells and stones (the one certain animation of their visits to Cromer) and also ran a menagerie of pets in what the house agent had rather ambitiously called 'the sun-lounge', a glassed-in arched passage that ran the length of the house on the garden side - for the building was on a slope. There were mice, guinea-pigs, a cage-full of screeching budgerigars (Leo constructed the cage for her) and a very large and lethargic white rabbit called Muncher - aptly named, for munching and its associated procedure was about all it could do in the confined space. Sally ruled over this assembly of creatures like a commissar. Nobody was allowed to touch them except herself, and the animals' misdeeds were fiercely reported at meal-times. 'I'm very cross with Muncher. He has eaten none of his lettuce leaves.' 'The budgies are naughty - they've pecked and broken one of their plastic pots. Would you please stick it, Dad?'

Though she sometimes thought Sally was eroding one of the most precious things in her old relationship with Leo, their hilarity, Jocelyn was glad she at least heard no more about the Bromfield Academy, the local private school he had talked about before. She became increasingly confident they would survive.

In the early part of a hot July when Sally was thirteen, an unfortunate incident took place. Sally had marked her arrival into puberty with characteristic sang-froid. It was Jocelyn more than Sally who worried at the first tell-tale signs of blood on the sheet. 'Oh, do stop fussing, Mum,' she said. 'I know what's happening. It's perfectly normal. I'm beginning to grow breasts and become a woman. So what?' So what indeed. Jocelyn retired, and waited.

She had already diagnosed how other children regarded Sally. That they didn't greatly like her was plain. But it was also clear they feared and admired her devastating truthfulness. Would this cavalier insouciance survive in the new sexually-aware precincts into which she was stepping?

The first she heard of the happening was Leo on the phone in the hall. She was aware of something in his voice and rushed to the landing to listen. Leo was just putting down the phone. 'Oh God,' he said.

'What's happened?' she asked, alarmed, too. Leo had sat down on the chair by the hall table.

'It's Miss Thorpe. Sally's made a complaint.'

'Complaint? What about?'

'I must go down there at once,' he said, jumping up again. 'It's quite terrible. That woman should control things better. She lets them do as they will.'

She thundered down the stairs. 'Leo, what's happened?'

'Two boys made an indecent attack on her. Apparently they interfered with her clothing. Sally reported them.'

Jocelyn continued to be concerned, but - where it mattered - she had already begun to relax. Nothing had happened, she was sure of that. Sally had reported them, *that* was the crisis, if crisis there was.

At this moment they heard the gate go outside. It was Sally. Leo fell on her, cosseting her, asking her if she was all right, almost weeping with anxiety.

'Stop panicking, Dad. I'm perfectly all right. I made such a noise the boys ran off. They'll be expelled,' she added triumphantly.

Jocelyn saw that her shirt was slightly torn on the top buttonhole, and her skirt was held with a safety pin. There was no difficulty getting the story. Sally was explicit. The boys had seized her and dragged her into the boiler house. They had demanded that she undress. When she refused, they had tried to drag her clothes from her. She started to scream - effectively apparently, the boys ran off. 'They're animals,' Sally said.

She then explained that Miss Thorpe had tried to make her stay until her father or her mother came to fetch her. She had refused. She wasn't going to let a couple of hooligans interfere with her life.

Was the damage hidden? Would it resurface? What further traumas awaited someone so blindly self-assured as Sally? Jocelyn asked herself all these questions, as did Leo. But it wasn't long before she saw that the worst fear lay in another direction.

'She must leave that school,' Leo concluded at the end of the evening. Jocelyn was coming to the same conclusion. Some revenge might be planned against Sally if she stayed where she was. She couldn't imagine that any of the pupils, even the girls, would take kindly to someone who had grassed in this way, whatever the provocation. Sally was only a moderate performer academically, but perhaps she could somehow be admitted to one of the comprehensives a year early? What Jocelyn didn't like was that at a certain point Leo went very silent. 'She must certainly leave that place forthwith,' were his last words on the subject.

She knew what was in his mind, but thank goodness he didn't say it, for there was no question now of Sally going to a public school. Their finances were on a firm footing again, but there was no surplus of that order - for one had to think, not of one year's fees, but four or five. It rather irritated her, however, that Leo left it entirely to her to make the arrangements with the two schools. You would think that having played the major part in reacting to the unfortunate incident he would have wanted at least to participate in the solution. It was as if, a public school being out of the question, he was being aloof. It was she alone who arranged that Sally wouldn't return for the remaining days of the current summer term and that she would go to the comprehensive in September.

They decided to go for a cheap holiday in the French Alps. They would take a chalet, and walk. Sally was going to look for wild flowers. One evening Leo came in in a state of suppressed excitement which was palpable. Not much later, when she asked him what was up, he said, in Sally's presence, they weren't going to the Alps. He had cancelled the booking.

'Why?' asked Jocelyn. 'We can afford it this year.'

'We're not taking a holiday, because Sally's going to Roedean next month. I've just fixed it today.'

Like the unexpected returning pain of an old injury, fear surged in Jocelyn. 'But we can't possibly afford it, Leo - even if it were a good thing.'

'Of course it's a good thing. You'll love it, Sal. Lovely buildings, really classy teachers, charming girls. I've been down there. There'll be no question in a place like that of any unpleasantness of the sort you've had to undergo.'

She was furious. 'How dare you, Leo,' she said. 'How dare you take a decision about Sally's future without consulting me - without consulting Sally, either. Even if we could afford it, which we can't, she may not want to go to a public school. Do you want to go, Sally?'

Sally was indulging a new habit of reading at mealtimes, which Jocelyn disapproved of, especially as it implied that the conversation was of secondary interest to her. Needless to say, Leo thought it should be allowed. Sally raised her head, looked between her parents, and shrugged. 'Don't ask me,' she said. 'I dare say most schools are much the same.'

Jocelyn and Leo postponed the debate until Sally had gone up to her room. It raged all that evening. They did have enough money for at least a year's fees, Leo said. And after that, she pursued? After that he would earn it, he said. How? He had plans. Plans he would not reveal, she supposed, like gambling on horses? No, not gambling. What then?

There was a long pause, a pause she would remember, one that even at the time she wondered would not prove to be a turning point. 'I've bought something,' he said quietly. 'Something that's going to make us a mint in six months. I've bought the entire equipment from a gymnasium which went bust in Coventry. We find the premises, we set up a club, and then we either run it or sell it as a going concern. There's no opposition in the town. We can't miss. And Sally will have the chance she needs.'

9.

On her return from seeing off Sally and Ken at Totnes Jocelyn felt she must throw herself into some work. She immediately changed into trousers and an old lumberjack shirt, stepped into wellingtons, and went up to her chrysanthemum bed behind the greenhouses. Henry had given her the job of caring for some three hundred chrysanthemum plants, whose blooms would be sold in the shop in the autumn. Last year's roots had been lifted from the long bed last autumn, cut back, and stored in boxes in the row of brick and glass frames. In the spring, under Geoff Applecote's tutelage, she had cut the new shoots, potted them in damp compost mixed with grit, covering each pot with a plastic bag held with an elastic band. Now they were rooted, they were ready to be planted out.

She loved the physical work as a contrast to the office, and asked Henry to give her more when he felt there was something she could be trusted to do. The evening had turned a shade cooler, and she was soon immersed in the task. She did a row at a time. First she double-dug and manured a length of soil and soaked it with the hose. She drew her string marker taut, then set about the planting. She tapped the bottom of each pot with her trowel, slid out the firmly-rooted plant, and tucked it into the warm moist soil. Finally, at the end of each row, she put in the canes, taking care not to damage the roots.

'You haven't wasted much time getting back to work.' In her absorption she hadn't noticed Henry approaching.

Happily, she straightened up to ease her back and wiped sweat from her brow with the back of her gloved hand. 'I felt like it.'

He perched on the edge of the parked barrow and looked down at her work. 'You've developed a routine with these.'

She laughed. 'Geoff told me how to do it.'

'You've improved on what he said. That's a good idea planting a row at a time, you don't have to tread on dug soil. Is that the idea?'

'Well, yes.'

The last visitors and the rest of the staff had gone some time ago. They had the place to themselves. A blackbird was hard at it on a lower branch of the Canadian maple beside them. Above a pair of buzzards were doing their evening searches in long silent circuits. Around them, relaxing for the night, lay the ordered area of greenhouses and seed-beds, beyond these the well-built limestone wall to which the fruit-trees were espalier-ed. They were silent a moment, savouring, Jocelyn felt, the beauty of the place.

She expected he would refer to Sally and Ken, but in a moment he rose from the barrow. 'You're enjoying the work, I won't disturb you. Come in for a drink, will you, later?'

After a day of sunshine, the work, and a bath, she felt good. She put on a fresh cotton dress, and felt young in a way she hadn't done for some time. Henry was waiting for her. He, too, had changed - into grey flannels, a clean shirt and a silk necktie. He wasn't the sort of man who ran his eyes over a woman's body as if it might or might not turn out to be his property, but she was aware of him taking in her appearance. He led the way out on to the terrace where he had drawn two of the iron chairs to the matching table. On one of the seats he had thoughtfully put a cushion from the room. With a hand on the back of the seat, he moved it back an inch, motioning her to it. 'I thought it might be a Pimms-ish sort of evening, don't you?' he said. 'Perhaps, though, you'd prefer something else?'

'Pimms'd be lovely. I haven't had one for years.'

'Pimms it is then.'

He went inside. She thought what she had already thought. She had thought it particularly this week-end, quite irrespective of, and before, Sally's remarks. Why *should* he have gone to such trouble? Was he about to make some approach now?

She couldn't believe he was. If so, why would he have - deliberately it would seem - set the scene here within full view of the bay-window above? Surreptitiously, she glanced up. The head was not in view. The window was shut, but their voices? Delia would surely hear them, and if it pleased her she could move into position to observe.

He returned with glasses and the elaborate drink, mixed ready in a jug with all the verdure, on a tray. He poured and handed her the glass. 'The visit was an ordeal for you, wasn't it?' he said, taking only a minute sip at his glass.

She was thirsty after the digging and had taken a gulp at hers. She was startled by the unusual outspokenness, and nearly had a spillage. 'Ordeal?'

'Sally.'

She looked away quickly. 'I suppose it was a bit. I've seen Ken several times of course, but not quite in his newly-declared role. He's nice though, don't you think? I think I approve of him. Sally will make rings round him, but that's what she wants. Probably it's what he wants, too.'

'I didn't mean Ken - and the relationship. I mean just Sally. She's the problem, isn't she? Don't get me wrong - I think she's sweet - but she's, well, a bit critical, isn't she?'

'Of me?'

'Yes. I could feel it the moment I met her in your flat. I felt almost as if I'd kidnapped you in her eyes.'

She stalled further. 'She has some misgivings about me coming down here certainly. How perceptive of you to notice, I didn't realise it was so obvious. But you were marvellous, Henry, thank you so much. You really headed her off. I think you won her completely, especially last night.'

'It was in my interest to do so - as far as your staying here is concerned. But again, that isn't quite what I mean. Sally is - or let's hopefully say was - critical of your coming here, OK. But she also has a different opinion about her father, hasn't she?'

'Leo?'

'About what you should do about him.'

She stared at him. 'Why do you come to that conclusion?'

'The conversation on the first evening - about rent-a-muscle. The air was buzzing with innuendoes, wasn't it?'

'What you said was an innuendo?'

'Not initially, no. It arose naturally out of the conversation about crooked tenants. I did once have a crooked tenant myself, in a flat we owned in London - which we had to let when we went abroad. But I knew as I was saying them that my remarks had other applications. Sally knew they had, too, didn't she? She made no effort to conceal what she was thinking. Look

Jocelyn, I'm sorry, diving into this when it may be distressful to you. If it is, please say so.'

'No, it's not distressful.'

'Good. If you're sure, then what I did want to say is this. I'll say it, then shut up. Even before Sally came, it occurred to me - when you told me about Leo - that there's a possibility he might find you here in spite of your precautions. You've obviously faced that possibility, too, or you wouldn't have said what you did to me about changing your name - being careful, and so on. What I want to say is that, if it were to happen - and there's no reason why it should - I hope you'll call on me to help. Now you're here and not living on your own, it *should be* a relatively easy matter to deal with I'd have thought - without messy embroilments with the law.'

She had a peculiar feeling. His features were filled with a goodwill and a concern that were entirely decent and admirable. But for a moment she had the same thought she'd had on Friday with Sally and Ken - that he was taking over her life just a little too busily. What business was it of his, by what process of thought did he assume it might be? And what was he contemplating - a couple of Commando blows on Leo's neck as in that semi-dream she'd had? She was immediately ashamed of her thought. He meant it well. She suspected he had planned this whole conversation to please her.

At this moment she happened to look up, really to escape his gaze. Framed fully in the window above - behind Henry, who was facing her - was the face of Delia Bordeaux, looking down on them, her features distorted with unequivocal hatred. She met the woman's eyes momentarily. In this, she tried to be fearless, she tried to communicate to Delia what she had attempted to say once already - that she was here doing a job no more and that she was sitting here simply because she had been invited to do so. She expected Delia to withdraw. She didn't. It was herself who had to look away.

The incident had taken no more than a couple of seconds. Henry, awaiting her answer, was unaware of what had happened. Under cover of his preoccupation with her problem, she strove to compose herself. She did so by returning to Henry and his offer to protect her. How devious of her not to accept it as it was intended, as an act of common decency. 'Thanks, Henry,' she said. 'What you say is certainly a comfort.'

He was happy enough to pass to a subject less fraught - the plans for the tea-room, to be called 'the refectory', which were now through. Work would start in the early autumn. She was determined not to let Delia's presence above disturb her. She joined in the conversation. After half an hour of pleasant talk they split up to go their separate ways, he to a cold meal Edith had left him, she to a Spanish omelette. She felt ravenous.

She had the first inkling there might be trouble from Geoff two days later. She had just taken a group round and was walking with them to their bus in the car park. Geoff was weeding the centre bed. As the bus pulled away she stopped to talk to him.

Geoff was a taciturn man and a hard worker, but it was warm and he was pleased to rest for a moment. They sat together on the dry wall that surrounded the raised bed. Geoff mopped his neck with a large handkerchief.

Conversation didn't come easily to them, though silence was never an embarrassment. Jocelyn had learnt from Geoff that, especially in the presence of the garden, communication could take place between people without speech. But on this occasion Geoff was ready enough with a topic.

'Vesuvius erupting then a bit?' he said. She arranged her features to enquire what he meant. 'Mrs Bordeaux - Edith says she's never known her quite like it, and that's saying something.'

'You mean she's being ruder than usual?'

'Rude? I wouldn't say that's the word for it. Reckon there isn't one in the language when she gets into her stride. Edith says her face was like - well, Vesuvius, when she went up today.'

'Does anyone know why?'

'She doesn't need a reason, does she? Apparently, this time she's going for Henry, too. And that's new - to this extent anyways. Edith heard them at it last night before she left. Hammer and tongs. She heard Henry shout and the door slam. Henry looks shaken, didn't you notice this morning? Not himself at all. And he hasn't been about all day.'

She thought back. She recalled he had flitted rapidly in and out of the office early on. She had assumed he was preoccupied about something. She had been late in for lunch after talking to a new travel agent from Torquay. She had registered that, like her own, Henry's food had been put to keep warm in the Aga and that he didn't come in while she was there. Somewhat harassed with the first afternoon visitors imminent, she hadn't noticed any particular atmosphere.

'Edith and I think he ought to institutionalise her. It's not fair on anyone to have to bear a thing like this.'

'I doubt if he'll ever do that.'

'I think you're right there. When Henry Bordeaux decides something he doesn't change his mind. I've often thought I'm glad I was never a war enemy facing a bloke like him.'

The news fell on her like a blow. Could it be something to do with herself? Of course it must. A further panicked thought occurred to her as she walked away from Geoff. If Delia really was kicking up about her presence here, would she be forced to leave? She was fairly sure Henry wouldn't dismiss her, but if her presence here was causing him unnecessary suffering wouldn't she have to go of her own accord? Was that what Delia was banking on?

She had promised herself a cup of tea and a sit down after a busy afternoon. She found her footsteps taking her to the kitchen, however, not to her flat. She must have more information if it was available.

'Cup of tea going?'

A gloved Edith was sitting at a tableful of silver. She was working at this moment on the elaborate épergne that stood on the dining-room dresser. 'Course, dear, help yourself.'

She plugged in the electric kettle, switched it on, and sat down. Edith worked furiously with the 'putting on', her forefinger covered with the cloth thrusting busily into the elaborate crevices of the Victorian ornament.

The subject, avoided at lunch as she now realised, was now palpable. Jocelyn had never gone in very much for woman-to-woman relationships, which too often seemed smugly cosy, but she and Edith had slipped into one. They saw eye to eye on most things and their relationship was classless.

'I've an idea what *you*'ve come to discusss,' Edith said after a few moments. Simultaneously she raised her eyes ceilingwards and gave a little thrust of her head. 'You've heard no doubt?'

'Geoff's just been telling me, yes. What's upset her, do you think? It must have happened before.'

'It has, but I'll tell you one thing, I've never heard her shout at Henry as she did last night. And I've certainly never heard Henry shout at her.'

There was a pregnant silence as Edith finished the putting on and began to muster the clean rag for polishing. Should she probe further, Jocelyn wondered? While she debated, Edith had more to say. 'I'll tell you another thing. That Damon Gillespie was here this afternoon with another man and a woman whose names weren't mentioned. Up with her for an hour. When he came before there was trouble. I wouldn't trust that man beyond the garden gate. Certainly not inside it.'

'Gillespie?'

'Her lawyer.'

Her heart missed a beat, leaving a numb feeling in her chest. 'Why would she want to see a lawyer?'

Suddenly Jocelyn was sure not only what the answer to her question was, but that Edith knew, too. Her fear came out involuntarily, in a rush. 'You don't think it has something to do with my being here, do you? She couldn't be . . . you know what she said to me that day when I went up to try to talk to her?'

Edith raised her eyebrows. 'I could make a good guess. If it's what I think it is, it would be just the kind of thing she would say - you'll pardon me - to an attractive woman like yourself. She's always been scared wet Henry'll fall for someone else and ditch her. Now she's got the threat, as she sees it, on her doorstep.'

'But why the lawyer?'

There was a heavy pause. Did Edith know that Delia owned Combe - if what Delia had said on that score was true? She was not kept wondering very long. 'Why the lawyer? I've little doubt. She owns the place, you know.'

'You mean she'd threaten Henry in some way?'

'I certainly do mean that, yes.'

Jocelyn found herself blushing. 'But if this is true it's monstrous. She has no grounds whatsoever to think such a thing. She did make the silly charge that evening I went up. I made it clear then how absurd the idea was. Henry has nothing to fear. She can't threaten without evidence. She's mad.'

'She's mad all right, and that's why it won't stop her.'

'You mean she imagines I'm vamping Henry and that she'll say if he doesn't get rid of me she'll sell the place over his head?'

'Something like that, I shouldn't doubt.'

Jocelyn pulled herself together. 'Edith, do you think I'll have to go? If things really are as we're imagining, I think I'd feel obliged to. If she has got this obsession she'll make that threat. I think you're right.'

'Henry won't hear of your going.'

'I should never have come here.'

'You mustn't say that, dear. How were you to know the set-up? I'm sure he didn't tell you.'

'He certainly didn't.'

'Well, perhaps the creature's only threatening. Perhaps she's got away with it before and thinks she can again. My guess is that this time Henry'll stand up to her and she'll be forced to back down.'

'But Henry shouldn't be in the position of having to challenge her.'

'He will. I'm sure of it. If I heard aright last night he's probably done so already. If you take my advice, Joss, I'd just lie low and let events take care of things.' Edith smiled briefly. 'I'd say Henry has an incentive now to do what he should have done a long time ago.'

'Edith, what do you mean?'

'I mean he knows which side his bread's buttered. He knows you're the best thing that's happened to the place since he started. He's never been good at the business side or at dealing with people. You are. He won't want to lose you.'

Jocelyn was beginning to feel uncomfortable. Was this all Edith was meaning? She wasn't at all sure she hadn't made a clever last moment adjustment in her last statement. She knew one thing - she was going to talk to Henry, whatever attitude he took. She got up. 'Where is he? Do you know?'

'No, I don't. He never came in for his lunch. Geoff says he hasn't been in the garden all day. He's gone out in the car most likely, probably to get away from her.'

She went out before Edith could say more.

Lie low, Edith said. How could she? How could she allow these calumnies to be abroad without talking to Henry? In her surge of feeling she went to the garage. The door was shut. She opened it. The Land Rover was there. She went to the terrace and looked down the garden. He was nowhere in sight.

As she stood there the house, the garden, seemed to be held in a strange stillness. She looked up at that window. It was as usual, the curtains drawn severely back, like a spying eye. It frightened her. Henry almost never went out without saying where he was going and what he was doing. Was it possible he could do something foolish? Was he capable, in an extremity - one he might never have had to face before so starkly - of putting an end to his suffering? What did she know of his surely tortured inner workings?

She remembered again how, in that first week, he hadn't allowed her to discuss Delia with him. All that bottled down - and now the possibility he could lose the one thing he had constructed over the ruin of his life. Should she go back to Edith and discuss this new dreadful possibility with her? She didn't want to. Goodness knew what Edith was really thinking - very possibly that there *was* something between Henry and herself.

She went up to her flat and slumped into her chair. Several times, thinking she heard noises, she jumped up to look through the window. The third time she saw Edith and Geoff emerging from the gate at the far end of the house with their bicycles. Geoff mounted and began up the drive. Edith, slower, had a large carrier bag to wedge into the handlebar basket. Powerless to move, Jocelyn watched her put her foot through to the far peddle and launch off.

Numbed with worry, Jocelyn went down and into the house again. The aching silence frightened her further, the pictures, the furniture just so, the grandfather ticking with an indifferent gait. She had another dreadful thought and crept up the stairs almost to the landing. There, too, through that door, there was silence. She imagined what could be behind it, the two bodies, blood, horror.

She dismissed this as melodrama. If something like that had happened, there would surely have been shots or some tumult that Edith would have heard. Edith must have taken up Delia's lunch, and that afternoon the lawyer had been. Just at this moment there was a stir. Delia was there all right.

She went back to the flat. Should she do a bit of work in the garden? That would be the best way to make time pass. She couldn't bring herself to make the effort. Eventually she sat down with some sewing.

The first she heard was a step on the outside staircase up to her front door. Made of iron, it had a resonance which was immediately audible. She flew to the door. It was Henry - Henry unflustered and looking entirely normal. Relief must have given her a comic look.

'Joss, it's only me. Sorry, have I startled you?'

He came in easily and sat at once, unbidden, in the other chair. 'I'm exhausted. You couldn't raise a cuppa, could you?' His eyes, ranging the small bookcase, saw the bottle on top, Ken's present to her. 'Belay that, a small whisky?'

He took a large gulp of the whisky to which she had added water by his instruction. 'I've been out on the estuary all day,' he said at last. 'I'd intended to be back at lunch-time, but my mind was elsewhere and I forgot to check the fuel. I ran out plumb in the middle. I tried to row back, but the tide had turned some time before and was by then in full ebb. I suppose I could have made the shore if I'd felt like the effort, but it was more pleasant to go with the tide. I just handled the tiller and drifted all the way down to Dartmouth. Someone gave me a line and I got ashore to fill up.' He paused, drinking again. He had drained most of the glass. He put it down. 'I expect by now you know what it's all about?' he said.

'I didn't until Geoff told me something a couple of hours ago. Then I talked to Edith.'

'Who had it all sewn up no doubt.' He smiled. 'Edith knows things even before they happen sometimes.'

She felt the ground beneath her was insubstantial. 'I gather Delia's being difficult.'

'It has gone beyond any kind of reason. The lawyer came today, did he?'

'Er - yes. Edith said someone had been - and another man and a woman with him.'

'The trouble is she means it. Incredible as it is, she is perfectly willing to sell this place over my head.'

'Sell?'

'Yes. Delia owns it, legally. It was mostly her money, or rather her father's we used to buy it. Her father was a very rich man. That was all arranged before - it happened. Before there was any question of irrational distrust.'

She braced herself. 'It's because of me, isn't it?'

'No it isn't, not essentially.'

'I wanted to tell you before. Do you remember that evening after I had gone in to try to talk to her? She made it clear then she thought I had designs on you. She also told me she owned Combe and would use it against you "if necessary." And that's what she's saying to you now, isn't it? Either I go, or she sells the place. It *is* about me.'

'No, it's not. It's about the mental illness she has suffered, or allowed herself to suffer, because of her injuries. It's not about you, and you're not leaving here - not that is, as far as I'm concerned. What she's saying, as you know, is total nonsense.'

'But you'll lose Combe?'

Interlocking his fingers, he looked sideways towards the window. 'Possibly, but not necessarily.'

'What do you mean?'

'That engine conking out, and a few hours on the river, have given me the chance to really think things through, Jocelyn, and I've decided. Undoubtedly, she's changed her will, as she has often threatened to do before. The couple who came were probably the witnesses. But this time I'm not giving way to blackmail. In the past I've always appeased her. This time I'm not going to. Maybe I shall lose the garden, but I've decided to tell her that if she doesn't abandon her offensive illusions I shall cease to look after her. She will go into an institution. My doctor advised me to arrange it years ago. There are limits beyond which no one can be expected to go. I'm going to tell her this evening - now.'

'Henry, don't. There's a much easier solution. I'll go. It's quite ridiculous that I, a total stranger in your life, should become a catalyst in this way. If I go, she'll calm down. You won't lose the garden. Employ a man and everything will be normal again.'

He threw back the last of the whisky with a violent movement unnatural to him. 'That's a way out I don't consider for a moment You're not leaving here by any wish of mine. I realise how terribly embarrassing this must be for you, but I hope more than I can say that you'll stay. This is what I came here to say to you - as well as to tell you the decision I've made about Delia. It may be that Delia, faced with the stark alternative I'm going to put to her, when she realises I mean it, will pull back from the abyss. It's certainly in her interest that she does. No institution, psychiatric or otherwise, will give her the care that I, and Lorna and Edith, have. But maybe Delia will go through with it, nonetheless. She's capable of savage vindictiveness. I just felt you should know, in advance.'

He rose, and hesitated, as if he were about to say something else. Whatever it was, he thought better of it. He thanked her for the whisky, and left.

10.

Jocelyn got over her anger about Leo's arrangements for Sally's education but Sally herself seemed to enter a sulk about it. 'You would like to go to Roedean, wouldn't you, darling?' Jocelyn asked her when they were alone. She got another shrug. 'If Dad thinks so, I suppose.'

Jocelyn didn't like to make any kind of counter-propaganda about the place which would have seemed like treachery, but she did mention to Leo at a right moment that Sally didn't seem ecstatic. 'Oh, she'll love it when she gets there,' he said with a careless laugh. 'She'll see the difference from the little pond she's been swimming in up here.' That Sally might find the new environment out of her depth he didn't mention.

From another point of view Jocelyn was not so chagrined about Sally's impending departure from home for two thirds of the year. It was from this time she diagnosed a new sharpness in Sally's relations with Leo. Leo had been enthusing again about the gymnasium, which was now set up and ready to open. '*Why* are you starting a gymnasium, Dad?' Sally asked.

'To improve the physique of our degenerate townspeople,' joked Leo. 'We'll probably start producing gold medallists at the Olympics in a year or two.'

Sally had a new adult habit of stopping her eating when an idea of importance had engaged her. She put her knife and fork down on her plate and tucked her hands under her chin. 'Is that the real reason?'

'Why certainly, Sal. "Mens sana" - whatsit.'

'"Mens sana in corpora sane," you mean,' supplied Sally primly, with her not so newly fledged, and devastating, accuracy. 'But will people want that? It's not much *fun* pretending to row a boat or pulling an elastic handle in and out. I'd rather jog or swim or go for a walk, or play games. I'm sure most people would.'

'Business men and women, in a city, don't have time for all that. Their exercise has got to be concentrated. You'll see, they'll flock to "Olympia", we'll be turning them away.' Olympia was the name Leo had thought up for his health centre.

'I think you're doing it to pay my new school fees,' Sally said. 'I do hope the place doesn't go bust.'

Leo laughed this off, too, but not before Jocelyn noticed the little imp of terror that put its head above the parapet for a moment in Leo's eyes. She remembered the same look during the horse-racing episode.

Maybe it was as well Sally wouldn't be around from the middle of September. Leo could probably do without too much overt honesty in the coming weeks. Jocelyn had learnt enough from working at The Yard to confirm her previous understanding, that their business depended above all on producing contagious confidence. She had even come to admire Leo in a way she hadn't done hitherto. She saw that it was not just foolhardiness to appear confident when things weren't so good. It often took courage. And the Sallys of this world, so adept at removing bungs from barrels, were not so good at filling them.

Now that the school was a fait accompli, she gave Leo all the support she could. She ran The Yard single-handed. Leo just came in on auction days. She hardly saw him, for he was at the gymnasium every evening until ten or later. It seemed, after a slow start, things at the gymnasium were going well. The advertising had been extensive. Leo said there was a steady stream of enrolments. He thought they might even start breaking even on the current account in the new year. The bank, he said, were cheering from the touch-line.

She had a silly superstition about not visiting the gymnasium. But one evening after it had opened, he invited her to come and inspect it and she felt she couldn't refuse. She was impressed. It had a good site on the first floor of a substantial block near the town centre, and the equipment seemed to be brand new. Screwed into the newly-sanded and polished parquet floor were gleaming chrome bicycles equipped with dials which told you your speed and the number of revolutions completed. There were lifting and pulling gadgets, ropes, suspended rings, wall bars and a vaulting horse (to be used by school-children during the daytime when adults would be thinner on the ground). In a corner were two punch-balls. There was a ladies' and a gents' dressing-room with showers installed, a storage area, and a small room which Leo intended to turn into a bar when the licence came through, and a minute office. The place smelt of the floor polish and of fresh paint.

'Today I engaged the aerobics teacher,' Leo enthused, 'and we enroled our twentieth customer.'

Maybe it would work. Jocelyn was ashamed of the several private thoughts she'd had about it.

Joss was doing well at The Yard. She heard that a largish house in their road had become vacant on the death of its aged occupant. She went to see the house agent who was handling the sale and won the contract for the sale of the contents, apparently against several larger firms from other towns. The house itself had already been sold, and the new owner wanted the contents sale done at once - at The Yard, so that the house could be cleared for decorators.

She'd had the main delivery of the important items, which were already on display for viewing. These included an exquisite Queen Anne bureau, a carved Carolian chest, and two sets of genuine Chippendale chairs. There were also a number of nineteenth century watercolours by well-known, catalogued artists. Leo said each of these would fetch more than a thousand. She put them in the separate, smaller room, which had iron bars on the windows and a door with a special lock.

One September morning she was overseeing the arrival of the lesser items. She had a local firm doing the removal, and Jocelyn knew the three men who had come with the van. Clutching her clipboard, on which she had the inventory for checking in the items, she was chatting with them in the loading bay as they began to unlock the back of the vehicle and let the ramp down. She saw the two men approaching. Both wore very clean whitish macs with belts and with collars turned up. They would have continued behind her into the show room and not spoken had she not turned, smiling, towards them.

'Just look round if we may?' said one of them.

'Yes, of course, though it's not official viewing till tomorrow.'

The second man was going to say something else but was clearly cautioned not to by a slight movement made by the other. The two men went inside.

It came on to drizzle and she moved inside the door to do the checking as the men brought the items in. From this position she could see the viewers on the far side of the room peering into the locked silver case. The more junior one was taking notes in a notebook as the elder man said things.

Later they wanted to see the pictures. She unlocked the door for them and, as Leo had told her she must, stood by it while continuing to do the checking in. Though she had never seen the men before, she imagined from the methodical way they were going about their inspection of the lots that they were dealers, probably from another city - maybe even from London.

She began to be suspicious. They looked respectable enough and had behaved courteously outside, but they didn't seem to be doing quite the sort of thing dealers did. She recalled that when looking at the furniture in the main room they hadn't been running their hands over the goods, pulling out drawers, looking at the feet of chairs and tables for signs of worm. Now, looking at the pictures, they didn't seem to be interested in the works themselves, but in their captions and the names of the painters - which Jocelyn had made clear on typed cards placed below the frames. Could they be criminal in some way? She would certainly tell Leo about them this evening. Just when she was wondering if she should phone Leo, the men finished their work. She felt they had been uncomfortable about her presence, looking on. But as they left, the man who had spoken before thanked her with scrupulous politeness.

It was a busy day, Leo didn't come in until after ten that evening, and she didn't in the end tell him about the men. He was always laughing at her fears and scruples, which she never used to have but which somehow arose frequently since the betting incident. He had once jokingly called her 'a nitpicker extraordinary,' she didn't want to give him more ammunition. In retrospect she thought the two men had been ordinary buyers.

The auction was a week later. Leo was at his best, Jocelyn thought. He could be waggish if he sensed his audience was receptive, but he had become much more straightforward in recent months with the higher value goods they were handling and especially when there were dealers present who didn't usually respond to auctioneers' witticisms. The room was packed. All the folding chairs they put out in the body of the room were occupied, and there was a throng standing on both sides. The sale went briskly. The bureau was knocked down at over four thousand, one of the Chippendale chair sets for nearly ten. The pictures were scheduled for the early afternoon. As they ate sandwiches in the office Leo was ecstatic. 'With this crowd the pictures will go for the maximum,' he forecast.

They hadn't had many watercolours of this value and Jocelyn was not au fait with the prices, but Leo was right, the first half dozen went for sums she wouldn't have imagined. There were a couple of French dealers there who had clearly come for the pictures. They hadn't bid for anything else.

Jocelyn's job during the sale was to stand by the entrance to make sure no one absconded with anything. She couldn't therefore always see exactly what was going on at the front. She heard Leo's gavel knock down another picture for the highest price gained so far for the collection - three thousand two hundred. There then seemed to be a disturbance with someone else's voice raised, not Leo's. She stood on a chair and saw two men advancing towards the dais. They were the same two she had noticed a week before, wearing the same light-coloured raincoats. A hush was falling over the room.

'I'm sorry, Mr Cunningham, we must interrupt you,' she heard clearly. 'Police.' A badge or a card was flashed. 'I'm going to have to take possession of the last lot just sold.' Jocelyn saw the man consult a paper he held. 'The same goes for the second picture sold - lot number three hundred and twenty-nine. For the present I suggest the two sales are declared by you to be null and void. We have reason to believe that both pictures are forgeries.'

The pictures were produced by Ben, one of the overalled assistants they employed for sales. The men left with them, carrying one each, accompanied by the babble of astonished whispering which was now succeeding the hush.

Jocelyn tried to halt the policemen at the door. 'What's happened?' she asked. 'Did the vendor know these pictures were forgeries?'

'You'll be hearing the details very soon, Mrs Cunningham. But since you ask, I must tell you that - no, the vendor didn't know these two pictures were forgeries. The vendor didn't possess them. They were inserted among the artefacts of the sale at a very late stage in the proceedings.'

'But they arrived here by separate delivery with all the other pictures. I checked them in myself, and of course they were on the inventory.'

'Doubtless you did, it was your husband's inventory, wasn't it? We shall be requiring to speak to you as well as to your husband - this evening, as soon as the sale is over. I've left a written note for your husband to this effect. My colleague here will be remaining, to accompany you both to the station.'

'You're surely not accusing us . . .

'At this point I'm accusing nobody. All I'm telling you is that these two pictures are not originals and that they did not form part of the vendor's property. Now, if you'll excuse me, Mrs Cunningham.'

Stunned, for several moments Jocelyn stood there in the porch watching the man leave. When she came to, the other man had gone back into the room. Her instinct was to rail against him. She overcame her impulse, what could be worse than to do that? She had to believe it had nothing to do with them. Most likely someone connected with the family had put the pictures in - or anyone could have. The forgeries, if such they were, could have been slipped into the empty house and hung at any time before Leo had done the first inventory and valuation. The house agent perhaps, or someone employed by them? They would have been able no doubt to detach the sum raised for the two pictures from the lump sum and the vendor wouldn't notice.

Somewhat reassured, she listened to Leo, who had resumed the sale and was making light of the interruption. 'Sorry about that little interlude, ladies and gentlemen. Clearly there does seem to have been some irregularity concerning the said lots, an irregularity, I hasten to add, for which this firm has no responsibility whatsoever. I'm glad, on behalf of the two gentlemen who bought the pictures, that they've been saved from what might have been a most unfortunate purchase. Now, shall we proceed to the next group of lots, the china and porcelain - all fine forgeries of course.' The titter that followed the riposte was less than full strength, but it was a titter nonetheless. Jocelyn took strength from the fact that Leo was so unfazed.

When the sale finished, she and Leo were usually frantically busy for another couple of hours, supervising the payment for and the removal of sold lots. The policeman tried to prevent them from doing this, but eventually, seeing there was no one else who could do it, allowed her to stay providing Leo went with him. His colleague would wait for her, he said. In the circumstances she hardly had a chance to exchange more than a word with Leo.

'Lot of old cods, Joss,' he said airily within the policeman's hearing. 'It's probably this Canadian cousin who's inheriting. Slipped them in for good measure. Quite a good wheeze. Though you wouldn't have thought he'd've bothered. If he's made as much on the house as he has on this sale he's going to be sitting pretty.'

She was thankful for the work. They usually aimed to clear most of the stuff the same evening. The majority of purchasers were more than ready to take their property right away if they had the transport. They were afraid it might vanish if they left it until the morning.

Everyone had gone. She did a last scout round to make sure nobody was in any of the side rooms. The staff had left. She switched off all lights. The policeman was waiting.

'Right, I'm ready,' she said.

The man had been busy with his mobile telephone and was just rehousing the aerial. 'It won't be necessary for you to come to the station tonight, Mrs Cunningham. I've just been speaking to the Inspector. I'm afraid your husband has been arrested and charged with the fraudulent sale of two forged pictures. You'll be required to give evidence, if you choose to - a spouse has the right to withhold evidence - but I understand that no charges are to be made against yourself.'

The man offered to take her home. She had duplicate keys of their own car, parked outside, and declined. She asked if Leo had been granted the right to see a lawyer. The policeman didn't know. He would assume so, he said.

At home she rang the police station. Leo was being held in the cells overnight, she was told. She asked if she could come and see him, but was told she couldn't. She asked if he had seen a lawyer. They said he had, and supplied the name.

She phoned the lawyer, whose name she had never heard - they didn't know any lawyers. He informed her in a voice she thought lordly that he couldn't yet make any comments on the case, but that it was likely he would obtain bail for Leo.

'Bail?' she said, 'for how much?'

There was a distasteful pause. 'I gather there's a gymnasium, as well as the auction business. I imagine the court will accept these as security for whatever sum is fixed.' The tone sounded uninterested.

Leo walked into The Yard at midday the next day. He was jovial. He had been bailed. 'It's a frame-up of course,' he said in front of Vince, their assistant. 'They don't know where to look for the villain, and I'm someone at hand to grab.'

With Vince there, she didn't like to ask the questions which had been swirling up in her mind all night. They shut up the place and went home for lunch. Alone, she fired her anxieties at him. 'The police surely couldn't have charged you so quickly if they hadn't thought they had something to go on.'

'Oh, they've got something all right. Apparently this isn't the first time these forgeries have been planted in sales. The police have been on the look out. Just before I made my on-site inventory, this Inspector Jacklin viewed the place. He claims the two pictures weren't there then. Someone must've slipped them in in the half hour or so before I arrived. There's no doubt the pictures were there when I did my list.'

'So they can't prove anything. Someone could have entered the house during that period.'

‘That’s what I pointed out to them.’

‘So why have they charged you?’

‘They say that after their visit they had the place under surveillance and no one went in before I arrived.’

‘Someone could have been hiding in the building all along.’

‘I pointed that out, too. They say they searched the house from top to bottom.’

‘Leo, it seems they’d decided you were up to something before they started.’

‘Right in one.’

‘But why? Why should they suspect you, out of the blue like this?’

Leo looked towards the window. His expression was one of philosophical endurance. ‘Because they say it’s not the first time forgeries have been through our saleroom.’

‘But we’ve had no valuable pictures through that I remember.’

‘Not pictures - silver, and furniture. That’s what started them apparently. Three Louis Quinze chairs, for instance. Remember them - about a month ago? One of them was a clever copy, they say. The purchaser discovered it and went to the police.’

Jocelyn was beginning to feel a coldness in her stomach. She strove to collect herself. ‘What did the lawyer say?’

‘What do lawyers usually say?’

‘He agrees you’re innocent?’

‘He agrees nothing. We didn’t even discuss it. It was just the bail he was arranging. I’ve to see him again tomorrow.’

What worried her most was Leo’s stoic, almost determinist attitude. She thought sometimes he accepted he was doomed, that whatever evidence they had against him would prevail. He made jokes about it, but the humour carried none of that light-hearted certainty in himself and in his view of the world which, she often thought, was what had most made her fall in love with him. He was superficially debonair still, but it seemed to her to be a new variety veined with masochism.

She wanted to go with him to see this lawyer, Phillip Plymstock - who lived in a large house outside the town. No doubt his fees would be commensurate with its dimensions. Leo refused to allow her to come. ‘No, Joss, no reason for you to be involved. I'll handle this rubbish. A few days and the police will be forced to drop the charges. Plymstock's a pompous ass, but I'm told he's the best around. He's a solicitor, but he does the court work as well.'

The next day Leo went to see Plymstock. After an hour's conversation, Plymstock said he wasn't prepared to take on the case. Apparently he told Leo he didn't take on fraud cases unless he was assured of the innocence of the defendant. He couldn't be so in Leo's case. Later, a bill arrived for three hundred pounds.

Leo went on trial two months later with another Nottingham man, Swinscoe, a painter who was accused of forging watercolours in the style of known nineteenth century masters. Swinscoe had been under suspicion by the police for several years for this probably lucrative adjunct to his legitimate work, but as he had been very crafty in the disposal of the copies - he had certainly sold several overseas - they hadn't been able to gather enough evidence to charge him. A month before Leo's arrest the police had been alerted to his possible involvement with Swinscoe by the Louis Quinze incident. As it turned out, the chair proved to be a hare - it wasn't a forgery. But as a result of the suspicion Leo was followed. The police had a clandestine photograph of him meeting Swinscoe in a pub. There was also a recording of their conversation. There was no doubt the two had been plotting to put the two pictures through Leo's sale. The proceeds were to be halved. Swinscoe got five years, Leo two.

11.

When Henry left her flat, Jocelyn felt a loneliness starker than any she had experienced since Leo first went to prison. What was it that seemed to make her a victim in life, as if by design? Sally for example would surely never have the problems she'd had to face. Sally would simply turn her back on anything that didn't accord with her immediate needs. Why hadn't she walked out on Leo years ago? Why didn't she walk out on all this now? The garden, stretching down to the estuary in the slanting evening light, which earlier that day she had imagined as a Shangri-la, a haven from her difficulties, seemed now oppressive, too set out and ordered. 'Walk out now,' she heard Sally's voice saying loftily, 'before you make a further idiot of yourself.'

She would probably have to go now anyway. How could she stay if Delia meant what she was saying and Henry was going to lose the garden? What would she, or he, gain by her continued presence? Whatever he said now, if she went he would appoint a man to do her job and everything would go on as it had before her arrival.

But she thought then of the reality of arriving at Sally's flat, which she would have to do until she got another job, Sally's unspoken self-justification, Ken's Christian solicitude. She sat down. No, not tonight. She wouldn't do another flit so precipitously. Henry's threat might work, Delia might back down. She would wait at least until tomorrow, until the verdict was clear. She should eat something, she thought vaguely, but she couldn't summon the energy to go to the kitchen. She continued to sit there in the chair, staring through the open window as the last of the day's light ebbed. Subconsciously she listened for voices raised in the main house. A pair of owls began calling to each other sinisterly - like conspiring lovers, she thought, bent like the Macbeths on some evil purpose - but the house was silent.

She must have dozed. She woke feeling chilled. It was almost dark. She got up, closed the window. She looked at her clock on the miniature mantelpiece. It was nearly ten. She knew she wouldn't sleep if she went to bed, but did so - really to get warm.

She slept fitfully, and consequently overslept. She knew at once how late it was from the strength of the sunlight. Horrified, she saw it was after nine. She jumped out of bed.

She was at the dressing-table when she remembered her comb was in her handbag in the sitting-room. Going in to get it, her eye was caught by something flashing in the park. To her alarm she saw it was a police car. Just at that moment an ambulance emerged from the drive. Transfixed with fear, she saw it make a wide sweep. It stopped out of sight at the far end. She threw on the rest of her clothes and rushed down.

In the office were Betty, Brenda May, and Edith. Betty, seated, looked pale and scared. Brenda, standing, was staring at Edith as if she had seen something supernatural.

Edith, clearly herself upset, turned as Jocelyn entered. 'Very tragic news, I'm afraid, Joss. Mrs Bordeaux has died.' Jocelyn stared, too, conscious at one level of a shameful relief - it wasn't Henry. 'She must have died some time during the night. I discovered her about half an hour ago when I took her breakfast up. When I first entered the room I thought she was still asleep - until I saw her face. It was terrible - greenish, the eyes were open, and there was an unpleasant almondy smell. I knew at once she'd gone.' She paused. 'If it was suicide, it can only have been poison, how else could she have done it?'

Jocelyn made herself think. 'Suicide,' she said, 'why should it be suicide? She could have died naturally.'

'Not much chance of that, I'm afraid. The colour of her face - and that smell. She'd taken something.'

'Where's Henry?'

'Upstairs with the police. I called him of course after I'd found her. He went in to look at her, then at once called the ambulance - and the police. He also called Lorna to tell her not to come in.'

They all stood, neutralised. Upstairs a door opened, there were voices, but not Henry's. They heard two people coming down the stairs. It was the ambulance men.

Jocelyn intercepted them in the hall. Even they looked shaken. They glanced at her - with distaste, she thought - and would have left without speaking.

'Are you leaving?' she asked.

'Not required for the present, no,' said one grudgingly.

'You mean Mrs Bordeaux's body is being left here?'

'For the present.'

'But why?'

'Police orders.'

'Did Mrs Bordeaux poison herself?'

The men exchanged a glance, but said nothing. They filed out, then faltered by the front door, realising it was not the one they had come in by. Edith led them firmly to the back door in the kitchen, which was nearer to the ambulance.

Perhaps fortunately, Betty's baby began to cry. Betty lifted him out of his cot and walked him up and down. The three of them fixed on this thankfully as some kind of normality. When the child was pacified, it seemed momentarily a little easier to cope. Edith returned, and they all agreed the best thing was to get on with the work as normally as they could. Though a question was in all of their minds, Jocelyn was sure, they put it to one side. 'Maybe,' Edith said, 'however dreadful, it may work out for the best. Maybe she realised she couldn't go on, and took the only way out. It could be a mercy.' They accepted this with nods, as a formula for carrying on. Edith went off to the kitchen, Brenda May to the shop. Nobody asked the dread question. If Delia had poisoned herself, how had she come by the means and how had she administered them? Had Henry somehow been involved?

Jocelyn began to open the post. As soon as she could, she started dictating the necessary answers. The sooner Betty got working on something the better, she thought. She looked very shaken and kept looking towards her now sleeping baby. Was she wondering if she should remove him from this now benighted house lest he contract some contagion from it? And both of them, Betty and herself, Jocelyn was aware, were listening for developments upstairs.

An hour later they heard another vehicle arrive. There was a party due which she was taking round the garden. She went out to see if it was them. It was another police car, a transit. She guessed at once who they were. Two men and a woman had the back open. They were taking out equipment - a tripod, a camera, lights, two large metal boxes.

Unavoidably her mind went back to last night when Henry came to her flat. His mind had been made up from those silent hours he had spent floating on the ebb tide. An ultimatum to Delia - that was certainly what he had fixed on. 'You won't leave here by my wish,' was what he had said to her. But if Delia wouldn't give way - what precisely had he said about that? Had he said anything? She was sure of one thing. From all she knew of him, he would have thought it through in total detail, with all the eventualities covered.

She could swear he had said or implied nothing beyond the fact that he might lose the property. But at the end, just as he was going, there had been something, hadn't there? He had been going to say something else, but held it back. What had he been going to say? Had he, could he have, contemplated an ultimate step? Had he been going to say something to her that referred to it, however obliquely?

As she stood there, she heard the bus turning into the gate at the top of the drive. She contemplated handing the job over to Brenda May, the shop could be closed for an hour. In the end, she didn't. What good could she do, with the police still here?

When she returned to the drive with the party, the first police car had gone, only the Transit remained. She said goodbye to the visitors and rushed into the kitchen. Geoff was sitting at the table with Edith.

'He didn't do it,' Edith said, looking at her. 'He's incapable of such a thing. If that was ever in his mind he'd've done it years ago. Henry makes his mind up. In my opinion, she wanted this to happen. She fixed it like this so it would.'

'They haven't arrested Henry?'

'No, but that's what's in their minds, isn't it?'

'Where is he?'

'In his room.'

'You've spoken to him?'

'When the police left I went up. He was just sitting there in the window. I asked him if he was all right. He said they were virtually accusing him of murder.'

'What did he say then?'

'Nothing. I said of course it was nonsense and that how could they prove something that didn't happen. He just smiled. Then he asked me to leave him alone.'

'He said nothing else?'

'No. When I was at the door he asked if you were taking the group round. I said you were.'

Geoff was nodding in her direction. She felt acutely embarrassed. Really to escape, she went out. 'I'd better go up and see if there's anything I can do,' she said.

At the top of the stairs she paused. The door of Delia's room was open. Through it, she heard the forensic team at work. One of them said something, and through the crack in the door she saw a bright light flash. What a ghoulish job, photographing corpses. She hurried along the landing and knocked on Henry's door. His voice sounded firm, as usual. He was sitting in the armchair which he had pulled into the window bay.

'Interested group?' he asked, as if nothing were amiss. The only unusual thing was that he didn't get up nor make any arrangement for her to sit. There was a long cushion round the bay. She went to sit on that, facing him.

'Edith says . . , she began.

'They think I poisoned her,' he interrupted. 'It's perfectly understandable they should think that. The motive was there, you can attest to that. I told them what I told you last night - that her behaviour had become unacceptable and that I'd made up my mind to present her with an ultimatum. I might have known Delia would have the last laugh.'

'You did tell Delia what you'd decided?'

'Oh yes. What amazed me was that she took it very calmly - almost as if she'd expected it. She did actually *say* she'd expected it.' He grimaced. 'She said it proved that what she'd been saying was true. I ignored that of course and asked her what she intended to do. Was she going to stop all this nonsense, or go off to a home? She laughed at that. "I'm not going to any home," she said. She said I ought to have the intelligence to know she'd never accept that. How did I propose to force her into a home? Was I going to get her certified? I ignored that, too - though on this point she was right. I might at one time have been able to get her certified, but after all this time I doubt if it'd be possible. To other people she's always been perfectly rational. No, I told her, I wouldn't have her certified. If she wasn't going to be reasonable, I'd simply leave the place. She'd be forced to sell and make whatever arrangements she decided for herself.

'"Oh, really," she said. "You'll just dump me, will you? After all these years of dutiful service you'll throw me over. Amazing what a man will do when . . ." You can imagine the rest of what she said. Finally, I couldn't listen to any more. I got up to go. I made it clear again that I meant what I said. Her last words were these: "Dear old Henry, you never did have much brain, did you? A soldier of course. Soldiers aren't meant to think, are they?"

'When I left her I thought she was bluffing, though I was pretty depressed because I thought I'd have to go pretty well the whole way before she realised I meant what I said. It just never occurred to me that . . .' He frowned, gripping his left wrist and holding it above his lap.

She waited a moment or two, then gently probed. 'It was poison she took?'

'Apparently.'

'Do you know what poison?'

'Not for sure, though I heard two of the forensic men talking. I caught the words hydrocyanic acid. Apparently it has a smell of almonds, which Edith said she smelt. I think when she called me and I went in I noticed a faint whiff of something like that.'

'How did she get hold of it?'

'I just don't know. The only people she's ever seen have been Edith - yourself that brief time - her hairdresser, Mrs Lipstock, who comes once a fortnight, Lorna, and me. Edith and Lorna are of course out of the question.'

'Mabel Lipstock then? Edith told me once Delia was always civil to her. She could have offered her money.'

'No, it wasn't her. Delia would never have asked a woman like her. They've never been that close, and it would have been a frightful risk to take.'

'Gillespie, the lawyer? He came yesterday, as you know.'

'Lawyers are hardly in the habit of handing out poison to their clients, are they? Least of all Gillespie, who'd always think first of his own skin. Gillespie came here, I am quite sure, to change Delia's will. The man and the woman who accompanied him were the witnesses. And if she'd decided what she was going to do, she'd almost certainly have planned it days ago, how else would the will have been ready for signature - which means, incidentally, it can have had nothing to do with my ultimatum last night. No, I'm afraid the way the police see it is plain. They haven't made much effort to conceal their thoughts. They don't think it's suicide, but murder. You can see how reasonable a conclusion that is. It would have been the easiest thing in the world for me to have slipped the acid or whatever it was into her ready-made whisky and water jar. She liked to have a nightcap which helped her sleep. The container was near the bed and she drank through a tube suspended above the bed.'

It was at this moment Jocelyn knew beyond all doubt Henry was innocent. Nobody could have faked the look on his face. Just for an instant the mask fell. She saw the stark misery and total bewilderment. It was all she could do not to put her arms round his shoulders. What he said next was also so out of character it added to the proof of his innocence. 'Perhaps I should confess to the crime. It would save a lot of hullabaloo.'

Jocelyn felt a sudden access of strength, which surprised her. 'Of course you're not going to confess to something you haven't done,' she said. 'There can be no possible evidence they can produce apart from a suppositional motive. If it ever went to trial, which I can't think it possibly could, there are several witnesses here to attest to your integrity. Someone else delivered that poison to Delia and you've made it plain how she was able to administer it to herself. She could even have had it for years hidden somewhere. She could have got it into the bottle herself, couldn't she, with that claw thing?'

He smiled a little at this and stretched forward his hand.

'Thanks, Jocelyn. I really thank you for that - overstatement about me as it is. Yes, I'll soldier on, I suppose, if I'm allowed to. After all, as Delia said, that's what I am, a soldier. Whatever happens, it won't do the garden and its reputation much good, but I dare say I'll weather that, too, given a little time.'

She squeezed his hand. She was on the point of saying they were all there with him to help do the weathering if any of that became necessary. She shrank from this, true as it was. Henry preferred emotions to be implicit.

12.

Until the trial Jocelyn had outwardly consented to Leo's fiction that he was innocent. But on the second day, when the police tape was produced, she slipped out. She could imagine Leo looking up and seeing her seat suddenly empty and the despair this would cause him, but she couldn't help it. She couldn't be a witness to his humiliation.

Sally had been at Roedean for nearly a term. Jocelyn had wanted to tell her right away about the accusation. Supposing she read of it in a newspaper, or someone else did and told her? 'It won't necessarily get into the national papers,' Leo insisted, 'a trumped up provincial storm in a teacup like this. I'm innocent, it'll blow over, Sally need never know it happened.' When she got home from the trial, Jocelyn went straight to the telephone. She asked the Headmistress straight out if she had by any chance heard what had been happening to her husband. There was a pause before the reply came.

'I'm very glad you've called, Mrs Cunningham,' she heard. 'I'm afraid, yes, as it happens we have heard. A housemistress saw notice of the trial in a newspaper today - Sally's housemistress as it happens. Oddly, she and I are just about to meet to decide what we should do.'

Jocelyn explained why she hadn't phoned before - her husband, who had been claiming he was innocent, hadn't wished it. But now his conviction was certain she said she thought Sally should be told. She would be driving down tomorrow, if that was convenient, to tell Sally herself. She would rather do this than try to speak to her on the phone.

Jocelyn was impressed by the lady. Possible repercussions on the school must have been on her mind. She might well have been wondering, too, if Jocelyn was also involved in the crime. If she was thinking any of this, there was no hint of it. In her voice was nothing but sympathy and understanding, there was no gush. After a brief word of condolence she kept to the practicalities. If it was in any way in their hands, they would try to contain the news until they had all talked, she said. It had been quite a small notice in the paper, on an inner page.

She felt a moment of guilt at shutting The Yard - and the gymnasium, on whose front door she had to leave a cryptic note announcing a 'temporary' closure. Leo had taken no steps apparently to cope with mystified or angry clients, and his two employees were nowhere to be seen. But she left the town the next morning. The legal aid lawyer defending Leo had phoned to tell her that after the tape evidence Leo had withdrawn his plea of not guilty, and that it was now certain he would be sentenced. Her heart was wrung, but what could she do for him now? She couldn't have visited him even if she had felt up to it.

After a while her feelings subsided a little. There had been a light dusting of snow during the night. The motionless winter landscape induced a sensation of suspension, almost of an anaesthetic. As she journeyed on the endless motorway, it seemed she might be insulated against the sharpest pain.

The bleakness of the school on cold windswept cliffs overlooking a lead-coloured Channel was belied by the warmth of the Headmistress's reception in the chintzy, homely room. While they waited for Sally and the housemistress, tea was served by an intelligent-looking, unschooly secretary.

'I'm afraid I'll have to withdraw Sally,' Jocelyn said at once when the secretary had left them alone. 'I don't know how exactly our finances will be now, but I'm quite sure we'll no longer be able to afford the fees.'

There was an extraordinarily generous offer to help. The Headmistress said that, anticipating that this might happen, she had already consulted some key members of the Board of Governors on the telephone. She couldn't preempt the Board's collective decision, but she was reasonably sure some 'adjustment' could be made to 'tide them over the difficulty.' What she was certain of was that the girls surrounding Sally would support her in 'the distress she's bound to feel.'

It was immensely civilised and humane, Jocelyn thought, so much so she for a moment greatly rued that Sally would be plucked from such a good influence. But the adjustment turned out to be half the fees. She knew even this wouldn't be enough. The gymnasium would be unlikely to function and would almost certainly have to be sold, if it could be, to recover the purchase debts. Profit from The Yard, she knew, which would now be reduced by the need to pay for an auctioneer, would never on its own foot the kind of triannual bill being talked about.

Sally entered, looking composed. She allowed her cheek to be kissed and sat with a new ladylike turning aside of her knees on the edge of the homely sofa. Her fine dark hair, parted in the middle and swept back to a small pony tail, already made her look two years older. Jocelyn's heartbeats faltered. Maybe she would care terribly. Maybe Leo had been entirely right about sending her to a public school, to all this courtesy and good breeding. But the news, which Jocelyn suspected she either knew or half-guessed the gyst of, didn't ruffle her composure. 'I see,' was all she said when told the news and that she would be leaving Roedean.

There were only a few days until the end of term. Jocelyn took Sally away at once. They returned to Sally's house to pack up her things, then drove into Brighton and for the night found a double room in a boarding house overlooking a Regency square.

Jocelyn told Sally no more than was necessary, and they avoided further talk about it that evening. But on the journey back north the next morning Sally soon made her attitude plain. There had been a small renewal of light snow during the night. The white backcloth to their progress seemed to reverse the role it had played yesterday. It served now to throw Sally's remarks into even sharper emphasis.

'I'm so terribly sorry, Sally darling,' Jocelyn began. 'For you. You were beginning to like the place, weren't you?'

'Was I?'

'It seemed so. When you came in last night, you looked - so part of the place.'

'I don't think so, specially.'

'But you'd found friends - the teaching's good.'

'I never thought it'd last.'

A profound dread began to overtake her, greater than anything she had suffered so far. 'But you couldn't have thought that, Sally. You couldn't have foreseen that Daddy would be tempted as he has been - that he'd do what he's done.'

'Not exactly *how* of course. But if it hadn't been this, it'd've been something else, wouldn't it?'

She took her hand off the steering-wheel and put it on Sally's leg. 'No, darling, we mustn't think of it this way. You as much as said it yourself that day - do you remember? You asked him why he bought the gymnasium. He made a joke about it, but you knew why he'd bought it, and said so. He has been very foolish, but what he did he did for you.'

Sally looked away sharply. 'I never wanted him to. You never wanted him to. You knew it would get him into trouble. I never wanted to go away to school on those terms. Leo's a crook, and that's all there is to be said. He wants to be something he isn't.'

The harshness shocked her. It was also the first time Sally had ever called her father Leo. It seemed like a final slipping of any moorings to him.

She wanted to cry all of a sudden. A residual sympathy unlocked itself. Poor darling Leo - in every other respect a worthy, amusing, lively, likeable man who had used to make her ache with love. He was still all those things. Why should society punish him for one transgression, one faulty gene perhaps which made him want to go faster than realities allowed? She thought of Leo now, fully, as she had not allowed herself to do before, locked up with other men who had done awful things, but many of whom were also perhaps ninety per cent decent, taking exercise, eating communal food, hearing the cell doors clang to as they were caged up again like animals. All Leo was guilty of was an ideal.

She was catapulted from her reverie. Sally was speaking again, calmly investigative. 'Why did you marry a man like that, Mum?' she was asking.

'Why? Because I loved him of course.'

'You must have known what he'd be like even then - weak and unstable.'

'You really mustn't speak of your father in this way.'

'Why not? It's the truth. Why *did* you marry him?'

Jocelyn could not keep the hardness from her voice. 'I've told you why. And you're being uncharitable.'

'Uncharitable, am I? And I suppose it was charitable of him

to have such a silly snobbish idea about my education. Are you telling me *you* feel charitable about that?'

'I'm not sure what I feel yet. All I know is that it's wrong to be vindictive. People are as they are.'

'And can't change, I suppose.'

'Some people may find it more difficult than others probably, yes.'

Sally gave a refined haughty sniff, newly acquired. 'Well at least he's out of the way for a time. How are we going to live, by the way? Have you thought about that? The gymnasium'll be a dead duck, that's for sure. Am I going to have to get a job?'

She readily seized on this, a mundane subject she could get to grips with. 'No, of course not. You'll go to one of the comprehensives as we'd planned before. You're right, the gymnasium will have to be sold probably, but I shall go on running The Yard, as I have done. I'll just have to hire someone to do the selling on sale days. We'll make ends meet somehow.'

'And the house?'

'The house will probably have to go, too.'

'*That*'ll be no loss. It's a silly white elephant.'

They filled the rest of the journey with such practicalities. She hadn't begun to think of them seriously until now. In the end she almost welcomed Sally's pragmatic attitude. Forced by it, she began to construct a likely strategy.

The lawyer got Leo's consent to power of attorney for her. The responsibility brought her a swift realisation of the position. When she went to see the bank manager it was at once obvious that 'smiles from the touchline' had ceased to be bestowed. In their place was a predictable summary of the 'position'.

'With no driving force to run it, Mrs Cunningham, the gymnasium is not going to generate the kind of funds necessary to service our loan, let alone repay the capital. If you were to appoint a manager that would only compound the problem, you'd have to pay a large salary. And I fear a second mortgage on your house is already a part of the loan collateral. If you cannot sell the gymnasium for the price at which the building lease and the equipment were bought, the house will also have to go.' The tone included her in her husband's felony.

It was a lot worse than this. Unbelievably, Leo had no clause in the gymnasium leasehold which allowed it to be assigned. The landlord wouldn't budge. If he didn't change his mind and himself sell the lease to someone else, she could be stuck with the rent for the rest of the five year period. The irony was that she couldn't even convert it into their living quarters. It was business premises and couldn't be used for domestic purposes.

She didn't care about the house, and she knew Sally didn't. But it soon became obvious The Yard would also have to go - on which, it transpired, Leo had secretly taken out another partial mortgage to pay for Roedean. This hurt. She realised she had begun to think of it as her own business, bought with her own money. Nonetheless, after all the anxiety-making comings and goings, she found, with the job at the clinic she got herself, she could rent a small semi-detached house in a different part of the town and, with the remnant of her own money, live modestly.

The two years were not an unhappy period. She had feared Sally's vindictiveness against Leo was the front for a deep wound within her which would manifest itself in even worse ways as time went on. How could she after all avoid being Leo's daughter - by an act of will acquire a sort of filial decree nisi? But if there was such residual damage, it never showed. Sally adapted to the comprehensive as she had to Roedean. The teachers were adjudged 'stupid' or 'all right', facilities 'adequate', her classmates 'what you'd expect.' She was almost certainly doing better academically in relation to the other students than she would have done at Roedean, and she made a few acceptable friends with whom she did the standard teenage things at week-ends and in the holidays. Jocelyn began to think that, paradoxically, Leo's imprisonment was, as Sally had claimed it would be, a release for her. Sally might not be at home for so long after he came out.

She was allowed to see Leo once a month. At first the visits were an ordeal. He was broken, abject, and though he insisted he was well-treated, looked haggard. He didn't even bother to beg her forgiveness this time. He said she should drop him and marry someone else. When she told him about The Yard, she wasn't sure he listened. He never asked about Sally.

Then, on a visit she made in the late spring of the first year, she found he had miraculously perked up. She could see the change as soon as he appeared at the door of the large room and marched to the table where she was already seated. There was a noticeable lift in his step. 'Joss, I'm over the worst,' he said at once. 'If you'll have me back I can start afresh. I've been a bit down, but I've done some thinking. I can't take the religious bit of course, but the padre here's a decent bloke. He's been helping me. He says I've got to reform, which I don't need him to tell me, and that I've then got to ask you if you can forgive me. Can you? Can you give me one more chance? I can admit now I was wrong about Sally. I'll always support her when she wants it, so of course will you. But she'll just have to take her luck in life. I see that now, and probably it's healthier and better for her. I was having pipe dreams, folie de grandeur.'

It took her by surprise. She had steeled herself to deal with his depression, not with this. 'Forgive you?' she said, 'I'm not sure it's ever been a case of that.'

'Of course it has. I've wronged you terribly, turned your life upside down, lost everything. Above all I deceived you. That's what I need you to forgive me for, so I can start again.'

Was he ready for a really full discussion? Was she? She approached warily, on another track. 'You're asking me if I'll have you back. I should've thought that was obvious from my coming to see you and continuing to write to you.'

'You'll be able to love me again? If not now, some time?'

She hesitated several moments. 'I don't know about that, Leo, not yet. I was able to before, this time we'll have to wait. A home will be there for you, but how I'll feel I can't forecast.'

'You'll love me again. I'll work for your love. You're what my life's about.'

They left it there. Challenged to look, she found that that same dead thing still lay in her - whatever he had said. But she could see he had taken heart from the exchange. She carried home with her the look of hope and renewed energy on his face.

Could his hope and vivacity and restored confidence also be hers, as it had been in the past? She considered the Christian ethic of turning the other cheek. What an irrelevance it was. As if things like this are *decided.*

'Sally, Daddy's coming home tomorrow.'

She had chosen a Friday night to tell her, when they had just been to the cinema with a nice school friend of hers to see a sentimental Australian film Sally had raved about. Sally's interest in the male sex, rather delayed by modern yardsticks, was dawning in a predictably idealistic format, a format well satisfied by certain film productions. Now, the friend departed, they were making her favourite supper of packaged fish, chips and frozen peas in the minute kitchen.

'Oh no,' she said to the news of Leo's return.

'He's won a six months' remission. Isn't that good?'

'Good? I think it's terrible.'

She tried to ignore this. 'I thought we'd do something special to welcome him tomorrow night. I've bought steak.'

'I don't like steak.'

'Daddy does.'

'Joan and I are going to the disco tomorrow.'

'You could put it off for once, couldn't you, as it's a special occasion? Daddy'll be very hurt if you aren't here.'

A more calculating look succeeded the annoyance. 'How long have you known he's coming out tomorrow?'

'A few days. It's been a sudden decision apparently.'

'A few days - and you tell me now. No, I don't see why I should have to let Joan down actually. I shall go out, Mum. You can be alone with him. It's probably better that way.'

Perhaps it was better if Sally was going to be like this, but she felt a sharp tug of fury at the girl for her cool surfing over life's difficulties. Leo could blame her for Sally's absence.

She went to the prison in the car to pick him up. She saw him emerge from the small door and turn back to shake hands with a warder. He was wearing the same clothes he had worn at the trial and carrying the small case she had taken him with one or two necessities. Looking round, he saw her pulling the car across from the meter where she had parked, and waved.

He opened the door before she had fully stopped, and got in. She was prepared for an embrace, but as if sensing her difficulty he just patted her arm. 'This is the best moment of my life,' he said as they moved off. 'I feel newly born.'

As it was Saturday, Sally was still in bed when they got in. No incentive, not even the desire to avoid her father's homecoming, was stronger than her determination to lie in. Jocelyn called up the stairs as they squeezed into the small passage known as the hall. There was no stir. 'She'll be down in a minute,' she said to Leo in apology.

'Never mind, let her sleep,' said Leo, whom she had seen looking expectantly up the stairs behind her. 'What I want right now is an egg and bacon if there's one going, made by you, and which isn't floating in greenish oil.'

They went into the kitchen. He sat at the table, and she began to cook. To fill the space, she spoke about her job at the clinic. She felt he was genuinely interested, but inevitably lurking was the question of what he would do now The Yard was no more. Not now, she prayed. Let this painful subject be postponed. But to her surprise he took it up quite naturally when she had run out of things to say about the clinic.

'I think I shan't try to get back into the auction business. I'll try to find something quite menial to do. Petrol station reception, something like that. It's probably a necessity anyway, but I want to be a nobody. I am one, so why not recognise it and be one?'

This could have been masochistic, but she didn't think it was. It seemed it was something he had been thinking sensibly about. She was composing a response, when there was a thump above, then footsteps coming down the stairs. The subject was postponed.

A dressing-gowned Sally entered, Leo rose. 'Hi, Sal.'

'Hallo. Mum, Joan and I are going out skating this morning. Do you know where my tartan skirt is? I can't find it.'

Leo sat down again. He looked more stunned than wounded. Jocelyn did the worst thing. She flew into a rage. 'Sally, is this how you welcome your father home?'

She turned to Leo perfunctorily. 'Welcome home,' she said neatly.

'You've grown.'

'One does.'

'Sally, you're behaving quite abominably.'

'Am I? I'm sorry. I suppose I'm just behaving as I'm feeling.'

'Leave her alone, Joss,' Leo said calmly. 'It's natural. It's natural for all three of us to be strange at first. We all just have to wait a bit. Let things slot back into place. There's time. Heaven knows, I know the meaning of time now.'

By that evening Jocelyn saw that he had changed, that his humility was genuine and undirected by despair. But it scared her. What was he if he didn't have that dancing audacity and cheek? An unskilled garage employee - did she want that? How would it work emotionally between them? Of one thing during the evening she was sure. When they had dined *à deux* in candlelight, and his voice was so gentle, she was swept by a profound pity for him. Here, now so starkly revealed, was that deep vulnerability she had noticed almost at their first encounter. How could life be lived without compassion? Mistaking her emotion for something else, he got up in the middle of the meal and, standing by her chair, put his arms round her. 'Oh Joss,' he said, 'can you really love me again? It's all I want. It's life to me. Can we really start again?'

She accepted his kiss and later gave him what he wanted. In a sense, after the long deprival, though it was not as before, it gave her something too. Could one rebuild a life this way? Was pity enough? Would it lead her back?

13.

'Now you say Mr Bordeaux spoke to you the evening before Mrs Bordeaux died?' said Detective Inspector Becket. 'Where would that have been? In the office perhaps?'

'No, it was after office hours.'

'Where then?'

'It was here.'

'He came up to your flat to speak to you?'

'That's right.'

The pause was fractional but enough to tell her what was coming. 'And that was quite a normal thing for him to do, was it, to come to your private quarters?'

'No. Henry is a very sensitive man. Since I've been here, he has always been very careful not to intrude on my privacy in any way, and apart from when I first arrived - and I think once when my daughter and her fiancé came down for a couple of nights - he hasn't been in this flat. But in the circumstances of that evening, I think it's understandable that he should have wanted to speak to one of his staff. He knew we all knew that Mrs Bordeaux was being difficult, and of course I was involved in the way I think you know.'

She was aware she might be saying too much. 'Involved because of what Mrs Bordeaux was saying about you?'

'Yes.'

'Why do you think Mrs Bordeaux made this accusation against you?'

'One can only conjecture. The view of Edith Applecote, who has known her much longer than I have, is that ever since the disaster in India she lived in a neurotic terror that Henry might cease to look after her in the devoted way he did. When I went up to see her once - soon after I arrived here - it was clear then to me what was in her mind.'

'She thought you might have an affair with Mr Bordeaux?'

'She accused me point blank of having come here to set about ensnaring him.'

'I see. And how did you react to that?'

'I was initially shocked of course. But on reflection and at that time, it made me even more sorry for her. I thought, as Edith did, that it was part of her deep anxiety.'

'You say "at that time." Did you come to alter your view?'

She thought carefully, looking strongly at this policeman's face. What sort of a man was he? Obviously, first, a policeman engaged on what he thought was a potential murder case. But she thought also, from his appearance and manner, he was probably intelligent. Anyway, what was the point of concealment? If she was to help Henry it was surely essential to establish there was nothing to hide.

'It's funny, isn't it?' she said. 'People who most need our help, often do the least to excite our sympathy. I have to say, yes, I did alter my view of Delia Bordeaux, certainly at times. However explained in psychological terms, I think she was in part an evil woman - and evil, I've always thought, is quite capable of acting on its own without any necessary motivation or explanation. It is, as much as goodness, a force of the spirit. I don't know of course what she was like before the air crash, but afterwards she seems to have become almost entirely selfish - and malign. Edith will tell you a great deal more of this than I can, as she has suffered from it, daily, a great deal longer than I have. I've no doubt Lorna Standish, the care worker, will give you a professional view on this.'

'And she became even more malign since you arrived?'

'Possibly, though I can't be the judge of that.'

She saw Becket stopped by the frank line she was taking. Drawing breath sharply as if in irritation, he shifted his approach. 'It seems to me from talking to the others, Mr Bordeaux's attitude to his wife also changed in the last month or two.' He left a space, she didn't fill it. 'What did he say to you when he came up here to speak to you that evening?'

'He told me his wife had threatened to sell High Combe if he didn't sack me.You probably know she owned the place legally.'

'And what was his attitude to that ultimatum?'

'He said he had no intention of sacking me. He also said that he was, that evening, going to tell Delia that if she didn't stop being so silly he'd cease to look after her, and that she'd have to go into some sort of a home.'

'That was pretty strong wasn't it, considering how well he'd looked after her all these years? How did you react to that?'

'I was horrified. I told him I thought I should go. I said he should appoint a male to do my job. Even when he refused to countenance this and had gone off, I thought I should go. I even thought of going that very evening.'

'Why didn't you?'

'Because, to be quite honest, I suppose I have to say, first, I didn't want to go for my own reasons. I've been very happy in my job here. It's been a solution to a problem of my own which we don't need to go into. But I also hoped that when faced with Henry's determination, which maybe he'd never shown her before, Delia would back down. I'd always hoped that somehow I might find a way of getting on good terms with her, perhaps help her. I thought there might be a better chance of this if Henry made her see how groundless her fears were.'

'Then, in the morning, you learnt that she was dead?'

'Yes.'

'How did you feel about that?'

'Stunned, naturally. We all were. Though . . .

'Though what, Mrs Hammond?'

'Though I have to say I think it was in all our minds that, dreadful as it is that someone should take their own life in such a way, ghastly as it was immediately for Henry, it could in the long run be a blessing. It's difficult to believe there was anything much in life for a woman so mentally disabled and diseased.'

She didn't regret being frank. She felt it was giving her the initiative. Again she sensed he was stopped by her openness. Has the truth some intrinsic power, even with policemen?

She was forcing him to change track once more. 'So it's suicide you posit. What makes you so sure it was suicide?'

'It wasn't murder. Your forensic people are wasting their time.'

'Oh?'

'Henry Bordeaux didn't murder his wife - if that's what you have in mind.'

'Very categoric. Are you telling me it never crossed your mind that he might have, or the minds of the others?'

'No, I'm not actually. In the morning, when we were all together in the office discussing the news Edith had told us, it was something we all probably thought of - the gross provocation, the apparent motive was there. But it was only a few minutes later that I became as completely sure as it's possible to be that Henry was innocent.'

'Why was that?'

'The others suggested I should go upstairs to Henry. I thought I should. He was sitting in his bedroom. I knew then.'

'How did you know?'

'Inspector, I dare say from investigating crimes you develop a nose for what is and what isn't the truth. When your nose tells you something, I wonder if you can always say exactly why it has communicated its message? All I can say is that, talking to Henry, I knew his behaviour to his wife the previous evening had been exactly as he'd told me it was going to be.'

'Namely?'

'That he told Delia, no doubt for the umpteenth time, that there was nothing between him and me, that she was making it all up in her mind, and that if she didn't stop being so paranoid he would call her bluff - even if she carried out her threat and sold the estate - and she'd have to go into some sort of care.'

'Which Mrs Bordeaux no doubt translated as further proof that her husband was carrying on with you?'

'It's very possible.'

'At which point, what you're saying is that after her husband's departure Delia Bordeaux helps herself to some hydrocyanic acid - this is what killed her, forensic have told us. She takes some of this lethal substance, which she has acquired from an unknown source and stashed away somewhere. During the day, before she is put to bed, with the claw gadget she operates with her teeth she puts the stuff into the whisky jug beside her bed, from which she is in the habit of taking a nightcap and from which she can drink by means of a tube suspended over the bed. Is that what you're expecting me to believe?'

'I have no means of knowing how it happened. As I say, I was only once in that room, and know nothing of the arrangements made for her comfort. All I'm saying is Henry didn't poison his wife. He's incapable of such a thing.'

There was an abrupt change. Becket gave a little laugh. 'I see you're valiant, Mrs Hammond.'

'What do you mean?'

'What I say. You defend by taking the offensive.'

'I've no idea what you mean.'

'You don't? I'll have to tell you then what I think. I think you and Henry Bordeaux are having an affair. For years, with the courage he no doubt displayed in his career in various operations, Bordeaux has suffered what was almost unendurable, the loss of his two children, and the conversion of a once beautiful and no doubt loving wife into a selfish harridan. Feeling guilt perhaps that he has survived intact when his wife is suffering in this abominable way, he eschews any possibility of putting her into an institution, engages the expensive services of a nurse, and nobly undertakes himself a large part of the immense burden of looking after her. He does this for years. These years, however, take their toll and do not, it seems, earn him the gratitude one might have expected from the patient. He begins to falter, to question, as anyone would, what the point of goodness is when it is so signally unrewarded Then he appoints you, an attractive divorcée, to his staff, and offers you a flat on the premises. He's a shy, almost a retiring man, but he responds to your no doubt sympathetic presence. At last, he thinks, he has an audience to whom he can pour out his anguish. He does so. You listen. You have also no doubt, as you hint, had your emotional problems. In your conversations you find you are soul mates. Affection grows. At last it is confessed. You *are* soul mates, and partners in affliction.

'But there's an obstacle. Henry's wife is no fool. She knows what's going on. Her diagnosis is no idle one. The threat she makes to sell her property is perhaps bluff - though she did undoubtedly alter her will - Gillespie has already hinted to me how she altered it - we'll probably never know if she would have carried it out in her lifetime or not. But she makes the threat, and it is this which drives Bordeaux, a decisive man I should guess, to total exasperation. I think when he came to see you that evening it was to make the final decision with you. The poison must have been already obtained - it is not a substance easily come by. You then planned together to rid yourselves of the one obstacle to your happiness. The rest was easy. There's no one else on the premises at night other than you two. One of you, probably Bordeaux, put the unnoticeable poison in that vessel, knowing the chances were your victim would drink that very evening and that in probably about two minutes she'd be dead.'

'None of this is true.'

'If it isn't, you're going to have to prove the acid got there in another way.'

'I should've thought it was your job to do that. If Delia took poison she got it by some means or other. She could have had it for some time. There's another point, incidentally - the lawyer, and the will. The afternoon before she died, Mrs Bordeaux summoned her lawyer to see her to change her will. Why did she do that just a few hours before her death, and well before the conversation she had with her husband that evening? Doesn't it indicate she'd planned to kill herself some days before and that that conversation simply determined the timing?'

'An excellent point, Mrs Hammond. You are quite right, there had been several telephone calls between Gillespie and Mrs Bordeaux in which Mrs Bordeaux had made plain the changes she wished to make to her will. This is what enabled Gillespie to bring the actual document for her signature on that afternoon, and two witnesses.'

'Well then, there you are. She was planning it days before.'

'Right, she was planning the change to her will. But what you are leaving out, or rather getting wrong, is her *motive* for doing so. I've not yet interviewed Gillespie for a formal statement, but I have spoken to him on the phone. He did not wish to give me the full picture on the phone, but he told me there was no doubt at all in his mind that Mrs Bordeaux was wishing to change her will in view of "some terrible fears she entertained." At the interview, when the will was legalised, Gillespie has said Mrs Bordeaux made clear to him what these fears were. What she feared was that for "various very classic reasons" - those were Gillespie's actual words and I have no doubt what he meant by them - her husband might seek to put an end to her life. Gillespie believed her, but he did not, tragically, act upon this statement quickly enough. Had he done so at once and contacted the police, the tragedy might have been averted. Gillespie is of course distraught at his omission.'

'I wonder if he is distraught. If Mrs Bordeaux did say that to him, he probably thought she was over the top, which is how anyone who knew the poor woman would probably have interpreted her words. That was why he did nothing.'

'But that is not what Gillespie *says*, and I can see no reason why a respectable and respected lawyer would wish to perjure himself. Can you really, on mature reflection, continue to think what you have just suggested, Mrs Hammond?'

'Gillespie has known Mrs Bordeaux a long time. It is quite likely Mrs Bordeaux has poisoned his mind against her husband. He might well be seizing an opportunity, perhaps without realising it himself, to implicate Henry Bordeaux. For that matter, one has to think he might even have been the means . . .

She checked herself too late. The inspector pounced. 'The means of her acquiring the hydrocyanic acid, is that what you're now saying - a suggestion, incidentally, rather at odds with what you have just said, that Gillespie was duped by Mrs Bordeaux?'

Jocelyn realised she was exaggerating and losing the brief initiative she felt she had taken earlier in the interview and was in danger of appearing absurd and in a panic. She allowed Becket to terminate their conversation on this bleak note.

She pulled herself together. She realised that if she didn't keep a clear head, nobody might. The day after speaking to Becket, on the second day after Delia's death, she took Henry his lunch on a tray in his bedroom and sat opposite him on the window seat.

'Is that contraption on the table beside the window in Delia's room the telephone? I've just been in to look.'

Henry hardly stirred. Pensive, he didn't appear to have heard her. 'I've been thinking,' he said. 'If they arrest me, maybe send me to prison, I really shan't mind so much. I'm quite sure she'll have disposed of this place in her will. That's why she saw Gillespie that afternoon and made sure she recorded her wishes and had them professionally witnessed. And perhaps, if she has terminated things in this way, for me as well as for herself, she'll have been right to. When we lost the children and she was so terribly damaged, I was inevitably injured, too, with her. I've never been religious in any liturgical sense, but I've always thought that religions have a way of institutionalising tribal realities. In Christianity, marriage is a "sacrament." They clutter it up with a lot of words like that, but I think there's a reality there nonetheless. I think the word sacrament means that if you have deep feelings about someone, fall in love and marry them, maybe have children, whatever happens, you cannot ever rid yourself of that experience. It becomes part of you, part of your nature, even of your body. To deny it has existed is to deny yourself. It would be like denying your parents, or denying history - as the Communists and other revolutionaries have tried to do. In the long run history reasserts itself. This is what Delia has been saying to me. Maybe I should have poisoned her, and myself at the same time, a kind of male funeral pyre.'

She feared for him, not the least because of her own experience. Hadn't she often been tempted to blame herself for Leo? 'No, Henry,' she said at once. You're being understandably self-critical. Of course I agree with what you say about marriage in general terms - ideally. You loved Delia, and that fact has an indelible quality. The love arose from something in you as well as from how you saw her. But the fact is Delia ceased to exist as the person you loved. It was another person you were looking after all these years. I - I've had the same experience in a different, less terrible way. What I'm saying is I do think I know what I'm talking about.'

He looked at her, drawn by the force of what she said. 'You must do, of course, yes.'

'Leo changed, too - or rather, in his case, circumstances exaggerated what otherwise might have remained only a small and controllable part of him.'

There was a long silence. Steam rose from the hot food on the table beside them. Melting ice in the glass of water released an imprisoned air bubble and clinked against the side of the glass. She felt her power to influence him, as she had all too briefly felt the power to influence the policeman. 'The telephone - in Delia's room,' she repeated more gently, 'she was able to use it, I presume, if she was phoning Gillespie?'

He looked away, frowning, making himself concentrate on what she was saying. 'Yes. I had a special contraption rigged up for her years ago - a speaker and a microphone. She could set it in motion with her chin.'

'How did she dial?'

'When she touched a bar with her chin, it connected her with the exchange. She just said the number she wanted.'

'And she used it often?'

'No, very seldom, if ever. In the early days she did quite a bit, yes. She ordered things, which were delivered. That's why I had the thing installed. I thought it would help her stay connected with the world.'

'In the early days, you say?'

'She soon grew tired of it. I felt sometimes she didn't use it just to spite me, to show me there was nothing I could really do to alter her appalling dependence on me.'

'She never made personal calls?'

'Only, ever, to one person, as far as I know. And that didn't last long.'

'Who was that?'

'She has a brother who lives up country somewhere. They never got on. I should imagine he was less than sympathetic about what had happened to her. The calls soon ceased. I met the man only once. He didn't impress me.'

'Henry, don't you realise? If she had that phone and used it recently to speak to Gillespie she could have used it to get someone else to bring that stuff.'

The fatigue in his eyes alarmed her further. 'I suppose so. But who? We know it was no one here.'

'Have you any ideas?'

He thought. 'No.'

'You've got to think. Is there no one in the neighbourhood she knew - recently, or before?' He shook his head despondently.

'Look, you've got to fight this. It's not like you to knuckle under. There's another thing I've been thinking - the estate. If she has disposed of it in some way, that can be fought, too. I've no idea what the law is exactly, but surely there's something about a surviving spouse's right to property? It's certainly true for women. Also, I'm sure there must be some provision for any improvements a tenant has made. Absurd as it is, I suppose in the eyes of the law you could be seen as a sort of tenant. You've doubled or tripled the value of this place by what you've done.'

There was a flicker of interest, no more. 'On that score, let's wait and see the will, shall we?' He looked towards the food, not from any appetite, she thought, but to rid himself of an unsavoury subject, and possibly herself.

Henry warned her Gillespie was coming again. She answered the door, and took an instant dislike to him. She could see he guessed who she was. As she opened the front door, his flat bespectacled reddish face regarded her with a dull contempt. What exactly, she had already wondered, *had* Delia said to him? Was it as Becket had reported, and did he, too, therefore regard her as a murderess or an accomplice? Because of this, she made no effort to be polite. She confronted him, saying nothing, forcing him to speak first.

'I've an appointment with Mr Bordeaux,' he said irritably.

She led him without words to the sitting-room and closed the door behind him. Henry, she knew, had gone up to one of the greenhouses to talk to Geoff. She went out to tell him.

She thought Henry had been a little less listless since they had spoken. 'Right,' he said, 'well, here goes.' He gave Geoff a rueful smirk as he went off.

They were closeted a very short time. From the office Jocelyn heard Henry show the man out. No words passed between them in the hall.

She wondered if Henry would come into the office. She doubted if he would say anything in front of Betty, but she would know at once whether the news was good or bad. But he went back into the sitting-room, closing the door.

She had to endure the whole afternoon. Henry didn't appear. Betty left. She stayed deliberately in the office, though she had nothing particular to do. Finally, Edith popped in. She was sure that Edith, like Geoff, knew what the visit had been about and what hung on it. Deliberately, nothing was said about it. 'I'm off then,' Edith said. 'Geoff, too. We've got company tonight.'

A prescient stillness descended on the house. Henry, she was fairly sure, was upstairs. She had heard his footsteps earlier. Would he come down? How long would she wait? She drew up the small step-ladder, mounted it, and began to enter the day's bookings on her new wall chart. Absorbed, she didn't hear him. 'It's the worst,' she heard behind her. He was standing in the doorway. He came in and sat in Betty's chair. 'The place is to be sold. Patrick gets the entire proceeds.'

'Patrick?'

'Her brother - the one I told you about.'

'But - I thought they didn't get on.'

'So did I.'

She climbed down and leaned against her desk. 'She can't have done that.'

'Well she has.'

'Did Gillespie make no comment.'

'A man like Gillespie doesn't make comments - though, reading between the lines, I'm sure he did say to the police exactly what Becket said he had. Clearly Delia made her accusation to him that afternoon. She seemed to have foreseen that I was on the point of making some kind of ultimatum about not looking after her if she didn't stop being paranoid, and she changed her will.'

'You mean she told Gillespie she thought you and I were having an affair?'

'By implication from the way he spoke, she must have done.'

'So Gillespie thinks you and I killed her?'

'Certainly that *I* did. Delia has no doubt paid him enough to condition his mind whatever he really thinks.'

'Did you ask him exactly what Delia made up about us, and what he told the police?'

'I made one oblique attempt, but I could see it wouldn't get anywhere. I just listened. I wanted him out of the place as soon as possible.'

'You're going to fight the will?'

'I don't know. I won't have the chance if I'm locked up.'

'You're not going to be locked up. Even if Becket believes what he said to me, there's no evidence on which any jury could convict. It's your word against Delia's - and Gillespie's. I know which I'd go for if I were a disinterested party. And now there's this legacy. Surely you can prove that Delia disliked this brother? If you can, her act of leaving him everything can only be seen as further evidence of her desire to hurt you.'

Henry sighed, gripping his head at the temples. 'I'm really not sure I want to, Jocelyn. You're being wonderfully sweet and loyal, when you have no cause to be at all. But I do wonder now if I feel like going on with this place anyway. Delia's ghost would always haunt it. I doubt if I could ever be happy here.'

'Surely the truth is that Delia's ghost has *been* haunting the place, now it's laid. Henry, you have the chance of real happiness again. You must seize it. You must fight to establish the truth about Delia, and you must fight for the possession of Combe.' She jumped up and went to the wall chart. 'Just look at the bookings we've had in the last few days. I think on an extrapolation of this summer's figures you could raise a bank loan and buy the place if it has to go on the market. And it might not have to go on the market. You must get your own lawyer in.'

Was there, like the momentary resuscitation of a dying fire, a flicker of the old enthusiasm? If there was, it couldn't be sustained. 'You're quite marvellous to care,' he said, 'but I'll have to see.'

'It's not only you I'm thinking about, but Edith and the others - and me. What am *we* going to do if this place folds?'

He looked concerned. 'They'll get other jobs, so will you.'

'After a charge of murder, even if unproven?'

She saw he hadn't considered this. 'They won't involve you.'

'I don't know. Becket, as I told you, seems to have pretty fixed ideas on the subject.'

'He doesn't mean them.'

'I'm not as confident about that as you are.'

She thought she had made him think about it. How ironic it would be, she thought afterwards, if it turned out to be an assertion of her own self-interest that made him change his mind. It had been her tactics to make him think so.

14.

On the way back from work Leo bought the evening paper to glance at the runners for tomorrow's races. With Jocelyn's knowledge, he had a weekly flutter. He didn't open the paper till he got home and was installed in the sitting-room.

'Cunningham to be Minister.'

He usually skipped the front news page, but this was a secondary headline and it caught his eye. It was like a trap being sprung in his stomach. He looked quickly towards Jocelyn. Her head was bent over a sock she was darning. Sally, thank goodness, was upstairs doing her homework. Sally was more capable of noticing things than Joss these days. He looked back at the paper.

'Sir Matthew Cunningham,' he read, skimming the paragraph, 'a rising star in the party . . . tipped by many as a future prime minister . . . his first post . . . when asked about his ambitions, Sir Matthew refused to be drawn. " I just have a job to do," he said.'

The first numbing shock was followed by tremors of panic. A minister - it must surely come out. Sooner or later there would be a picture. The likeness was plain - and coupled with the name? He should of course have told Joss right at the beginning. In those days it wouldn't have mattered. But even now he could manage it somehow, couldn't he? 'Look at this, Joss, my brilliant, titled, ass of a half-brother has got his bum on the Government front bench. But of course Matt always *would* have done, now one comes to think about it. A born ladder climber, a veritable steeplejack - they should've called him Jacob. He won't stop till he reaches the pearly gates.' She would be surprised at the first mention, but he could surely laugh that off to advantage. Hadn't their marriage started because of an unspoken agreement to live in the present not the past? Matt was as irrelevant now as he had always been. Later when Jocelyn went upstairs he went out and stuffed the paper in the dustbin.

He remembered his last (chance) meeting with Matt on a pavement in the City years back. 'An auctioneer?' Matt had said, palely contemptuous. Leo could conjure now the skin pulling even tauter over those high white cheekbones. 'Odd thing to choose to do, isn't it?'

He had laughed easily. 'Odd, Matthew? I wouldn't say it's any odder than what you do. We both sell junk. Yours is just the verbal variety, that's all.' Matt had walked off in a huff. He had definitely got the better of that exchange.

Surely he could live with Matthew's new appearance in his life? Hadn't it been predictable? And what was so amazing about having a semi-relation you hadn't thought to mention to your wife because of his irrelevance? His silence *implied* the irrelevance. The thought got him through the next day or two.

Jocelyn saw the picture on the front page of *The Times* the next day only because one of the doctors at the clinic pointed out the name as a joke. 'Relation of yours?' She took it as a joke.

It was only when the doctor had left the room and she was taking a closer look at the photograph that she thought there was quite a likeness - the chin, the setting of the eyes. A cousin perhaps? She was only mildly interested and would have forgotten about it had she not seen the same paper on a news stand that evening on the way home. She'd had to make a few purchases. They didn't take a daily paper. She bought a copy.

When she got back, Sally was in the kitchen and saw the paper sticking out of the basket. 'A daily paper? Unlike us, isn't it? *The Times* at that.'

Jocelyn told her. Sally's interest kindled ominously. She took the paper as if it were some precious document and, kneeling on a chair, spread it on the table. 'You're right. It's a relation all right,' she announced. 'Quite a close one, I'd say. So, what's he been hiding from us this time, do you think? Do you think he's the black sheep of the family and he doesn't want us to know?'

Jocelyn was already wishing she hadn't bought the paper. 'Of course not. It's probably a distant cousin - or no relation at all.'

From the bedroom she saw Leo coming up the street. There was something of the old jauntiness in his step. She had been afraid when he took the porter's job at the hospital, but it seemed to be working out. By his own accounts at least he was making friends with everyone - the other staff, the patients, even the doctors. She believed it. Leo had never had trouble making friends. She didn't go down at once. She had decided how to play it. Because of Sally it might need playing. She heard their voices below. There didn't seem to be any ructions. In a while, when she heard Sally going up to her room she went down.

He was sitting in the kitchen on the high-backed chair parked against the wall between the fridge and the washing-machine, doing nothing. The newspaper was still on the table where Sally had left it.

'Good day?' she said cheerfully. She went to the vegetable rack to get an onion. It was early, but she would start the meal, she thought. He didn't answer. 'I had quite a slack day.'

His gaze, which had been blank, focussed. 'Oh yes.'

'Anything exciting at the hospital?'

He got up, not answering. He would have gone up to wash and change, a habit he had developed with the new job. 'Did Sally show you the paper?' She nodded to it.

'Yes.'

'*Is* it a relation?'

He looked at her menacingly. 'You know damn well it is, so why ask?'

'I - wasn't sure. Who is it?'

'Who is it, you ask, all innocence. It's my goddam brother, that's who it is. Matthew bloody Cunningham. On his way to the top of the mulberry bush.'

'Brother?'

'Half of one, yes. *Enough* of one.'

'But I never knew you had . . .

'I never told you, did I? Why should I tell you? Any more than you told me more than a few words about your lot. Our "lots" were irrelevant to us in those days, weren't they?'

'Leo, what on earth are you talking about? Our family backgrounds *were* irrelevant, yes. We agreed they were. That was what was so marvellous. Have you forgotten how we used to look at other people and see them writhing in family traditions they couldn't escape from. We thought of ourselves as marvellously free. We started with ourselves, just as we were. So why should you now . . .

'Why should I now what?'

'Well, why should you apparently be so upset?'

'Upset, am I?'

'It appears so.'

He turned away to the window so that he had his back to her. His voice was constrained. 'Our daughter obviously thinks family connections are vital.'

'What does Sally know about it?'

'She appears to think I should be something like Matt, a minister, probably prime minister by now.'

'How can she think that, the silly girl. What did she say?'

'She didn't have to say much. I know what she thinks.'

She was faint with disgust but she made herself touch his arm. 'Sally is sometimes a malicious, wicked child. How can you listen to her? Now tell me about Matt. Tell me about your childhood. There's something, isn't there? What is it that makes you so hurt by this?'

He thrust away from her. 'I'm not hurt, just realistic. Sally isn't malicious, she's right. Matt was right. A mere auctioneer, now a hospital porter. What kind of father for anyone is that?'

'But we've been through all this. I thought we'd always taken the view . . .

He faced her for an instant. 'We've always taken the view that success doesn't matter, right. Once, when we were young, that made sense. Now it doesn't any more. Sally expects more than youthful indulgence from her father. No wonder she despises him, and rightly.'

She could no longer rein her anger. 'You've got to stop this, Leo. This is what is indulgence - your attitude. If Sally is thinking what you say she is, she's wrong. Sally, for whatever reason, is a little prig. I fear for *her* if she doesn't begin to grow up soon. The only thing you ever did wrong was to stop thinking about life in the way that made me fall in love with you. I thought you'd refound yourself.'

He went blank suddenly. 'Did you?' he said. 'Well, maybe that's what I've got to do then - if you say so.'

He brushed past her roughly on his way upstairs.

In an unchanged mood of rage she went straight up to Sally. She was doing her prep in the little room. She saw at once from her manner of righteous application that she was not guiltless, that this absurd idea of Leo's was no mere construction of his own.

'Sally, just what have you been saying to your father?'

She went through the motions of being tiresomely interrupted in her work. 'Saying?'

'You've deeply upset him.'

'Have I? If he's upset, I'm sorry.'

'You asked him who Matthew Cunningham is?'

'A natural enough question, isn't it? You must have been curious, too, or you wouldn't have bought that paper.'

'And when you heard he's your uncle?'

She shrugged. 'Naturally, I expressed interest. Rather a distinction, isn't it, to find we have someone important in the family after all?'

'What do you mean "after all"?'

'We are otherwise, you must admit, rather mediocre.'

Her rage exploded. 'People are mediocre if they think they are. Sally, I'm going to tell you a home truth. I don't know why, but you're growing into a very stuffy, prim little girl. If you go on like this, sooner or later you're going to come down with a bad crash. People aren't automatons that can be pulled this way and that by the application of some prissy little principles. You know as well as I do that Leo has had a problem, one that is based on his idea of your welfare. You know, and you deliberately used your knowledge to hurt him just now. Can't you see, you silly little ass, that Leo loves you, and that all you can do is throw his love back in his face? If this silly incident has repercussions, I warn you, I shall find it very difficult to forgive you.'

She had the decency to cry - that is to say, tears were coursing down her cheeks. But there was no sound of weeping. The white face turned to her was impassive, unforgiving. 'Did you forgive him when he went to prison?'

'I love him.'

'I said forgive.'

She gave up. How can you morally persuade even a child, perhaps above all a child? She suppressed her anger and cleared the decks. 'I think you should think about it, and then in some way of your own choosing, show your father that whatever has happened you love him.'

'I don't love him.'

'Then that you respect him as an individual - as *any* individual if you can't accept him as a parent.'

Sally turned back to her table. Jocelyn left her. She felt mostly a loneliness that was like solitary confinement. To live in the same house with two people for different reasons so removed seemed like a punishment. What had she done to deserve it?

The situation went into a freeze. She ransacked her brain to think of some way of reintroducing the subject with Leo. Had he really, all through, harboured these feelings of envy and inferiority, in thrall to a brother he never saw? Had this been behind all the other incidents? She tried to remember the few references there had been to his past in the early days. She had gathered that his mother had died and his father remarried. She had understood he held no brief for his stepmother. She was sure there had never been mention of a sibling from his father's second marriage, yet all these years the memory of Matthew had been there like a dormant explosive.

The two of them lived on together, going to work, returning in the evenings, saying normal things, performing normal acts, but the consciousness of the brief bitter exchange that evening remained. Her nature revolted at the silence. Not so long ago it had been Leo's nature, too, to be open. Even the worst things had never been unreferred to for long. But now she began to think that it would go on like this, that this stupid sulking doggedness would become a habit, that it was useless for her to say anything because he would refuse to talk.

One hot August afternoon - the temperature was in the upper eighties - the senior doctor at the clinic thought she was looking tired, which was true enough. He suggested she went home early. His daughter was there, on holiday from school - she could help the other person on duty behind the desk. Jocelyn didn't really want to go home. Work was a solace these days. But she went.

She got into the car in the park. The interior was stifling with the close heat of the city. She opened both doors. Obligingly a little breeze got up. Feeling the relief, she was suddenly overwhelmed by a nostalgic love for Leo, which she hadn't felt for a long time. There was no malice in Leo, only a conditioned lack of confidence. She felt glad suddenly that it was apparently this envy which had probably always goaded him, and not simply avarice. It was understandable, human, *curable.* She could help him to cure himself, with an application of a sense of proportion and of humour. She was overcome by a desire to be with him, now, at once, just as she had used to feel in the London flat waiting for him to come home in the afternoons. If she could be with him and show him this new feeling of hers that she understood and sympathised, surely, hand over hand, things could be restored to normal.

There were three hours before he would be home. She thought she would go to the hospital and surprise him. She had only once been there when she'd had to drive him because of a bus strike. He had shown her round and introduced him to the people he worked with.

The hospital park was full. When she eventually found a space it was miles from the building where Leo worked. She began to feel silly. Who went to see their husband during working hours unless there was an emergency? And she would have to ask for him at the desk, she shrank from that. Perhaps she should just wander about the building and hope to come across him. This is what she did. She walked along stuffy corridors and peered into the wards. Nurses, sick people in the beds, regarded her. A sister asked her if she was looking for somebody. She pretended she hadn't heard. She didn't find him. She remembered he had shown her the laundry rooms in the basement. Feeling an intruder, she took a lift down.

There were two orderlies sitting with their white jackets unbuttoned on two of the large baskets having a smoke. She felt an ass, but having got this far she was determined not to retreat. She approached them. 'Do you know Leo Cunningham by any chance?'

The men looked up at her. 'Leo?' said one. 'Of course. That's to say we *did* know him.'

'You mean he's been transferred to another department?'

The men exchange glances. 'You a friend then?'

'I'm - yes, that's it, a friend. I was hoping . . .

'I'm afraid you won't find him here. He left about a month ago. Said he had a better job.'

She went home and sat in the shade of the rowan tree in the small garden behind the house. She endured the sounds of high summer, the ubiquitous hum of insects. A child was splashing in a home-made plastic pool next door. She found the squeals, the occasional barking of a drowsy dog, the mother's confident authoritative voice, obnoxious, but tried to shut them out by thinking. It was Sally, she was waiting for, she decided.

Sally came in soon after four, looking cool. 'Any tea going?' she called amicably from the open kitchen door. She was already a young woman, it occurred to Jocelyn. She was slipping into womanhood as easily as she did everything else, no fuss, no nonsense. She continued to sit. 'I want you to come here a minute, Sally. There's something I have to tell you.'

There was a tentative approach. 'What's this, something happened?'

She told her to get herself another seat before she would begin. This time, she had told herself, it was to be different. She wasn't going to treat Sally like a child any more. This had been her mistake. She made her voice matter of fact.

'I had the afternoon off from work. I thought I'd go up to the hospital and see Daddy. I've only seen the place once before. I thought we could have a cup of tea in the canteen or something. He wasn't there. His colleagues told me he hasn't been there for some time. It appears he's got another job without telling us.'

She had certainly caught Sally off guard. For a moment, before she remembered to be cool, she looked almost vulnerable. 'So?'

'I don't know quite how "so". It's possible he's done something quite reasonable, to earn more money. Perhaps he aims to surprise us. On the other hand, judging by the past, and because of what happened over Uncle Matt, I have to think it may not be like that. He could have got the sack and been afraid to say, or he may be getting himself into more trouble. Either way, I intend to talk to him about it. I know how difficult it's been for you to cope with having a father who went to prison, but I want you to help me. If I talk to him alone I don't think he'll listen, but if we do it together - if you'll be there when I ask him what he's doing, in an understanding and sympathetic frame of mind - I think there's more chance of getting a sensible answer.'

There was an unexpected look of interest. 'What do you think he's up to?'

'I don't know. I'm sure it's nothing sinister. We'll do it in an ordinary way if we can, not accusatorily. I'll simply say what happened and we'll play it by ear.'

The ploy seemed to work. Sally said she would do her best.

Leo didn't come in at the usual time. Soon after seven the phone rang. Sally, awaiting a call from her boy friend, got to it first. From the top of the stairs Jocelyn heard a brief exchange, then Sally hung up.

'It's him. He's not coming back tonight. Something about the hospital wanting him to go with the ambulance somewhere. I thought he'd left the hospital.'

At supper Jocelyn questioned Sally further. Sally was gulping her food. She'd had a call and was going out. Her answers were less than interested. 'It could be those men at the hospital got it wrong,' Jocelyn said. 'Perhaps he's changed to the casualty department or something.'

Sally managed just one contribution. 'He certainly sounded rather pleased with himself,' she said.

15.

Henry's lawyer, a man called Potter, came. The two were closeted for a couple of hours. The coroner postponed his hearing. The police came and went, Becket interviewed them all again, but Henry was not arrested.

Since the funeral Henry had hardly been seen. Jocelyn knew on two days he took the boat out on the estuary. He didn't appear for lunch, and when not on the river seemed to spend a great deal of time in his room. On one day Edith, who took midday food up to him there when he was in, said he was sorting papers. He had them all over the floor, she said. Half the food they took up to him remained uneaten.

Jocelyn found herself running the place as best she could, but on the fourth day there were two important decisions to be made involving quite large sums of money. She heard him upstairs and went up to him. He was in his chair in the window with a photograph album on his knees. She began to speak about the business straight away. He asked her distantly to deal with everything as she thought best. 'You mean we spend the money?' she said. He nodded. She didn't think he had really taken in what she said. On the other hand she didn't feel he was displeased she had come up. She lingered, and after a moment made a sounding. 'The police haven't been for a couple of days.'

'No.'

'That has to be good news, don't you think?'

'Is it?'

'If they thought they had a case, they'd surely have charged you by now?'

He looked up, placed his hand on the open page of the album, and showed some interest. 'Possibly. Peter Potter's inclined to think so. There's after all no evidence against me. Do you know they went through the house with a teaspoon and removed all my clothes? Searching for traces of the acid, I suppose.'

'Which they won't find. There's also the fact they've held up the inquest. That's surely encouraging. If the police had found any evidence to charge you, it would have happened with a verdict of suspicious circumstances or something.'

'Potter thought that, though of course there's an alternative less satisfactory explanation for the delay. They think the evidence will be there and are waiting to tie the ends of a case against me.'

She hesitated. Was he really better able now to discuss things? It seemed so. 'Did you also discuss the legalities of Combe with Potter?'

'Yes. He was bulging with stuff about it.'

'Encouraging?'

'Yes. You had the right idea. I do apparently have some rights. Not your improvement line - apparently, in general terms, if a tenant improves a property it simply puts more money in the landlord's pocket, he can charge more rent. But I have, it seems, an "automatic right as a spouse" - I think that's the phrase. Potter's probably being optimistic, but he says I'm entitled to at least half the value of the place.'

'But that's marvellous. With that as collateral surely you'll be able to borrow, and buy out this tiresome relation? Surely he'll sell, if you make a good offer? He can't be interested in the property for itself.'

'Oh he isn't. He has already announced he intends to sell it.'

'There you are. You appoint a neutral valuer, and you offer to buy out his half at the price fixed. Why should he disagree, when he realises what the law is? If he sells to you he's assured of the money, and is shogged of all the expense of a sale.'

'That's also what Potter's suggesting. You should have been a lawyer, Jocelyn.'

'So?' There was a long pause. Geoff was cutting the grass round the fringes of the drive on the other side of the house. The throbbing cut suddenly, seeming to expose an immense and frightening tension. Henry's face darkened.

'Potter has approached Murdoch's solicitor and he agreed to put the suggestion to his client. Murdoch's turned it down flat. There'll have to be a case.' Henry's voice was clipped, executive. It was the kind of tone in which she could imagine he gave orders in the heat of battle, shorn of human consideration, concerned only with the elimination of the enemy and of survival.

'Murdoch's Delia's brother, isn't he?'

'Yes.'

'Why doesn't he like the idea? It's so much in his interest.'

'He clearly doesn't think so.'

'What does Potter think?'

'He's mystified. He got the impression between the lines that Murdoch's lawyer thought a settlement out of court was the best way.'

'Is it vindictive then, in some way? Does Murdoch somehow blame you for Delia's death?'

'I suppose he must - though I find it hard to believe he'd care very much even if he thought I'd been involved. He was perfectly vile to Delia. Washed his hands of her years ago.'

'Then why should he act like this?'

Henry was looking disinterested again. 'Patrick Murdoch's a rich dynast - made a lot more money than he inherited, in business. He probably thinks because Delia put up the original capital for Combe, the capital belongs to him and his family by right. Maybe he's thinking of putting some relation in here, I don't know.'

A thought was beginning to occur to Jocelyn. She sat on the window seat, frowning. 'Henry, you don't think, do you, this man could have supplied the poison somehow?'

'Of course not.'

'*Why* not? Don't you see, he's the only person with a mercenary motive? He stood to inherit this property when Delia died. He maybe knew that.'

Henry smiled. 'This time, my dear, I'm afraid you can't be right. I've told you, Patrick hasn't been near this place for years. He and Delia never spoke.'

'But they could have done, on the phone. How exactly did that phone gadget thing work? When you first put the phone in I think you said Delia pressed a button and got on to the exchange, who put her through. One doesn't of course go through the exchange now, but you can if there's some difficulty. Delia had only to say she was disabled and I'm sure the operator would have connected her. She could have made her plans, called her brother, and asked him to get her the poison.'

'But even if Patrick had agreed, which I cannot contemplate, how would it have been delivered? Not by post. You or I open all the mail. Delia knew that. Delia's had no mail for months.'

'He could have come here, or had someone come.'

'In broad daylight, with everyone buzzing about?'

'At night. He could have forced a window somewhere and got up to her room. You're at the other end of the building. I certainly wouldn't have heard. Your dog sleeps pretty soundly, too, doesn't he? I've never heard him bark at night. There's another posssibility. If Delia did phone him, if he's the sort of man you say, he could at first have refused to do what Delia wanted - until she offered to leave him Combe. And if it did happen this way, that's why Delia summoned Gillespie that afternoon, to fulfil her side of the bargain by changing parts of her will.'

Henry's interest faded again. 'No, Joss, you're very sweet to think all this up. But there was only one reason Delia changed her will - to spite me. She was doing what she said she would do if I didn't act as she wanted. She's had the last laugh.'

'But have the police interviewed Murdoch?'

'I'm sure they haven't. Why should they?'

'Because Delia left him everything. He has to be a suspect?'

'I cannot believe it.'

'You should at least ask Potter what he thinks, shouldn't you?'

He didn't answer this. A frightening look of intense fatigue came over his face, combined with that element of inalienable decision. He shut the album and put it on the floor. 'No, Joss, I've had plenty of time to think in these last days, and I've made up my mind. What I've decided is that if I'm accused of Delia's death I shall of course state the truth, but go along with whatever the jury decides. If I go to prison I shall accept it. In a way I feel guilty. I didn't encompass her death, but I did make that ultimatum she so clairvoyantly anticipated. It was in a sense an act of murder on my part. Whether they accusc me or not, if Potter gets for me what appears to be my legal due, I shall see that all of you are compensated for your marvellous loyalty. If I'm not accused, or found not guilty, I shall take what remains of the money and push off somewhere, maybe go and plant tea or nuts or something if you can still do that. I couldn't go on here.' His eyes were dull, but for a moment a light kindled in them as he looked at her. 'I'm really sorry to have got you into this mess, especially you, with your own difficulty. I profoundly wish there was a way of arranging for you to stay on here.'

There were a number of other things that were lining up to be said. She could see it would be useless. The element of self-immolation that had been there before had gone. Henry had made up his mind. He didn't have the mental equipment for wavering.

The hours lapped. They were all busy. She allowed the work to suppress her thoughts. She imagined the others were doing the same. They didn't talk about the situation. If she had any notion, it was that since there had been no arrest, as with a storm cloud that had threatened and moved away without rain, light would steadily return. There would be no murder charge, the coroner would pronounce 'suicide while the balance of the mind etcetera.' Perhaps even Murdoch would have second thoughts about Henry's offer, or there would be a court case and Henry would win. Henry would recover his zest for living and his passion for the place. Accustomed by living with Leo to endure and hope, she endured and hoped.

Two evenings later she didn't finish until nearly eight. In her flat she poured herself a more than usually liberal glass of gin and tonic and put her feet up on the sofa. Hearing a car in the drive, she craned her neck. It was the police. She saw Becket get out with a constable. The driver remained.

She stood up and saw the two men appear below and ring the front door bell. Something in Becket's stance told her what they were about. She rushed down. When she arrived, Henry had opened the door and was listening to the ritual warning. She stood off, watching. She realised then Henry was addressing her.

'Jocelyn, I'd like you to take over the running of the place, if you would, until this business is decided. It may be the truth and reason will prevail. If it doesn't, Potter has all my instructions.'

The constable accompanied him upstairs. Meanwhile, she stood with Becket in the hall. 'This is madness,' she said. Becket had turned aside. He didn't answer.

Henry came down with a small suitcase. He looked composed, even relieved, she thought. He gave her his bunch of keys. 'Perhaps you'd kindly do the locking up, Jocelyn, and let them in in the mornings. I suppose I'll get some bail, so I should be back.'

Becket turned to her. 'I am presuming you will remain at this address, Mrs Hammond. If for any reason you do not, I must ask you to inform me where you may be contacted. You will certainly be required as a prosecution witness.'

The constable handcuffed himself to Henry's wrist and the three men departed.

She was neutralised with shock, the more so when she realised that from any outsider's point of view Henry's likely guilt stood out a mile. Hadn't this been her own first reaction, and probably Edith's and that of the others? She could imagine the trial, the tireless piling up of the allegedly sympathetic evidence of what this war hero had suffered over the years, the innuendoes of his understandable search for solace in the arms of this female assistant so recently appointed - with no professional qualifications for the job. Then the accumulation of an overwhelming desire to be rid of it all would be described, leading to the last desperate act for which no one else had any motive. She could see how there would not need to be any hostile witnesses. Her own evidence, that of Edith and the others, attesting to Henry's qualities, asserting their belief in his innocence, would compound the prosecution's case. She could hear the rhetoric. Yes, all this - Henry Bordeaux was indeed a loyal, temperate, decent man - who would deny this? But wasn't he also human? And, crucially, what did the jury make of the evidence of this recently divorced woman who had every reason to find the defendant a happy way out of her own difficulties? Hadn't she, and the happiness perhaps her appearance at his house offered him, provided the final incentive for an act which could by some be construed merciful for the victim? Finally the jury would look at Henry and note his magisterial calm in the witness box, his dignified one word answers, even the dignity of his one central lie as they would assert it was. How could they not conclude what the prosecution would so eloquently suggest, that here was a man who, goaded beyond all endurance, and perhaps even humanely believing that what he was doing was an act of euthanasia, acquired the poison and slipped it into the bedside drinking vessel, which it was his habit to top up with whisky? She could imagine the judge summing up, cautioning the jury that in deciding upon their verdict they might well be swayed by those suggestions of humanity on the part of the accused which the prosecution had cited. They might well, in view of these, be tempted to usurp his own (the judge's) duty of sentencing and bring in a protective verdict of not guilty. What they had to do was simply to decide whether or not Henry Bordeaux was guilty of poisoning his wife, nothing else. It would be for himself, the judge, to weigh any mitigating circumstances which might allow the sentence to be modified if the defendant were found guilty.

She drove herself almost to the point of hysteria with these imaginings then, back in her flat after locking up the house, began to feel vulnerable from another point of view. She hadn't fully realised until now how reassuring Henry's presence in the main house had been to her. She was alone on the premises. Supposing Leo chose this moment to come? There had been short pieces about Delia's death in the national press. One paper had mentioned her own assumed name, with an innuendo about her relations with Henry which must surely come near libel. Though it was illogical - why should Leo notice the name Hammond, which he had never heard? - she imagined him somehow sniffing out the truth between the lines as he was so adept at doing, then coming here, exploiting her weakness in some diabolical way, even assaulting her. She thought of phoning Sally. In present circumstances just to hear her matter of fact voice would surely be a comfort.

Then she began to recover herself. Perhaps it was thinking of Sally which helped to do this. She didn't phone Sally. If Sally hadn't phoned her, the chances were she and Ken hadn't seen the notices. All to the good. Time enough for Sally's opinions and self-justifications when the trial started, if there were to be one, when she would have of course to be told.

She got to sleep finally and in the morning woke freshly and with one idea predominant. Of what possible use to Henry was the kind of thinking she had been guilty of the night before? Perhaps Henry had been right with his compliment, perhaps she did have something of 'a lawyer's mind' - certainly a stark sense of relevance which Leo had once called honesty. She had been conscious all through, as surely Potter must now be if he was going to do anything to help Henry, that what was crucial was Delia's telephone. She concentrated on this now. As far as she knew, only two people had spoken to Delia in her room since she had been at Combe - apart from Henry and Lorna - the hairdresser and Gillespie. If all of these were eliminated as the source of the poison, the telephone had to be crucial. Why was no one thinking of this? Delia must surely have spoken to someone, surely fairly recently? She herself had carefully checked the second quarter bill at the end of June. All the calls had been accounted for. At nine she phoned the telephone accounts office. She asked if it was possible to have an interim statement with all calls listed up to date. At first she was told it wasn't possible. She insisted how important it was. At last they agreed that it could probably be faxed if she had a machine. She pressed, and got a sort of promise that it should come through in two or three hours.

She couldn't concentrate in the office, but fortunately she had the place to herself. Betty was sick. Twice the machine started rattling. She jumped up, only to find they were booking enquiries. The third time it was the telephone account. She waited impatiently for the typing to stop, then tore off the sheet and took it to her desk. She had hoped that Delia's phone would be listed separately somehow as it was connected differently, but the charge for this exceptional service was in the rental and there were no separately detailed calls. Most of the places named were familiar to her, as she had made the calls herself. Then her eye lighted on one that stood out because of its length - an unusual number of units which she calculated as a twenty minute call.

None of the business calls were longer than five minutes. Then she noted the date - exactly a week before Delia died. The destination of the call was Cheltenham. She flew to Henry's private address book, which she knew he kept in a drawer near the phone in the sitting-room. Murdoch was not listed. Never mind, she thought. As soon as Henry was bailed she would tell him. He must surely take note of the call.

In the late morning, Peter Potter called. He wanted to come to see her in the early afternoon if she was free. He wouldn't say what it was about, but she imagined it would be something about bail. She couldn't wait to tell him, too, about the number. He would know where Murdoch lived. If Murdoch had had a conversation with Delia on that date, it had to be relevant.

In the meantime she had another thought. If Murdoch, or his emissary, or anyone else for that matter, had delivered the poison to Delia, how had that person entered the building? Had the police thought about this at all? She couldn't believe, in their certainty of Henry's guilt, that they had. Certainly she had seen no one prowling round the building. She couldn't believe the entry had been made in daylight. Who would have risked that, when to be seen would inevitably be remembered after Delia's death? And if someone had got into the house at night there must be some evidence of entry - which must surely have been through a window, no doors had been tampered with. She began an immediate search of the building.

Almost at once, she found something. All the windows had safety locks. There was one, in the most obvious place - the downstairs toilet beyond the kitchen, on Delia's side of the house - whose safety lock had not been screwed home. The ordinary catch in the centre of the window was turned to the closed position, but a knife inserted between the two small windows would have taken care of that easily enough. She opened the window, climbed on the toilet, and turned her head sideways to look at the wooden outside edge of the lower window. She drew her breath sharply and exclaimed. There was no doubt, there seemed a number of scratches just below the catch.

She hadn't told Edith what she was doing, but her gasp must have been more audible than she thought. Edith appeared. 'What's up?' she said, wiping her hands on a cloth.

'Look at this, Edith. The safety lock isn't bolted, and there are knife marks on the outer edge of the window.'

Edith didn't move. 'No, that's nothing, I'm afraid. Henry always leaves that one undone in case he locks himself out at night. It's been like that for years. I'm the only one who knows about it. He told me because he thought I might need to get in at some time, if he were ill or away. And I know he did use the window once or twice. That accounts for the marks.'

Jocelyn was on the point of blurting her theory, but stopped herself. It must surely be, first, for Potter's ears. She got down from the toilet and managed, she hoped, to make herself seem disappointed. 'Oh well, it was a thought,' she said.

She went back to the office. Pulses now seemed to have broken out all over her body. Disappointing? Of course it wasn't disappointing. Who knew about the open lock? Only Henry and Edith, and presumably Geoff? But almost certainly Delia would have known, too. Henry must have mentioned it to her at some time. And if Delia knew, she could have told the intruder, told Murdoch? How easy it would have been for Murdoch or someone on his behalf to get in.

When Potter arrived, she took him into the sitting-room. Both of them, she thought, felt awkward sitting here in Henry's house in his absence as if they were intruders. She asked him first about bail. He frowned. 'I'm afraid the news on that front isn't good,' he said. 'The police argued in court this morning that "in Henry's agitated state of mind", they advised against it. At large he might well be tempted to leave the country. Anyone looking less agitated than Henry cannot be imagined, but incredibly the magistrate took the police's word. I'm quite sure the real explanation of the police plea is that they're unsure of their case and don't want Henry outside organising his defence.' Potter went on to say that he thought really it was a good sign. The prosecution knew they were on thin ice. He'd already had preliminary words with counsel, who had agreed it would be 'one of those cases in which evidence was almost entirely circumstantial and which would depend largely therefore on the character and credibility of the defendant' - this having to be a bonus for Henry, who was so patently honest.

Potter then got on to what it was clear he had really come about - her own testimony. 'Mrs Hammond,' he said suddenly, in a new voice as if all that had gone before was an unnecessary prelude. 'I've already heard Henry say this, but I would like first to clear with you the most obvious drawback there could be to Henry's defence . . .

It had been on the tip of her tongue to interrupt him with her news of the phone call and the toilet window, but it was at this moment she knew she probably wasn't going to mention it. How would Potter react to the news? Probably Murdoch lived nowhere near Cheltenham, and the call was one of Henry's to someone he knew there, she thought, a supplier perhaps she hadn't yet come across, or a friend. What did she know about people he knew? She had no wish to appear foolish to this irritatingly confident man. And if the call had been to Murdoch, how would Potter react? Quite probably like Henry. 'So what?' he would think. 'So Delia had spoken to her brother, maybe knowing it would be their last conversation. Perhaps she had even told him she was changing her will. How was that going to help Henry? It could even hinder his case if he was seen trying so desperately to shift the blame on to someone else.'

Henry thought a lot of Potter. She had already decided she didn't care for him. To her he seemed a lot more interested in his own prowess than in Henry's predicament and how he was to be got out of it. She certainly didn't like the probing he was now indulging in. 'It is most important, Mrs Hammond,' he began, 'that, however awkward it may be for both of you, I know the precise truth about your relations with Henry. The prosecution will press for all they're worth. We must be clear in advance what we're going to say.'

'What is to be said will be simply the truth,' she found herself saying tartly. 'Henry and I were not having an affair. The idea came from Delia's imagination. What I said to Inspector Becket needs no alteration, and it will be what I'll repeat in the witness box if I'm called.'

It was plain Potter didn't believe it. He tried from another angle. If there had been no thought of 'such a relationship' from her side, could it not have been in Henry's mind? Had she done or said anything, perhaps unwittingly, which could possibly have given him encouragement? She had to curb herself. She mustn't be too rude, she thought. She realised that if she wasn't going to tell Potter what she knew, there was something she must have from Potter before he went. If she wanted it, she mustn't antagonise him more than she had.

It wasn't until right at the end she managed to slip it in. Not surprisingly in view of Henry's arrest, the matter of his rights to the estate took second place. She did eventually, however, mention this as they were walking out to Potter's car. She asked him if this was going forward.

'Oh yes, that's in hand,' he said dismissively. 'It's hardly, though, my major consideration at present.'

She was sorry she had allowed her feelings to show and hadn't been more friendly. She knew what was in his mind. To her the disposal of the estate *would be* the major consideration, he was thinking. She would be worried about her own position, her job. She forced herself to ignore this and persist. 'Do you know this man, Murdoch?' she asked as casually as she could manage.

'Not personally, no.'

'Where does he live? Henry said up country somewhere.'

Potter was less than interested. 'Oh, in the family house apparently. Place called Whiston Hall.'

'Where is that?'

'Somewhere on the edge of the Cotswolds, I believe, just outside Cheltenham. It's a Cheltenham lawyer who has written to me. Why do you ask?'

She again came as near as she had been to blurting. What was she up to, concealing evidence from Henry's lawyer, when Henry wouldn't be bailed? But she was guided now by a strong instinct. She took refuge in being brisk. 'Oh, nothing much,' she said. 'I was just curious. I never met him.'

Potter frowned at such further irrelevance, said goodbye and drove off.

16.

The next day, a Saturday, when Leo was due back, Jocelyn forced herself into a state of neutrality. The two orderlies could have been wrong about Leo leaving the hospital. Leo would return with some perfectly reasonable explanation. It would turn out that she needn't have spoken to Sally.

Being the week-end, the clinic was closed. It was still very warm. She felt the need to talk to somebody. Not about Leo, she'd never had the least inclination to do that, which to her would have been a betrayal, almost a form of adultery. What she wanted was just to talk - about anything, to confirm to herself that there was such a thing as normality. She had made no close friends in Nottingham. Sally was out all day, and Leo had said he wouldn't come until the evening. On impulse, at midday when she had done the chores she usually did on Saturday morning, she lifted the phone to speak to an amusing woman called Judy Callow whom she had met in the clothes shop where she had done the part-time job. Judy, whose husband was a rich manufacturer of bathroom fitments, like her had been bored and done the job for a few weeks. They had sometimes shared a sandwich lunch in a coffee shop, and when they had both given up the job met once or twice in town. Judy answered the phone. She recognised her at once and was loudly pleased.

'*Jocelyn* - that shop, my fellow sufferer. How are you?' Jocelyn asked her if by any chance she was free that afternoon and if so if she could come out and see her. 'But of *course*, darling. When am I *not* free in the daytime? Come on out now, right away. Have some lunch and a swim. The fridge's *sinking* with food.' Elated, Jocelyn jumped straight into the car.

It was a large modern brick and timber house, the timbers arranged in diamond shapes, well out of town in an executives' suburb on the edge of the forest. She felt her old car was out of place as its worn soggy tyres made heavy weather of the deep and immaculate pink gravel. But Judy must have been watching for her, she came bursting out of the door.

'This is just what I needed. How did you know how bored to the withers I was?' She opened the car door.

Jocelyn had been wondering if Judy knew Leo had been to prison. Of course she must know, she thought - after the publicity. She would have interpreted her telephone call out of the blue as a *cri de coeur.* But Jocelyn had decided that of all the people in the town who could be called her acquaintances Judy was the least likely to want to dwell on the fact. It was quite likely there would be some quick reference and that would be that. Their relationship had been of a carefree laughing sort. They had never discussed anything serious.

She seemed to have judged accurately. It could have been yesterday they were working together in the shop. Judy launched into a list of her current '*ennuis*', the most prominent of which were Barney's business dinners which seemed to happen extremely frequently and consisted of 'men who either wanted to touch you up or consign you to conversational limbo, and women whose conversational gambits were wanting to tell you about the shortcomings of their hairdressers, about their children - and their other possessions.' Finally, she said, there were these 'frantic' holidays Barney kept insisting they took, abroad, which were 'just a lot of flies, overtanned flesh and gastro-enteritis.'

Jocelyn fell thankfully into the old groove of listening and being amused, for what she had liked before about Judy was the merry way in which she described 'these banalities' she claimed enmeshed her. She constantly ran down Barney - apparently the source of her sufferings - but concurrently you felt she must have some affection for the man to mention him so frequently. Why else would she put up with her life? She had no children, apparently had 'money of her own', and surely had the panache to walk out today if she chose. They ate a haphazard salady lunch in the kitchen, off odd plates. Judy pulled food out of the fridge and a cupboard, on impulse, in bits, as they occurred to her.

After a while Judy asked Jocelyn what she was up to. Jocelyn told her about the clinic and how she enjoyed the coming and going. She concentrated on some of the amusing things which had happened. Judy said how much she envied her for having something positive and useful to do. She 'somehow just couldn't quite get round to it.'

Jocelyn began to think Judy didn't know about Leo. Perhaps she imagined he still ran The Yard. 'Now, are we going to swim?' she said as they finished washing up the few items they had used, and as if they had for the moment used up all the interesting topics they could talk about.

Jocelyn laughed. 'I haven't brought my suit,' she said. 'In my haste to come I completely forgot you said you had a pool.'

'I can lend you a bikini. Our tits are about the same size. Come to that, why do we bother about suits? There's nobody about. I often go in in the nude when no one's here.'

They took off their clothes by the heart-shaped pool. For a moment Jocelyn felt self-conscious. She had swum nude with Leo several times in deserted places, but oddly it seemed strange with another woman. It was only momentary, the water was delicious. The swim finished off her cure.

They dried themselves on Judy's huge towels which were as woolly as fleeces, redressed, and had tea under a sunshade beside the pool. Jocelyn was thinking of Sally coming home, possibly Leo, and was looking surreptitiously at her watch as Judy dropped the bombshell. 'Oh, I forgot to tell you, I ran into Leo the other day,' she said, casually. Jocelyn's pulses stopped. 'That's to say I didn't exactly run into him, I saw him - in someone's garden.'

'Garden?'

'Yes. Isn't that what he's doing now? I heard he'd given up the auction business, and assumed that's what he's turned his hand to. I was visiting Vi Turnbull. Vi's not really my type - too rich and half-buried in it - but she's lively and decorous. Living alone, she craves company and inveigled me into going over for tea - she only lives over the way. She was gassing away about some new fabulously expensive picture she'd bought. I happened to look through the window and there was a gardener busy setting up a sprinkler-hose thing Vi has. I was immediately sure it was old Leo - though you know I really only saw him once or twice when we were in that shop. I asked Vi, and of course it *was* Leo. I asked her if Leo liked the job, but she'd say nothing about him except that he'd been with her a few weeks.'

Driving home Jocelyn felt physically numbed. Her mind was still there, but it was as if it no longer presided over a body. She was amazed at the way things had ended with Judy. She hadn't been able to reply to her statement about Leo. Judy hadn't pressed her. This was not, she thought, out of tact - she wondered even if Judy *did* know Leo had been to prison. It was simply, she thought, because something else had occurred to remove her attention, something of more importance, men being anyway no more than a sort of common predicament women shared.

'Look, it is splendid your appearing out of the blue like this, Jossy,' she had said on the way out to her car, 'we've simply got to do it more often. Perhaps we could go off on a jaunt together when Barney goes away next - which he's always doing, as if this place is just another of the hotels he visits.'

This, and her own assurances that they should do some things together, filled their closing moments. There was nothing more about Leo doing the gardener's job. Leo, Judy seemed to imply, as Barney was to her, would be on the periphery her existence.

Was Leo ashamed of working in a garden? Had he got the sack at the hospital and was it that he didn't want to tell her? Surely if he had got the sack his two colleagues would have known? But perhaps they hadn't known, she thought with a ray of hope. She realised she wanted him to have got the sack, wanted shame to be the cause of his changed job. Shame she could cope with, it could even be a source of sympathy. Then she remembered his story of going away. Why had he needed to go away overnight, into a week-end, and why had he invented the story of the ambulance, if he was working as a gardener? Why had he been away overnight?

Because of what had happened, she had left a bit earlier than she needed to, with time to spare before Sally came home. As she was about to turn on to the main road back into town, she had a sudden thought that there could have been a mistake. It might not have been Leo Judy saw. She had only seen him twice, some years ago. It could have been another man with the same first name. Wasn't it checkable, she thought? Further back she had passed a phone box. She turned and drove back to it. She was in luck. There was a local directory on a hinge. Fumbling, she found the name. There was only one Turnbull in this posh neighbourhood. She noted the address.

She didn't hesitate. A cold inner necessity seemed to have taken her over. The cul-de-sac road was not difficult to find, it was next to Judy's. It was deserted. She cruised past the motionless houses, each set in large gardens, looking at the names on the gates. Vi Turnbull's place was a mansion at the end. Largely shielded by a wall and trees beyond it, it was set back some way from the road. From a glimpse of the roof and the upper storey it seemed to be the only one that wasn't modern. Had it been the original big house of an estate? On either side, the wall was broken by large wrought-iron gates, black with rather tartily gilded knobs on the top. Both gates were shut.

She had imagined herself parking, going in, ringing the bell, putting the question brazenly, perhaps to a servant. Faced with the gates she had cold feet. Supposing the woman herself opened the door? She did not even want to park here. 'Go home', she told herself, this snooping was demeaning. But she couldn't bring herself to do this, either. She remembered that half-way down the road there had been a side-street with more, rather smaller, neo-Georgian dwellings with an open-plan lawn running down in front of them. She turned round and drove back to this street and parked anonymously. She pushed her bag under the driving seat and locked the car.

She walked back quickly to the house, uncertain what she was going to do. As she drew nearer she saw there was a lane running away on one side of the property between the brick wall which continued round the side of the house and an overgrown hedge. Thankful for the cover, she dived into it. The wall was high, at least twelve feet, but after a hundred yards there was a wooden door, also newly-painted black. If it was open couldn't she just have a quiet look?

She hesitated, looking both ways. There was still no one about. The gate would surely be locked, but she tried the latch. It lifted, and the door opened. Inside was a mossy path under a canopy of tall bushes. The house was well-shielded by these. Feeling breathless, she went in quickly and shut the door behind her.

She scrambled up a bank to a place where there was a full view of a wide lawn and beyond it the three-storey Victorian house. She first searched the garden - what was visible of it. No gardener was in sight. Her eyes returned to the house. At ground level was a sort of loggia. Above this was a balcony over which a striped awning was stretched. There were canvas chairs set out. In one sat a male figure. She could not fully see his face which was obscured by the top of the balustrade that ran along the balcony. It seemed to her he was leaning back as if sunbathing, his hands behind his head.

She watched, transfixed - she couldn't have said for how long. After a while she saw a movement in the room through an open window. A woman in a white dress appeared with a tray of drinks. The male figure, who was naked to the waist, rose and took the tray from her. It was Leo. He put down the tray on what must be a table. She then saw the two embrace.

They held each other briefly, then, separating, sat in opposite seats. She could no longer see them clearly beyond the balustrade.

Leo didn't come in that evening. He phoned at ten to say he wouldn't be back until tomorrow evening. There'd been a hold-up, he said. Still, they shouldn't grumble, it was all overtime. She made no attempt to remonstrate, simply listened, then when he had finished put the phone down.

She knew it was over. Money, status, and Leo's feelings about Sally's future were one thing, this was quite another. Strangely it might seem, in view of Leo's instability in other directions, the thought of infidelity had never entered her head, either for him or herself. She had looked at other people and noted how they came and went with each other, and marvelled. Were Judy and her husband faithful to each other? She doubted it. She had thought that she and Leo were different, that they were just two people chosen by the fates out of a thousand to be satisfied with each other, like people who win lotteries with huge odds against them. Now she thought she had just been naïve, guilty of wishful thinking, even smug. Why should she and Leo be different from other people? By what right had she claimed immunity from the common human predicament?

If this were so, were not by the same token forgiveness and reinstatement possible? She tried herself with this, but found it immediately non-acceptable. However quirkish, she was not made that way. 'My word is my bond' - that was the phrase wasn't it? - though in her case it was not so much an imposed mental discipline as a ready-made state of mind. She had thought Leo identical in this.

One aspect of the matter was a kind of relief. So it was over, was it? All the anguish of the last years had been because of the indissolubility of their union. Now there was no more a union, now the union she had imagined they enjoyed had proved to be a myth, wouldn't things be easier, as they appeared to be for Judy? In the next hours she waited, imagining it was like being in the period between a death and a burial, a space of stilled becalmment.

The next day Leo walked in in mid-afternoon when she had put up the sunshade in the garden and was sitting under it mending clothes.

'Joss, how nice - got in earlier than I thought. They let me go, though I'm paid for the day. How's things?' He walked up to her, bent, and kissed her on the side of the head.

There was no point in beating about. '*They* let you go?'

He pretended not to hear. He sat on the short flight of steps that led from the dolls' house balcony on to the lawn. 'Garden's looking untidy, think I might give it a go in a minute.'

She repeated her question. He turned to her, feigning blankness. 'What do you mean?'

'You said the hospital let you go.'

'Of course.'

'But you're not working at the hospital.'

He looked back at the garden as if his mind was still on the jobs he would do. 'No, I'm not as a matter of fact.'

'So where are you working?'

He made a semblance of pulling himself together, of rather tiresomely being made to go into unnecessary detail. 'Joss, they made me redundant. You know - all these hospital committees and economies. I was ashamed. I thought you'd think I got the sack for another reason, something I'd done. That's why I've been keeping it dark. I got this gardening job. Actually, it's quite a bit more money. My employer's very generous.'

'She does seem to be.'

Her missile hit him. She saw the terrified look, then the further retreat - to a prepared position? He stared at her in a semblance of amazement. 'You know who's employing me?'

'Vi Turnbull. Pretty well-off, isn't she? You might say she can afford to pay you well, as well as providing other benefits.'

'How do you know her name?'

'Does it matter?'

There was a flush of - what, surely not pride? 'I think it does,' he said in a gross semblance of being indignant, of being the wronged party. 'Have you been following me or something?'

'Does *that* matter? You're sleeping with her, aren't you?'

This at least put paid to any extension of the indignant line. He was frankly at bay. He had a long think this time before he spoke, leaning to grasp an ankle as if it were sprained.

'It's not as you think, Joss. I met her at the hospital. She was a patient in a private ward which was on my cleaning beat. I thought she was a lonely person - I liked her - and we got chatting while I worked. Chatted about all sorts of things - art mostly. She's a collector and knows quite a lot about a lot of stuff. Then one day - I supposed she'd realised I wasn't the usual type who took an orderly's job - she asked me if I liked the hospital work. I told her it was OK, that I had no complaints. She asked me then if I'd like to come and do her garden. Someone she'd had doing it had left her. The salary was good. I accepted.'

'And it just slipped your mind to inform your family about it? Even now you prefer to tell me the hospital made you redundant.'

He lowered his head. 'I was going to tell you.'

'And you're sleeping with her.'

He made a movement intending to imply anguish. 'I've really fallen for her, Joss. I didn't know it when she asked me to do the gardening job. But it happened soon after I went there. We

- probably want to put it on a permanent basis. I thought for a time it was just a flash in the pan, that it would blow over. That was why I thought up these stories. I thought I could get rid of it, leave her, and maybe go back to the hospital. But after the last three days I've realised it isn't going to blow over. It's the real thing. I'm sorry, Joss, really, that it's happened like this. I would've been telling you about it. But our marriage has been over for some time, hasn't it? Because of what I've done - I freely admit that - I'll never be able to forget how I wronged you. Because of it all, a new start is better - for both of us.'

His hypocrisy disgusted her. She drove through it ruthlessly. 'What you mean is that this woman's rich, and that'll give you the status you need to compete with your brother.'

That got him to his feet. 'You would think that of course, it's natural. But I'm not going to answer what you say. I don't want a row with you, what's the point? It's agony to think about after all the good times we've had together, but I'll just move out now, without fuss, with a couple of suitcases. That's the best way.'

He left the house as Sally was coming in. From the kitchen Jocelyn saw them encounter by the small gate. Leo, encumbered by two huge suitcases, stood aside to let her pass. Sally did so without a word or a glance.

'Another outing with the ambulance?' she remarked as she came in. 'Must be going for a bit longer this time?'

'He's left us,' Jocelyn said.

'Good riddance,' Sally said.

Six months passed. She was rather surprised how anguished she felt. Hadn't she been in training for this for years? Apparently not. Leo in love with another woman? She couldn't believe it. A positive thing was that Sally changed. She became more light-hearted, almost on occasions skittish. But this hurt almost more than her recurrent memory of that scene on the balcony. How could Sally rejoice in her father's departure? It was grotesque. She had to stop herself showing her disgust at Sally's levity.

She had kept one photograph in her bedroom of Leo and herself in front of the Doge's palace in Venice, Umberto, their guide, lurking in the background. A street photographer had insisted on it. At this stage of their holiday nothing had been decided, but on her face, and Leo's, was already their imminent happiness. Sally was helping her clean the room. Jocelyn saw her pick up the frame as she was dusting the table it stood on. 'Shall I bin this?' she said.

Jocelyn flew into a rage which took her as much by surprise as it took Sally. 'You'll do nothing of the sort,' she shouted, snatching the photo from Sally's hands and stuffing it into a drawer.

Even Sally was fazed. 'All right, keep your hair on.'

It was established then that there was a no-go area where Leo was concerned. Sally was to know it and tread no more within its precincts. Jocelyn's past was her past, preserved, whatever had happened thereafter.

She had a reaction to this when the quick flames of her anger had died. When Sally was at school the next day she did dispose of the photograph. It was the day the rubbish was collected. She quietly slipped it into the bin just before the vehicle arrived. Sally had been wrong to trespass so callously on the love which had once given her life meaning and which was responsible for her - Sally's - life, but she was right about their present existence, which must now be paramount.

Judy phoned. Jocelyn had thought she couldn't go to her house again, so close to where Leo was. In the moment of the call she said she would, and arriving at Judy's place she found she wasn't affected at all by that other house. Judy knew what had happened. There had been local gossip about their millionairess who had taken up with her gardener. Jocelyn told her very simply what had happened from her point of view, and included in the story Leo's gaol sentence.

'Well rid of him then, are you?' was Judy's single comment. Jocelyn began to suppose it was just possible she might come to think so.

She was even prepared for a new revelation Judy made to her not so long after. Judy gave the news in her usual give-away style, not at all as a headline. 'You've heard of course?' she said, when they'd had a swim and were drying themselves, as if apropos of very little.

'Heard what?' Jocelyn asked.

'That your Leo's done a flit. Vi told me, as cool as a cucumber. She really is a card, that woman. Only took up with the man as a lark, she told me, and he took it seriously apparently - thought he was on to a good thing no doubt, and that he'd marry her and her millions. When she told him otherwise he scarpered and took with him for good measure two quite valuable silver trinkets.'

Jocelyn's heart stumbled - was this a reflex conditioned by all her past anxieties? 'You mean the police are after him?'

'No, I don't think they are. Vi did think of calling them but had second thoughts. She's quite reconciled to her loss, she said, even pleased. She said she was glad the poor sod had got something out of it, and he could have taken a lot more. I say, you don't mind about it, Jocelyn, do you - now?'

Jocelyn got back control of her heartbeats. 'No, I don't mind about it,' she said.

'It's irrelevant now he's out of your life, right?'

At home she pondered what she had heard, at a kind of remove. Had it after all been the woman's fault? Had she led him on, in her wealthy boredom perhaps, unconsciously flattering his wounded dignity, lighting false hopes? Jocelyn could imagine it, but she censored this line of thought. What difference did it make? She wouldn't allow herself to entertain such a flabby mitigation of his act. Her marriage was dead, beyond resurrection. It had been dead for a long time, only given the semblance of survival because of her wish to think it otherwise. This was the fact of the matter and this was how it must remain.

17.

Sally's voice had never spoken so clearly in her memory as it did after Potter's departure. 'What is it about you, Mum?' she had said once. 'Why do you have to be a perpetual coastguard scanning the seas for people in distress?'

She debated this in her present predicament. Had she ever involved herself out of her own necessity in other people's disasters? 'Yes, you have,' Sally's voice came back. 'With Leo, and now with this man Henry Bordeaux. You say you aren't sweet on him, but here you are getting enmeshed again. It's his mess, not yours.' Persuasive, even taking into account her daughter's infinite capacity for oversimplification.

Was she 'sweet' on Henry. The starkly posed question made her think. That Henry had some especial regard for her she had never doubted. But the crisis of Delia's death had surely revealed the limits of his feeling. He had talked of money if he went to prison, decent arrangements for his ex-employees, but this was hardly the language of love. And her own feelings? Attraction certainly, admiration and deep gratitude without doubt, but surely a regard which was short of love?

All right then, given that, why this mad enterprise she contemplated, which had suggested itself in barest outline, she realised, at that moment she had heard from Potter that bail was refused? Why *hadn't* she passed the buck to Potter? She reassured herself. She hadn't told Potter for entirely pragmatic reasons. It wouldn't have helped Henry. What trust had she in the processes of law and the passionless objectivity of its practitioners who, like aloof Levites, passed by on the other side of the road where humanity lay bleeding? And that - mere practicality - was enough motive. How could one ever ultimately disentangle the reasons for what one did?

She stepped clear of her self-doubts. She had already imagined Henry's conviction for murder. How would she be able to live with the thought that she had funked this one chance to prevent it? She then had a thought which dropped into her mind with the finality of a chestnut falling heavily from a tree in autumn. It was something Becket had said which seemed to have stuck in her mind and now, just when she seemed to need it, played itself back to her. It was something to do with his confirmation that it had been hydrocyanic acid which killed Delia. 'A substance exceedingly difficult to obtain,' were the words he had used to describe it.

So, if difficult to obtain, who had thought of doing such a thing, and who had been able to perform this difficult task? Delia herself could have thought of it maybe? But Delia wasn't a scientist as far as she knew, and there were no reference books in her room. If there had been, someone would have had to plant the book on her lectern in order for her to be able to operate her page-turner. And how would she have obtained such a jealously guarded substance? Had she left the means of her demise to Murdoch then, if he were the villain?

She went to the library and tried one of the encyclopaedias for hydrocyanic acid. See 'Prussic Acid,' it said. She swapped volumes. Almost at once, under 'Uses', her eye fell on the phrase 'used in large quantities in the refinement of gold.' She flew to 'Who's Who', which was kept in the office, she had often used for secretarial purposes. Feverishly she pushed the thin pages with her finger. There were several Murdochs. Her eye lighted on the Cheltenham address and Whiston Hall. 'Murdoch, Anthony Edward Montague.' There was educational material, Eton and Balliol she noted impatiently, no mention of a wife or children, details of the career, then 'currently' director of three companies. She whistled aloud - the third was 'Batholomew Metal Refining.' She rushed to the phone, got the number of the firm from directory enquires, and dialed. She asked the operator point blank if the company refined gold. After a dither she was put through to a man who asked her who she was. She didn't answer but put the question again. After a pause the man laughed. 'What've you been doing, skin diving?' he said, 'Spanish bullion you want melting down, is it, perhaps?' Then he gave the answer she wanted. 'Yes, we refine gold,' he said. She thanked him, muttered something about her boss needing to know, and rang off.

She now knew for sure she was going to carry out her mad entrerprise. It wasn't too busy the following day. To cover her absence, Jocelyn told Edith she had to cope with a problem Sally had. She said they were meeting half-way to London.

She had recently spent money on her car which had reduced its unreliability, and decided to go by road. She was thankful for the privacy the old machine offered. The need to concentrate on the driving might also ward off bouts of cowardice, she thought. Nonetheless she did several times think of turning back. It was a crazy shot in the dark, and almost certainly a wild-goose chase. The gold business was just a coincidence, with a significance her own mind had manufactured. Murdoch would have a simple explanation for his telephone conversation with Delia, and she would look a fool. There was another consideration which terrified her. Just suppose her hunch was right and the man had connived at Delia's death? Couldn't she be in some danger with a man who could kill his sister? Nobody knew where she was - supposing she disappeared? Wouldn't the world draw an obvious conclusion, that she had joined Delia in suicide because her lover had been charged with murder, and out of remorse at her complicity in the deed? The fact that Murdoch couldn't know she had gone away without telling anyone where she was didn't entirely console her.

She also wished she hadn't called Murdoch's number last evening, which she had also got from enquiries. It would almost certainly have been better to drop in on him out of the blue and risk his being away. If he was guilty of something he would by now have had time to think what he was going to say. She hadn't even got a definite appointment from calling. A fruity male voice had answered - she gathered he was some sort of a servant, a butler perhaps. Mr Murdoch was 'in residence,' yes, the man said, though he was out at that moment. Could she make an appointment to see him tomorrow? Mr Murdoch didn't empower him to make appointments. She'd had to think fast. 'I must see him,' she'd said. 'Tell him it's very important and that I'll be there in the early afternoon. I'll wait - hours if necessary. I'll even stay overnight in the town if I have to. Tell him it concerns the recent death of his sister.'

The man began to ask her to call later. She said this was difficult and that she was sure that in the circumstances Mr

Murdoch would see her. The name was Hammond, she said, and rang off.

The house was important enough for its name to be printed on the ordinance survey map she found in Henry's library. It seemed to be half-way up the escarpment which rose above the town. She skirted the town on a ring road, turned off it, and began to climb a steep wooded slope. She went past a posh-looking drive flanked with laurels which, though conspicuous, had no gate or name, and had to retrace her steps after asking in the next village.

The drive was tarmacked and wove through beech woods. The large impressive eighteenth century house then revealed itself beyond a wide circular drive in. She drove up to the Cotswold stone portico whose ochre pillars supported an unadorned classical tympanum. One side of the bowed front door was open. Within was a porch and a further, closed, door with opaque glass.

There was a small modern electric bell beside the door, which she pressed. She had moments of weakness as she stood waiting. After a long silence there were brisk footsteps. The inner door opened to reveal a dapper figure in dark trousers and a multi-coloured silk waistcoat. He confronted her, running a busy hostile look from toe to head.

'I'm Jocelyn Hammond. I've come to see Mr Murdoch. Perhaps it was you I spoke to on the phone yesterday?'

The man's shiny red face confronted her implacably. He kept his hand on the handle of the open door. 'I very much doubt if Mr Murdoch'll see you,' he said.

'You mean he's out?'

'I didn't say that. I said I doubt if he'll see you.' His voice had an actor's resonance.

'You gave him my message?'

'Yes.'

'Then perhaps I could wait. As I told you, the matter I've come about is important.'

The man didn't move. 'What's it about?'

'I'll explain that to Mr Murdoch.'

'He says I'm to ask you what it's about.'

'Just tell him I'm here, if you would. Meanwhile, if I could perhaps come in and wait somewhere?'

A slight anxiety was replacing hostility on the man's face, perhaps he wasn't so formidable as he had tried to make out. As she made a move forward, his hand dropped from the door. Passing him, she waited while he preceded her into the beautiful long hall, floored with black and white flagstones and furnished with gleaming antiques. The walls were hung with armour and a couple of large ornately-framed oil-paintings. Opposite the elegant oak staircase, which curved up to a landing, the man opened a door.

'In here then,' he said, motioning her with a jerk of his head.

She entered a fawn-carpeted drawing-room filled with more beautiful period objects - she noted immediately a walnut bureau, two lovely matching later eighteenth-century tables against the wall, a jardinière, abundant lamps of differing shapes and colours, and heavy damask curtains of a rich red colour with pelmet to match. The chintzed sofa and armchairs, toned with the curtains, looked well-used and comfortable, and on the walls were more impressive-looking pictures one of which, a portrait of a lady in a large feathery hat, looked like a Gainsborough. She sat in one of the armchairs.

Silence resettled. Surely a man of this taste and importance couldn't be the sort of villain she had imagined, but the chances of his seeing her had to be minimal, she thought. The servant, if that was what he was - from his rudeness she suspected he might be rather more - would reappear to tell her so. She shouldn't have mentioned Delia, used some stratagem. Neither should she have used her own name. It was possible Murdoch knew it. As far as she knew her name hadn't been in the papers, but Delia could have mentioned it to him. What would she - could she - do if the man returned to show her out?

She waited ten minutes, twenty. She contemplated a preemptive foray round the house to find Murdoch. She was on the point of doing this when there were leisurely footsteps and the door opened. A small chubby man appeared with a large pink head, wearing a creased greenish light suit and double-lens glasses, resembling Evelyn Waugh in a bad mood. As the man had done at the front door, he stood in the doorway, confronting her, looking extremely disagreeable. She saw the likeness to Delia at once.

'Who the hell are you, and what do you mean by barging in on me like this?'

She had risen. 'My name's Jocelyn Hammond. I'm a friend of Henry Bordeaux. I've come here to ask you some questions.'

She thought an interest showed momentarily. 'Questions? What nonsense is this? Are you a lawyer?'

'Perhaps if we could both sit down and if the door could be closed . . .

'You've really got a nerve. I've more than half a mind to chuck you out.'

Nevertheless he came into the room, put his hands in his pockets, and threw himself sulkily into the corner of the sofa like a schoolboy. He didn't shut the door. Amazing herself at the strong resolution and clarity she felt, she advanced to the door herself to repair the omission. She wasn't having the multicolour waistcoat overhear. She returned to her seat. She had decided before that she would start with the problem of the estate, and plunged to the heart of the matter without preliminary. She thought her voice sounded calm.

'You, or your lawyer, have heard from Henry's lawyer, I believe?' He didn't answer. 'I understand you have, and I'm sure you're aware that a husband does have the same rights upon a deceased wife's property as the other way round. I'd've thought it was obvious that a lawsuit would profit no one except the lawyers.'

'I'm aware of no such thing. What I am aware of is that my sister has left me her property and that I'm selling it. The money was originally my father's. It, and any interest it may have earned in terms of capital appreciation, belongs to my family. That's the end of it. I've instructed my solicitor on the matter, and he has already contacted a house agent.'

'I think you'll find things won't be quite as easy as that. You've inherited the estate - that much is clear. But even if it isn't your wish, you'll be forced to yield a large proportion of its worth to your brother-in-law, who has been responsible for making it such a beautiful and profitable place. You'd be obliged to do this anyway, even if there hadn't been these enormous improvements and even if a very sizeable commercial goodwill was not involved as well as the property, no part of which might be adjudged to be yours.'

His hostility, perhaps reined by an initial uncertainty or curiosity, broke through with full force. 'Who are you?' he said.

'It really doesn't matter who I am. Enough to say I'm a friend of Henry's.'

'I know who you are, you're that woman he employed. Delia mentioned you now I think of it, *and* told me what you've been up to.' His face shrivelled into a sneer. 'So I see, I see why *you're* interested. Bad luck Delia arranging things as she has, isn't it? You thought you'd made yourself a comfortable future by, first, wheedling a flat on the premises, then setting to work to vamp Delia's husband. And now, poof, it turns out the man's a murderer, you're his accomplice, and the estate's gone. Hammond - that's your name, of course. You're wasting your time here.

'Am I? We'll see about that, or Henry's lawyer will. I think you'll find you'll get a much better deal if you accept the settlement which is being offered. However, that isn't principally what I've come about, which - you're right - isn't directly any of my business. What I've come about is something a great deal more serious. I notice with interest that you own to having spoken to your sister recently.'

'"Own", what do you mean? Of course I've spoken to my sister. Why shouldn't I have done?'

'You hadn't done for some years, I gather from Henry.' He continued to stare at her with patent hostility. 'But you did very recently, on a single occasion, right?'

'What if I did? Of what possible relevance is this to you?'

'Of considerable relevance, a relevance which will certainly also interest the police.'

He remained impassive but something surely had glinted in his eyes? Fear, could it possibly be fear? 'I haven't the slightest idea what you're driving at,' he said.

'I believe you do. You know for sure, judging from what you've just said, what has happened. You know that Henry has been accused of murdering Delia by means of poison and has been arrested.'

'I certainly do. I read newspapers.'

'Then I have to put a simple question to you. Why haven't you contacted the police about that phone call Delia made to you, only a few days before she died?'

'Why should I?'

'Because it has an obvious bearing on the case which is being brought against Henry.'

'Has it?'

'You know it has.'

He lifted his chin, his jaw twitched, and a smirk momentarily replaced the scowl. 'It certainly has,' he said. 'This is the first sensible thing you've said. If the police know what Delia said to me it will be even clearer that she was poisoned by Bordeaux.'

'What did she say to you?'

'I've no reason to tell you, but since you ask, and since you talk about informing the police, I will. I'll tell you exactly. The police will indeed be very interested to hear what Delia said to me. You're right, she did phone me - a week before she died. She phoned me to say you and Henry were having an affair and that she feared Henry was going to kill her so he could marry you. She told me she didn't care, that she no longer wished to persist with life in these circumstances. She told me she was going to change her will in my favour, that if her husband was going to behave in this filthy despicable way she was at least going to deny Henry the estate.'

'Which you happily connived in.'

'Not at all. That is to say, let me correct that. In one sense - not the one you're implying - I did unwittingly connive. I didn't believe the accusation she was making. It wasn't the first time she'd complained to me about Henry's lack of attention, one way and another. In the early days of her affliction she used to do it frequently, and I'm afraid to the point of tedium. You aren't the first woman he's looked at, you know. But going on past experience of Delia's tantrums, as before I didn't take any notice.

What Delia craved for of course was attention. I imagined that was all she was up to again. I had no idea that this time the accusation she was making was true. Yes, do by all means go ahead and inform the police about Delia's call. I'm indeed surprised they haven't contacted me on the subject before. The call must be recorded on Delia's telephone account. I daresay you may also find yourself being arrested as an accomplice if all this gets out. I'm only surprised from what Delia told me you haven't been already.'

Jocelyn felt her stomach had disappeared, but she also now had the strongest intuition that the man was lying. What was it - a sudden rhetorical irony and an overelaboration in his speech, which had replaced the defensive venom? She summoned all her strength. She was aware again of the possible consequences of what she would say, but a kind of recklessness came upon her. If he was innocent, he would laugh her out of the place, she thought. Well, let him. And if her shot in the dark hit its target she wouldn't at this moment consider what he might do to her. She strove to keep her outward appearance calm.

'You aren't telling the truth,' she said. 'Delia didn't phone you for the reason you're saying. It's quite possible she told you that Henry was having an affair with me - though this is totally untrue she'd made the same accusation to my face right back in the spring, quite a short time after I started the job. But she didn't tell you she feared Henry would kill her. She phoned to tell you she'd had enough of her appalling existence and that she wanted to take her own life. She asked you to deliver to her the means of doing so. I don't of course know exactly what you said to each other, but a good guess is that either Delia said she was going to change her will and leave the estate to you, or you made it a condition of your cooperation. It hardly matters which it was. Either suited Delia as a last way of hurting the man who had cared for her so devotedly all those years. She'd obviously decided to make it look as probable as she could that Henry had killed her.

'You then delivered the poison, hydrocyanic acid, and she set about changing her will, which she completed on the very day she died. All *this* is why you haven't contacted the police about the call. You were not going to go anywhere near the police if they didn't contact you. If they did interview you, you were going to tell them the lies you've just told me, and no doubt pretend you'd been protecting Henry by your silence.'

He had thyroid frog eyes. They and the whole of his squat body seemed to bulge larger. 'This is total, laughable rubbish, whose pathetically naive motive is plain.'

'Is it? I ask myself why then, if what I say is rubbish, you visited Combe, which you hadn't done for years, just days before Delia died, and after the phone call.'

He gaped at her. 'Of course I did no such thing.'

'I'm afraid I saw you with my own eyes. That's why I'm here.'

She watched him. He wasn't a good actor. She saw the fear, yes quite definitely now the fear which leapt, the flush that ignited his cheeks. 'You must be mad.'

'You said just now you knew what my motives are. I'm afraid you're entirely wrong about them, too. Quite apart from the fact that there's never been anything between Henry and me, you won't know something else about me. You won't know that I don't sleep too well, and that when I can't sleep, sometimes in the summer I walk, as I was walking that night. I now realise I saw you leaving the house, in the way I guess you'd arranged with Delia.'

'You're quite demented. I haven't been near the place for years.'

'Deny it as you will, I'm prepared to swear on oath that you did. It will be your word against mine. I wonder which of us a jury would believe?'

There was a silence. Until this moment she had kept her nerve. Suddenly it began to waver. She was convinced her bluff had at least partially worked. If her guess hadn't been right in every detail, it was right enough. She thought of that sinister servant or whatever he was lurking outside. She thought of running for it, but at once abandoned the idea. Somehow she had to get hold of herself again and play it to the end.

She had made him think, she saw. He was doing his best to compose a sour whimsical amusement to cover what must be his racing thoughts. He gave a sniff which was nearer a snarl. 'So you saw me creeping about Delia's place in the dead of night, did you? Then why have you done nothing until this moment, I ask myself? Why haven't *you* told the police? Why *haven't* the police been here to interview me? And now Henry's where he should be - in gaol - why hasn't he told the police to save his own neck?'

She collected herself for the final lie. She had foreseen that if she got this far this is what he would ask. 'I'll tell you. On the night I saw the male figure, which I didn't know then of course was you, I went into the house immediately afterwards to wake Henry, thinking, as he did, that the man I'd seen was a burglar. Though nothing was stolen, we continued to think it must have been a burglar, disturbed perhaps by my presence in the garden. I went on thinking this until the morning of Delia's death. Henry and I both knew Delia knew nobody locally who could have supplied the stuff. It was then I had the thought that you were the one person who might have a motive for delivering poison to Delia, and that the figure I'd seen that night could have been you. I'd had a good view. I began to question Henry about your appearance. He was too shocked to answer properly, but what he said was enough to make me wonder. He said you were short and tubby, those were his words.'

'So, if this is so, why didn't Henry immediately tell the police?'

'I've told you, Henry was traumatically shocked by Delia's death and was already, that morning, developing a deep fatalism. He wouldn't entertain the idea you were involved and wouldn't allow me to pursue my theory. I tried to persuade him that he should tell the police, so they would investigate, but he refused. I thought when they arrested him and was refused bail he'd say. Apparently he hasn't. It seems now that if needs be he's prepared to go to prison and leave things as they are. It's this which has impelled me to act. OK, I have an axe to grind, my job's on the line, so are those of my colleagues, but that isn't my principle motive in coming up here. My motive is that, apart from caring about what happens to Henry, I'm just not prepared to allow a terrible injustice of this order, especially as now, having seen you, I'm as sure as I can be that you are the person I saw in that garden. I am totally determined not to let you get away with this.'

'With Henry's undying gratitude to come to you I've no doubt.'

'Henry doesn't know I'm here, nor if you behave in your own interest ever will he.'

'Oh, it's nobility of that order, is it? And I suppose you're going to tell me his lawyer doesn't know, either. In your single-handed Florence Nightingale act you have not thought to bring him in to your little fiction? One can understand why of course. A lawyer would scarcely countenance it for a second.'

'I was going to tell Henry's lawyer yesterday when he called, but I didn't because a much better idea occurred to me, which a lawyer couldn't possibly be a party to, certainly not a lawyer like Potter. It occurred to me that you and I could do a very satisfactory private deal. What it amounts to is, in a sentence, this. We do a deal, now, or I go to the police tomorrow.'

He gave a grotesque sneering giggle. 'A deal now is it I'm being offered?'

'Though you gave Delia the means to kill herself, it could just be considered a mercy to herself, and in the longer run to Henry, that she died. Henry and I were never having an affair, but Delia's agony, in addition to what she already suffered, was that she imagined we were. If it hadn't been me she fixed upon, it would have been someone else. As you have hinted, I was probably not the first object of her imagination. I have thought about this long and hard. I consider that what you did, in view of the fact that it has rewarded you so handsomely, is despicable. But I have to say that if your act were to go unmarked it wouldn't, viewed in the way I suggest, be such a crime to allow it to do so. I'm proposing two things. First that tonight you phone the police and tell them you've only just heard that Henry has been charged with Delia's murder. You'll tell them about Delia's phone call. You'll say she told you she'd had enough and intended to take her own life in a way she didn't specify. She also told you she was going to change her will and leave you the estate to punish Henry for the affair she imagined he was having with me. You can say what you like about your own reaction to the call - and no doubt to the action you'll say you didn't take afterwards - but these points you must precisely say. Second, you must agree to a deal on the estate. You'll agree the estate won't be sold - which would be a gross injustice to Henry - but that you will accept the offer which has been made to you - cash consisting of half its value, as a property not a business, and fixed by an independent assessor agreed by both parties. The latter, in my view, is a great deal more than you deserve.'

'You're totally crazy.'

She rose. 'You take it or leave it. I'll give you until midday tomorrow to contact the police, the day after tomorrow for your instructions to your lawyer to reach Henry's lawyer concerning the estate. If either doesn't happen I'll go to the police. If both do happen I shall play no further part. I shall not even tell Henry I've been here, ever.' She rummaged in her handbag, drew out a card, and threw it on the small table. 'You won't need that, but there it is in case you should need to communicate further.'

She paused, to give as much drama to her parthian shot as she could muster. 'There's a final point. As you no doubt know, it was hydrocyanic acid which killed Delia. It's interesting, isn't it, that this substance is used in the refinement of gold, the very activity of one of the companies of which you are a director. I understand it is a chemical extremely difficult for the ordinary citizen to acquire. I'm sure this is a detail which will especially intrigue the police.'

He also rose. She had a last thought that he might attack her. But he did nothing of the sort. 'Get out of here, you silly lying bitch,' he said. 'Get out before I screw you.'

He turned, and made towards the door, wrenching it open. She heard his heels on the uncarpeted tiles of the hall, then a slammed door beyond. Thankfully, she noted that Waistcoat didn't seem to be in the offing. She hurried across the hall and escaped, leaving both front doors open in her haste.

18.

When Jocelyn left Patrick Murdoch's house she drove as fast as the traffic allowed. Her one idea was to distance herself from the place. She didn't realise how exhausted she was until she had driven several miles and saw the blue motorway sign looming. She had eaten nothing since a scanty breakfast before starting and couldn't face the long stretch of unravelling concrete which lay ahead. Half a mile ahead she could see a posh-looking modern multi-storey hotel she had noticed on the way up. She turned away from the motorway and made for it.

In the lift coming up from the toilet on the basement floor she saw food advertised in what seemed a round-the-clock bar-restaurant. No doubt it would cost a fortune, but she decided she must eat. With food in her stomach she would recover her strength. She sat at one of the bar seats, ordered a glass of lager, then from the glossy plastic menu chose 'lasagne special.'

She realised not only how exhausted she was, but also how low in spirits. She might have felt elated that her visit had gone off as well as it had. She had been certain Murdoch was lying, and still was. She was as sure as it was possible to be that he had been concealing something. But it was a mad impulsive expedition she had undertaken. If Murdoch had been responsible for the poison, he could very easily have used someone else to deliver the stuff, and if he had done it himself it might not have been at night - in either of which cases he would know her remarks about recognising him were patent nonsense, and therefore that her ultimatum was worthless. The most likely outcome of her ill-advised venture was either that he would continue to do nothing, or that he *would* phone the police, but not to clear Henry in the way she had demanded. He would tell the same story he had told her. He would say the reason Delia had telephoned him was to tell him her suspicions that she and Henry were plotting to kill her. By her rash intervention she had quite possibly sealed Henry's fate. The prosecution would pounce on Murdoch's evidence. How would her pathetic last-ditch attempt to rescue Henry appear but as the last throw of his despairing lover? She herself could be on an accessory to murder charge.

She forced herself to stop conjecturing, but this was only to drift into further gloomy thoughts about her life in general. She was again assaulted by the idea that there must be something in her own nature which predetermined her involvement in disasters. It couldn't just be bad luck. Perhaps her problem all along had been chronic naivety, she thought. Life had seemed so easy after the death of her parents in Ely. She had imagined she had only to reach out to grasp happiness. With how much greater blindness had she believed this after meeting Leo and going to Venice with him. For those years before Sally was born it seemed the belief had become reality. But all along she had been *constructing* her content with her mind, closing her eyes to emotional reality. She had been making the most elementary mistake of all of thinking that, if you thought something strongly enough and people seemed to concur, they were thinking in the same way as yourself. If she hadn't been so self-deluded, wouldn't she have seen that Leo was not as he seemed, that he was not at all, like herself, an independent spirit, but a man enchained by an unhealthy ambition to compete with this successful brother he never saw? Surely, if she had looked, she would have found the evidence? She even questioned her own independence. Could one use that word about someone so innocent and gullible? And now, here she was again, not blinded by love this time it was true, but still deeply involving herself in the affairs of a man she hardly knew.

'Your lasagna all right, madam?' The chef behind the counter, who wore the full absurd regalia - white overalls, apron, tall hat and all - was regarding her. She thought it wasn't the lasagna he was asking her about. Did the palor of defeat and disillusion show on her face so obviously?

'Oh fine, thanks, fine.'

To escape his watchful eye, she ordered an ice-cream and made an effort to pull herself out of her maudlin reverie. She forced herself to think practically. By the time she was back on the motorway she had made a decision. If nothing happened tomorrow, she would go to Potter and tell him everything, let him make of it what he would. As for what happened next, like Henry she would tell the truth and just accept her fate. She understood his state of resignation a lot better now. There is a point surely when the energetic struggle against injustice becomes undignified. Let others examine their consciences. Perhaps that had been her problem all along - she had been too aware of other people. She would borrow a leaf out of Sally's book.

She was thankful to find when she got back that Edith and the others had gone home. Edith had left a note through her front door, saying she had made her a mini steak and kidney pie in case she was hungry. All she had to do was stick it in the Aga. The veg were all ready to cook, too. She was grateful, but didn't feel like it. She had a stiff gin and went to bed early.

The next day was busy. Betty was still away and the phone rang constantly. As well, there was two days' mail to see to. She was glad of this. Edith came in to castigate her for not eating the food and obviously hoping for a chat. She hadn't told Edith yet Potter's bad news about bail. The busy phone gave her her excuse for continued silence. She thanked Edith for her kindness last night, explaining how tired she had felt, escaped from her questions about Sally's 'problem' with a minimum of deception, and got on with the work.

But active as she was, she worked only on the circumference of her mind. She was waiting for the one call which would release her from agony. Would it be from the police if it came, from Potter, from Henry himself? She envisaged the effect of none of these people calling, the lengthening period of silence. She foresaw the arrival of the police car, Detective Inspector Becket at the front door, the once uncertain look on his face, which she had induced with the truth, replaced by a sardonic certainty in his own false conclusions.

Lunch time came. She would have liked to take her food to the office, pleading Betty's absence and the need to be by the phone. She couldn't raise the energy to make the excuse. In the kitchen Geoff came in, also Brenda May. She decided she must tell them Henry had been refused bail. They were appalled. At least their indignation made the running as far as conversation was concerned. The police were harangued by all of them in turn for their unjust behaviour. She took refuge from their questioning in repeating Potter's ritual optimism. She was sure it would be all right in the end. It gave her no pleasure that they seemed to look to her these days. Why should they, she thought irritably? They had all been here a lot longer than she had.

During the afternoon she had two groups to take round. She had to ask Edith to listen for the phone and take messages. She was most of the way round with the second lot when Delia's bell went. She had arranged with Edith to use this signal to summon her if anything important came up. She apologised to the group, explaining they were short-staffed today, and ran out from the dahlia beds where they were admiring the massive woolly blooms, to be in view of the house. Edith was on the Italian terrace, gesticulating. She began to run up the path towards her.

'It was the lawyer, Mr Potter,' Edith said. 'He wouldn't wait but wants you to call him at this number immediately.' She handed her a slip of paper. 'Is it good news, do you think?'

'How did he sound?'

'Couldn't say. He wasn't giving anything away.'

She went into the office, sat for a moment to recover her breath, then dialled the number, which wasn't Potter's office. Someone else, a woman, answered. 'Oh yes,' she said when she asked for Potter, and put down the phone. There was quite a long pause. She could hear Potter's voice in the background, talking to someone else. Surely it was going to be bad news, why would there be the smallest delay if it were otherwise? The talk stopped and there were two or three heavy footsteps.

'Mrs Hammond? Glad I've got you. Sorry if I've called you in from the garden, but I've just had a message from my office. I'm in a client's house. Are you alone?'

'Yes.'

'Well, it sounds as if I've one item of good news to report to you. It appears on the estate issue my arguments have been persuasive after all. Murdoch's lawyer, McAlpine, called mid-morning, and it seems Murdoch has bowed to reason. He's going to settle, I gather from my secretary, roughly on the terms I proposed. We'll have to wait for it on paper, but it was good of McAlpine to give us prior notice like this. It *isn't* of course the main thing, as we both know, but I thought it'd cheer you all up at Combe to know this. It'll no doubt also put Henry in better spirits. I'll be informing him as soon as they'll allow me to.'

She wanted to detain Potter, question him further. Had this lawyer said anything else? But he was in a hurry to go. 'Just thought I'd let you know at once,' he repeated. 'I must say, it's most gratifying when on rare occasions good legal sense is acknowledged,' he finished. 'Goodbye.' The line went dead.

Her instant reaction had been to exult. If Murdoch had complied on this, surely he must also have phoned the police about Delia's phone call? Her huge bluff had, unbelievably, worked. A moment's reflection destroyed her joy. How was this likely? If Murdoch had given way on the estate, there was only one reason. He was doing so to destroy any accusation which might be made against him of having desired Delia's death for his own profit. Here he was, it would be alleged, embarrassed by the legacy from his unfortunate and deranged sister, doing the decent thing out of guilt at not taking her call seriously. But on the charge against Henry he was digging in.

Jocelyn could not imagine his mere appearance in the witness box would inspire any more confidence in the jury than it had inspired in her, but this deed of generosity of his, and what Murdoch would, under questioning, with false reluctance convey about Delia's telephone call - these would weigh. She returned to the group with these thoughts swirling. It was difficult to keep her mind on the job for the remainder of their visit.

The reaction of Edith and Geoff, whom she immediately told, was typical, she thought. They didn't know for sure about the contents of Delia's will - she didn't think Henry had said anything. But they must have guessed, knowing Delia owned the place. This news could mean their jobs and income might after all be secure. But not for a moment did they consider this, they were both at once as disappointed as she was. Henry hadn't been bailed. This was what weighed with them.

They went home, she shut the place up and went to her flat. To give herself something to do, she decided to repair a couple of plates she had broken. She had just got one glued and held by an elastic band and was propping it delicately in a tray of sand purloined from the greenhouses, when she heard a step on the iron staircase which led to her front door. Startled, she let the plate fall back in the sand and fled to the window. It was Henry.

She opened the door before he got to it. He stopped one step down from the top, holding the rail with one hand and in the other carrying the small suitcase he had taken when he was arrested. He was looking up at her, grinning. 'Sorry, Joss, a bit of a shock probably. I should have phoned. But I'm in a state of something near shock myself and couldn't get home quick enough. I still can't believe it. I feel I must have escaped.'

It was almost a similar feeling she had - that she must get him inside quickly, that someone would be on his heels. She actually glanced across the empty car park to the entrance drive where it curved away into the rhododendrons, expecting a police car.

'You've got bail? Potter didn't say anything.'

'I don't think Peter knows yet. No, not bail. It seems I'm released altogether.'

'You mean they've dropped the charge?'

'I can't believe it, but it seems so.'

She withdrew a little for him to enter, and as he put down the case, sat himself on the minute settee, and glanced towards the bottle on her sideboard she couldn't fail to recall the last time he had done precisely this on the evening of Delia's death. Beneath a warning stricture she was already giving herself, a bright beam of triumphant hope was dawning. Without prompting this time, and to give herself time, she went for the whisky bottle and the glass. She topped the drink with water remembering this was the way he liked it.

'It appears you were partially right,' Henry said, as she handed him the glass. 'Murdoch has been involved. He delivered no poison - we still don't know who did. But it appears he did speak to Delia days before she died. She phoned him to say she was going to take her own life and that she was going to leave him the estate. It appears he didn't take the call seriously. Delia had made melodramatic statements to him in the past. He did nothing about it. I suppose what then happened really shook him, which probably accounts for the emotional instructions he gave to his lawyer about the estate. But then he must have heard about my arrest. He phoned the police yesterday evening apparently. They've been to see him and checked his statement. His evidence lets me off the hook. The charge is dropped. I'm told the coroner will hear the case again and now almost certainly accept suicide. They're saying Delia could have had that poison for years. I don't believe it. I still think she got it somehow much more recently. But it's now hardly relevant.'

Jocelyn strove to control her triumph. She must not let him see, she must not ever by the smallest implication let him gain an inkling that her feelings were an inch more than just relief and happiness for him.

'Thank God,' was all she could manage, as she filled her own glass. In a little while she told him about Murdoch's change of mind over the estate, which he didn't know about.

'I must say it's strange,' Henry said when he had absorbed this. 'Murdoch behaving in this way. I have to change my mind about him somewhat. He could easily have left me in the lurch about Delia's telephone call. I'd probably be facing years in gaol if he hadn't owned up. And now he's done the decent thing over the estate. The man must be human after all. I've no wish to see him again, but I shall have to write and thank him.'

She let it rest here. The letter would prove to Murdoch that she had kept her promise not to tell Henry about her visit. In a little while she set about a meal, the first, she was aware peripherally, she had cooked for him on her own ground. Was he also thinking this, and did they both make tacit provisos on the subject? She certainly did. She remained his employee, she told herself, and that was how it would go on.

A single consideration remained that night when he had gone - that she would be able to keep her coup secret. That she must do so she was absolutely sure. There were a great deal too many nasty worms in the can if it were ever opened, not the least of them being her uncertainty about how Henry would view the act of perjury on her part which had saved him.

PART 2.

19.

It was early November. The season had been extended to accommodate several groups who had responded to an initiative Jocelyn had begun in the middle of the summer. She'd had a single sheet printed and distributed featuring a good photograph of the garden taken in autumn. There had been a surprising response. But now this, too, was over, and as the promotion work had dwindled and was occupying less than a quarter of her time, Jocelyn was more than happy to don trousers and wellingtons and join Geoff and Henry in the huge amount of clearing up.

Geoff and Henry were busy together at the bottom of the garden removing a thicket of bramble, brushwood and small trees which had got a hold in what they called The Spinney, an area which bordered the estuary. The idea was to create a winding path through a new rock garden, which would be planted with coastal flowers. They had a large bonfire going to dispose of the cleared material. Jocelyn was dealing with fallen leaves on the lawns and paths. If they were allowed to stay they would moulder and make later collection more difficult. For clearing the lawns Henry had designed his own push cart with revolving scoops that spun the leaves into a large canvas bag. It worked also on the level paths, but the steeper ones and the many steps had to be swept and collected by hand. Near the greenhouses was a huge compost pen into which the leaves could be fed. Working further down the garden, it was unnecessary labour to make the journey to it each time. Geoff had constructed two other hidden compost pens for her, one half-way down and one at the bottom.

October had been wet and windy, but they were in the middle of a surprisingly mild spell. Late in the afternoon when she had just finished clearing the last of the leaves, she sat down on the bench by one of the bridges over the stream. The smell of the still smouldering fire below hung pleasantly on the air. She had worked all day, but felt fit - healthier than she had been for a long while. Through the afternoon she had heard the angry noise of the petrol saw echoing through the trees below. While she was sitting, it stopped abruptly. The light was fading fast, probably the two men were knocking off, too. She thought she would wait for them to come up. Now the clocks had gone back they usually had a cup of tea together indoors at this time. Neither appeared, but as she was about to get up to put her tools away she saw Henry emerging alone from the trees below. He saw her and waved. She waved back.

It pleased her to see the energetic way he came up the path. In the last weeks he had been a different man. He had always been highly active, but he seemed to have acquired even greater vigour since Delia's death and his release from arrest. He threw himself heartily on to the seat beside her, like a young man, his lumberjack shirt open almost to the navel.

'We've almost finished the clearing,' he said. 'Tomorrow we can start on the landscaping. The boulders, and the small shingle for the path we're making, should arrive by barge from Dartmouth in the morning. Then we'll have the nice part, the planting. I've found a place up on the north coast that specialises in the kind of stuff we'll want. We'll go up together one day soon if you'd like to come, maybe next week-end.'

'Love to. Though I won't be much use. I'd hardly know sea-wrack from sea-anemone.'

'That's two names for a start.'

'I'm showing off. We used to go to Cromer when Sally was young. One of her hobbies was collecting flowers for pressing. They're the only two I remember.'

He smiled, and looked around appreciatively. 'I say, Joss. You've really got the autumn under control. We've never been so clear of leaves at this time. You've worked like a trojan. Is there anything you can't do?'

'I love the work.'

'I'm so glad. You know, when you first came I did wonder if you'd cope with the physical side.'

'You made that rather clear.'

'Did I really? I suppose there's a category for that sort of male assumption.'

There was unexpectedly a situation. She had seen Geoff putting the tools away in the bottom shed and assumed he would join them. She saw him now mounting the path on the far side towards the greenhouses. In a few moments he disappeared behind the rhododendrons. They were alone in the rapidly darkening gloom. Henry leaned forward slowly, putting his elbows on his knees reflectively.

'You know, Jocelyn, don't you?' he said in quite a different voice, and not looking at her. 'I expect you've known from quite early on, maybe before I did - or before I was able to admit it to myself. Am I right?'

'Know?'

'That, from my point of view, Delia was right. I was attracted to you right away, when you first came down here to see me. I knew that. But it wasn't until I was sitting in that police cell contemplating my navel that I fully came to understand my feelings for you - that I came to realise you're the most wonderful person I've ever met - that I'm in love with you.'

Did she know? Her lack of surprise indicated she did in some way. But that didn't prevent an instantaneous ignition of excitement and joy. She looked away to hide the look which must have leapt to her face. She looked up at the dark house in which no lights shone on this side. Could this be her home, this garden hers too, to share? This was her first involuntary thought - of which she was immediately ashamed. How could she put before her feelings for Henry, whatever they were, a purely material consideration?

'What you say makes me feel deeply happy,' she said after a moment.

'You did know then?'

'I thought you found me a bit attractive, yes. I found you attractive on that first evening, too. But no - I didn't think you felt as strongly as this.'

'I know what the textbook says. That I'm on the rebound, that I'm relieved - yes, I'll say it, it's what I feel - relieved that Delia has gone and that I'm a free man again, that I'm snatching at the first lovely woman who comes along. But it's not like that, not at all. Of course I've looked at other women. There was one not so long ago, who thought she was going to rescue me from my predicament - which was for a time flattering. But I never felt anything like this with her, and we didn't have an affair, nor did I have one with anyone else. You're so - sincere. You don't lie to yourself, and that's quite a rare quality, you know. It makes me a little apprehensive even. I know when you give me your answer, it'll be an entirely truthful one. All I can say, Jocelyn, is that if you have any percentage of the feelings for me which I have for you I shall, well' - he gave a little laugh - ' think I made a rather good appointment.'

Her joy swelled. It was not what you would call the most romantic of declarations. He had not, in textbook fashion, swept her into his arms and kissed her. He had, she knew, a certain rather dogged methodicalness - maybe long years of looking after Delia had conditioned him to putting mental processes before emotion. But he was no stereotype, and when he said something important, as he had now, she knew he meant it with all the force of his strong character. She was moved to depths she had forgotten were there.

And yet - what was the matter with her? - at the same time she felt a restraint. Had he planned this? Not the time and the place, which had been more her doing than his. But she thought he probably had planned it, even the words. She hated herself for doing so but she couldn't help thinking of that day in Ely, the way Leo had danced into her life, the entire *thoughtlessness* of it. How could she compare this entirely wonderful man, in any respect, with Leo? And yet when the light sprang on in the greenhouses high above them as Geoffrey reached them, warm and light-hearted as she felt, it seemed like a reprieve. She rose, and when he did the same took his arm in both of hers.

'You've made me feel immensely happy,' she repeated. 'So has this place - and the work, everything. I think I feel happier than I have for many years.'

There was a silence after this. She knew he was hoping she would say more. But she sensed he realised she couldn't for the moment go further. After a few moments he straightened. 'Shall we go up and have some tea?' he said.

As they mounted the steep path, she still held his arm He put his hand on hers. From a distance, to a stranger, they might appear like a vintage married couple, she thought.

In a curious way it seemed she almost filed what Henry had said to her. Or it was like an unopened birthday present, still wrapped, to be kept for the day? As she set about her usual evening routine, she chided herself for this. To Henry, she doubted if her behaviour was at all strange. In his estimate, a man proposed, a woman disposed. A delay in her answer was therefore to be expected, even proper - especially in their circumstances. To her it was, well, chideable. Shouldn't one, by all her own canons, know such things at once?

Why was she being so much less than spontaneous? Was it, she thought, because 'the proposal' was - in a certain way, now that it had happened, certainly in the eyes of others, predictable? She imagined how Edith would take the news, if news it turned out to be - surely in the 'I-always-knew-it' category, accompanied of course by warmth, the best of best wishes, 'Henry's a very lucky man,' etcetera. She could envisage with even greater certainty how Sally would react, as she had over Delia's death and its unpleasant aftermath - all to be expected, given the situation. 'It was written all over the walls, Mum,' she would write, 'you were the only person who couldn't see it coming.' Was this why she was behaving like this? Was it sheer obstinacy?

Or was it in some way her secret about Patrick Murdoch that was making her drive with the brakes on? She had doubly decided she would never tell Henry what she had done. What would be the point? Every day that passed it seemed more likely the incident was closed. Convinced by Murdoch's reluctant but effective evidence at the inquest - Murdoch had not looked at any of them in the eye during the hearing and disappeared immediately afterwards - the coroner had pronounced Delia's death to have been suicide. The estate had already been valued, and on the back of the past summer's figures the bank had been more than eager to make the loan to pay Murdoch his legacy, on the security of the property. Combe was now, but for the mortgage, Henry's - a triumph for which Potter was taking all the bows and, no doubt, a handsome amount of cash for his pains. Why raise the matter again, when it could have incalculable consequences? But could it be this lack of frankness which was somehow inhibiting her? He had said she was truthful. She had a rash impulse to tell Henry after all, but quickly disposed of it. It was as unnecessary to tell him now as it ever was, and no, she couldn't really think her encounter with Murdoch was the cause of her reticence.

Her main concern that evening was that she had been churlish. She knew it had been on the tip of Henry's tongue to suggest they ate dinner together in the house. A moment of lingering on her part as they walked up would have been sufficient to release the invitation. She hadn't lingered. After tea with the Applecotes in the kitchen, the three of them did some work together in the greenhouses, and at five-thirty she slipped away to her flat when Henry was talking to Geoff at the other end of the building. She hoped he would pursue her to the flat. She knew he wouldn't. Their habit of principled care on this matter would continue to prevail until she signalled its demise.

It was partly to repair this, the next morning when they were alone together in the office for a few seconds, that she asked him if he was going to the nursery on Saturday and whether he did want to her to come. Betty was in the offing, she was on her way back from the kitchen where she had been changing the water of a vase of chrysanthemums. He didn't need to answer. His radiant smile made her feel guilty again. He would fix it at once, he said. Could she be thought to be playing cat and mouse? She abominated that idea.

She spent the remainder of the week in a rage of thoughts she had no power to calm. She knew that raising herself the matter of the nursery was tantamount to saying that by Saturday he would have her answer. Did it also mean her answer would be yes? All day and for a good deal of the nights she was both defence and prosecution in a furious almost non-stop debate - like the hare playing himself at tennis in the old cartoon, she thought grimly. It was her life with Leo, she kept telling herself, which was making her question what was surely obvious - the habit of doubt and restraint she had been obliged to adopt all those years. Wasn't this now totally unnecessary? Apart from those first idyllic years with Leo, had she ever before felt so happy and relaxed? How could she equivocate like this? If Henry had freed himself from a psychological shackle which was surely far weightier than hers, why couldn't she?

It seemed she heard everybody's voice on the subject except her own. She heard Ken's measured Inns-of-Court tone replying to a request from herself for advice. 'Well, Jocelyn, you've obviously got to know each other very well after what you've both been through together. He's a thoroughly nice man. It was obvious to us he was very fond of you when we came down that time.' She heard what Ken wouldn't say but would think. 'And it does very neatly solve your little problem in another direction, doesn't it? Married, Leo will never dare pursue you.' She heard Sally's verdict, leaving aside the I-told-you-so which, whether spoken in words or not, would lurk in the tone. 'If you want to remarry, at your age you're not probably going to do any better now, are you? I'd grab it.' She heard also Edith's warm, home-baked encouragements, already listing the wedding meats.

By Friday she was no nearer a decision. She was terrified she would say yes because she couldn't think why not. Worse, she thought she might not say anything at all but just fall into his arms and let that decide. Would she wake up in his bed and then know? What sort of a situation would that be if she found then she didn't want to marry him? What was this kind of thinking - a medieval trial by love-making?

As if to show itself as indifferent and as little cooperative as possible, the weather changed and a gale blew all through Friday night. When she woke it was still raging, bending the trees, racing thick grey clouds across the sky, hurling bouts of rain against the windows. Would he decide not to go, she thought? If he abandoned the trip would she be relieved? Of only one thing she was sure - she *wasn't* sure what she would say to him. As if blown to her by the gale, a saying of Leo's came to her, a variation on the proverb 'if you have nothing to say, don't say it.' 'If you don't know, don't.' But she wouldn't have this. She was deeply fond of Henry Bordeaux, she argued. She would permit no glib aphorism to prompt her.

A look at Henry was enough to tell her he hadn't even thought of not going. They had agreed to get away at half past eight, before 'the troops came on parade', as he put it. She was glad she had dressed for it - a warm tartan skirt, woollen tights, and a new three-quarter length waxed coat for bad weather outside. They met in the hall. 'The north coast should be a sight in this westerly,' he said.

He was in the best of moods, full of the confidence which had no doubt won him his high military rank and which had prompted him to conceive of Combe. For a good deal of the way he talked about the plants they were going to buy. He had brought a catalogue which had a table of all the plants mentioned with information about colour, soil condition, flowering time and duration listed opposite each name in columns. As he drove, they selected names. She looked them up, read what it said and, if one looked a possibility, wrote it down with the catalogue number on a clipboard notepad he had prepared. She was pleased to note he didn't know much more about coastal and marine plants than she did. 'As far as I'm concerned it's new territory,' he confessed. Several times he asked her opinion about what they might buy. It would be so easy, she thought once, in this professional intimacy they had bred, to slip into almost an assumption of their union.

He had decided to take a devious but shorter route across Dartmoor rather than the obvious one skirting it on its eastern side, 'so she could see the moor in its winter mood.' Actually, the winter mood precluded panoramic views. Soon after leaving Ashburton, they seemed to be up in the clouds, and for most of the way were restricted to the sight of a hundred yards of sodden grass and heather on either side of the narrow road. She had to keep her nose glued to the map. At each small crossroads they slowed, lowered their windows, and craned their necks to look at the signposts. 'Sorry about this, Joss,' he said once. 'Bit of a boob. I should have been more sensible.' She caught herself being glad. Was it because of the distraction it offered, or because of a shared, slightly dangerous enterprise and the feeling of close proximity it induced?

The journey probably took a good deal longer despite the 'short cut.' It was after midday before they reached the coast and the shoreside nursery near Bideford. The manager knew they were coming but they hadn't fixed an exact time. On the gate hung a 'closed till 2 pm' sign. There was nothing to do but wait. They went into the town and found a pub. They were both hungry and thirsty. They had a pint each, and a huge plate of sandwiches scattered with cress and tomato slices was delivered to their table. They were surrounded by a festive group of men in suits who were apparently celebrating someone's birthday.

Then it was the nursery for two hours. A length of beach and the grassy area of dunes behind it had been converted into an attractive and unusual garden for a display of the plants in their natural habitat. Behind the dunes were less attractive plastic-covered tunnels. The man was knowledgeable and diligent. First, blown to bits in their waxed coats and wellingtons, they made a tour of the garden, Henry taking notes on the clipboard now covered with a sheet of plastic to keep the page dry. The wind was marginally less, but the rain had increased. Beside them huge Atlantic-size rollers rode in like lines of horsemen, arching into foaming crests which roared and crashed beachwards. A few gulls stood above them, mewing and beating their wings then, turning, soaring down in long sweeps from which they mounted again to battle with the wind. The warm salt air was heady. The wildness pleased Jocelyn. She remembered a winter day outing to the coast with her father.

They had a long session in the tunnels, which were lined on either side with row upon row of plastic boxes containing cuttings and seedlings. One tunnel contained the larger species in nine and twelve inch plastic pots. She admired the intent way Henry listened to the garrulous nurseryman, asking questions whenever he wasn't sure of something, and she was pleased when he frequently asked for her opinion. They reached a decision-making phase, and it was the salesman's turn to take notes of the long order.

Then they were alone again in the Range Rover whose boot and back seat were packed with as many of the smaller plants as they could carry, the rest would be delivered. She guessed what might be in his mind - a hotel to obviate the fatigue of a long journey in the dark. She was prepared to agree. She imagined drinks beside a large open fire, a discreet candle-lit dining-room, perhaps that rush of overwhelming tenderness she would feel which would at last put an end to her wavering. In fact they drove in silence for at least five miles until the heating in the car had reached the comfort mark and she had shed her coat.

'Have you been thinking, Joss?' he said suddenly, 'about us?'

'Yes, endlessly.'

'You're not sure.' She was immeasurably startled, and tongue-tied. 'I know I shouldn't probe and should let you take your time, but I have to ask just one thing. Is your - indecision - for that's what it is, isn't it? - something to do with your estimate of me, and your feelings for me, or is it otherwise?'

'Otherwise?'

'I don't know. It's probably grossly insensitive of me, probably arrogant - trying to find a reason for your feelings other than that they aren't sufficiently strong - certainly I'm being very impatient - but I've had the feeling, long before the other day when I told you I love you, that you are somehow . . . detained. Do you remember that conversation we had in my room after Delia had taken her life? We talked about the commitment of marriage, the psychological, perhaps even in some way the spiritual commitment we've both felt in our not entirely dissimilar situations - even when neither of us is religious in any formal sense, and even when by many people's standards that commitment might be thought to have legitimately expired. You remember that discussion?'

'Yes.'

'For me of course it's now become very simple, with Delia dying. For you perhaps it's less so. What I think I'm asking in a terribly convoluted roundabout way is whether Leo is somehow still in your thoughts?'

She felt at last an emotion, though the one she least expected, a tempest of unaccountable outrage. 'Of course not, I've divorced him.'

'I know, but . . .

'But what?'

His tone was tentative but his purpose resolute. 'Well, I suppose what I'm asking is whether you *have* divorced him - on all levels?'

She was overwhelmed with what could only be raging anger. 'Christ, for a Commando you're a bit lacking in dash, aren't you? What am I supposed to do, go on my knees all the way to Buckfast Abbey to convince you? No, whatever my feelings are, or aren't, they're nothing, *but nothing,* to do with Leo Cunningham. Leo is a weak conster, who fooled not only me but himself all his life and broke the vows we took by going off with another woman. You intimated once that if he ever dared to put himself in my vicinity again you'd do a rent-a-muscle act, remember?'

He was still gentle, but stood firm. 'Aren't you perhaps illustrating my point?'

'What the hell do you mean?'

'You're angry at my suggestion. Doesn't that suggest there's something in what I say?'

He was then silent, so was she. For long seconds they drove on down the empty dark road, the tyres swishing, her head turned away from him. She felt her pulses racing, like an engine out of control. *Why* was he so impossibly controlled and English, so maddeningly decent? How dare he suggest she had feelings of this kind? Why the hell didn't he just sweep her up and take her to bed if that's what he wanted? Why this *debate*?

But at the top of her rage, something seemed to break in her. She found her anger, if that was what it had been, had gone. Substituted was a drenching self-pity which arched over her like those waves. She was going to break down, she realised. There was no other way she could get through. She put her hands over her face and burst into tears.

He slowed the car gently and pulled into a long lay-by separated from the road. He switched off the engine and the lights and put his hand on her shoulder. 'Joss, my dear, I think, I hope, I understand.'

'You don't, you can't. I don't understand myself.'

She reached an apogee of sobbing. He gave her his large handkerchief. Several cars swished by, their headlights sweeping over them impersonally. She felt herself passing the worst of her strange disturbance into a new area in which she was aware of his strength and understanding beside her. Steadily a new feeling of relief and gratitude spread. Was it possible to maintain your independence yet at the same time to depend on someone? Had she forgotten this in her years of total responsibility?

She was aware he had physically withdrawn from her a fraction. 'You know, I don't think we should drive home tonight in this muck,' she heard, 'we've had a long day. At Moretonhampstead there's a five star hotel. I suggest we stop there and give ourselves a treat. If they aren't full, we'll have a slap up dinner and a bottle of very good wine. I mean single rooms, of course.'

She dried her eyes and blew her nose. She was going to say no, that she was all right, why not get back, but he restarted the engine, and they drove on, for some miles neither of them spoke. What had happened, she thought? Would he think less of her because of her weakness? Yet, against her mind, as the crisis receded and her head returned to normal, she was aware of a sense of well-being diffusing involuntarily again throughout her whole body. Had something after all been decided?

A little later it became even clearer. 'I'm glad we're stopping,' she said. 'It'll be nice, and fun. I'm feeling better. I'm so sorry.' He stretched a hand, placed it on her knee, and squeezed. She put her hand on his. It was coincidental with these movements that she knew they would have a double room in the hotel.

Jocelyn had made up her mind, and because of this did not consider that the decision could be difficult to implement. They drove the rest of the way to Moretonhampstead in virtual silence, the rain drumming evenly on the windscreen, the wiper whirring and twisting mesmerically. Once or twice Henry made commonplace remarks - about the rain, about the wind which cuffed them periodically like someone handing out blows, about how far away it must be now to the hotel, and he again questioned whether there would be room for them without a booking. Perhaps he should phone he said, but they saw no phone box, not even a sign of life, in two dark villages they went through. The commonplace exchanges fed her content. She felt so at peace, so *right,* she could not imagine that her decision could be otherwise. It was only when they had entered the gates of the posh hotel and were approaching the parking area she realised he couldn't know what was in her mind. She panicked. How on earth would she actually say it - now, when three-quarters of an hour's silence had congealed his statement about two single rooms?

'There aren't many cars, it should be all right,' Henry said as he drove past the parking area and entered a covered porch. A uniformed man came out to take their non-existent bags. Henry leaned across her to lower the window on her side. 'No luggage,' he said to the man, 'last minute decision, hope you have room for us.' The man said there should be no difficulty about that this evening. Still leaning, Henry opened her door. 'You get out, Joss. No need for both of us to get wet.'

She was going to tell him then but the man was standing to help her out. She got out and went in. She thought she would go straight up to the reception desk and register for them, present him with the fait accompli, but the size of the hall and the decor somehow put her off. Besides, would Henry like it this way? She stood just inside the door, waiting meekly for him to come in and feeling like a teenager.

Henry came in, shaking the waxed coat he had thrown over his head and stamping his feet on the huge mat. 'What a night,' he said loudly to the girl at the desk who was looking across at him, smiling a welcome. Nearly, she funked it, but there was a split second when it was possible and she seized it. She approached and took his arm.

'A double,' she whispered in his ear, aware of the girl. For a dreadful moment he looked at her in astonishment and she thought he might think she meant whisky. Then mercifully she saw the look of recognition and the joy on his face.

But an instant later he knitted his brow responsibly. 'Are you sure?' he said quietly, putting his hand on hers, unaware now of the audience. For answer she pulled him towards the desk. Heaven knew what the girl would be thinking at what she had witnessed, but having taken the plunge and seeing his doubt she felt bold. 'We prefer one bed if you have it,' she said, looking the girl straight in the eye. With this, any lingering possibility of embarrassment was annihilated. The awkwardness, if any, would come later, between them.

There was none. In the room Henry took her in his arms. His kiss was gentle, controlled, but also she noted, with an additional peripheral pleasure, nervous. He was in love with her, his whole resolute tenacious personality fastened on her. She was aware then of a kind of dissolution. It was as if that part of her mind, normally so active, which recorded and processed the moment by moment minutiae of existence, closed down. Her 'decision' became an overwhelming convulsion as she gave herself unconditionally to the enchantment of the evening and of whatever might lie beyond it.

20.

Secretly Jocelyn had misgivings over giving up her small flat over the garage in which she had been so happy. It was of course a totally impractical thought. The relevant question which arose was whether - in the main house in which she would now live - their bedroom was to be Delia's or Henry's. Henry was at pains to suggest that she would 'probably not want it to be Delia's room.' She replied that she really didn't mind about this. They would be redecorating it, didn't he think - perhaps largely re-furnishing it - and surely Henry knew enough about her to her know she wasn't superstitious? But the more she told him she didn't care, the more he seemed sure she was trying to please him and meant the opposite. She finished by giving up and asking him to decide. He chose his own room, when she knew he preferred the other one. She had a private laugh. If she had been a gene nearer the sort of woman who cared about such matters, she supposed it might have been the cause of a dispute. As it was, she accepted the decision light-heartedly. 'It was in this bay-window, with you standing beside me, I had my first view of the garden,' she said. His pleasure in this warmed her, and confirmed she had been right to do as she had. What did a room matter to either of them if the psychology of its occupation was right?

Henry had scruples about an immediate announcement after their return from Moretonhamstead. Would it be seen as indecent haste after the tragedy of Delia's death? This time she spoke her mind plainly. 'You must of course decide, Henry,' she said, 'you know your people better than I do. But I'd take a bet they're all waiting for it. My guess is that Edith was marrying us off weeks ago.'

'Oh, you think so?' Henry said, amazed.

'Shouldn't be surprised if she's got the cake made and stashed away in one of the freezers.'

'Was it so obvious then?'

'Not to us. But Edith's like a truffle pig. She can smell romance yards down.' He continued to look doubtful, but did decide to let it be known. It would be impossible to keep it secret anyway as soon as the furniture arrived and she moved into the house. The effect was gratifyingly genuine. Betty, Brenda May, even Peter Potter and other people who came to the house from time to time, fired broadsides of congratulation. Geoff's taciturnity was temporarily suspended. He shook her hand as if he were trying to drag her arm loose from its socket. 'We're all so pleased,' he said, 'it'll bring the place alive again.' Conversation was notably lighter, laughter without that muted conditional quality which it had suffered from before. Jocelyn was borne along by it. So obvious an outcome did it seem, she was soon able to forget the curious resistance she had offered, which was still inexplicable to her.

It was an enchanted winter of happy labour. They rose together at seven in the dark, made breakfast together, planned the day. Usually she was detained for an hour or so in the office, dealing largely with next summer's bookings which were coming in much earlier this year. As soon as she could she was out digging, heaving and planting for the rest of the day with Henry and Geoff. When it rained heavily there was always a mass of work waiting in the greenhouses.

Edith's pleasure in their union had been patent, but once the news was absorbed Jocelyn discerned an unexplained tension between them. Was it that Edith's tenure of total domestic power was now ended? It would be entirely understandable if this was the case. Jocelyn determined to use the first opportunity to put the matter straight. A couple of days later she happened to go into the kitchen. She witnessed an unprecedented event - Edith sitting at the table apparently doing nothing. She didn't move as Jocelyn entered. 'Are you feeling all right, Edith?' she asked.

'*It*'s not right,' Edith said after a moment.

'What's not right?'

'You ought to be giving me orders now, menus and the like, not me carrying on as before as if nothing had happened.'

She saw what the trouble was. 'But, Edith, nothing's changed. I've no *need* to give you orders.'

'Yes you have. There must be a heap of things you want done differently.'

'But there aren't. I - Henry, too, I'm sure want you to do exactly as you always have. You do all the midday cooking, and cleaning routines, as ever. Henry and I will probably usually be doing our evening meal, but he often did that before in the winter, didn't he? And I'm sure there'll be many days in the summer when it'll be marvellous for me if you can look after our dinner, too.'

'But the lunch menus?' Edith said. 'You should be telling me what you want.'

'Not a bit. How can I improve on your delicious lunches? You're a much better cook that I am. I want us all to carry on just as ever.'

Edith wouldn't believe it. For a week or two the atmosphere continued - until half-way through one morning when Jocelyn was in first from the garden for coffee. She was already feeling hungry and asked Edith what was for lunch. The tension suddenly went. Edith broke into surely one of the broadest smiles recorded in the history of Devon.

'Well, you're Henry's lady all right, that's for sure. You're going to live for that garden, as he does. Chicken risotto's what for lunch.'

They both laughed heartily.

Jocelyn was greatly relieved. And when she thought later about Edith's comment she supposed she had been right in a wider context than lunch menus. The house and its functions would no doubt inch by inch work its way into her consciousness, become an integral part of her psyche as houses were supposed to do in the female make-up. But for the moment it was simply the very lovable place where she ate and slept and loved Henry. Had this not always been the case with her concerning dwellings? In relationships she was par excellence an intensive cultivator, but environmentally she was a nomad.

That she did love Henry she had known that first night in the hotel. How could she not when he was, as he said and demonstrated, in love with her, when he was so grave and sensitive, so attentive to her smallest shifts of sentiment. She was maybe not 'in love' herself, whatever that phrase meant, but she loved him with a steadfastness which she was sure would grow - under the benign and silent witness of the lawns and beds and paths and woods they tended. He, like herself, was unattached to any family he cared about. They had each other, their concentrated view of each other, uncomplicated by other views, other intrusive loyalties, other histories. Was this not, if belatedly, her original perhaps her rather particular vision of life, which she had so mistakenly believed to be reciprocated by Leo?

She had a dutiful correspondence with Sally. This, she sometimes rather shamefully admitted to herself, was from no initiative of her own, but from what she was sure was a kind of chanted catechism of Sally's. In Sally's mentality one wrote to one's parents - to one's parent if one happened to be pruned of one of them. Her letters, like her personality, were factual. I did this, Ken did that, we did the other. Seldom was there comment unless it was castigation of someone else's stupidity and lack of common sense. Even her inventory of new possessions, which she continued to acquire from the very ample salary the estate agent company paid her for her no doubt invaluable services, carried with it no particular materialist joy. The items were necessary, they were things you had to have 'if you had any sense.' But Jocelyn read these letters with an increasing affection. She was so glad her earlier fears for Sally seemed to be proving so groundless. Perhaps Ken, as a lawyer - himself concerned with the application of finite values - appreciated this geometrical certainty. She felt proud even, in a distant sort of way, of this very effective and attractive fellow female she had produced. In her own letters back - yes, 'back', she always felt she was replying to Sally - she tried to be equally factual. Her instinct in any communication was to try to rumble her feelings about this and that, to catch them out as it were, slithery elusive items as they always are. She desisted in Sally's case, knowing they would irritate her.

Undoubtedly it was for this reason she hadn't yet told her about herself and Henry. How could she state this in purely factual terms? 'Oh by the way, I forgot to tell you. Henry and I are now living together. I'm living in the main house, and I suppose one of these days we'll get round to some sort of ceremony - civil, I imagine. We've really all been too busy to give it much thought.' How would that look in cold handwriting? And of course there would be the inevitable response, whatever form it took. 'Of course, I always knew you would. I think I remember saying so when we came down.' Jocelyn nonetheless upbraided herself for this reticence of hers. How many mothers in England would forbear to tell their children they were going to marry again, unless it were from shame of some sort? Yet she continued to be silent, and the longer she left it the more difficult it became.

Suddenly it was too late. Just before Christmas, which Sally had announced she was spending with Ken in the Caribbean - off the next day - she wrote that they had decided to be married in May. There was an off-hand suggestion attached to this. Did Jocelyn think there was any chance of 'doing it' at Combe? It would be 'quite nice.' It was a lovely place and Henry Bordeaux had been so very kind before. They would pay of course - Ken's family were offering 'to stump up quite a bit.' Was it at all possible, or 'would it complicate things?'

Jocelyn was thrown into instant panic. She had imagined already that this was what she and Henry would offer if and when a wedding took place. But she saw at once how foolish she had been in not telling Sally about Henry and herself. Wouldn't she now be obliged to do so?

Henry's reaction to Sally's news didn't improve things. 'But how marvellous, Joss,' he said at once. 'Of course they must have the wedding here. And why don't we make it a double bill? That'd be a laugh. Bridegroom and bride's substitute father on the same day. Might qualify for the Guinness book of whatsits. What do you say?'

She abominated the idea. Why, she thought? Why was this? Was she mad? Wasn't it just the right thing? She couldn't control her face quick enough.

'You don't like the idea?' Henry said.

She floundered. 'It's just that I haven't told Sally about us yet.'

He was astounded. 'You haven't? Why not?'

'I don't know. You saw what Sally's like when she came down here.'

'The bossyboots angle, you mean?'

'Yes. And something else. I don't quite know myself.' She calmed herself and went to put her arms round his neck. 'Actually I do know. I know very well why I haven't told Sally. What we have is ours, no one else's,' she said, 'not even Sally's. Perhaps least of all Sally's - Sally having, I'm afraid, the unwitting power to disrupt and discomfort.'

She saw him struggle to understand. Then, with relief, she saw he had. 'Yes, I can see. Of course. And, now you make me think about it, it's just what I feel, too, really. I was getting carried away. Well, in this case my suggestion is we quietly do our deed as quickly as possible, before Sally gets the same idea I just had of a double whammy.'

Jocelyn was delighted, delighted Henry felt the same as she did, delighted above all perhaps at the outrageously circumstantial reason there was now to be for their nuptuals. A shotgun wedding if ever there was one, Sally having provided the barrel in the ribs.

Nonetheless she took seriously the ceremony in the Dartmouth registry office, as Henry did. 'Neither of us is religious,' he said, 'but we've got to have a tribal war-dance round us, don't you think, a solemnity, a vow taken.' It was precisely what she thought - it was to be a solemn pledge in a public place and the pouring of a libation or two in front of their fellow workers at Combe, if they would come.

They were married on New Year's Day. They had thought to have a few days in Paris afterwards. As it turned out, a large consignment of shrubs arrived very late from the nursery, which had been held up in the Christmas mail. They decided they would rather deal with these. Jocelyn wrote to Sally the day after, an entirely factual letter which she would get on her return from her holiday - there had been no Bermuda address to communicate with. She congratulated Sally on her engagement to Ken, hoped they would be very happy, and said she and Henry would of course love her to have the wedding at Combe. She contemplated making her own news a P.S. as a joke to herself, but resisted the temptation and made it a last, one-sentence paragraph. It did, however, almost echo the 'Henry and I are living together' phrase she had imagined in jest before. 'Henry and I were married in Dartmouth yesterday,' she wrote. After all, she thought wryly, it shouldn't be so amazing a revelation to Sally, as she had forecast it so accurately.

Spring was early. The first daffodils were budding heavily in the middle of March. Jocelyn couldn't believe she had been at Combe nearly a year and that in a couple of weeks she would be beginning her second season. She was now back in the office with a vengeance, dealing with a torrent of applications. At this rate they would be paying off the mortgage in five years not twenty, even with the money they were spending on plants and improvements. The building of the new refectory had been postponed, but was now rescheduled for the autumn.

One late afternoon soon after they had reopened, she had just finished with a group and had gone upstairs to the bedroom to wash her hands. She had done the usual thing on the way round, spotted weeds about to choke young plants and was unable to resist the compulsion to pull them, with no gloves on. Having finished with the scrubbing brush in the bathroom, she was sitting at her dressing-table, one of the few pieces of her own she had salvaged, via Ken and Sally, from Nottingham. Thank goodness, she thought, as she reached for her bottle of 'Intensive Care', Henry's expectations of her femininity did not extend to immaculate hands. Her eye was caught by an object on the sill of the bay window, half hidden by the curtain. Her heart gave a thump then seemed to stop. She half-rose to get a full view of it. What was Henry playing at, or could it be Edith? Without doubt it was Don Quixote, one of the pair of fine wood carvings Leo had brought back from a sale in their very early days and which she had once treasured. She thought they had been sold with the rest of the stuff in Nottingham. The thin loony knight, bearded and be-lanced, sat in his familiar posture leaning uncomfortably forward on his meagre mount. She got up and moved the curtain back, expecting to see Sancho on his donkey. He wasn't there.

She thought the carvings must after all have escaped the sale and been in a box of small objects Sally had thoughtfully rescued for her, and which she had never opened, not wishing to have anything of this nature to remind her of a past which was to be obliterated. She thought Henry had put the box in the attic. Perhaps Henry, or Edith, had been up there, seen it, and for some reason pulled this out for her. But why put it there, half-hidden behind the curtain? Why just one of the two pieces? And it didn't seem a sensible action certainly for Henry to have taken. He knew what she felt about the box and its contents.

She went straight up to the roof, which was attained by a pull-down ladder. She found the box. She was sure it was pristine, neatly taped just as Sally had posted it. She went down to Edith, who knew nothing about it.

Now thoroughly alarmed, she waited impatiently for Henry to come up for tea. It was all she could do to stop herself going out to him. Normally they had their tea in the kitchen with the others. She laid their tea on a tray and took it into the sitting-room as soon as she heard him come in. They did do this sometimes when they had things to discuss. She asked him point blank as he came in. He knew nothing. He saw her distress.

'Are you sure it hasn't been in a drawer somewhere?' he said. 'Perhaps you put it there absent-mindedly and then pulled it out thinking maybe to dispose of it somehow.'

'I'm certain. I haven't seen the thing since I left Nottingham.'

She saw him searching for other possible explanations. Did he include the one she hardly dare contemplate? She saw that, if he did, he wasn't going to admit to it. 'It's Leo,' she had to say at last. 'He's been in here, in our bedroom, today. I *know* it.'

'Of course he hasn't, Joss. For a start how could he have got hold of the object? He couldn't have known about the parcel in the roof.'

'He didn't have to. You remember, the night I left Nottingham he was in the vicinity and I was expecting him to come to my house. Later that night, or probably the next, he'd've gone to the house, found me not there and almost certainly forced a window and got in.'

'Sally didn't report anything amiss, did she? She went up there soon after.'

'She wouldn't have known what he took.'

'Well, if he did take the object, how could he have got in here without someone seeing him?'

'Very easily. Probably when I was taking the group round. There were a lot of people in this afternoon. No one would have recognised him among the throng. You wouldn't. He probably bought a ticket like any visitor, then had only to wait his moment to slip into the house, probably through the front door. Betty wouldn't have heard anything. She keeps the office door shut to keep the dog out. He walked in, up the stairs, found our room, and could have been out again in a few seconds.'

Henry gave a humourless laugh. 'But what could he possibly hope to gain from doing this?'

'I don't know. But that he did it I'm now quite certain. He wants me to know he's found me. There'll be something else, then another thing, until sooner or later I *shall* know what he wants.'

'There's only been one thing he wants, isn't there, and that's money? He must know he's not getting that.' She was silent. 'As for intrusions, if that's what he's up to, that's soon fixed. With all these people on the premises and the house often empty, I've been thinking for some time we should have some sort of a security system. We haven't got anything very much to nick, but a couple of cameras at strategic points would be a good idea. This persuades me. I'll also inform the police about this intrusion, if that's what it is. If he were foolish enough to come again we'd have him.'

'It won't be any use.'

'Why not?'

'Supposing you got a picture of him entering - he'd only have some explanation.'

'If I catch him I'll give him something to take away with him.'

The memory of his previous threat to do this made her shudder. If Henry indulged in any kind of rough play, the only result would be that Leo would sue him for assault and win triumphantly. Suddenly, with a further shrinking of the spirit, she knew exactly what Leo was up to. She knew this sly invasion was no prank, no ordinary con for money. This was the opening shot of a continued psychological war, for which, initially at least, Leo held all the crucial armour. If he was here in the neighbourhood, he would know for sure of her present circumstances. He would know there would be no money with Henry involved in the action. What else had she to lose which he could take?

'I still don't believe it,' Henry was saying. 'There'll be a simple explanation for the Quixote figure. I'm sure something or other has slipped your mind, as it usually has when one's lost something. Afterwards you can't think why you forgot.'

This was the ordinary healthy thing to think, she thought. For the remainder of tea, in Henry's cheerful and protective presence, she was just able to think it, too. In one of her fits of absent-mindedness - which could, she was well aware, accompany a period of concentration on something else - somehow she herself was the cause of the mystery.

Why should she care now about Leo? Was it cowardice on her part? If so, was not even cowardice a kind of disloyalty to Henry? And what foundation was there anyway for cowardice in her present circumstances? What more could Leo take from her that she hadn't already given?

Such questioning was pointless. Her dread stubbornly remained. She discovered something else. The following day, when she had to go in to Dartmouth to shop, she found herself looking about her, looking for that athletic figure which she imagined would be standing on the other side of the street, watching her, hands in pockets, his feet overlapping the curb - as he had waited for her that day in Cambridge many years ago. Wasn't there another element? When she found he wasn't there in the street waiting for her, wasn't there in a certain way a kind of anti-climax? Was it that she wanted to vent on him her stored wrath for all the harm and anguish he had given her and regretted she had not had the opportunity?

A day passed. Nothing further happened. Her wariness, her tense expectation would diminish, she told herself, as by an innate curative process nature in time seems to erode anything unpleasant that happens. There were even periods in which other explanations for the appearance of the carved figure still seemed possible.

Two days later she was in one of the greenhouses pricking out into pots the new chrsyanthemum shoots from the overwintered parent plants. Heaped on the plywood slab on which she worked were two piles, one of compost, one of sharp sand. She cupped the umpteenth pot into the compost to fill it and felt the plastic come up against something hard. Rummaging with her other hand, she drew out Sancho Panchez.

Still holding the figure, she swung round in fear, expecting to see Leo behind her. There was nobody. In the adjacent greenhouse she could see Geoff sifting something, his good-natured features as ever absorbed in the task. She put the plump figure down on the bench and stared at its realistic representation, the legs dangling at the donkey's sides. With this purely physical act, all Leo's personality was arriving in her mind simultaneously. It was surely no accident he had chosen these two objects. Did he wish to remind her of that comic, perhaps eccentric indifference to the world they had once shared? For the first time she recognised there could be, not menace, but a comic element in this charade he was playing. Was he reminding her of the fun and the laughter they had shared before Sally appeared in their lives - their idyllic exclusiveness, their unencumbered ability to love each other? Was he asking her if she found this same zany humour with Henry?

She dismissed the thought. Of course he wasn't. This was her own psyche still trying to excuse him, to make some sense of the years she had wasted, not Leo's. She decided this time not to worry Henry. Let Leo play whatever games he chose. Not to be able to ignore him *would* surely constitute a disloyalty to Henry.

21.

Days passed, Leo did not appear, and there were no further manifestations of his presence in the neighbourhood. Could it be that for some reason he'd had second thoughts? After all, with Henry now in the equation, what could he do which would not humiliate himself? Had this at last sunk in?

As if to justify optimism, on the following Saturday she and Henry spent a particularly pleasant evening. To celebrate the last of their freedom before the season began Henry suggested what he called a 'Gala Dinner', just for themselves, a special menu which they would cook together. They dressed up, and Henry brought up a special claret from his cellar.

Later they made love. Though she hoped Henry didn't know, she had gone through an initial period of difficulty with sex. Was it that she had been so long without it, or did she still associate it with all the unpleasantness of her past? She felt sexy, but in the act, patient and sensitive to her response as Henry was, she had never quite reached the pleasure which was there waiting, she was sure, but which always eluded her. Tonight she broke through to what Leo had used to call in their good days 'the jackpot.' It was a good expression - implied, the miraculous conjunction of numbers, the ecstatic pause as the event was registered, then the profligate spilling of pleasure to all parts of the body. Henry, she was sure, had probably diagnosed her difficulty to date, and knew this occasion was something new and special. She knew this from the way he held her afterwards.

Henry woke first, feeling lively. Seeing she was still sleepy, he said he would make breakfast and bring it up on a tray. She felt guilty, but accepted and was glad she had. His pleasure in providing the hearty meal, which included bacon and eggs, reminded her of when she first arrived at Combe in the early morning to take up her job. Laughing at their hunger after the meal they had eaten last night, they demolished everything.

Putting the tray aside, they took up the papers Henry had also brought up, Henry his *Sunday Telegraph,* she *The Sunday Times.* Normally she went straight to the book section. Political news had never had more than marginal interest to her. But casting a cursory eye on the front news page, something caught her eye. The headline seemed to be some new accusation of sleaze against the Government. Her eye descended a few lines and she realised what she must have seen and subconsciously recorded. It was a name - Sir Matthew Cunningham. In a minor panic she detached the news section from the rest and began to take in the headline: ***'Minister In New Sex Scandal.*'** The main picture was of Matthew leaning out of the driver's window of an expensive car. On the kerb, slightly bending, her arms across her chest as if she were cold, was the obvious prostitute. She read. It appeared Cunningham had been snapped in this compromising moment by an anonymous 'source', who had no doubt sold his rich gleaning to the paper for a large sum. 'In a wish to preempt further embarrassment to the Government,' the Minister, who was one of the Under Secretaries of State for the Environment, had immediately tendered his resignation to the Prime Minister, who had 'regretfully' accepted it. A photocopy of the exchange of letters was also printed at the bottom of the page. A further article of comment in another section of the paper described this latter act as 'swift footwork' on the part of the disgraced politician, as was his personal statement of guilt and shame at this 'very shabby, one-off deed,' and the similarly predictable statement from Lady Cunningham that she was 'standing by' her husband in 'this hour of calumny'. The wife appeared in another picture in which she was, literally, standing by her husband - holding hands with him outside their London house like two shy siblings at a party.

Jocelyn put the paper down on the eiderdown and stared sightlessly through the window. Henry stirred beside her. 'What's up? You look as if you've seen a ghost.'

'In a sense I think I have.' She picked up the news section again and tapped the photograph with the knuckle of her forefinger. 'That's Leo's half-brother.' Henry took the paper, read a few lines, and put it down. He waited for her comment, looking at her. 'I never told you about this man,'she said. 'I suppose he was indirectly the cause of Leo's trouble.'

She had a feeling of gross distaste. She didn't want to think about it. She wanted to toss the paper on the floor and get on with the book reviews. She knew this was impossible. Henry wanted, needed, to know. She should have told him long ago, but because of her own mental embargo on the subject of Leo, she had told him almost nothing except in abstract terminology. She had said Leo had been dishonest, sycophantic, and unfaithful. She told the full story now bleakly, factually.

'Leo's father married again - hence this younger half-brother. I never knew about him. Leo was almost totally silent about his family, as I was about mine. I thought his silence had the same reason mine had - because there was nothing to say. It turned out not to be like this at all. I found out about Matthew in much the same way as this.' She nodded towards the paper. 'His elevation to a Government post was reported in the papers and I happened to see it. Matthew looks a bit like Leo and I thought they might be related. I was quite prepared to think, as I always had, that the reason Leo hadn't mentioned Matthew was because he was an irrelevance to him. It very soon appeared he wasn't at all an irrelevance, but the mainspring of most of his behaviour over all the years I'd known him. He was jealous of Matthew. Leo's dishonesty about money was not, as I'd been prepared to think in better moments, just because he wanted the best for Sally, which I think he did, too - but because of status, for himself. He must have known Matthew was "rising in the world," whatever that means. He was going to do the same by becoming rich. Even his silly affair with a rich woman seemed to have something to do with that. Then when she grew tired of him he ran off with some of her valuables.'

'And now the catalyst has fallen from grace.'

'It appears so.'

There was a silence. Henry, she knew, was curious. Of course any man would be in this circumstance. If only he could just drop it here, she thought, shoot it in the dustbin where it all belonged. If only they could go on reading the papers.

'It could conceivably have a good effect on Leo, I suppose?'

'It's possible.'

'Envy appeased and all that. It could even help him to lead a more satisfactory life.'

'Improbable,' she said, and fell silent.

He saw her mood and seemed to decide to appease it. He picked up his reading spectacles again. 'Well let's hope it does anyway,' he said. 'And maybe if he has been nosing around here he'll clear off.'

This made it worse. Paradoxically, as they re-fastened themselves on their reading, she thought perhaps she would have liked to discuss it. *Would* it alter Leo? Would his brother's frailty demonstrate the groundlessness of his own obsession? If it did, how would this affect him? They wouldn't know - hopefully they would never know - but to have talked about it might have laid the new ghosts she suspected would be liberated in her mind. She found she couldn't take her usual interest in the new books published. Very soon she got up. 'Shall we saw logs this morning?' she said, going to run a bath.

She heard the teasing in his riposte. 'I thought we were taking it easy today?'

Correspondence with Sally had escalated to two letters each a week. As Jocelyn had forecast, Sally had shown no surprise that she and Henry were now married, and this matter had occupied a minimum of notepaper. 'We're so pleased for you, Mum,' was the key and definitive phrase. The unusual volume of wordage concerned Sally's own wedding which was now six weeks away. She and Henry were methodically making the arrangements, which were largely a matter of negotiating with other people to do things - a printer to do the invitation cards, the vicar, caterers, hoteliers for guests, a florist, and so on. This did not prevent Sally from 'reminding' her of things which were already under way. Jocelyn understood. She was too busy to come down, and it had always been difficult for Sally to believe that anyone could be as efficient as she was. Jocelyn was meticulous in answering every query fully, taking care never to say anything which could be construed into a charge of Sally being a fusspot. She tried to make it sound as if Combe House efficiency was the result of Sally's meticulous promptings. A fortnight after the garden was opened for the summer, and three weeks after the appearance of Sancho Panchez, there was a bombshell. Leo had written to Sally. She enclosed a photocopy of the letter.

PO Box 231
Post Office
Kensington High Street
W.C.1.

My Dear Sally,

Yes, this is your Dad, your very recalcitrant but remorseful Dad - on the warpath, you'll say, though I'd call it the peacepath. I've heard, never mind how - as you may know to your cost, I've always been good on information-gathering - I've heard you and Ken are to be married at a westcountry venue under your mother's auspices.

Now I know what you've thought of me since you were quite a little girl. You thought me (quite correctly and, as it turned out, clairvoyantly) improvident. You thought me too much of an optimist, not too much given to the splendid kind of accuracy and straightforwardness you have in such plentiful supply! But I do believe you always made one little error in my direction. I don't think - for very understandable reasons - you ever quite appreciated how much I've always loved you, which remains as true today as it ever did. Maybe you did know, but chose to overlook the fact, which would also be entirely understandable in the circumstances I created for you and your mother. Anyway, with this credential as it were (I mean my loving you), however you remember me, what I'm asking is whether you would consent to my giving you away at your wedding. I'm the last person in the world to talk of "rights" - a father's right for example to see his daughter wed. People are as they are in my opinion, and don't deserve to be straightjacketed by words like that. No, it's not rights I'm after. Perhaps what I'm asking for is charity. It would warm more than the cockles of my heart to lead you up the aisle and to sit, if permitted, in the front pew to hear you take your vows. The warmth would stay, even if - God forbid - I never saw you again, for the rest of my life.

A last point. I could imagine, even if by some lucky chance you are moved on your own behalf to meet my request, that you wouldn't do so in order to protect your mother from further contact with me, as you have been doing ever since she left Nottingham. Let me only say that I know, too, of her circumstances, that I wish her well in them, and have no wish to disturb the happiness I am sure she has found and deserves. After the service in the church I would depart, and naturally - even if this were contemplated, which I'm quite sure it wouldn't be - wouldn't expect to take further part in the proceedings.

I send you my love, my darling Sally, even though I dread that you may not have read this far.

Your ever loving Dad.

Jocelyn returned to Sally's letter, of which she had read only the first words announcing Leo's letter.

'I've just had this, if you please. Thought it would interest you as Exhibit Zilch. I haven't replied of course. Ken says we should discuss some arrangement to remove him if he should try to muscle in on the day. It does seem he knows where you are, which I suppose doesn't matter much now?'

The rest of the letter again concerned the wedding.

Weak at the knees against all her will to be otherwise, Jocelyn knew at once to whom the letter was really addressed. Had Leo called off the dogs? Of course he hadn't. It reeked of Leo's cunning to ring the changes and to choose this roundabout approach. As he had no doubt calculated, the letter, in addition to the arrival of Quixote and his stout companion, picked up all the equivocal sentiments she had been having and played on them, just as in their first meeting he had with such uncanny insight picked up her state of mind then. In the letter he had referred to the undoubted truth of his love for Sally. There was the request for 'charity'. Could he have guessed that she would have read in the press about Matthew's disgrace and wondered if this could affect him in some way? Every fear she'd had before crowded back on her.

Feeling a coward, after lunch she took the letter to Henry in the sitting-room where he had gone to read the paper for a few minutes. He would have to know anyway, she argued. They presumably would have to make some plans to cope with Leo if he did turn up. She adopted a practical tone.

She might have known he would see through her attempt to be offhand. He at once put down the newspaper and gave the letter all his attention, holding it at arm's length as if *a priori* it would be distasteful. Then he frowned, putting the letter on the small table beside him. 'My dear Joss, how very upsetting for you,' he said, carefully. 'I suppose this does confirm he's been down here snooping. Obviously, he *is* on the warpath, and we'll have to assume he'll be here for the wedding.'

'I suppose we will.'

'We can certainly keep him out of the reception, but it may be difficulty stopping him entering the church.'

She tried out a wild abandon. 'Oh we can let him come, can't we? I doubt if Sally will be fazed. She'll just ignore him, I can picture it.'

'You mean *you* wouldn't mind?'

'I wouldn't like it, but it's Sally who matters, and I'm sure Sally can be relied on to put the poor man in his place.'

He looked at her more sharply. 'You almost sound sorry for him,' he said with a laugh.

This forced her to define her feelings. She sat down, thinking. 'I don't feel sorry for him,' she said after a moment, 'he certainly has no right to give Sally away. But maybe he does have a right at least to witness his daughter getting married.'

'You think he'll behave?'

'I think there's a good chance. Leo might want to embarrass me, but not Sally.'

To her dismay, she saw Henry pick up the paper again. 'Well, if that's how you feel, Joss, it's fine by me,' he said. 'Let the man come then, if Sally doesn't mind. If there were any trouble I suppose we'd manage to deal with it somehow.'

She saw that further discussion would be redundant. She was no longer weak at the knees. Henry was washing his hands of what he saw as an irrelevance. Perhaps it was an irrelevance, but that didn't prevent her from her feeling the onset of a heavy foreboding.

22.

After long thought, Jocelyn wrote Leo a short note.

'Dear Leo,

'Sally has passed me your letter, which she tells me she has no intention of answering. I understand her feelings, which are similar to my own, and there's no question of your giving her away at her wedding. She doesn't wish it, and has in fact asked my husband, Henry, to do the honours. But I do think, as Sally's father, you have a right to witness her marriage. I therefore enclose an invitation. I would only ask that you read into this no more than what is there - a simple courtesy. I also ask that after the wedding you leave us all alone and indulge in no more of the tricks I believe you have been up to lately. As you must realise, you and I are totally finished. I now have a new life with prospects of great happiness. I hope that you, too - if what you say about yourself is true - will be similarly lucky, and I wish you well.'

She was going to put 'Yours sincerely,' pondered over alternatives, finally just signed herself, 'Jocelyn.'

She also spoke to Sally on the phone, telling her what she had written to Leo. She said that as he seemed to have discovered where she lived and where the wedding would be, there was nothing anyone could do to stop him entering the church for the service, and that it seemed better to keep things on this courteous level. After some discussion, Sally said she 'supposed' Jocelyn was right about the service, though she had no intention of talking to him. She 'presumed' he wouldn't be admitted to the reception at Combe. Jocelyn replied that she didn't think they should prevent this, if he wanted to come - which he might not after her letter - it might only lead to an unpleasant scene. Sally said she thought nothing could be more unpleasant than having him there 'among my friends, and Ken's.' But it appeared she accepted the inevitable. In subsequent letters she made no further mention of the matter.

Jocelyn felt something of a relief when this exchange was

over. She felt she had done the right and charitable thing. She had also taken the initiative, always so important in her relations with Leo. This had the curious effect of muting her previous anxieties about him. Not to have invited him would have given him the initiative - with his twisted way of looking at things.

To close the matter she thought she must tell Henry what she had done, and chose what she thought was a good moment after lunch, when he was standing by one of the sitting-room windows with his nose in a reference book. She stated baldly that she had invited Leo, to the reception as well as the church, as it seemed churlish not to.

He seemed to have what he wanted from the book. He snapped it shut and returned it to the shelf. 'Churlish?' he said.

'Yes, I think even Sally accepts that a father has the right to see his daughter married.'

'Sally's keen, is she?'

'I didn't say that, no. I said she's accepted it as a necessity.'

She hoped the matter would rest here. But to her disquiet he sat down on the arm of the one of the armchairs as if there were more to be said. 'So Sally has accepted it because you made her, is that right?' he went on.

'I suppose you could put it like that.'

He gave a little laugh. 'Isn't the truth, Joss, that in some remote way *you* want him to be here?'

The tone alarmed her. She strove to keep rancour from her voice. 'Why should you think that?'

'I don't know - you do seem to be rather going on about it.'

'I'm not going on about it at all. The situation has arisen and I'm trying to cope with it as best I can. Naturally, I thought you should know what I've done about it.'

He got up with an abrupt motion. 'OK, Joss,' he said, 'it's your affair and I'm not going to interfere. Let the man come then.' He opened the french window door and went out onto the terrace, severing any reply from her.

She was taken aback for a moment. Perhaps she was wrong, she tried to think. Perhaps there could be some covert element of wish-fulfilment in herself which she hadn't recognised. But she couldn't accept there was. Could it be then that in some mild way Henry was jealous?

She tried to forget it, but she knew from the set of Henry's jaw and the way he spoke to her that the matter was continuing to rankle with him. She would like to have discussed it again, to make clear that he was misjudging her motives, but didn't she have experience of his reticence on emotional subjects? It was back to the first days last summer when he had refused to discuss Delia. And talking of Delia, couldn't he see that these last rites of hers on behalf of Leo were the exact counterpart of his own scruples over her? Didn't he remember the discussion they'd had after Delia's death about bonds not lightly to be put aside? How could he apply this to himself and not to her?

Later, in a calmer frame of mind, she made a less dramatic decision. All she had to do, she thought, was carry through her original purpose. Leo, if he bothered to come, would be at the wedding. With any luck he would try no tricks. She would say a few words to him, and she would be gently freed from a last mooring, the matter would be forgotten. She felt happier at this, and the very mild expression of Henry's annoyance ceased to rankle.

As the wedding approached, activity obliterated everything but fleeting thoughts on the subject. Ken's parents came down to inspect the site. Given Ken's amiable disposition, they were predictably pleasant - Ernest Playmore, an upper crust ex-merchant banker with a large estate in Kent, and his diminutive wife, who was a pillar of several charities. Delia's room was used for the first time to accommodate them. Ernest, it seemed, was no farmer or horticulturalist - he rented his lands to others - but he was nonetheless enthusiastic about Combe and its success and wanted to know everything about it. As his interest seemed genuine, Henry responded. Jocelyn found the going heavier with Theresa Playmore. Gardening to Theresa was a subject concerning, not actual contact with the soil, but the difficulty of engaging satisfactory people to work for her. They were saved by a discovery of a common childhood interest in birds. They managed on this, and on reminiscences of childhood linked to bird-watching. Henry had been going to refuse Ernest's offer of financial help for the wedding, despite the fact that three-quarters of the guests were going to be their friends and Ken's but, in the agreeable atmosphere, accepted gracefully. The Playmores approved greatly of the setting for their son's wedding and, apparently, of the (amended) provenance of their future daughter-in-law. Leo, rather naturally, was not mentioned, though presumably they had been informed about him by Ken. A week later Ken and Sally descended with a mountain of luggage. Sally, running her eye over the arrangements, could find no fault. With Ken and Sally, too, no mention was made of Leo. Inasmuch as she now thought about it, which wasn't much, Jocelyn assigned his possible appearance a low priority. Leo hadn't replied to her letter, and there had been no further intrusions. It was just possible her letter had put him off and he wouldn't come.

It was not until the night before the wedding when, with a curiously antique bowing to tradition, the pair were sleeping apart - Ken with his parents in the house of friends they knew near Totnes, Sally at Combe - that any reference was made to Leo. In the middle of dinner, which they were eating by candlelight in the dining-room, Jocelyn had gone to the kitchen for the pudding. Returning, she was aware Henry and Sally had been discussing something and stopped in the middle of it. Sally made an attempt at a cover-up, with a mooing noise at the sight of the cream-and-raspberry topped meringue she was carrying. Jocelyn had caught Sally's words, 'I absolutely agree.' She knew at once they had been talking about Leo.

'What do you absolutely agree about, Sally?' she said, putting the plate down on the table and licking her fingers which had encountered the sticky sweet juice. They exchanged glances.

When had Sally ever shrunk from a challenge? It was she who answered. 'Leo,' she said, bluntly.

'What about him?'

Jocelyn looked at Henry, who had picked up a spoon and started playing with it. But again it was Sally who answered. 'If he's to come to the reception, they're a number of things he could try on, Mum. You must see this.'

'Like what?'

'For a start he could try to make a speech and say something ghastly, or muscle in on the act somehow. I really don't want that and, whatever we think, Ken's parents aren't going to see it with the kind of tolerance we might muster. They're very proper and traditional. Another thing, he's bound to drink too much.'

'Leo never had that problem.'

'He may well have by now. Anyway, it's prudent to make some plans to deal with him - in case.'

'A chucker out, you mean?'

'Bluntly, yes.'

She thought she faced it fairly. 'That's possibly wise, though I'm pretty sure it won't be necessary,' she said.

'I hope you're right.'

'Leo never did the obvious thing.'

'He certainly never did the *right* thing.'

She began to serve the food. A cool head was all she needed, she thought. It would be all right if she just kept calm. 'All right, you and Henry make a plan. It's wise. All I ask is that, if Leo behaves - which I think he's likely to - we all make an effort to produce a minimum level of civility in his direction. Particularly you, Sally. There's one thing in his letter which was undoubtedly true. However you criticise him, he always loved you. I think you know that.'

It was a moment or two before they got the conversation back to normal. Henry did not contribute. He had now the perfect credential for his point of view about Leo. It was Sally's wedding, in relation to which, at this moment, he was conveniently merely the host - and Sally was totally on his side.

It was showery, but warm, and as if it were a contribition to the occasion, just before three a spell of sunshine was vouchsafed. Jocelyn arrived in good time at the little church with its red sandstone tower and clock. Whatever protocol did or didn't prescribe, she thought it would be a good idea to meet some of the alien guests and get some of the gracious act over before the service. They came thick and fast, the cars queuing in the tiny lane to enter the field they had hired from the farmer for the parking, including the black morning-dressed posse of Playmores, the people they were staying with, and the bridegroom (resplendent in grey, top hat and all). She saw Leo come through the lych gate as she was talking to one of their party, a garrulous Kentish woman who bred horses and had known Ken 'since he was a stripling.' As their eyes met, inevitably she remembered that afternoon in Ely when she had stood outside the cathedral on that little piece of lawn talking to the Dean. Leo had observed her then, just like this, and seen at once how politely uninvolved she was. Would he also note the similarity? Why wasn't Henry here, she thought, whose robust presence would defend her from such aggressive memories? Why did they have to endure all these wedding do's and don'ts, which had condemned her to deal with Leo alone?

She looked away and took with her the indelible impact of Leo's appearance and his look. He had obviously made some effort, his suit wasn't new or smart but presentable. And there was no cynicism in his grin, only - surely - regret, warmth, concession. She found she was breathless as she re-faced the woman, who had shifted the topic of conversation from Ken to the likely high cost of fodder this year. Later, when she was beginning to think she must go inside, she saw Leo standing off, alone, under a yew tree. He wouldn't approach her, she saw. Before entering the church she made a sudden resolution. She went up to him.

'Hallo, Leo,' she said, 'I'm glad you've come. Sally's looking lovely.' She held out her hand.

He took it, holding it fractionally longer than was usual. 'She's not the only one,' he said.

'You look good, too,' she replied quickly.

They were, perhaps for the first time in their lives, at a loss what to say. They stood, eyes averted, looking at the other guests, who had begun to enter the porch. She pulled herself together. 'Well, I suppose I'd better get inside and take up station.' At the last moment she had another rash impulse. The initiative - she must keep the initiative, she kept telling herself, regardless of anything else. 'Do you want to sit with us at the front?' she found herself asking. She looked him briefly in the eye.

'No. Henry wouldn't like it, would he, neither probably would Sal. And I'd stick out like a sore thumb in this suit. I'll sit at the back.' He paused. 'And leave afterwards.'

'No, please come to the reception.'

His face lit. 'You mean it?'

'Of course.'

'Thanks.'

She swung away. She heard her heels banging with unnecessary force on the polished tiles of the aisle as she cut through the milling crowd of well-dressed people being shepherded by the ushers, the country organ fluting manfully. She entered the front pew and gave a brief glance at the Playmore front bench on the other side of the aisle. They were all facing forwards steadfastly. Though she hadn't prayed since Ely days, she knelt on the hassock and held her temples, spreading her hand over her face. This was as much as anything to hide, and steady herself. She found her blood was still pumping. Poor Leo, was she the only soul here with a kind word in her heart for a man down on his luck?

The small church was full. Wide spreads of white flowers stood with passionless stillness by polished brass railings. They waited, listening for the presence of the hired limousine outside, the slammed doors, then the presence there would be at the west end door behind the congregation. Decently delayed, but not too much (Sally would have made the calculation to the second) their anticipation became reality. The bride and her surrogate father arrived. Craftily informed, the parson appeared from the vestry and stood at the altar steps, hands crossed over his breast as if he were a saint expecting martydrom, the organ limbered up for its windy rendering of the time-worn tune and plunged into it. The stately progress began. Jocelyn could picture Sally turning her head to left and right, bestowing her smile through the veil. They drew level. Henry, resplendent in his morning suit, delivered his charge to Ken, and stood aside.

She didn't listen to the service, her mind gliding over the past, Sally's past - her early days when Leo had whirled her in his arms, visits to Cromer, the day at school when Sally had routed with scorn the boys who had molested her, Roedean and their dismal retreat from its homely excellence through that winter landscape, Leo's coming out of prison and, through it all, Sally's behaviour, her unbelievable consistency, now this. What part had she and Leo played in the girl's maturing? Almost none, it seemed. Sally had arrived, used what facilities she and Leo had been able to provide, and now had a great deal more sensible arrangements for her future which would certainly make her early life with Leo dull by comparison. Jocelyn wondered if all would be well, as she had wondered about her unnecessarily in her early teens. But it was difficult to think of Sally being unhappy.

She thought then of Leo, in the shadows at the back of the church - surely in some way a new Leo. Was it possible he could have staged the modesty and humility he had shown outside? It was all she could do to stop herself looking round. She was attacked by another gust of emotion. If only she had known more about him in the early days, known about Matthew, could it have been different? Surely in those salad days she could have danced him away from such absurd envy? Even that Turnbull woman - had it been entirely Leo's fault he had been so weak? She thrust aside these thoughts. What was she doing? Her duty today was clear, wasn't it? No mad U-turns, no histrionics. Her intention must not be muddled, in any way modifed. They were singing a hymn now, holding up their hymn books. She transferred the book to her left hand, surreptitiously slid the disengaged one inside Henry's arm, and sang more lustily.

At Combe, she did her duty in a daze. She had first to stand with Henry to receive the guests, a correctitude neither Henry or herself had wanted but which Sally had insisted on. 'Ken's lot will expect it,' she had said. She dreaded the situation of Leo confronting Henry. Would they shake hands? But the queue dwindled to the last guests, and Leo hadn't appeared. Then later, when Henry had made a brief speech, when Ken and his best man had given polished and eloquent performances, she saw him standing at the back of the ring which had gathered round the white linen-covered table. He must have slipped in quietly. There was no glass in his hand, he was just watching Sally intently, a look of simple pleasure on his face. She waited until the fuss had died down and Sally was exchanging a word about something with Ken. She went up to her.

'Take Leo a glass of champagne, Sal,' she said. 'I don't think he has one. He's over there, at the back, making no trouble.'

Sally coloured. 'I really don't want to, you know,' she said.

'Go on. You should - on your wedding day. It's probably the last time you'll see him.'

'*That* has to be a good thing.'

'Won't you do it?'

'Can't you - if we must?'

She looked towards Henry for support. She thought Henry had deliberately turned away to joke with Peter Potter. She felt a surge of alienation and resentment. Surely on a happy day like this a little common decency was not asking too much. Resolute, she seized an empty glass from a tray of reserves, filled it from one of the still unused stand-by bottles, and made for Leo.

'You haven't got any champagne.'

He stood amiably, hesitated, then accepted the glass. 'I'll drink her health then,' he said, and took a sip, looking in Sally's direction. 'You're right, she looks beautiful.'

'Leo, are you - all right?' she asked.

'All right?'

'Have things - improved, as you said?'

'I could never use the word improved after losing you.'

'I was referring to your attitude to things.'

For a moment there was a glimpse of the old Leo, as he smiled. 'You really want to know?'

'I'd like to know you're all right.'

'I haven't been in trouble again, if that's what you mean.'

'Money OK?'

His smile faded, and he looked away with a bored look. 'You won't believe it, me of all people. A couple of months back I came into a legacy.'

'But - that's marvellous. A lot?'

'An indecent lot.'

'So you're able to live off it?'

He avoided the question. 'I get by fine.'

'You've been able to get going on a business again?'

'Well I have actually - but that had happened before the windfall.' She could see he wasn't interested in the money question. He was looking at her intently. 'God, I've been a fool, Joss.'

She closed a door in her mind. 'We're not going into that.'

'No.'

She changed tack quickly. 'I saw about Matthew.'

'Yes, the silly bugger.'

'Not the success story you thought after all.'

'No.' She could see the subject was central to him, but he began at once to gather himself, as if pulling himself forcibly from it. 'Look, I'd better go,' he said. 'I can see Sally doesn't want to speak to me, and I'm making things difficult for you. I'm grateful to you, Joss, for letting me come. It's meant a great deal to me - just to be a witness. Looks as if old Sal's done herself all right. Though' - he paused, the old humour breaking through- 'though frankly, her bloke looks a right ponce to me. But I would be prejudiced against lawyers, wouldn't I?'

She smiled. That's all that needs saying, she told herself. She had done her duty, and kept her end up, her dignity. She could remember today with a calm mind now. It was only that dignity and initiative didn't seem to be as relevant in dealing with Leo, just as it used to be. She had a rash desire to detain him. He had told her nothing about himself, nothing about Matthew and his attitude to him, nothing about Quixote and Panchez. She flicked a glance across the room to Henry who, she saw, received her look, but immediately looked away. It brought back all her former feelings in a rush. Charity was all she was asking for, she thought. She made a quick decision. Flushing, she turned back to Leo.

'I'll meet you in Dartmouth tomorrow afternoon, two thirty at the Royal Castle Hotel. I want to know you're all right before we part company.'

He didn't answer, but seemed to shake his head. Then he left without looking at her again, without looking at Sally. He threaded his way quietly through the throng and out of the far door that led into the hall.

23.

Some time ago they had asked the Playmores and their hosts to stay to supper after the wedding, but happily they'd had to decline because of their hosts. Henry had a nice idea. He suggested they had a small do just for Edith, Geoff, the others and their spouses, all of whom were involved with the wedding. They had all been delighted to accept.

It was a warm and fitting conclusion to the day, with all the right connotations. Jocelyn had done the new food in advance herself, leftovers would not have been appropriate, and Henry had made sure there was plenty of champagne set aside. As they sat down to the meal in the cleared sitting-room, drawing up chairs to the table which still had its white cloth for the wedding fare, Henry seemed restored to full cheerfulness. When they had eaten, Edith made a toast to 'the other happy couple', as she put it. Henry put his arm round her waist and kissed her cheek. Then Geoff, a good deal less than sober, proposed health 'to Combe'. They all drank to that.

But for Jocelyn, over the goodwill of the evening there was a cloud. She had intended to tell Henry about the meeting she had arranged with Leo when the guests and the catering firm had gone, but a few locals like Peter Potter lingered. Then in the few moments they had upstairs before going down to the supper, Henry was busy talking about the day. She thought, now it was over, Henry had decided to put Leo from his mind. The longer she left it, the more ashamed she felt, but having failed to seize an early moment she came to think it would be better to say nothing. She would do what she had intended, on her own, as she had done what she intended today, then leave it. Perhaps, she wouldn't even go. Leo's odd head-shaking at her suggestion could well have meant he wouldn't be there.

In the morning Henry was up when she woke, whistling in the bathroom. 'Think I'll get out and fix that fence this morning, or the cows'll be in again,' he said as he appeared, naked, towelling himself vigorously. She had decided on waking she *would* be going to Dartmouth, and nearly blurted it then. She'd just mention it casually, she thought, as if her arrangement to meet

Leo was no more than a daily chore. But she imagined herself saying it - 'oh, by the way, I'm meeting Leo in Dartmouth today. I just want to be sure he's all right before he clears off.' She knew it wouldn't come out like that. He would spot the falsehood as quickly as he would spot a malignant fungus on a plant or a tree. She funked it again.

Did she really care about Leo then? Of course she did, as Henry had cared all those years for his smashed happiness. She went about the real clearing up that morning - the re-hoovering, the proper dusting and polishing which an outside firm could not be expected to do, and the restoration of the furniture to its proper positions. But all the time she thought of Leo, and what had befallen him. Was he all right? How much happier would she be if she could know he had somehow reformed? Sense advised her not to find out, to do what Sally had done, turn her head aside. She couldn't do that. Her fear now was that Leo wouldn't be there - for in what new limbo would that strand her?

There was no difficulty in leaving the house. Henry came in for lunch, sweaty and happy from his exertions. He had embarked on the whole fence, not just the bit which had been broken. 'It's all rotten and will go again if I don't tackle it,' he said heartily. It would take him the rest of the day. 'What are *you* up to?' he enquired once, aware he had been talking too much. When she told him she was clearing up, he just nodded. He probably presumed she would be spending the afternoon at it.

There were two ways to Dartmouth by car, right up to Totnes and down the other side of the estuary, or the much shorter road to Kingswear, then the ferry across the water. She chose the latter route, left the car on the Kingswear side and bought a passenger fare. In the sunshine, which had now re-established itself over the showery weather of yesterday, she stood on the car deck as the rickety vessel churned between its restraining chains. Ahead of her lay the old town, rising to the Naval College. Upstream were two small grey naval vessels moored side by side like neatly seated cats, the lower estuary was littered with Sunday leisure craft. Was he there in the jumble of houses ahead of her? She imagined him sitting in the hall of the hotel -

waiting, wondering, too, if she would come. Alternately, she imagined the place empty of him. Would that end the matter?

He wasn't in the hall. The hotel was in the throes of doing a big lunch for some party. Presumably he would be in the bar or the lounge, wouldn't he? In the stuffy corridor on the way to the lounge, which smelt of food, she passed a red-faced man walking unsteadily on his way back to the dining-room from the toilet. He stood aside for her to pass, leering. She opened the glass door. At first, as her eye swept the small tables and armchairs, she thought it was deserted. It was only two-fifteen, she told herself in a panic, she was ridiculously early. Then she saw him rising from a chair near the window, folding a newspaper.

His smile of relief and pleasure moved her. 'Jossy, you've come - and early,' he said. 'I was laying bets with myself. Lost heavily I'm glad to say.'

To cover her feelings she indulged in repartee. 'No intuition these days?'

He took her seriously. 'Oh yes, still a good deal of that. That's one thing I've never lost.'

'Shall we sit here?'

They sat at the table in the old bow window where he had been, which looked like the poop of a galleon. It commanded a fine view of the estuary and the steep wooded hill beyond. She thought they should order something. 'No need - unless you want it,' he said. 'They're all too busy with the binge-up to notice. Anyway I stayed here last night, I'm a guest.'

She didn't really want to plunge in. It would have been nice just to sit, to listen to the vibes through more ordinary speech, maybe even joke a bit. She thought it would be possible for them to joke. Now they had met beyond the scrutiny of the others, it seemed remarkably easy. She thought he might have been feeling the same about a relaxed chat, but she saw him forego the pleasure. She saw him force himself to respect her motive for coming.

'So, you really want to know about me?' he said at once.

'Yes.'

'Where do I start?'

'Wherever you think. Where are you living, what are you doing?'

'I'll start with Matthew.'

'All right, but it's you I want to know about.'

'Then I'll start with Matthew. It's relevant.'

He stared out of the window. 'Matthew was being blackmailed,' he began, 'apparently by someone he'd done down in business years back, though whoever it was had been very careful to cover his tracks. That picture the papers got of Matthew with the woman was taken ages ago. Whoever it was had been taking money from him for a year or more. Then I suppose there was one demand too many. Matthew had been soaked dry - and probably because of his new job the ante had been upped. Anyway, he decided to call it a day and threw in his cards. The blackmailer presumably collected another large sum from the newspapers.'

'You've seen Matthew?'

'Oh yes. I called at his London flat - about a couple of weeks after the story broke. He was out when I arrived, but his wife Naomi, was there. I'd never met her before, but when she heard who I was - Matthew had never told her of my existence - she told me everything. She said she'd known nothing about it until that week or two before. Matthew hadn't even had the courage to tell her, she'd had to read it in the press. Then she discovered from Matthew about the blackmail and its results. Their country house was mortgaged to the hilt and would have to be sold. The London house was rented, and the amount would now be too high for their dwindled resources. They'd have to move somewhere a lot smaller. I asked Naomi how she felt. She said she didn't know. She was going through the act of the dutiful wife. She thought her eventual feelings would probably depend on Matthew and how he behaved.'

'How was he behaving?'

'Badly apparently. Turned against everyone, including her, despite the hypocritical photo she allowed the press to take of them together outside the flat. He seemed to think it was everyone's fault but his own.'

'But the prostitute? There was no doubt he'd been with her?'

'He'd been with her all right. But that was Naomi's fault apparently, for staying in the country too much and not supporting him in London - that's how he was seeing it.'

'How awful for Naomi.' She paused. 'You saw Matthew, too, you say?'

'Yes, he came in when I was there.'

'Did he treat you civilly?'

'Far from it. He wanted to know what the hell I was doing in his house and told me to get out. As a matter of fact he was quite right about wanting me to go. I didn't much like my own motive for being there.'

'What was your motive?'

'Curiosity. I pretended sympathy of course, but what I really wanted was to see for myself, in the flesh, that the vision I'd been chasing all those years was a crazy phantom, that Matthew was as fallible as I'd been. That's what I was feeling then.'

'But you changed?'

'I suppose I did, yes.'

'How?'

'You won't believe this, but in a few days I found I was feeling sorry for Matthew. Really. In the few moments I was with him I'd seen all the workings of that gene we must share - the rage at our redundant and irrelevant family past, the self-disbelief and the despair it had bred, the need to cover it up with some kind of ladder-climbing. In Matthew's case of course that had been politics, in mine money - social position. Then, only a month afterwards, something utterly extraordinary happened. If I was religious I'd be building a shrine or something, throwing up a statue of Our Lady and starting a cult. Someone phoned me in the place where I live. I was out and my landlady took a message. I phoned the number and found I was on to a lawyer. Was my address so and so, and was I Leopold Edward Cunningham? He sounded like the returning officer declaring an election result. When he was convinced I was, he asked if I'd call at his office, and bring identification. If he hadn't said it was something "I might consider to my advantage", I'm not sure I'd've gone, I thought it must be my past backfiring again. Well, I went. Very posh premises near Lincoln's Inn. I still got the feeling something distasteful was coming, the man seemed to find my presence in his office an assault on propriety. But the nitty was that because of Matthew's disgrace I'd been left a considerable sum of money, to wit about half a million.'

He paused, as if amazed anew. 'But - that's marvellous,' she had to prompt. 'Who was the benefactor?'

'That's just it, that's what makes it so bloody miraculous. It was nobody I ever remember. Apparently she was a relation - some sort of distant cousin who'd been in her nineties and had no children or grandchildren alive. She'd left all her money to Matthew, but because of the case had gone right off him. She must have known of my existence - but not obviously of *my* brushes with the law - switched her will at the last moment, then kicked the bucket before she'd even had me traced. I guess the lawyer'd had a hard time finding me and obviously didn't think much of my address when he did. How about that for a Dickensian happy-ever-after ending?'

'But that's incredible. So now you're . . .

'Saved, that's the word for it. The Salvation Army couldn't have done a better job.'

She began to feel there was something he was withholding. He was looking sheepish. 'You haven't blown the money?' she said anxiously.

He gave a quick laugh. 'The question to be expected. Touché - and yes, I suppose you might say I *have* blown it.'

'What on?'

'Ah, that would be telling.'

'You've gambled it?'

'A good way of describing it, though this time it's yielded the jackpot.' He saw her distress. 'It's all right, no cause for alarm. Everything's under control.'

'Leo, what have you done?'

Her spirits sinking, she saw him toy with some new evasion. 'Oh, I don't know,' he said, fidgeting, 'the rest isn't perhaps so interesting.'

'I want to know.'

He hesitated, then seemed to make up his mind. 'All right, I wasn't going to say, but it may, again, conceivably amuse you as a footnote to everything. I gave the money to Matthew, or most of it. It was really his anyway.'

She gaped. 'You gave it to Matthew, and he kept it?'

'He didn't know it was from me. I didn't yet have my hands on the legacy, which isn't going to come through for ages, but on the strength of its being on the way I got the bank to lend me what I wanted. I got a solicitor to have it delivered by hand, in cash, anonymously "from a well-wisher".'

She still couldn't get her mind round it. 'But how do you know he accepted it if it was anonymous?' she managed to say.

'A good question. I was of course as interested in that as you are, and nosed around a bit. Matthew's flat was in Westminster. Round the corner was a booze shop where I was sure Matthew - and probably Naomi, too, from the manner in which she was putting it away when I went to see her - were customers. I was right. Fortunately the man was a gossip, and so, it seemed, no doubt out of exasperation, was Naomi, who'd been spilling a lot of beans in his direction. I got the man talking on the "bad-luck-on-old-Cunningham-round-the-corner" line. I told him I used to know him. Yes, but didn't I know, there'd been a windfall from a well-wisher, I was told? Lady Cunningham had been in and said so. They'd be staying in the flat after all. Apparently the man didn't only sell drink. He seemed to throw in a buy-and-sell gossip service as well. He finished with a lot of crap about ill-winds and how some people always land on their feet.'

Jocelyn strove to gather her scattered thoughts. 'But it's astonishingly good of you to do what you did.'

'I don't know, now I look back it all has a sort of inevitable symmetry.'

'What do you mean symmetry? It was a wonderfully decent act. It's probably made all the difference to your brother, and therefore to Naomi - the thought that someone cared, as well as the actual money.'

'Maybe. But I take no credit for it. It's just the other side of an equation. The human brain seems constructed in this way. Tilt it too far one way and it tilts back on you to compensate.'

'Are you trying to tell me giving Matthew this money was *involuntary*?'

'Yes, I really think it was. Certainly I take a hedonistic view. Apart from persuading you to marry me, it's the most satisfactory thing I've ever done and was entirely in my interest. It's rid me of the tentacles of my past at a stroke. A top shrink couldn't have thought up a neater solution. All I regret is that I didn't have the opportunity before, or that I'd had a clean mental slate to start adult life, as you had.'

She removed herself from his ambit for a moment. How could she absorb this extraordinary turnabout? Was it true even, she asked herself, in a desperate attempt to break out of her feelings? Was this just another of Leo's clever ruses to win her sympathy? There was something at the back of her mind and it only took her a moment to remember it.

'Why did you plant those wooden things at Combe?' she said, in another voice she didn't recognise.

His tone also changed. He had been confident, almost reserved, now he was nearer the Leo she knew - rash, quick, covering the ground like a dog on a scent. 'Ah yes, that's another matter. I'm sorry about all that. All that took place when my other life was still in progress, before the Matthew story broke. I actually read about Matthew's débâcle when I was down here. I'd found out where you lived through Sally. She had to be knowing where you were of course. When she announced her engagement in the papers in the winter I kept watch. I thought she'd be writing to you. I watched her going to work each morning. I was sure sooner or later she'd be writing to you and post the letter on her way. I thought I'd wait until the collection was made and tell the man I'd posted a letter with the wrong address or something, and try to get it back. It didn't work, there was no letter, or she didn't use that box. But just before Christmas she and her man went on holiday. I broke into the flat and found a letter you'd written. You'd carefully put no address, but the letter was still in the envelope, stamped Totnes. In the letter you mentioned the word Combe. I came down here and the rest was easy. I found out you were married. I saw you and Henry working together in the garden, apparently so content. It got to me. I couldn't believe you could have found someone else to love in the way we used to. I had to let you know I knew where you were. I put Don Quixote in your room, yes, which I took from the Nottingham house as a memento - and Sancho in the greenhouse. I was going to go on doing things. I had a mad idea somehow you couldn't love Henry, and that when you knew I was around, after a time I'd take shape and something miraculous would happen. I confess I wasn't very clear what. Then, while I was still down here, the Matthew story happened. It changed everything. I knew I had to see him, to make sure the story was true. I left here and went back to London. I saw Matthew as I've described. Then those few weeks later the money arrived like manna, and everything changed.

'It wasn't long before I realised there were symmetries other than my own to be established. You also have had to redress a balance. I realised finally I no longer have a claim on you, that I'd run well past my expiry date. But I did want to see Sally married - and yes, I did want to see you, like this, just once more, in a proper way. That's why I wrote to Sally. I'd've been content with what we exchanged yesterday - I know what it cost you to do what you did - but you were kind enough to suggest this meeting, which is a bonus. I shall put it on the shelf with my other mementos.'

A door opened in the corridor outside the room, and a burst of noise fell out. The lunchers were breaking up. Two men and two women came laughing into the lounge looking for something. A bag was found by the fireplace by one of the men. Out of it stuck the handle of a squash racket. He lifted it in their direction. 'A healthy body and a filthy mind,' he bawled at them, then belched. The women screeched with further laughter.

When they had gone, Leo got up. 'I'd better go now. I've checked out of my room. Just got to hop into the car. I did treat myself to quite a decent second hand car.'

She also rose, confused. 'But what'll you do now, Leo? All this is the past. What of your future?'

'My future's going to be OK. All I ask is that you put in a

good word for me with Sal when she's settled down. I'd like to see her from time to time.'

'Of course I will. But what are you going to do for a living?'

'Not the auction business certainly.'

'No. What then?'

'Something'll turn up. Don't worry, Joss. You don't have to worry about anything now except your life.'

'I wouldn't mind seeing you sometimes - if things really have changed, but Henry . . .

'Doesn't see me in a very favourable light. Of course he doesn't. I don't blame him. I wouldn't if I were in his shoes. He looks a really nice bloke.'

They were at the point of departure. She wanted to stop it, but there was no way. She saw he wouldn't allow it. It was this which told her above all else that he had been telling the truth, this was no bid for sympathy. He held her hand, then raised it to his lips. 'Little green fingers,' he said, looking at them. 'They'd make any blossom bloom.' He looked her in the eyes once more, then left. At the door he paused for a last jaunty wave - the old Leo.

24.

She drove back from Dartmouth like the wind. She could only think of Henry and the predicament she had landed herself in. It was barely four, but he might well have come up from the garden and seen her car gone. Then she met an oncoming car on a corner and passed it with inches to spare, the hedgerow slashing at the windows. This was absurd, risking an accident. Of course she must tell Henry where she had been. What had she to hide? If so, what was the hurry? She slowed down.

As she took off her coat in the hall, she heard a clink of crockery in the kitchen. She went to him at once. He was sitting at the large table with a cup of tea, studying a catalogue, pencil in hand. She knew at once he guessed where she had been. The frown was overstudious. She had already decided to come straight out with it.

'I've been in to Dartmouth to say goodbye to Leo,' she said as she went to the dresser to get a cup for herself. He made no answer, and turned a page. 'I thought it was only decent when he'd come all this way, and Sally was so, well, Sallyish. I fixed it with him at the wedding.' He made no comment. She poured from the brown pot which was sitting on the Aga. The milk bottle was on the table. 'I'm glad I did,' she continued, grabbing it, and sitting opposite him. 'It's drawn a proper line instead of leaving a blank space.'

He took a sip from his cup and sent her a brief glance. 'Remorseful, was he?' he remarked. The tone was spare.

'He wasn't actually. There've been some remarkable new developments in Leo's life. I really think he's changed.'

'That has to be for the better, I imagine.'

She seized the horns. 'Henry, I do want you to know about it, if you don't mind, even if it's distasteful to you - and I can understand if it is. I want just to tell you for the record if nothing more. When I've done so, that'll be that, it can be laid to rest. But I do hope we'll always tell each other things.'

'Relevant things, certainly.'

'This is relevant - to me.'

He pushed the catalogue aside. 'Fire away then,' he said. He folded his arms like a schoolboy in a first eleven photograph.

It wasn't the best emotional environment, but it was an environment. She told him factually what Leo had said, and concluded by saying how much better it made her feel that Leo, too, now had some chance of happiness.

Now she had said it, she felt ridiculous. He was right, it wasn't in any way relevant to their life. While she was talking, he had been playing with the pencil, his eyes cast down. Now he was nodding in a tolerant way.

'So,' she said after a moment and after drawing a deep breath, 'did you finish the fence?'

What more could she expect from him? It had been perhaps foolish of her just to blurt it out like that, but what else could she have done in the circumstances? The banality of their exchange left an unpleasant void. Considering the sympathy and forebearance she had given him over Delia, he could have shown, surely, a modicum of interest in the outcome of what had been after all a very large part of her life. She would have preferred it if he had been angry at her unannounced rendezvous. Anger exposes its perpetrator as well as attacks its opponent, it can be regretted and forgiven, anger spawns its antidote. An unpleasant thought struck her. Leo, in the matter of his surely legitimate presence at the wedding, had behaved with rather more dignity than Henry - and Leo was the loser. She brooded also on what Leo had said about equations, and the redress of disturbed balances. Had her equation been squared by their encounter?

The busy summer resumed. Their life settled. How easily, Jocelyn thought, activity, the impedimenta of life, closes over what we like to think are the finer moments, the occasional flashes of insight and revelation. As they went to bed at night, she sometimes questioned that she had ever had qualms about her last meeting with Leo, and about Henry's less than sympathetic comments on it. She questioned once more her own talent for introspection, which might well be thought - at some Olympian tribunal where such matters are judged - not so much to interpret or uplift life, but simply to stop it in its tracks when it didn't need stopping.

By the end of the summer Jocelyn had adjudicated her behaviour over Leo's visit as somewhat juvenile. She didn't stop thinking of Leo and wondering how he was faring, but she could see it had been over-simple on her part to expect that she could share her thoughts about him with Henry. How often, for that matter, did they discuss Delia? It was no doubt the experience of any second marriage. You had these two rooms at the top of the house which must be kept permanently locked. She and Henry re-found the tenderness and concern for each other which, she soothed herself, had only temporarily been disturbed. She even thought she discerned sometimes an extra element in Henry's attentiveness to her, as if he wished to atone for their brief estrangement. She appreciated anew how admirable his non-verbal approach to life could be. Perhaps because her own parents had seemed to suffer from such a self-denying and life-protracted silence, she had always been a blurter. She and Leo had been mutual blurters - with the one tragic exception on his part. But the alternative thesis did not have to be like that of her parents. Henry exemplified the - surely quintessentially English - technique at its best? One communicated through deeds and glints in the eye, not through the overt - this was what he posited. Perhaps in time she also would become like this? *Per forza,* she thought with grim humour. Henry wouldn't change to her way.

In September they decided to take a holiday before the sun completely disappeared, even though they were still busy. 'Let the troops run the place for a few days, do them good,' Henry said. 'And we could call it a honeymoon. Do you realise we haven't had one yet?'

She had forgotten. Apart from the two wedding week-ends, theirs and Sally's, they had been at it solidly. They thought south-west France - fly to Toulouse and hire a car. She bought two Michelins, the main red one for hotels, and the green regional guide for sightseeing. They spent an evening picking hotels. She was warmed to find their expectation of the holiday fitted exactly. They decided on a peripatetic journey with one night stands. First they fixed what they wanted to see, then chose accommodation accordingly. She booked the first two nights on the phone. They left the rest to when they got there. They might want to change their minds.

The evening before they were due to go, Peter Potter came to supper. Henry was asking his advice about a legal matter concerning the refectory, which in view of the settlement with Murdoch was going to be built after all that winter. Because of the delay, they'd had to re-apply for planning permission, and their neighbours - whose house was some five hundred yards away - had remonstrated to the committee, which they hadn't done originally, on the grounds that if cooked meals were to be supplied, they could be assailed by obnoxious smells. Henry was confident they had no case, but he wanted to be sure.

Jocelyn had not amended her view of Peter Potter, who had seemed to her at the time of Henry's arrest to overestimate himself - as if the law was not, as she regarded it, a necessary but rather clumsy point of reference when human affairs got out of order, but a kind of holy tablet of morality of which he and other lawyers were the priestly custodians. They, the rest of mankind, were apparently their flock. She suspected Henry might have come to have much the same view of Potter, but she knew he respected and was grateful for his acumen, as (apparently) illustrated over the Delia affair. She programmed herself for an evening of appropriate hospitality.

Potter and Henry dealt with the business. Potter, after labyrinthine to-ings and fro-ings, agreed with their own assessment of their neighbours' challenge. They finished the modest meal and went back to the sitting-room. Jocelyn took out some embroidery, an atrophied habit she had recently revived. Topics of conversation were suddenly thin on the ground.

'Oh, I met someone the other day who'll interest you both,' Potter declared suddenly into the silence. 'I must have mentioned to you before, Henry, that we have a kind of West Country lawyers' pow-wow once a year. This year it was up in Cheltenham. Guess who I bumped into - Patrick Murdoch's solicitor, Roger McAlpine. Because Murdoch was, in the initial stages anyway, so difficult, I'd always imagined somehow his solicitor must be the same. Far from it. McAlpine turned out to be a most agreeable fellow. I shouldn't probably tell you this, but we fell inevitably to discussing the case. I'd always imagined that it must have been McAlpine's advice - after he'd received my broadsides - which changed Murdoch's mind about the very generous offer we made, and which also prompted him to phone the police about Delia's telephone call. Interestingly, apparently it wasn't. As I guessed, McAlpine had originally advised Murdoch to settle on something like our terms, but when Murdoch dug his heels in he felt he had to go along with his client's position. On second thoughts he concluded there was a case to be made for resisting our challenge to the will. I have to put in that McAlpine probably also saw the chance of the conveyancy business coming his way if this place was sold up. But then, as we know, quite unexpectedly Murdoch suddenly caved in and wanted to settle after all. He said he'd thought about it and decided he didn't want to be bothered with a matter that had become extremely distasteful to him. The deal we'd offered got it all out of the way at a stroke, and so on. Now the interesting thing is that McAlpine didn't quite believe in Murdoch's reasoning. He had the quite definite impression there was some other unknown factor pushing him, something which wasn't being said.'

'You mean he felt guilty?' Henry said.

'That's what I put to McAlpine. But he didn't think it was guilt. His impression was that Murdoch was *scared* about something.'

'What on earth could he be scared about?'

'A good question, which I also put to McAlpine. McAlpine didn't know at the time of course about the telephone call which Delia had made to him a week before she died, but he very soon did when it came out in the press after the coroner's second hearing. He also knew Murdoch had been interviewed by the police. When he mentioned the matter to Murdoch he refused to discuss it further and said the matter was closed. Yet again, he said, he got this feeling that Murdoch was scared - shifty was the word he used - and was hiding something. One couldn't help noticing, too, how uncomfortable-seeming and uncommunicative he was at the inquest. An interesting little postscript, isn't it?'

To Jocelyn's dismay, Henry's attention had quickened. She could see he wasn't going to drop the subject. 'He most certainly *was* uncomfortable at the inquest. I'd call it shifty. I made an attempt to speak to him, to thank him again, but he practically turned his back on me. What was he hiding, do you think?'

Potter, Jocelyn thought, was beginning to realise he might have been indiscreet. She prayed he would act on his realisation and stop here. 'One may well ask,' he said, more blandly.

Henry was looking correspondingly more concentrated. 'Are you suggesting Murdoch may have delivered the poison?' he persisted.

Potter looked sheepish. '*I'm* not suggesting anything,' he said.

'Well, McAlpine then. Is that what he was implying, perhaps even saying?'

'He certainly didn't say that.'

'But that's what he meant?'

'I suppose he might have done. I can't say.'

There was pause. In her anxiety, Jocelyn had snagged her wool. She bent over the embroidery frame to hide the flush she was sure was igniting her cheeks. How could Potter be so tactless as to raise this matter again - so painful to Henry? She dared not look up.

'That's what you thought, wasn't it, Joss?' Henry said. 'You thought Murdoch was the only person who might have a motive.'

'Did I?'

'Of course you did - that dreadful morning when you came up to my room and were so marvellously supportive.'

'It was what anyone might have thought.'

'But "anyone" didn't think it, including me. It didn't occur to the police either, even after Murdoch got on to them apparently, and they went to see him.'

She prayed the matter would be dropped here. Of what possible interest was this to anyone now? But Potter was also looking at her. '*I* remember your being interested in Murdoch, too, Jocelyn,' he said. 'The morning I came to tell you about

Henry's bail. You asked me where Murdoch lived. Do you remember that? He was much on your mind wasn't he?'

'I suppose he must have been.'

There was another tense silence. Jocelyn had cleared the knot and continued stitching. She felt both men were looking at her, as if she were someone in the dock awaiting a sentence. She never thought she would ever pray for Henry's taciturnity as she did now. Let him for these few ghastly moments be the most insensitive dull-witted male imaginable, she thought. Let him fail to notice how agitated she was.

'Joss, do you know something you haven't told me?'

She contemplated lying only for an instant. How would she get away with it under this double assault? Wasn't there also an element of resentment still there in her somewhere, that desire to retaliate which she had felt before, *a redress of balances.* Why should she have to bear her secret alone? She tried to keep her voice as level as she could. 'Yes,' she said. 'I went to see the dreadful man. It seemed the only hope.'

'You went to see Murdoch in Cheltenham?'

'Yes. The day after the one you were mentioning, Peter. I went up in my car.'

'What for?'

She put the embroidery in her lap, and looked at Henry. All right, if she was going to have to say it she was going to say it all, and in front of a witness. What better one than this cocky lawyer who had thought he brought off the whole thing by the elegance of his legal prose? In the act, she was able to say it calmly, without emotion, almost disinterestedly, as if it had not been herself involved. She related what had happened and, before they could question her, also carefully covered in advance what she thought would be the ifs and buts.

When she had finished, she looked at them in turn. Potter had the modesty to look shriven. So much for his legal expertise having been the cause of the successful outcome. He was looking towards Henry. Henry was looking astounded.

'You did all that without a word to anyone?' was all he managed.

'It seemed the only way out.'

'It's incredible.'

'I assure you it happened.'

'Murdock could have harmed you.'

'The thought crossed my mind.'

'But why have you kept quiet about it all this time?'

'There seemed no point in it becoming known. Everything seemed to have had a satisfactory outcome.'

Henry began to look cross. 'That can't be the reason,' he said.

Did she have to say everything? It seemed like it. She became fatalistic. If she got blamed, she would know how to respond. 'I wasn't sure what you'd do,' she said. 'I thought you'd want to sue Murdoch, or have him charged or something. I didn't think that would be wise. It seemed better to me to leave things exactly as they were, not push our luck. For another thing, I had a selfish motive. I'd told a whopping lie. I'd said I'd seen Murdoch in the garden on that alleged night. I didn't fancy perjuring myself in a witness box and probably being cross-examined.'

'My God,' Henry said, 'you've known this all this time and said nothing.'

It didn't seem to Jocelyn the news was entirely pleasing to him. In spite of the tension, she had a whimsical thought. How about her period of silence qualifying in the non-blurtery stakes? Some marks due on that score, surely?

At least it broke the evening up. Sensing the uneasiness, and no doubt nursing the wound to his own ego, Potter soon decided he must go. 'Well, your intervention certainly seemed to do the trick, Jocelyn,' was the nearest he got to paying her a compliment. 'Not quite orthodox proceedure, but I have to say it seems to have been effective. It was certainly the day after your visit that Murdoch phoned my office, and the police. That stuff about gold-refining was a master-stroke. I bet, guilty or not, that made him sweat.'

Henry saw Potter to his car. While he was away, she resumed her sewing. Now she had said it, she felt a lot calmer, even relieved. She hadn't enjoyed her secret. Henry returned, looking grim. He re-sat himself in the chair.

'Patrick murdered Delia,' he said blackly.

'Is euthanasia murder?'

'It wasn't euthanasia. On Delia's part it could be said to be maybe, but not his. He stood to gain. He brought her the means to end her life knowing almost for sure that he was going to inherit this property. He could well have made it a condition for doing what he did. You cannot call causing someone's death mercy killing if a mercenary motive is involved.'

'He *could* have made it a condition, but it might well have been Delia's idea - which she put to Patrick, not necessarily to encourage him to do what she wanted, but also to injure you.'

'I don't believe it.'

'Does it matter either way? We're not ever going to know. If it were put to him, Murdoch would simply deny it. There's no transcript of their conversation. Nothing's changed.'

'Of course everything's changed. That man's a murderer, and he's got away with it. You should never have hidden this from me, Joss. He should be brought to justice.'

Her anxiety was reborn. 'No, Henry, that would be madness.'

'Madness to bring a villain to justice?'

'What good would it do? He didn't murder Delia. Undoubtedly Delia had decided to take her own life. If Patrick hadn't assisted her she would have found some other means. The difficulty was your being accused, and possibly being convicted, of murder - and the difficulty of the will and your losing the estate which was yours by any canon of moral right. Both those things have been dealt with satisfactorily. Force Patrick into the dock and goodness knows what will result. He'd undoubtedly say all sorts of ghastly things. He'd re-construe his behaviour after my visit in some way. You could even be accused again, so could I. No, Henry, I'm not always certain about things but I am about this.'

'I'm going to the police. It's my duty.'

'Duty? Is that the word?'

'What do you mean?'

'In my opinion, if you're really thinking of doing that it's some strange working of your pointless guilt again. It must be. What you're suggesting is masochistic madness. And you're leaving something out - me. You seem to have forgotten that if Patrick were put on trial I'd have to be a witness.'

'Of course.'

'You mean you'd expect me to stand up and lie in public, would you, in the way I did to Murdoch? You'd want me to say I go for walks when I can't sleep and saw him climbing out of the house that night?'

'That would be a small price to pay to get the man convicted.'

She lost her temper. 'Oh, I see. I'm to pay what you call "a small price" to satisfy this crazy vindictiveness of yours which, as I say, has a very suspect origin. I save your neck - and incidentally risk my own. Murdoch, as you surmise, could have quietly done me in that day and no one might have been the wiser. Nobody knew where I'd gone, I could have just disappeared. I save your neck - you don't think by any chance, do you, sitting on your macho Mount Olympus, that I might have an opinion at least worth listening to in consequence?'

'Joss . . .

'Don't Joss me. Frankly I think your attitude over this stinks. Because you're an ex-Commando used to giving heroic orders in the heat of battle, you think you can do the same in real life. Well I can tell you, real life can't be reduced to such simplicities. I'll tell you something else - I'm not *going* to perjure myself in court. If I were called as a witness I should say the exact truth and nothing but it. I shall admit to making up the walking in the garden story, and the reason for it - the hope of flushing Murdoch out of his lies. The fact that he acted on my proposal will be in your favour and go a long way to proving my point, but you realise the conclusions they'll draw from all this? They'll say that I was in love with you (rather proved by subsequent events, isn't it?), that we'd been having an affair all the time, and that we'd jointly plotted your ultimatum to Delia and her demise on that very night. *Now* can you see how daft you're being? You're almost as bad as Leo in one respect. He, too, was guilty of acting from a phoney male idealism. Have I to endure it twice?' She stormed from the room and upstairs.

The standard thing would have been to throw herself on the bed and weep. She felt like neither. Now she had said what she had, she felt totally calm again, not even angry. Was she a lot harder, she wondered, than she had ever admitted? Had this speech of hers been waiting all the time in the wings, tethered only by some ingrained conditioning to good behaviour - or, worse, by self-interest?

Automatically, she set about preparations for bed. She had a bath, lingered over it, half-listening for sounds downstairs. There were none. Had he gone out? What did she really know of him, she thought? Another woman had known him from early manhood, had borne his children. Who was she by comparison? She thought of Leo, in digs somewhere in London - Kensington was it? She began to think of their early days, until tears did start pricking. Of one thing she was sure. She wasn't going down to Henry. She shouldn't have mentioned Leo like that, which had been spiteful, but the rest of what she had said she meant and couldn't withdraw. She was tired of making emotional adjustments to save other people's pride.

She was in bed and about to put the light out when she heard him coming upstairs. His movements were slow on the stairs and the landing. He appeared.

'I'm deeply sorry,' he said at once. 'I was totally selfish and self-indulgent, and I'm entirely in the wrong.' He sat down heavily in the armchair which faced the bed. 'You're right about Murdoch. Things must of course be left as they are.' He paused as if to gather strength for the most difficult part of what he must say. 'And with astounding courage and clear sight, you saved me, Joss - from the law, and more importantly from myself. Though I'll try, I'll probably never be able to repay to you the service you've done me.'

25.

In the next years, Henry repaid Jocelyn a hundredfold for the service she had rendered him. This wasn't so much through any specific deeds of his. She had always enjoyed his daily thoughtfulness on her behalf, his imaginative tenderness. What was new was a whole change in his general attitude.

She thought that Henry's upbringing, his career in the Commandos, perhaps his early marriage to Delia - certainly its tragic later stages - had taught him a certain attitude to women. He had been modern enough in superficial manifestations, such as sharing the cooking and other domestic chores. Politically, verbally, he had subscribed to liberal values. But his instinct had still been gallant, old-fashioned. His gestures, his every voice inflection had implied that women were to be defended, honoured in an inner shrine, even worshipped. But at the same time they were expected to conform to the female role created for them by the historic male. What had shocked him about her visit to Murdoch was that she had stepped outside this assigned part. His instinctive reaction to what she had done for him was to feel humiliated, for by her act she had usurped his own role.

What she deeply admired was his immediate recognition that he had been wrong. His apology on that same evening had carried with it no element of the abject, there was not a shred of masochism about it, for at base it was an intellectual change which had taken place, which would be permanent. She remembered all those small but telling evidences she had collected of his former attitude - from that first letter he wrote her with the suggestion that a woman wouldn't wish to haul and draw - and saw that if these were to recur, as they inadvertently might, they would be instantly recognised and laughed about. They had broken through, she thought. She hadn't expected her life with Henry would ever contain that element of passion she had once enjoyed with Leo. She now began to think it could. If it did, it would not snap into flame as she and Leo had in those days in Venice. It would be an accumulative conflagration, and who is to say that this would not prove as all-consuming a fire?

A bond between them of inestimable strength was the garden.

Love it as she had done from the first moment she saw it, she hadn't thought she could ever be possessed by it as Henry was. But this, too, was coming about. The daily toil it demanded, the vision, planning, and the process of seeing it constantly through the admiring eyes of visitors, carried with it an implicit submission to its charm. It was a sadness that they would not have children, which paradoxically she might have been keener on than she had been with Leo, but less of one when they stood on the Italian terrace on summer evenings and felt that in some degree the garden was like an offspring, as much and as little of their own conception - for plants and trees are as wayward and unpredictable as new human life and as rewarding for this very contrariness.

A week-end in late June five years later the Bordeauxs were in London. Henry, an increasingly well-known and now influential figure in the flourishing British gardens industry - for an industry was what it has become these days - had now been elected to the committee of the National Gardens Association. It was a meeting of this body which accounted for their visit to London. The meeting had been on the Friday. On Saturday they enjoyed themselves. The weather was fine and they took a river trip down to Greenwich, had a delicious lunch in an outside restaurant, and in the evening went to the National Theatre. They had decided to forget money, which was becoming an increasingly lesser consideration, and stayed at the Hyde Park Hotel.

Someone he knew well on the National Gardens Committee, whose wife had gone down suddenly with a bad bout of flu, had offered him the spare seat for the Wimbledon men's singles final. Henry had declined it as it was just the one seat, but when he told Jocelyn that evening she insisted he rang the man up and ask if he could change his mind if it wasn't too late. 'But what will you do with yourself on a Sunday?' he had asked her in a kind of dismay. She laughed. 'You mean, the shops being shut, what could possibly be left for a mere female to do in London without her husband?' she mocked. She recalled that there had been a time when a leg-pull of this sort wouldn't have been in order.

He grinned easily, raising his hands in surrender. 'All right, properly arraigned. I'm still a male chauvinist, aren't I, when taken by surprise? Old habits die hard. But what *will* you do?'
She had this at hand. She had already noticed the Picasso Exhibition on at the Tate and thought she would like to see it. She hadn't mentioned it because she hadn't thought Henry would want to go. Convinced by her enthusiasm that there was no sacrifice on her part - Wimbledon certainly wasn't her scene, so she would be feeling no disappointment there - he consented. The seat was still available.

On Sunday morning, after a sumptuous and disgracefully late breakfast in their room, Henry went off like a schoolboy. He was meeting his friend for an early lunch. Left in the hotel room, she felt a moment of isolation and exposure as silence settled. The room overlooked the Park. Still in her housecoat, she watched the glinting traffic bowling along immediately below, and beyond it people on the grass strolling in the sunshine. Everyone in the world but her, it seemed for a moment, was occupied, engaged. What was she these days without Henry, without the furnishings of activity his love and their joint concern for Combe had brought her?

She lectured herself. Was this like her? She had in anticipation relished a day alone with no duties, no reponsibilities, in which she could allow her inner thoughts to come voluntarily from their corners. She *would* relish this salutary departure from habit.

She had a leisurely bath, enjoying the exotic bath soap and the huge fleecy towels provided by the unpretentiously classy hotel, and dressed herself at a corresponding speed. By the time she was downstairs and handing her key to the uniformed man at the desk and asking if he knew which bus it was to the Tate, she could almost imagine herself as a habitué of these luxurious surroundings until she saw a rich-looking elderly woman with huge glasses on a gold chain and with a miniature dog under her arm complaining disagreeably about something to the dark-suited man at the reception desk. She decided she was after all a happy one-off interloper.

On the top floor of a bus bearing her along the embankment,

she had an unexpectedly powerful recall of that period she had spent in London when she first married Leo. On so many days she had gone off alone like this to look at things. Briefly the memory startled her, as if a stranger had roughly tugged her sleeve. Could her present pleasure be compared with the quality of her joy in those idyllic youthful days? Wouldn't she have to force herself to think it could? No, it was merely because youthful memories are bolder, she argued, bolder because they are incised when the clay is fresher and more malleable. This doesn't mean that contemporary sensation is less profound. The power of nostalgia is always suspect.

There was a queue stretching round the path of the small green garden to the side of the stone classical entrance of the museum. Happily she joined it and was soon talking to a mid-Western American family behind her, in London for a holiday. How eager they were, she thought, how charmingly involved and unblasé the boy and the girl who, heads raised, listened to everything said by the adults and joined in. The father was absurdly complimentary about London and England. 'A great old city you have here,' he said. 'Makes us feel as if we're just kind of born.' In their company she did not notice the wait, and in no time, it seemed, she was buying her ticket and wishing her chance acquaintances a happy stay in England.

In the long hallway there was a modernistic display of moving tableaux. She gazed at a seeming example of perpetual motion, a contraption in which the outer of three heavy silver balls, all of which were suspended on long strings, swung and struck the other two and sent its neighbour but one flying up in the other direction, so to repeat the process from the other side. There was a creation with water along similar lines - at the top a fount of water falling on to the first of a series of tilted trays arranged on descending levels. In turn each filled up until, the point of balance being reached, it see-sawed and tipped its contents on to the next one down. There was a montage of Heinz Baked Beans tins arranged in a pyramid, and hoisted above for no discernible reason was a baby grand piano with a flowery pattern painted all over it and a garland of fairy-lights switching on, off. It was all zany, fun, designed perhaps to provoke, flush out (and so de-fuse?) the kind of pious outraged scorn she heard once or twice about her.

She entered the smaller gallery where the exhibition was and was soon immersed in the artist's prodigious world of fantasy. Only the one or two full portraits, some of the animals - especially the sculptures - and a selection of the still life, she thought were serious. Most of it, not so unlike the modernistic jokes in the entrance hall, was surely inspired doodling, which nonetheless, seen all together like this, amounted to the huge impact of Picasso's entirely original view on life. It was funny, she thought, how art - humour, too, for that matter - has to be repeated many times for the effect, the *persuasion*, to be made. Was it the same in life? Was it proliferation then, self-belief, guiltless insistance, which quenches criticism and ultimately triumphs? If so it was certainly an explication of her own mediocrity. She had seen two sides to most confrontations.

'Never had any doubts this guy, did he?' she heard at her shoulder. It was uncannily as if her thoughts had been speaking aloud. She nearly jumped out of her skin. Then she saw it was Leo. His smile of incredulity at their meeting was there, but as if that could wait he turned back to the famous pierrot picture, black and red, the figure wearing a wonky tricorn hat.

'You were thinking that?' were her first words to him after all these years. They carried, she knew, an equal postponement of conventional astonishment.

She saw the old merriment. 'You mean you were, too?' he said.

'I was more or less, yes - along those lines.'

'It seems we coincide about art then, as well as other things. Remember Leonardo - the St Anne picture?'

'Of course I do.'

'So maybe nothing changes so much after all.'

She couldn't think what to say in answer. Was something wrong with her knees? They felt as if someone had knocked out their locking pins with a mallet. 'Well how are you, Joss,' she hearh him go on, 'and why are you in London?'

'Henry has a meeting.'

'On a Sunday?'

'No, it was on Friday. Someone offered him a seat for Wimbledon today.'

'I see.'

She thought this sounded selfish of Henry. 'The man's wife was ill so there was only the one place. I wanted to see this, he didn't so much, so it all fitted in very well.'

It was much too long an explanation. As if he thought so, too, Leo looked away at the picture again. 'It's worth seeing all this, isn't it?' he continued. 'Nobody like this man ever. I mean - the Impressionists are all different, but they're a school, most artists belong to a school, but there isn't a Picasso school, is there?'

'No.'

'Even a scribble of his couldn't be by anyone else. That must be worth something. "I'm here, it's by me", it proclaims, like a cock crowing on top of the dung-heap.'

Jocelyn was beginning to get her knees back. 'Leo, it's incredible, bumping into each other like this.'

'Well, your being in London is unusual maybe. But given that you are, is it so astounding? We both like art, it's a Sunday, I'm not working, and this exhibition's on.'

'How are you?'

For answer Leo looked around them. The largely silent mob was seething with ever more articulate aggression as the degree of constriction grew. 'If we stay here we're going to get *heeled* from this scrum. A cafe and a sandwich, don't you think? Or am I going to have the trouble I had to get you to have dinner with me in Cambridge all those years ago? Have you seen enough of Pablo?'

She found herself laughing. 'No, no problem there - I mean about the cafe. And I've had my fill of Pablo, yes. *To* the cafe - there's one here in the building, isn't there?'

There was, but by the time they had fought their way against the incoming tide in the entrance hall, they were imagining the vast queue there would be there as well. 'Where's your hotel?' Leo asked, 'I presume you're at a hotel?' When she told him 'Knightsbridge' - she didn't like to say the name of the hotel - he seemed to take a decision. 'Right, roughly the same direction as my patch.'

He led her out of the building and within moments had secured a taxi. She wondered if this was wise, but he was holding the door open for her. She decided at this stage she could only get in.

As the taxi-driver slalomed his knowing way through the maze of streets, Leo kept up a barrage of talk about exhibitions. She wouldn't believe it, he said, but he had become a museum and exhibition freak, as she had used to be - perhaps he had caught the disease from her. As he chatted, so easily, she ran an eye over his appearance. He looked well, she thought, quite his old relaxed self - new-looking suede shoes, jeans, a nice clean sports shirt.

The coffee-shop, self-consciously chic, was in Sloane Street. Leo was handing a ten pound note to the driver before she could offer to pay. He tipped generously, she noticed. Was he flush despite giving away his windfall to his half-brother, was he back in some business? They entered the carpeted interior, foliaged with thick-leaved plants like a film-set jungle, and settled on a grey corduroy bench seat in a corner inhaling the exotic aroma of freshly ground coffee beans. The girl, not at all Sloane-rangerish as demanded by the decor and the district, archly adjusting the single orchid on their table asked how she 'might be of assistance to them.'

'With coffee,' said Leo. He picked up the glossy multi-coloured menu. 'And for me a "Caribbean Surprise" sandwich.' He gave the two words humorous emphasis and looked at Jocelyn for her choice. 'Squared,' he added.

'I beg your pardon?' said the girl.

'*Two* surprises.'

Displeased at such liberties, the girl withdrew. When she was out of sight, Jocelyn laughed. 'I see you haven't changed much.'

'Not in those ways probably.'

'Still iconoclastic?'

'Not always on purpose - as with that girl.'

'No, you're right. You always expected people to be on the same wave-length. It's not your fault when they aren't. Anyway people shouldn't use such dreadful expressions. You're totally excused.'

They appraised each other, eye to eye. 'It really is just as it was, isn't it?' Leo said. 'As far as the first proofs show anyway. It seems we can still leave out the grammar and take glorious short cuts when we speak to each other, right?'

'I hope so.'

'It's a rare pleasure. Speaking with most people is lumbersomely laborious.'

'I agree.'

He hesitated only a split second. 'Do you leave out the grammar with Henry?'

'Yes, these days.'

'Sounds as if you had a struggle.' He looked at the back of his hand. 'I suppose I did - do - too.'

She did not wish it but her heart dropped a beat or two. "You, too", you say?'

'I'm married to Tessa, yes. Not so long after I saw you in Dartmouth actually.'

'You knew her then?'

'No. Why do you ask?'

'I - I don't know. Yes, I do know - of course I know. You know, too.'

'Do I? Yes, of course I do. You mean if I'd had Tessa in the bag at that famous meeting you'd be thinking a little less of me in this moment. I'd've been acting from a position of strength.'

'And you weren't?'

'Why should I be modest, I never was? No, I didn't know Tessa then. Whatever faint hopes I had were still in your direction, until I saw what had happened to you, until I saw Henry and saw I was too late.'

For a moment an abyss opened at her feet. He must have seen her distress. His hand was on hers. 'It's not a cause for sadness, Joss - really. Not really for me, and I'm sure not for you.'

'No, it's just that . . .

'That the timing was wrong for us?'

'No - yes, but that's not what I was thinking.'

'What were you thinking?'

She checked herself on the brink of confession, but how had

she ever been able to stop going over the edge? 'I was reflecting more on the lack of grammar bit, reflecting how *quick* we always were with each other - just like this.'

He removed his hand, his face darkening. 'That's true,' he said. 'And that doesn't come twice. Tessa isn't quick like that. Am I allowed to suspect that Henry isn't, either? What we have here is two hare and tortoise situations if ever there was one - *in that way.* But of course there are compensations, aren't there? It was a massive compensation I saw in your Henry. After all it's the tortoises which win the races, isn' it? If I'm not careful, any moment I shall be guilty of a gross cliché.'

'You mean about things turning out for the best?'

He didn't answer this. 'Tessa's half my age,' he continued. 'Pretty, warm when she's feeling like it, practical - perhaps in a way she's not so unlike our Sally. Doesn't concern herself too much about the things that get under belts - the belts of the likes of you and me, I mean. For example, naturally, being the age I am, I was worried it wouldn't last, that she'd give me a run - as if I were someone pacing her for a couple of laps - and then that I'd be dropped panting by the wayside. It was ages before she even noticed it was on my mind.'

'And then?'

'I think I did almost lose her - not at all because of our age difference but because she thought I was being so stupid to think about it. "Do you think I can't make my mind up?" she said. "Do you think I haven't noticed you're a few years older than I am?" It was no gambit to save my feelings, she really meant it. She was furious. I'm deeply fond of her, so much that the gulf between us hurts. I look at her sometimes with . . . our child . . .

'You have a child?'

'Yes.'

'But I'm happy for you, Leo.'

'I'm sorry, I wasn't going to mention it.'

'Why not?'

'All right, why not indeed? Where was I? Yes, when I see Tessa with Anthea, being so practical with her as if she wasn't our child but arrived by post, somehow I . . . Well, I *am* still a dynast, you know, Joss, even without Matt in the offing and what I used to feel about him.'

'I'm glad for you, really, so glad. You know very well I'm not a dynast and never was. That's probably why I feel no envy about Anthea. Sally was quite enough for me, for one lifetime.'

He paused, putting on a new-topic face. 'How is Sal?'

'She's fine. Ken's at the bar now and getting serious briefs. It really looks as if the lights will continue to be green for Sally all down the boulevard.'

'No children yet?'

'No sign, and I doubt if there'll be any now. Sally's firm have just made her a director and I'm sure she's indispensable and knows it. She earns pots. You haven't seen her obviously, despite my hints to her.'

'No.'

'She's still a very silly girl in that respect.'

'Oh, I don't know. She's right probably - for herself. And I don't mind so much now. And incidentally I'm earning again. You'll never guess with what.'

'I don't think I will.'

' Posh City nobs' wine and grub bar. Really. I appease the midday Stock Exchange appetites - I'm almost opposite the place. Started in a small way with sandwiches at a great deal less upmarket an address. Now I oversee - strut about the champagne and oysters in a suit and talk to people, tease them a bit. I flatter myself they come as much for the chat as the champers.'

She was delighted for him, and said so. The coffee came. Leo thanked the girl nicely, but this was too late. 'You're welcome,' she pronounced musically, but aloof and defiant as she flounced away.

A precipitous silence followed her retreat. Leo put sugar in his cup and stirred. The preliminary agenda was dealt with and the moment had come, they both knew it had. Which of them would say it, Jocelyn wondered. Was the onus on her as it had been finally that midday in Venice when Umberto their guide had left them at the small restaurant and it was answer time?

Leo was watching the swirl of brown liquid as if it were a

maelstrom into which he might be sucked, and she knew increasingly the onus *was* on her. In a way he had made his statement, as he had on that other occasion. 'It's just different the second time round, isn't it?' she managed at last. 'I was thinking on the way to the Tate this morning - when I remembered how I used to go off to galleries when we lived in London and how happy I was - that it's wrong to make comparisons. I think you think that, too, don't you?'

'Wrong?'

'OK, not the right word, irrelevant.'

'Not irrelevant either.' He raised his head and looked at her with the full frankness of his blue eyes. 'We won't ever escape, *mentally,* Joss. I won't, anyway. For me it'll always be there, "unsunderably." The prayer book has the right word in the marriage service. Though only with that word - the rest of the phrase in which it occurs is balls. What it should say is that *once* it's there, no man, or woman, *can* put it asunder. Try to and, like an image on water, you can shy stones at it for all you're worth, shatter it, fragment it, but it comes together again. So in the end you don't shy stones, you gratefully include it in your life, make room, give it a place. The new relationship becomes tacitly - hopefully out of sight of our partners - a "marriage a trois".'

She had thought she had recovered from the weakness she had felt in the Gallery. She found she hadn't. But she knew she must not protect herself with a lie. She must not pretend she was any different from Leo in this respect, for she wasn't and never had been. It was for her, too, precisely as Leo said it was. Henry had sensed it, that was why he had got huffy at the time of the wedding. In a few moments she felt strong enough to say what she must.

'You don't only speak for yourself. It has been, will be even more now after this meeting, the same for me.'

His small nod indicated he understood what she meant, and that he was relieved, for had she not in an indirect and involuntary way pardoned him by her confession? 'One of these days we'll all go on a cruise or something,' he said jauntily, 'all four of us.'

knew Leo knew this. For how would Henry and Leo begin to get on, on what ground was it likely she and Tessa would relate? They would not see each other again. That was what Leo meant.